The
Campbell Sisters

Eileen Joyce Donovan

DX VAROS PUBLISHING

Published by:
D. X. Varos, Ltd
7665 E. Eastman Ave. #B101
Denver, CO 80231

Book cover design and layout by Ellie Bockert Augsburger of Creative Digital Studios.
www.CreativeDigitalStudios.com
Cover design features:
Collection of black women full length portraits silhouettes in different poses isolated on white background. Lady fashion style with dress, trousers, shoes, hat, bags. For logo, emblems, advertisement by Atflare on Adobe Stock, Red apartment building with a shop in the ground floor. Flat vector illustration. by Laura on Adobe Stock

ISBN: 978-1-955065-70-2 (paperback)
ISBN: 978-1-955065-71-9 (ebook)

for Donald, my eternal muse

CHAPTER ONE

Spring, New York City 1955

Helen didn't relish the role of oldest sister, even though all three of them were adults now. Peggy, the baby of the trio, still looked to her for guidance and watched every move she made, trying to model herself after Helen's actions. Carolyn, the middle daughter, was... well... Carolyn was Carolyn. How does one rein in a Carolyn?

As Helen walked along Lexington Avenue, the noise of the taxis' horns, the exhaust from the city buses, and the constant construction sounds from yet another building going up on the avenue jarred her nerves. When she spotted the Foundling Hospital's orphanage's iron railings, she thought how much like a prison they looked, despite the fact that they housed the only warm comforting home the orphans inside had ever known. She exhaled a deep breath and her shoulders relaxed as she anticipated the eager faces of her four to six-year-old group waiting inside to greet her.

Situated in the relatively peaceful and wealthy Upper East Side of Manhattan, these children would never see the poverty and abuse she witnessed growing up at the foot of the rough West Side docks of Chelsea.

When she entered the children's playroom, they greeted her with a chorus of "Good morning, Miss Helen."

"Good morning, children. It's a beautiful spring day outside so I think we should go to the playground. What do you think?"

The children jumped up and down, screaming their approval of her plan.

"But we'll have to settle down if we want to go. We can't walk through the streets like screaming banshees, can we/"

"No, Miss Helen," they said, calming themselves and forming a line.

"That's better. We'll stop by Sister Josephine's office to let her know where we'll be. We won't want her to think someone stole all of us away, would we?"

The children giggled at the idea of someone entering their fortress and running away with twelve children and their carer. Helen led her small group of children into the playground. She nodded to the mothers and nannies who sat on nearby benches, then sank onto an empty one to watch her group play.

The children loved coming to the Central Park's playground nearest the orphanage. And Helen savored her few minutes of peace and tranquility in this oasis of calm nestled in the midst of soaring skyscrapers and the congested noisy streets of New York City.

On their way to the playground, Helen watched the children laughing and talking to one another. She imagined taking this walk one day holding her husband's hand, and watching their children scamper ahead of them. Visions of a happy family life filled her head. If she could just find a decent man to marry. It seemed the only men she met were total jerks, or mommy's boys, or cocky wannabe gangsters.

At one time, after secretarial school, all Helen wanted was a job in a big company, maybe as a private secretary. She couldn't imagine spending her working day caring for orphans. But now, after doing just that for the past six years, she couldn't imagine a job that would bring her more joy.

Suddenly, a child's scream ripped her musings to shreds.

A dagger of fear sliced through her. On her feet in a second, she scanned the area and did a quick head count.

She reached eleven.

One was missing.

She ran to the nearest child.

"Where's Jimmy?" she asked, her voice quivering, her heart racing.

The little girl shrugged and shouted, "Jimmy? Jimmy? Where are you?"

The children stopped playing and looked around. Soon they echoed her call, and the peaceful surroundings turned chaotic.

Birds squawked and flew out from the trees.

Squirrels chittered and ran for cover.

Mothers and nannies grabbed their children and headed for safety. TV news coverage of the Robert Greenlease kidnapping, only two years before, burned into their minds.

A little boy tugged on Helen's skirt. "Miss Helen, I think I saw him go over there." He pointed to a clump of bushes that lined the 67th Street bike and foot path.

"Oh, dear God, no," she muttered, making a quick sign of the cross on her chest. "Grab hands everyone and follow me."

On shaky legs, she stumbled out of the playground. The children, used to obeying her orders, lined up and hurried after her. She stopped at the road that cut through the park. A small crowd had already gathered there. Women, who just moments ago watched their children enjoy this unseasonably warm sunny day in May, now huddled around a tiny figure lying on the ground. When Helen approached, they parted. Some cast disapproving looks her way. Others tsk tsked and whispered about the irresponsible attitude some young people had about their jobs. Particularly when it came to the care of children. Very few looked at her in sympathy.

Helen shoved past them and dropped to her knees alongside the little boy, and pushed the man crouched there away. Her circle skirt fanned out around her. The rough concrete dug into her knees the minute she hit the pavement. Jimmy lay in the roadway. He clutched his left arm and moaned. Tears streamed down his chubby cheeks. Someone's bicycle lay on the ground near him, the wheels still spinning. Helen's head swam, terrified that Jimmy was seriously hurt. Her breakfast clawed its way up from her stomach and she swallowed hard to keep it down.

"Jimmy, what happened? Are you hurt?"

"It's my arm, Miss Helen," he said between sobs. "I think it's broken, like Sarah's was. It hurts a lot."

"Can you sit up, sweetheart?"

"I don't know."

"Let's try."

Helen put her arm around his shoulders, coaxed him into a sitting position, and pulled a tissue from her pocket to wipe his tears. "Anything else hurt?"

4

Between sniffles, Jimmy said, "I don't think so."

"Let's get you back to the Foundling and have a doctor examine you. Can you stand?"

"I think so." Jimmy struggled to his feet and swayed like a toddler trying out his legs for the first time. When Helen stood, the trees wavered and spun around in circles before her eyes. Myriad consequences of what could result from this accident flashed through her mind. She couldn't imagine trying to explain this to Sister Josephine, her boss.

"Oh no, this isn't good. Come over here and sit on the bench for a minute until you feel steadier."

And I do too.

The other children gathered around the two of them. They stared at Jimmy, mouths hung open. No one spoke.

"All right, everyone," a man said, herding the onlookers away from the scene. "Show's over. No need to stand here gawking." He crouched down in front of Helen. "I'm real sorry, miss. I couldn't stop fast enough."

"What?" Helen looked at the man who was wringing his flat cap in his hands. His face was ashen and he ran his fingers through his brown hair. "What are you talking about? Who are you?"

"I'm the one who hit him, miss. With my bicycle. I was riding down the road, and he charged out through those bushes. I couldn't stop in time. I guess he was chasing after that ball." The man pointed to a little pink spaldeen that lay a foot away next to the curb.

"So, you're saying it's his fault?"

"No, miss. No. Not at all. I'm just trying to explain what happened. I know it's my fault. I should have stopped as soon as I saw that ball, but it all happened so fast, I didn't have time to react."

Helen looked where the man had pointed. "Jimmy, is that your ball?"

5

Jimmy looked down and rubbed his arm more vigorously, which was a mottled red and slightly swollen. "My arm really hurts."

"You didn't answer me."

"Um... yeah."

"Haven't I told you, all of you," she said, looking at the wide-eyed faces surrounding her, "that you can't bring toys to the park?"

The children nodded.

"You know the rules. No toys outside the playroom. And this is why."

Helen sounded firm, but her hands trembled and her stomach rocked like a small boat in a storm. "I can't even imagine where you got that ball. I've never seen it before."

"I think those people who came to see him on Sunday gave it to him," one boy said.

Helen pursed her lips and shook her head.

"Another rule broken. Jimmy, you know that we share all our gifts, don't you?"

He nodded.

"And you hid it from me and never said a word." Helen tossed her long auburn hair back over her shoulder and sighed. "Let's see if you can stand now."

"Miss," the bike owner said, "if you can wheel my bike, I'll carry the boy back to wherever you're going."

Helen hesitated for a moment and looked the man over before she said, "Children, each take a partner's hand again and stay in line so we can get Jimmy home quickly."

They grabbed hands and lined up in silence.

"All right," Helen said, "I guess we can make this work. Thank you, Mr. ... oh, I don't even know your name."

"It's Charlie. Charlie Sanders. And you are?"

"Helen Campbell. And these children are in my group at the Foundling."

6

"Ah, the orphanage," Charlie said.

"And hospital."

"Of course. All set?"

"Children, stay close to me and Mr. Sanders. We don't need another accident like Jimmy's, do we?"

"No, Miss Helen," they said in unison.

The entourage started the odyssey back to 68th Street and Lexington Avenue. And a strange looking group it was. Two adults leading, one carrying a four-year-old child, the other walking a man's bike, with a dozen children following like little ducklings.

"Don't look so worried," Charlie said to Helen. "We'll get them back safely. I'm no danger anymore, now that you've got my bike."

"Oh, it's not that. I know you didn't mean to hurt anyone. It's Sister Josephine I worry about. She's a stickler for the rules, and I know she'll blame me for this. I should have checked their pockets before we left. I don't know why I didn't. I always follow her rules and the one time I didn't, this happens. I'll be lucky if she lets me keep my job."

She looked over at Jimmy who was curled up against Charlie's chest, eyes half closed.

"Don't let him fall asleep. He may have a concussion. That was something my orientation course at the hospital emphasized. And he's got a pretty big lump on his forehead."

"Okay, okay, take it easy. I'll keep him awake and talking."

Charlie looked at Jimmy and said, "So, your arm's broken, is it? Well, I've had one or two broken bones in my life. It's not so bad. Everyone makes a big fuss about you and gives you lollipops and reads to you. And you have a wonderful story to tell all your friends."

"What bones did you break?" Jimmy asked, now wide awake and intrigued by the stranger.

"Let's see now. My nose – twice. Two or three of my ribs. You know, they're the bones over here," he said, tickling the boy's side.

Jimmy giggled and grabbed Charlie's hand with his "broken" arm. Charlie looked over the boy's head and winked at Helen.

So, that's why there's a kink in his nose. Probably one of those toughs from the docks. Just my luck. Meet a good-looking guy and he's a hoodlum, or well on his way.

As Charlie told Jimmy about how and where he had broken all these bones, Helen stopped listening. She could feel her shoulders relax and her whole body calm. Before long they were standing in front of the Foundling and Jimmy seemed to have forgotten his injury.

"I'd better get him inside and have a doctor check him over. Thanks, Mr. Sanders."

"Charlie. Please."

"Okay, Charlie."

"I'll carry him in so you can take care of the rest of them. Just find a place to stow my bike, would you?"

"Oh, sure." Helen propped it against the nearest lamppost. "Done."

She bundled the children through the front door and asked the receptionist to page the doctor on duty.

"I'll take Jimmy." She reached out to release Charlie from Jimmy's grasp around his neck.

"You sure you can manage him? He's not a lightweight. I can carry him wherever you're going."

"I'm afraid that's against the rules. Only employees can go past the reception area. Or prospective parents."

"Do you always follow the rules?" Charlie asked, a mischievous glint in his eyes. "Sometimes it's fun to break them, or at least bend them a little."

8

"Yeah, well, I broke one today and look where that got me."

"At least it let you meet one of the most handsome, debonair men in New York City. And I got to meet one of the prettiest ladies. That's two excellent results."

Helen could feel her cheeks turning a rosy red.

He is kind of handsome, even with a slightly crooked nose.

"Look," Charlie said, "this may not be the best timing, but could I see you again? Without all the kids?"

"I... I don't know." *What if he really is a hoodlum? He did just run over one of my kids. Although he seems genuinely sorry.* She always said she wouldn't let herself get involved with a strange man unless someone she knew introduced him. Now here she was on the verge of breaking another rule.

"Tell you what," Charlie said. "Why don't I meet you right here when you get off work today? We can grab a cup of coffee or a hot dog and then you can decide whether or not you want to see me again."

"I guess that would be all right."

"Wouldn't be breaking any of your rules, would it?" he asked, tilting his head, pushing his cap back, and giving her a captivating smile.

"Well... not really. Maybe bending them a little."

"Great."

They stood grinning at each other until one child said, "Miss Helen, I have to go to the lavatory."

"Oh, of course, Bobby. Thanks again, Charlie. I get off at four o'clock."

"I'll be waiting right outside." He lowered himself and stood Jimmy on the floor. "Think you can walk on your own now, pal?"

"Course I can. I'm four years old."

"That old, huh?"

9

Charlie looked up over Jimmy's head and winked again.

"See you at four, Helen."

He was out the door before she could answer him, or second guess her decision, something she always did. Maybe looking at both sides of a situation wasn't always the best way to live your life. She knew her idol, Harriet Quimby, wouldn't have thought twice about whether people would approve of her decision. Harriet did whatever she pleased, society's rules be damned. And a date with Charlie pleased Helen.

"Miss Helen, I really have to go," Bobby said, hopping from one foot to the other.

"Sorry, honey. All right, everyone, get in line and let's go upstairs. Jimmy, you stay next to me."

The children headed for the staircase. Helen shook her head and wondered what had gotten into her to agree to meet him at four o'clock.

Maybe Charlie's right, she thought, smiling. *Maybe I can bend the rules a little.*

But her smile disappeared when she rounded the corner and saw Sister Josephine. The children were telling her all about Jimmy's injury and Mr. Sanders. Her frown deepened as she listened to them.

"Helen," Sister Josephine said, "I need to speak to you in my office. Right now." The long skirt of her nun's habit swished in a wide circle as she turned and strode down the hall.

CHAPTER TWO

"How's Jimmy?" Charlie asked as soon as Helen opened the Foundling's front door.

"The doctor says he's fine. Just a bruise, but a sizable black and blue mark on his elbow that he's proudly displaying for everyone to admire."

"How's his head?"

"Again, just a bruise, and a beauty of a shiner. Thank God."

"And how are you?"

"Recovering from the tongue lashing I got from Sister Josephine, but surviving."

Charlie winced. "She's a tough cookie, huh?"

"The toughest. I guess I can't blame her though. She's got all these children to look after, and what turned out to be nothing could have been disastrous if we had been at a different playground and you had been driving a car instead of riding a bicycle."

"I don't even want to think about that. I wouldn't be able to live with myself if I killed a little kid."

"You! I'd want to die myself if one kid I cared for got killed. Especially if it was my fault for not following the rules, but fortunately that didn't happen." She brushed a stray hair away from her forehead and smoothed down her circle skirt.

"So, hot dog or coffee?"

"Maybe a hot dog. I couldn't get lunch down. My stomach was on a roller coaster ride, between Jimmy's accident and Sister Josephine's harangue. But I think it's finally settling down." With that, her stomach growled loud enough to be heard over the street traffic.

They both laughed, and Charlie said, "There's usually a hot dog guy by the entrance to the park. Feel like returning to the scene of the crime?"

"Sure. Why not. Don't they say you should get back on the horse as soon as he bucks you off? I have to go back there someday, so it might as well be today."

"Terrific." Charlie shoved his hands into his pants pockets and strode down the street. Helen ran a few steps to catch up to him.

"Uh, Charlie, think we could slow this down to less than the sixty-yard dash?"

"Huh? Oh, sorry. I got in the habit of walking really fast since I always seem to be late for wherever I'm going."

"Walking fast is fine, but your long-legged stride is about two of mine. And running in high heels is never a good idea."

Charlie slowed down and said, "Why don't you take my arm? That way if I start to race again, you can tug on it to remind me we're not at a track meet."

Helen slipped her hand through Charlie's arm, blushing a little.

"That's better," he said, patting her hand.

While they waited for the light to change before crossing the street, Helen asked, "What do you do when you're not bicycling through Central Park?"

Charlie rubbed his chin. "Well, right now, not much. I'm working with some kids who think they're tough. Teaching them the finer skills of boxing instead of the street brawling they think they're good at."

"You're a boxer? How exciting."

"Yeah, if you like getting beat up on a regular basis."

"Oh, you can't be that bad. No cauliflower ear. No visible scars," she said, examining his face. "So, that explains all the broken bones you told Jimmy about. I wondered about that."

They hurried across the street when the light changed.

A boxer, huh? I don't know how I feel about that. Not exactly a stable occupation. Not great for a family man. Wait a minute! You just met him. You don't even know if you really like him yet.

Charlie looked out the corner of his eye at Helen. Most times when he told girls what he did for a living, they shied away. Boxers didn't have the best reputations in the world. Not the type of man every mother hoped her daughter would bring home. But so far, Helen hadn't suddenly remembered a previous appointment, or just excused herself and walked away. Like some other girls he had met.

"So, where are you working with these little hoodlums?" she asked, a twinkle in her eye.

"The Hudson Guild Settlement House."

Helen stopped dead in the street. Her hand yanked hard on Charlie's arm and almost pulled him off his feet.

"You okay?" he asked.

"I don't believe it. I live two blocks away from there. On 24th Street."

13

Charlie stood facing her and pushed his cap back on his head. "Well then, I won't have any trouble finding you when I come to pick you up for our date on Friday night."

"Oh? Are we going on a date on Friday? Did you forget to ask me, or did I already forget you did?"

Charlie looked down at the ground, shuffled his feet, and shoved his hands back in his pants' pockets. "Sorry," he said, his cheeks turning pink. "I mean... well... would you like to go out with me on Friday?"

"Hmm. I'll let you know after I have my hot dog. I'm starving."

Helen smiled, grabbed his arm, and pulled him down the street toward the hot dog man. A grin stretched across his face.

~~~

"Wadda ya want on it?" the hot dog vendor asked, the pungent scent of sauerkraut overpowering everything.

"Just a little mustard," Helen said.

"The works," Charlie said.

"Ya sure ya want onions?" the man asked, glancing at Helen.

"Um, maybe not. Okay, skip the onions, but plenty of sauerkraut and relish and mustard."

While they watched him ladle on the condiments, an announcement came over the transistor radio perched on the vendor's cart reminding people that the championship fight between Rocky Marciano and Don Cockell would be broadcast live "tonight from San Francisco's Kezar Stadium."

"That should be a great one. Just hope I can stay awake for the whole fight." Charlie bit into his overflowing hot dog. Helen just smiled.

They walked into the park a little way and found a bench where the noise from the cars, buses, and taxies was somewhat muffled. They munched on their hot dogs

14

and the only sounds were the "Ummms" from the two satisfied customers. Helen leaned back, face raised to the sky. People passing might have thought she was enjoying fine French cuisine instead of a dirty water hot dog. Charlie, on the other hand, attacked his meal like he was afraid it would sprout legs and run off if he didn't consume it fast enough.

"Want another one?" he asked, wiping the mustard from his mouth with the paper napkin.

"No, I'm good for now. In fact, I should head home. My mother will worry if I don't show up soon."

"Can't you call her and tell her you met the most handsome man in the city and you're running away with him?"

Helen burst out laughing. "I don't think she'd like that very much. Run off with a man she hasn't met and passed judgment on? I doubt I'd get away with that. She'd have every cop in the city out looking for me."

"Well then, how about you just say you met a friend and you'll be home later?"

"How much later?"

Charlie looked at the sky. "Ten o'clock?" he asked, looking back down at her.

"What are we going to do until ten o'clock?"

"I don't know. Go to a movie? Eat a real dinner, not a hot dog? Ride the Circle Line around Manhattan? Whatever you want to do."

Helen fidgeted with her napkin, wiping her already clean hands.

"Please, Helen. I'd really like to spend some more time with you."

"Well... Do you think there's a phone in the park?"

"Probably not, but there has to be a drug store around here somewhere. They always have phones."

Helen didn't answer for a while. She crossed her legs, uncrossed them, got up, walked to the trash can, threw her napkin and hot dog wrapper away, came back, smoothed her skirt, dug out her mirror and lipstick, put some on, and finally said, "Well, come on. The drugstore's not going to come to us."

Charlie grinned, grabbed her hand, and pulled her out of the park and down 68th Street.

"Well?" Charlie asked.

"She wasn't altogether happy about it, but . . ."

"Swell. Where to?"

Helen was still thinking about what she wanted to do when Charlie said, "I know. Let's take a ride on the Staten Island ferry. We can watch the sunset, then we'll grab a bite to eat somewhere downtown."

"All right. I think I was on the ferry once when I was a little girl, but I know I haven't been on it in years."

"Oh, it's great. You can see the skyline and watch the sunset. All for a nickel."

"Okay, Mr. Big Spender, lead the way."

They headed for the downtown IRT subway station at 59th Street.

"This train'll take us to South Ferry," Charlie said. "Then it's a quick walk to the Staten Island ferry."

They hit the subway right at the end of the work day. Rush hour. New York City was emptying its offices into trains that would take the workers to every part of Manhattan, Queens, Brooklyn, the Bronx, and Staten Island. At every stop, the doors opened and spit some people out while even more pushed their way in. As the train got closer to the last stop, fewer people got on and Helen and Charlie finally had some room to breathe. South Ferry was the last stop and the remaining

16

passengers shoved through the subway's doors as soon as they opened. Then the flood of humanity hurled themselves to the stairs that led to the street. The masses moved as one towards the ferry terminal. Most people already had a nickel in their hands to jam into the turnstile that would propel them across the room to the ferry waiting at the dock.

Helen, a native New Yorker, was used to crowds, but never traveled during rush hour if she could help it. Sweat ran down her face and gathered under her arms. She could only hope it wasn't leaving big stains on her blouse. In the unruly pushing and shoving, she couldn't see Charlie. She knew she could make her own way home, but the evening he had planned sounded like fun and she didn't want it to end because she lost him in the crowd.

"Better take my hand," Charlie said, popping up at her side. "I don't want you to get swallowed up by this mob. Then I'd have to eat alone. And I hate eating alone."

He held out his hand and Helen grabbed it. When they reached the turnstiles, Charlie put his arm around Helen's waist, dropped a nickel in the slot, and nudged her through. In seconds, he stood next to her, hand gripped firmly in his, and led the way onto the boat.

"Do you want to sit inside or outside?" Charlie shouted over the din of people and the ferry's engines.

"Could we stand at the rail? That way we can see everything."

"I was hoping you'd say that. Let's head to the back of the boat. There'll be fewer people there. Once we hit Staten Island, everyone'll be in a rush to get off and I don't want you swept away."

"Get off? I thought this was a round trip."

"It is, but we have to get off and then get back on again. Something about Coast Guard or maritime rules, or some other nonsense. But don't worry, we don't have to pay again. The return trip is free."

"Oh good. I was afraid you'd leave me on the island if you had to pay another nickel," Helen said, a twinkle in her eye.

Charlie's cheeks turned rosy. "Gee, Helen, I didn't mean it that way. Why, I wouldn't care what it cost to spend the evening with you."

Now it was Helen's turn to blush.

They found a place at the rail towards the back of the boat just as it lurched away from the pier. The further they pulled away from shore, more and more of the famous skyline etched its way against the sky.

"The city must look beautiful from this boat at night," Helen said, "with all the buildings lit up."

"We'll come again, but later next time."

The ferry sailed past Ellis Island and the Statue of Liberty. It was the first time Helen had seen the famous statue up close. Like most native New Yorkers, she never got around to visiting the landmarks that people traveled from all over the world to see. The boat lurched and Charlie put his arm around Helen's waist.

"I'd better hold on to you so you don't go overboard."

Even though she doubted that would happen, Charlie's arm around her felt wonderful, so she looked at him and smiled. She was happy to listen to him as he pointed out various buildings in Manhattan. And while he did, she took a minute to take stock of his face. Before this time on the ferry, they always seemed to be rushing somewhere, or surrounded by children. Now she had time to study Charlie. He wasn't the Clark Gable type of handsome that most girls would swoon over, but he was pleasant looking. And honest looking, a quality Helen admired. None of that smirky, con man attitude she saw in so many of the men in her neighborhood. Their slickness and bombast sickened her. She knew her sister, Carolyn, fell for that kind of guy. But no, she decided Charlie was not that type. He was like a little boy, excited and full of enthusiasm about this boat ride, and, hopefully, being with her. His eyes sparkled with every unfamiliar sight he pointed out to her. His attitude was contagious. Helen was enjoying herself much more than she had thought she would.

The boat bumped against the pier at Staten Island and almost knocked Helen off her feet.

"I'd better keep holding on to you. I wouldn't want to lose you now. You okay?"

"I'm fine. Guess I didn't have my feet planted firmly enough. It's a lot like the subway when it jerks to a stop, but the ride's been so smooth, I didn't expect it."

"Well, by the time we get back to South Ferry, you'll be an old pro."

They followed the crowd to the ramp that would take them off the ferry. On solid ground again, Charlie looked for the signs that would direct them to the boat loading for departure.

"Over there, Helen. That one's leaving next." He grabbed her hand, and they hurried towards the adjoining pier. There was usually about a fifteen-minute delay before a boat would leave, but Charlie wanted to make sure they didn't miss this ferry and have to sit around the terminal. Like most bus or train terminals, it was a seedy mess. The floor was sticky from spilled drinks. Trash cans overflowed. And a distinct smell of urine and diesel fuel overpowered the salty sea air.

They clambered aboard and got a prime spot at the rail where they could watch the sun begin its descent. It was a clear evening, with just a slight chill in the air, a typical day in early May. Helen shivered when a breeze kicked up. It tossed her hair and a sea mist feathered across her face.

"You cold?" Charlie asked. "We can sit inside if you'd like, or I could get us a cup of coffee."

"I'm fine. It's wonderful being out here, listening to the seagulls, and feeling the mist hit my face. I don't like the beach that much. I always get too sunburned, then I suffer for days, so being on the water without the sun beating down on me is heavenly."

"I agree. I think if I had my druthers, I'd want a job on a ship. Somewhere where I could be on the water every day."

"If you love the ocean so much, why did you become a boxer?"

"Simple answer is I was good at it. Something I didn't tell you, I grew up near you. On 17th Street and Ninth Avenue. When I was a kid, I used to go to the Settlement House. One day, one of the guys who volunteered there, Joe, asked me if I ever thought about becoming a boxer. I hadn't, but he said he'd be willing to train me and maybe I could compete in the Golden Gloves. I was interested, and it sounded a lot better than just punching a heavy bag.

"Joe set up a training routine for me the next day. I had to learn how to move, throw punches accurately, stay on my toes. You know, all the things that real boxers do. The first time he put me in the ring with a sparring partner, I knocked him down in the first round. I felt terrible, of course, but thrilled. I never thought I'd be any good. Especially with the way Joe used to yell at me all the time. But the best part was Joe. He was so excited. He was sure the sparring partner he had picked would knock me down and shake some of the cockiness out of me. Even the guy I had just beat jumped up and congratulated me. And he told Joe he had a winner and should hold on to me all the way up to the title."

20

"That's fascinating. But I have to say, you don't seem like a boxer at all. I mean, you're polite and kind and gentlemanly and . . ."

"Didn't you ever hear of 'Gentleman Jim' Corbett or Professor Mike Donovan? They were two of the greatest boxers ever. And real gentlemen. *And,* Corbett didn't even really like boxing. Although Donovan did."

"So, are they your idols?"

Charlie looked out over the water as a sheepish grin stole across his face. "Sort of. But since I like boxing, I guess I'd have to say Donovan is my favorite. He even became the boxing instructor at the New York Athletic Club."

The ferry bumped into the dock and Helen fell against Charlie. His arms wrapped around her. "We definitely have to take this ferry again," he said, grinning at her.

CHAPTER THREE

After a lovely dinner at the historic Fraunces Tavern, the place where George Washington said farewell to his troops, Helen and Charlie took the subway uptown.

"I had a great time today," Helen said when they reached her tenement.

"Me too. So, are we on for Friday night?" Charlie asked.

Helen squinted her eyes almost shut and pursed her lips together. "Friday. Friday. Let's see. I might have to consult my social secretary to see if my calendar is open that night."

"Social secretary, huh?"

"Of course. All New York City society ladies have social secretaries."

"Oh. I guess I should've been calling you Lady Helen all day instead of just plain Helen."

Helen giggled. "Lady Helen. Has a nice ring to it, don't you think?"

Charlie rolled his eyes and shook his head.

"I'd love to see you again on Friday," Helen said.

"That's swell. Should I pick you up here or at the Foundling?"

"Are we going someplace fancy? Or will my work clothes do?"

"You don't have to dress up like Astor's pet horse for me. I'm not the fancy type. Not usually anyway."

"Then meet me after work at four o'clock. That way you can avoid meeting my parents for a little while longer. Mom can be pretty intimidating to prospective boyfriends."

"And am I a prospective boyfriend?"

"Maybe. We'll see."

Charlie's face glowed. He leaned over, gave Helen a quick kiss on the cheek, and sprinted down the sidewalk, leaving Helen in wide-eyed surprise. She touched her fingertips to the spot on her cheek where Charlie had kissed her and smiled.

Definitely a prospective boyfriend.

"I'm home," Helen called as she entered her apartment.

"Did you eat?" her mother asked from the living room. Judging from the sounds coming from the TV, Helen knew they were watching *The Millionaire*, and hoping they would be the next recipients of the million dollars.

"Yes, Mom."

Helen went into the bedroom she shared with her two younger sisters, Peggy and Carolyn. She kicked off her high heels, put them under her bed, and pulled out her slippers.

"Oh, much better."

"Who were you out with?" Peggy asked.

Helen ran a brush through her hair and sat on the edge of the bed. "No one you know."

24

"A guy? Was it a guy?" Peggy put her pen down and swung around from the desk where she was finishing up a recent assignment. In a few months, she'd start her second year of medical school, one step closer to her dream of becoming a doctor.

"C'mon. Spill. Who's the guy? Not someone from the neighborhood. Where'd you meet him? How—"

"Hold it. Gee, you're as bad as Mom. And keep your voice down or she'll be in here in a minute for a full interrogation."

"Okay, okay. But I want all the dirt."

Helen took a deep breath. She knew Peggy would pester her to death until she got every detail.

Sometimes she acts like she's still in high school instead of medical school. She's like a dog with a bone.

"I met him today in the park. I took my kids there, and he ran over one of them with his bike."

"What!"

"Girls, keep it down in there," their mother yelled from the living room. "We're trying to watch TV."

"Sorry, Mom." Peggy turned to Helen and in a quieter voice said, "He ran over one of your kids and you went on a date with him? Are you crazy?"

"It's not as bad as it sounds." Helen explained the situation to Peggy exactly as it had happened and how concerned and considerate Charlie had been about Jimmy's injuries.

"Guess he's not a total monster," Peggy said.

"More like a Prince Charming than a monster."

"Who's a Prince Charming?" Carolyn asked, coming into the bedroom and flopping onto her bed, only inches away from Peggy's. The three twin beds lined the wall like army cots in a barracks with just enough space between them to stand and stretch.

"This guy Helen met today."

25

"Really? Do tell."

Helen sighed.

"I'll tell her," Peggy said, and repeated the tale to Carolyn.

"Well, well. So, our little spinster might finally have a prospect," Carolyn said after listening to Peggy's account.

"Carolyn!" Peggy said. "Don't be so mean. Helen's not a spinster. She just hasn't found the right guy yet."

"As far as I'm concerned, anyone over twenty-five who doesn't have a steady boyfriend is a likely candidate to be a spinster for the rest of her life."

"Says the worldly Miss Carolyn Campbell," Helen said. "And since you're twenty-four, you'd better put a move on it. I don't see men knocking down the door asking to marry you."

"I have plenty of men interested in me. I just don't plan on marrying any of them. I'd rather use them to get what I want. I want to be one of those beautiful and sophisticated sought-after ladies who live uptown and go to all the finest restaurants, shows, and parties on the arm of some handsome man. But always elusive. Never caught in the trap of marriage."

"Sounds like you want to become a kept woman to me," Peggy said.

"And what's so wrong with that?" Carolyn asked.

"Carolyn, you can't mean that," Helen said. "We weren't raised that way. Why... why that's nothing more than becoming a high-priced prostitute."

"That's not the way I see it. Men have been using women for ages to get what they want. It's time to turn the tables. And I figure I'm beautiful enough to get any man I want. For as long as I want him."

Helen and Peggy exchanged glances while Carolyn pulled her pajamas out from under her pillow.

"I'm going to take a shower. Do you have to use the bathroom before I do?"

"No," both women said.

"Good, cause you can't rush beauty." Carolyn walked down the long hall to check with her parents.

"She can't really mean what she said, can she?" Peggy asked.

"Who knows with Carolyn. She's always been a bit on the wild side, so I wouldn't put anything past her."

"So, do you think this guy's the one?"

"I don't know. I don't really know him yet," Helen said, sitting on her bed.

"But you *do* want to get married someday, right? You always talk about it like it's so important to you, although I don't know why."

"Now you're starting to sound like Carolyn."

"I don't mean it that way. A lot of successful women never married. They had their careers to think about. Like me. Once I'm a doctor, I'll devote all my time to my patients. I don't plan on ever getting married. Besides, after the way the men treat me at school, I don't know if I could ever respect a man enough to want to marry him. He'd have to be awfully special."

"Well, the reason I want to get married is nothing as lofty as your ambition to heal everyone in the world—"

"I never said that."

"Just teasing. I know it sounds pretty ordinary, but I just want to find a guy who's wonderful and kind and one I can fall head over heels in love with. Someone I want to spend the rest of my life with, have kids with, watch them grow up and finally go out on their own to do whatever they want to do with their lives. And not spend my old age taking care of Mom and Dad, like Miss Clausen in 2B."

"Sounds like a *Father Knows Best* life."

"Kind of, I guess. But that's what I want. A nice peaceful life with a man I love who loves me."

"Dream on, dear sister. Fairy tales don't exist."

"Maybe they do."

Helen woke to a glorious Friday morning. The rising sun lit up her bedroom with a warm glow. The city's skyscrapers would soon overshadow that silvery sliver of daylight, but Helen enjoyed these few minutes of sunrise. She got up, washed, and dressed with more care than usual, for tonight was her second date with Charlie.

"You look nice," Peggy said, sitting on the edge of her bed and rubbing the sleep out of her eyes. "What's the occasion?"

"I'm meeting Charlie after work," Helen said.

"Oh, that's right. Better bring a jacket or a sweater in case it gets cool later."

"I know. I'd like to borrow Carolyn's pink cardigan. It matches this plaid skirt perfectly. And pink looks good on me."

"Ask her." Peggy leaned over and poked Carolyn in the ribs. "Hey, sleepyhead. Can Helen borrow your pink sweater? She's got a date with Prince Charming tonight."

"Huh? What?" Carolyn half sat up and squinted in Helen's direction. "Who?"

"You remember," Peggy said, "the guy I told you about the other day. The one who ran over one of Helen's kids."

"Oh, yeah. Him. Wait a minute. He ran over one of your kids? And you're going out with him?"

"You're impossible," Peggy said, "And half asleep. Just let Helen borrow your sweater, okay?"

"Yeah, sure," Carolyn said and lay down, pulling the blanket over her head.

"See, nothing to it," Peggy said.

28

"Thanks, Peg. I owe you."

Helen stood in front of the mirror to see how everything looked. She slipped the sweater over the pale lavender blouse. With the pink and lavender plaid pencil skirt, it completed the outfit perfectly. The blouse's Peter Pan collar lay flat on top of the sweater and complimented her brown Mary Jane heels and matching purse.

"Think I should wear pearls?" she asked Peggy.

"Where are you going?"

"I don't know. That's just it. Charlie wouldn't tell me."

"Then I wouldn't. Might be too fancy. Besides, I think that outfit looks great without jewelry."

"Okay. I'll just wear my tiny gold ball earrings."

"Perfect," Peggy said as she headed to the bathroom to get washed and dressed for school.

"Well, don't you look nice today," Helen's mom said when she came into the kitchen. "Just like a breath of spring."

"Do you think it's too summery, Mom?"

"Not at all. And it's supposed to be warm today, so it's perfect."

Helen poured juice into everyone's glasses and placed cereal boxes on the table while her mother put the coffee on to perk.

"Remember, I won't be home for dinner tonight."

"I remember. Who are you going out with?"

"Oh, just someone from work."

"Really." Her mother looked at her, shook her head, and sighed.

Helen ignored her mother's skepticism, drank her juice, and poured cereal into her bowl.

"Morning," Peggy said, bounding into the kitchen. She walked between the table and the sink to get to her chair in the corner of the room.

Helen sat next to Peggy. Once they sat down, their mother pulled up the drop leaf for the table so their father could squeeze into his chair, his back to the sink. That left the end of the table for Carolyn and their mother.

Morning logistics finished, everyone dug into their cereal. By the time they finished, the coffee was ready.

"So," their father said, "what do you girls have planned for today?"

Even after all their years in the States, Helen's parents still had an Irish lilt to their voices. Which wasn't surprising since most of their neighbors, and the men her dad worked with as masons, were from "the old country" too. It was hard to develop an American voice when everyone around you talked with a brogue.

"School," Peggy said.

"Work," Carolyn said.

"Work," Helen said.

"And?" her father said. "And don't be telling me there's nothing else, Helen. There's a reason you're not coming home to dinner. What would that be?"

"Nothing, Dad. Just going out with a friend."

"Would that be a male or female friend?" he asked.

Helen's face took on a rosy color, and Peggy and Carolyn fidgeted in their chairs.

"Dad, could I get up?" Peggy asked. "I have an early class."

"You'll sit right where you are until I get an answer from your sister." He turned to Helen. "Are you going to make your sister late for school? Or are you going to tell me who you're stepping out with tonight?" He folded his arms across his chest and rooted himself further down in his chair.

"Just a guy I met at work," Helen said.

"And is this the same scallywag that kept you out till all hours the other night?"

"Dad, I was home before ten."

"And even that's too late on a work night. Now, tell me, love, why isn't this beau of yours coming by the house to pick you up and meet your parents? What has he got to hide?"

"Dad, first of all, he's not my beau. And he's picking me up after my shift ends. It's just more convenient."

"For who? Him or you?"

"Dad, you're being old-fashioned. It's 1955 and I'm a grown woman. I shouldn't have to bring him home for your approval. I can make my own decisions about whether or not he's respectable."

Peggy and Carolyn squirmed in their seats, and their mother fiddled with her coffee cup.

"Paddy," she said, "we can discuss this later. The girls have to get to work and school."

Paddy threw his napkin on the table. "I'll not have my daughters traipsing all over town without me knowing who they're with."

He shoved his chair back, crashing it into the sink behind him.

"We're not done here, lass," he said to Helen. "I'll be waiting up for you tonight and you'll be bringing your young man home with you so I can get a good look at him."

"But Dad—"

"No buts about it. That's settled."

Paddy stormed out of the kitchen, his heavy steps rattling the dishes in the cabinet. He grabbed his lunch bucket from the top of the fridge, and his cap and jacket off the peg by the door. The slamming door echoed throughout the apartment.

CHAPTER FOUR

Charlie paced the sidewalk in front of the Foundling, hands thrust deep in his pants pockets, his flat cap pulled low on his forehead. When he reached the end of the building, he stopped, turned, checked his wristwatch, then continued in the opposite direction. Back and forth he went until Helen opened the front door. Charlie's pacing halted in mid-stride. He greeted her with an extended wolf whistle.

"You look great." A smile lit up his face. "Everyone'll be jealous of me tonight and wonder where I found such an angel."

Helen's face turned red as a cherry. "Charlie, stop. You're embarrassing me."

"Sorry, Helen, but I can't help it. You look like a movie star."

Helen looped her arm through his and they walked down the block.

"Where are we going tonight?"

"First, I thought we'd grab something to eat, then... a surprise."

"A good surprise, I hope."

Charlie smiled and thought, *I hope so too.*

They walked across town to a small restaurant on 8th Avenue.

"Anything exciting happen today?" Charlie asked after they were seated. "Anyone run over one of your kids?"

"Charlie! That's a terrible thing to say. Don't even joke about that."

"Geez, Helen, I was just kidding. I mean, that's how we met and all. I'd never want to see one of those little guys get hurt. I hope you know that."

Helen played with the food on her plate. "I do," she said, refusing to look at him. "That just sounded so mean."

Charlie winced and reached across the table for her hand. "I'm really sorry. Forgive me?"

She looked into his eyes. "Oh, Charlie. You look like a puppy who's been caught chewing on a slipper."

He frowned. "I wanted this to be a really special night and I've ruined it." He looked at his plate and shoved it aside.

"It still can be, Charlie. Let's start over. Tell me what you did today, then I'll tell you about my day. How does that sound?"

The frown on Charlie's face and the furrows on his forehead disappeared. The corners of his mouth curled in a tentative smile.

"You sure?"

"Of course, I'm sure."

"Okay, although my day wasn't too exciting."

As he talked, he dug into his pot roast and mashed potatoes. He had spent the day at the Settlement House working with another trainer to set up a schedule for sparring matches and regular routines for the boys. One young wannabee, Sean, had caught his eye, and he wanted to focus on developing his natural ability.

"You should see him, Helen. It's like he knows exactly what the other guy is going to do before it happens. I know some guys telegraph their punches, but Sean can see them coming even when they don't do that. And he sets himself up to block the punch and get in one of his own. He's a natural."

"Sound like you've found a winner. When do you plan on putting him in a real fight?"

"I don't think he's ready for that yet. I don't want to rush him. If I put him in too soon, he might get beaten and decide this isn't his game. I don't want that to happen. Not when he's got so much going for him."

"I'm sure you know what's best. I know nothing about boxing. I've watched a few matches on TV with my dad, and he took me to Sunnyside Gardens once to see the Golden Glove fights, but that's it. He's a big fan."

"Oh yeah?"

"Yep," she said between mouthfuls of her pork chop. "In fact, he'd like to meet you." Helen kept her head down and speared a slice of sweet potato as she said this.

"He's heard of me? Not many people follow the light heavyweight division. Most people are only interested in the heavyweights."

"Um," Helen said. She swallowed the slice of potato. "I'm not really sure if he follows your career. I think he's more interested in seeing if he thinks you're suitable to date me." She grabbed her beer and took a long gulp.

Charlie stared at her, mouth hanging open. Helen refused to look at him. Instead, she focused on the food still on her plate and waited for his reaction.

"You're joking, right?" She didn't answer him. "Helen? You can't be serious."

35

Finally, she looked up. "I'm afraid I am, or rather he is. He told me I have to bring you upstairs when we get home tonight so he can meet you."

"And what will he do if I don't agree? I mean, it's a little ridiculous. I'm thirty-eight years old, not sixteen. And you're old enough that he should trust your judgement about the men you date." Charlie drummed his fingers on the table.

Helen fiddled with her napkin and looked everywhere but at Charlie.

"Wait a minute. Helen, will he take it out on you if I don't agree?"

"What?" She stared at him wide-eyed. "You mean hit me or something?"

"That's exactly what I mean."

"Gosh, no. He's the sweetest man in the world. He'd never lay a hand on my mom, me, or my sisters. Not ever." Helen's eyes brimmed with tears. "He's old fashioned. I know it's silly, but that's just the way he is. He says as long as we're living under his roof, he wants to know who we're 'stepping out with,' as he puts it." She reached across the table and took his hand.

Charlie stared at her, but remained silent.

"Please, Charlie?" The tears finally breached her eyelids and rolled down her cheeks. "Guess *I've* ruined the night. You thought you did, but I did instead." She pulled her hand back across the table and placed her napkin next to her plate. "I've had fun, but I guess if you can't do this one little thing, spending time with me doesn't mean as much to you as it does to me. I'm sorry, Charlie."

She stood and started walking away.

"Hey," Charlie said, coming out of his stupor, "where are you going?"

"Home, I guess. Thanks for dinner, Charlie. It was nice knowing you, if only for a little while."

"Wait a minute. Come back here and sit down. You didn't finish your beer. That's a sin in my book."

Charlie grinned, jumped up, and pulled out her chair. "M'lady. Have a seat."

Helen laughed and wiped the tears from her face. "Does this mean you'll come up and meet my father?"

"I'm always willing to meet an adoring fan," he said, a twinkle in his eye. *Even if I think he's a jerk.*

"Here we are!" Charlie said. He looked up in adoration at the sign above the door.

STILLMAN'S GYM
TRAINING HERE DAILY
BOXING INSTRUCTIONS
see JACK CURELY

"It's called The World Capital of Boxing."

Helen looked at the dimly lit seedy stairway sandwiched between a GE Appliance Repair shop and a hock shop and felt her stomach drop. She had thought they might go see a movie, or go dancing at the City Center, not spend the night in a smelly gym.

"This is where I got my start and I still train here every day, when I'm in town. I can't wait for you to meet all the guys. I know you'll love them. They're the best guys in the world."

Helen gave Charlie a weak smile and hoped her dinner would stay down.

"C'mon." He grabbed her hand and pulled her up the filthy staircase. As they got closer to the top, the pungent stink of men's sweat and stale cigarette and cigar smoke almost choked her. At the top, a tired looking middle-aged man stood in the doorway, glasses perched on his nose.

37

"Hey, Jack, I want you to meet Helen Campbell. Helen, this is Jack Curley. He taught me everything I know."

"Don't go blaming me for your mistakes, kid. Fifty cents each to get in," Jack said, hand extended. "Nice to meet ya' doll," he said to Helen, looking her over from head to toe.

A blush crept from Helen's neck to her hairline, whether from embarrassment or humiliation, she wasn't sure.

"Thought we'd take in tonight's fight. What do you think Helen? Excited?" Charlie pointed to a man sitting at a desk in the corner. "That's Lou Stillman. He owns the place. He always sits right there so he can watch the door and make sure no one gets in without paying. And I mean no one. If some celebrity tries it, Lou yells, 'Pay up, ya bum.' He's great."

While Charlie talked, he pulled Helen over to the gallery seats. "These seats okay?"

Helen looked at the wooden folding chairs in a daze. "They're fine, Charlie."

"Swell. You want something to drink? There's a counter in the back that sells food at lunch, but they might still have some sodas or something."

"No, I'm fine." Helen couldn't imagine eating or drinking anything. It was tough enough to hold her dinner down. She knew the gym's stench would stay in her nose for days, and she'd probably never get it out of Carolyn's sweater.

"Hey, Charlie," someone called from across the room.

"Joe! Didn't expect to see him here tonight. Helen, mind if I go over and get Joe? He's my trainer. Gee, this is great. I really want you to meet him, okay?"

"Sure, I'll be right here when you get back."

Charlie squeezed her shoulder. "Save the seat next to you for Joe. I'll put my cap on my seat."

Then he bolted across the room. After he left, Helen looked around. The ceiling soared into a black void. Posters of past and upcoming fights were pasted or tacked on the columns and walls of the loft. On the balcony that ran around the perimeter of the gym, men punched heavy bags and speed bags while others shadow boxed and jumped rope. There were two boxing rings. One surrounded by the gallery seats, the other for sparring. While Helen looked around at the characters in the gallery and milling around the gym, two men climbed into the sparring ring. After a few punches, Lou Stillman yelled over, "Get out of the ring, ya bum. You call yourself a professional?"

Helen broke out in a cold sweat, assuming there would be a brawl any minute. Growing up where she did, she had seen knives pulled over lesser offenses. Instead, some men laughed, the boxers kept sparring, and no one stopped what they were doing long enough to pay attention.

Guess they're used to him screaming insults.

"Helen, I want you to meet my trainer, Joe Hayes. Joe, Helen Campbell."

"Nice to meet you, Helen," Joe said, pulling off his fedora and shaking her hand. "Whatever did a pretty young lady like you see in this bum?"

"Don't pay any attention to him, Helen. He just wishes he'd met you first. Joe, grab the seat next to Helen. That way, if she has questions about the fight, she can ask you to explain. She told me she doesn't know much about boxing."

"And where are you going to be that she'd have to ask me?"

39

"You know me, Joe, I can't sit still for too long when I'm in this gym."

"Helen, I think you'll be sorry he brought you here tonight. It's like he's got ants in his pants when he sees other boxers he knows or admires. He's got to go talk to them. But I won't desert you."

"You'll be okay if I leave for a minute or two, won't you?" Charlie asked Helen. "I don't want the guys to think I'm getting too high and mighty for them just because I brought the most beautiful girl in the city with me."

"I'll be fine, especially since I have Joe to take care of me."

"That's swell. Oh, Joe, look. There's Bobby. Helen, I've got to say hello. Bobby's just starting out, but I know he's going to be great."

"Go ahead, Charlie."

He was out of his seat before Helen finished talking.

"Who's Bobby?" she asked Joe.

"Bobby Bartles. He's from Queens and he's good. Charlie's right. He's going to be a great fighter."

"He looks more like a movie star than a boxer."

"You're right. A real leading man type. I hope he still has his looks after a few fights. Good-looking guys attract more women to the fights than some of these beat-up old timers."

"And do you really want more women at the fights?"

"Well... they're a lot easier on the eye than a bunch of broken-nosed cauliflower-eared men."

Helen laughed and started to ask another question when the bell rang and the referee jumped into the ring to announce the fighters. There wasn't an emcee or announcer like Helen had seen on the *Gillette Cavalcade of Sports* TV show she sometimes watched with her father. This was much more informal. The referee read the night's card and the two boxers climbed into the ring amid both cheers and jeers.

Charlie came back to his seat just as the bell rang to start the first round. The two men on either side of Helen could have been on another planet. They were so fixated on the action in the ring, it was like she wasn't even there. The bell rang again to signal the end of Round 1.

"Do you see the way Hank's flat footing it?" Joe asked. "He won't last long unless he starts to tap dance."

"You're right. And he's not covering his left side at all," Charlie said.

Helen sat mute while the two men critiqued the boxers' performances. The bell rang for Round 2.

"Did you see that, Helen?" Joe asked after one boxer landed a punch. "That's called an upper cut. You try to get in under the other guy's defenses and land one on his chin."

"That must hurt. I'm amazed anyone has any teeth after a punch like . . ."

Helen's voice drifted off. She stared across the ring at a couple who had just arrived and were trying to find two seats together.

"Helen? You all right?" Joe asked.

Charlie was busy discussing the fight with another boxer who sat on his left.

"Charlie," Joe yelled over the noise of the gym, "something's wrong with Helen."

"What?" Charlie turned and looked at her. All the color had drained from her face and she stared straight ahead, not responding to either of them.

"Helen," Charlie yelled, shaking her arm. "Helen, what is it? What happened, Joe?"

"I swear, I don't know. She was fine one minute, then the next, she turned into a statue, just staring across the ring."

Charlie looked over to where Helen stared. He didn't see anything unusual.

"Helen." He grabbed her chin and swung her head around to face him. "Helen, say something."

Her eyes focused on his and she shook her head. "What? What's the matter?"

"Oh, thank God you're all right. Joe and I thought you were having a fit or something."

"A fit? What are you talking about? Charlie, that makes no sense at all."

"Helen," Joe said, "we were talking and all of a sudden you stopped and froze. Scared me to death, I have to say. What happened?"

"I... I don't know. Maybe the fight... being up this close... I don't know. And... and I thought I saw someone I know."

"Do you want to leave, or go say hello to whoever you saw?" Charlie asked.

"No. No, I'm fine now. Honest. And it wasn't the person I thought it was. Sorry to have caused you both to worry."

"You're sure?" Charlie asked.

Helen nodded, but Charlie grabbed her hand and didn't leave his seat for the rest of the fight. Joe kept one eye on the fight and one on her for the next few rounds.

She was aware of their concern, but she knew what had happened had nothing to do with the fight or the gym. One half of the couple who came in late was her sister, Carolyn. And when the man with her removed his hat, and gave Carolyn a loving kiss, the gym's lights glittered off his gold wedding band.

42

CHAPTER FIVE

After the fight, Joe said, "Why don't we take Helen to the Neutral Corner? I'm sure she'd get a kick out of the place. And you never know who's going to show up there."

"What's the Neutral Corner?" Helen asked.

"It's a bar just down the street," Charlie said. "Everyone goes there when they leave the gym."

The best you could say about Neutral Corner was that it was a neighborhood dive bar. It was only wide enough for the fifty-foot-long bar with for a one-person line-up against the wall behind the bar stools. Cigar and cigarette smoke created a gray cloud that made it difficult to see anything from the front door. Newcomers had to squeeze their way through the crowded bar to reach the few wobbly tables and chairs that filled the back room.

"I'll get us some beers," Joe said after they wiggled through the bar crowd. "Unless you'd like something else, Helen?"

"Beer is fine, Joe."

Joe nodded and Helen watched him squeeze his way back to the bar and poke his fist between two men camped out on bar stools. He waved a few bills to catch the bartender's eye. A minute later, three beer bottles replaced the bills, and Joe headed back. The tables had filled up right after the fights, so Helen and Charlie leaned on the bar-height shelf that circled the room.

"Boy, it's really crowded in here," Helen said.

"Yep. Most of the guys have figured out who won the fight before the last round, so they head over here to beat the crowd."

"So, that's why the gym seemed emptier when we left."

"The really smart ones leave around the middle of the fight, unless it's a real close match. That way, they can get a seat at the bar. The corner up front by the window is, of course, the most prized spot. That way, you can look outside and see everyone who's coming in."

Helen looked towards the front window and wondered how anyone could see out. It looked like no one had washed it since the day the bar opened. The same couldn't be said for the bottles behind the bar or the glasses that hung overhead. They sparkled in the reflection from the big globe lights suspended from the ceiling.

"Here we are," Joe said, handing each of them a cold Rheingold. He took a long swig and said, "Delicious. Just what I wanted after that hot gym. You'd think Lou would open a window or something in that place."

Charlie laughed. "You know him. He thinks fresh air isn't good for you. I sometimes wonder if he ever leaves that place."

"I don't know. I've never been there when he's not there. Maybe he has a little room for himself in the back or something."

While the men talked, Helen looked around the bar. Most of the men were either hard-looking toughs wearing fedoras, or working men wearing flat caps like Charlie's. A few fit somewhere in between, like Joe, but there were no dandies like the man Carolyn was with tonight. The image of Carolyn and her well-dressed date flashed through Helen's mind. She didn't remember what he looked like. All she could remember was that gold band on his finger.

"How'd you like the fight?" Charlie asked, bringing her back to reality.

"It was exciting. I've never seen a real fight in person. I mean, the Golden Globes were fun, but they're only kids, not like these guys."

"You didn't mind all the sweat and blood flying around?" Joe asked.

"I have to admit, that wasn't the best part, but since none of it landed on me, it was okay."

They laughed at that and Charlie said, "That's why I didn't take seats in the front row."

"Thank you for that."

"Another beer?" Joe asked, draining his bottle.

"I think we'd better get going," Helen said. "It's getting late and my dad likes to get to bed by eleven o'clock."

Charlie looked at his wristwatch and cursed under his breath. "He's not going to be very happy with me then. It's already ten-thirty."

Joe looked at Charlie, questions written all over his face. He opened his mouth to speak, but Charlie shook his head, and Joe slammed his mouth shut.

"We'd better get going then," Helen said. "Maybe he won't mind too much. It *is* Friday, and he has off tomorrow, so he can always sleep a little later."

"I'll keep my fingers crossed," Charlie said.

"It was nice meeting you, Joe. I hope I see you again soon."

"Count on it."

"Oh, and thanks for the beer."

"Anytime, Helen. Anytime."

Charlie took Helen's hand and led her through the crowd, now somewhat thinner than when they arrived. He could only hope his first impression on her father wouldn't be a disastrous one.

"I'll go in first, to make sure my parents are still up. You wait out here." She closed her apartment door and left Charlie standing in the hall.

Only seconds after she left, head lowered, hands deep in his pockets, he started pacing up and down, past the other apartment doors. The sharp rap of his heels against the tiles echoed in the silent hallway. The thought that he might disturb her neighbors flitted through his mind, but he didn't care. If Helen's parents were going to treat him like a teenager, he'd act like one. And maybe if Helen's father was asleep, he'd wake him up. In an act of rebellion, he walked faster and with more purpose.

"Charlie," Helen called from the apartment door, "couldn't you stand still for one minute? You're making an awful racket."

"Guess I'm a little hot under the collar. I'm not used to being interviewed by parents."

"Don't think of it that way. He just wants to meet you. That's all."

"Humph."

"I won't let Dad keep you for more than a few minutes. I promise."

Helen wrung her hands, but she noticed a smile creeping along the corners of his mouth and a mischievous twinkle surfacing in his eyes.

"Oh, I can be nice, but it'll cost you."

46

Her forehead creased in a worried frown. "Cost me?"

"Sure, if I'm going to put on a show for your parents, you'll have to pay the piper, so to speak."

Helen stuck her chin out, her mouth set in a defiant scowl, hands on her hips, and said, "What's your price?"

"A kiss."

Her eyes widened, her scowl transformed into a smile, and her hands went from her hips to Charlie's shoulders.

"Is that all?" She leaned into him and pressed her lips against his.

Charlie, shocked at her ready acceptance of his terms, stood lifeless as a statue, hands still shoved in his pockets.

"Thought I'd get a better reaction than that," Helen said, "or a least *some* reaction. I must be losing my touch."

Charlie shook his head, trying to clear the petty behavior that clogged his brain.

"I didn't expect... that is, I thought maybe after . . ."

"Oh, shut up, Charlie."

This time he was ready. When Helen looped her arms around his neck, he pulled her close and met her lips with a fervor that made her gasp.

"Whew, I wish we didn't have to face my parents right now."

"Me too, but we'd better get in there before your old man comes out looking for me."

Helen grabbed Charlie's hand and pulled him into the apartment. They walked down the long hallway, each trying to wipe the silly grins from their faces.

"Mom, Dad, this is Charlie Sanders."

"Mrs. Campbell, Mr. Campbell," Charlie said. "Sorry I couldn't meet you earlier tonight. We were on a pretty tight schedule and I didn't think we'd have time for Helen to come home before our dinner appointment."

"Oh," Helen's mom said, "You took her to dinner, did you?"

"Yes, ma'am. Couldn't have her starving all night, could I?"

Helen watched her father through this exchange, her hands twisting around each other.

"I'm sure dinner didn't last until . . ." he looked at his wristwatch, "eleven o'clock."

"No sir. We went to a boxing match."

"Boxing, huh?" her father's eyebrows shot up and the gleam in his eyes replaced the squinty appraisal he had been giving Charlie. "I'm quite a fan of boxing. I sometimes go to the Sunnyside Garden fights, I do."

Helen's mother's head shot up. "And why is this the first I'm hearing about it, Paddy? When do you do that?"

"Aggie, it's no time to be discussing that. Not in front of Helen's young man."

"You haven't heard the last of this from me, Paddy Campbell."

He rolled his eyes and breathed a deep sigh.

"And did you enjoy the fight, Helen?" her father asked.

"Oh, yes, Dad. It was very exciting. Much better than the Golden—"

Her father coughed. "No need to be comparing things, pet," he said, waving his hand downward. "You can tell us all about it tomorrow. But right now, I think it's time me and your mam got to bed." He stood, walked over to Charlie, and extended his hand. "Nice to meet you." He looked at Helen, who was smiling up at Charlie.

"Maybe you and Mrs. Campbell can come to a fight with us sometime," Charlie said.

"Oh, heavens be praised. I think not."

"Aggie, there's nothing wrong with a good, clean fight."

48

Aggie glared at Paddy and Helen said, "I'll walk you to the door, Charlie."

"Goodnight, folks," Charlie said.

Helen pushed him out of the living room and down the hall. Once they were out of the apartment, she said, "Thank you, Charlie. You were perfect."

He took her into his arms and gave her a good night kiss that would assure she had pleasant dreams all night.

"He seems like a pleasant enough lad," Aggie said, settling into the bed next to Paddy.

"Too nice. He's been around the block too many times to be acting like an unbroken stallion. I'll be keeping my eye on him, I will."

"Och, Paddy, no man's good enough for your princesses. It's time Helen found someone. She's not getting any younger, you know. Or do you want her to remain a spinster and stay home taking care of you her whole life?"

"Course not, Aggie."

"Good."

"But I'm still going to keep an eye on him," he mumbled.

Aggie squeezed his hand. "Go to sleep, love. It was only one date. Maybe nothing'll come of it at all. Now, give us a kiss and turn out the light."

Paddy did as he was told, but a worried frown creased his forehead until he fell asleep.

CHAPTER SIX

"So, is he The One?" Peggy asked when Helen came into their bedroom.

"Maybe," Helen said. The smile on her face said more than words could. She slid her pajamas out from under her pillow and grabbed the jar of cold cream from the top of the dresser. "Wait a minute. Where's Carolyn?"

"Who knows. You know her. She'll climb up the fire escape and tap on the window when she's ready to come home if she thinks she won't be able to use her key quietly enough not to wake Mom or Dad."

Helen's frown prompted Peggy to ask, "Why the sudden concern? You know how she is."

"Yeah, I know. But tonight's different."

"Why?"

"It just is. Isn't that good enough for you?"

"Not in a million years. What's going on?"

Helen plopped down on her bed and scooped a wad of cold cream onto her face. While she smeared it all over to remove her make-up, Peggy grabbed some tissues and sat next to her.

"Here," she said, handing them to Helen. "Now, the truth. What's up with Carolyn?"

Helen lifted her shoulders and dropped them with a deep sigh. "I saw her tonight."

"So? What's so amazing about that? Seems she's out every night, somewhere or other."

"I know." Helen turned to face Peggy. "That's just it. She's out every night and Dad never asks to meet the men she dates. Why do I have to bring them home? Charlie's perfectly respectable. Not like her date tonight. But I bet Dad never met him. If he had, Carolyn'd be locked in this room until she turned forty."

"Whoa. Who is this guy? Where'd you see her? You have to tell me everything now."

Peggy pulled herself further up on the bed and sat cross-legged, waiting for all the details.

Helen wiped some cold cream off her face, spread another big glob on, and said, "Okay, but you can't tell Mom or Dad. Promise? I want to talk to Carolyn first."

Peggy rolled her eyes. "Of course, I won't blab to them. Do you think I'm an idiot?"

"Sorry. I'm just upset. I saw Carolyn tonight at Stillman's Gym—"

"He took you to a gym for your first date? Geez, he's weird. Who wants to go to a smelly gym on a date?"

"Peggy, shut up and listen, or I won't tell you anything."

"Okay, okay. Sorry."

"We went there to see a fight—"

"A fight! Like a street brawl?"

"Peggy!"

"Sorry. Go ahead."

"A boxing match, okay? Anyway, right after the fight began, Carolyn came in with a man. I probably wouldn't have even noticed her, but the guy kept asking people to

52

change seats so they could sit together. When he leaned over to kiss her, he reached up to take off his hat and that's when I saw his wedding band."

"A wedding band? Are you sure?"

"Of course, I'm sure. What else could a gold band on the third finger of his left hand be?"

"Don't know." Peggy shrugged and pulled at a loose thread at the bottom of her pajama leg. "Maybe it's a school ring or something like that."

Helen eyed her younger sister. "You know something you're not telling me."

Peggy shrugged again.

"Peggy. Look at me. You knew Carolyn was dating a married man? How long have you known? Did she tell you? When?"

"Geez, you don't have to give me the third degree. And she didn't tell me he was married. I just kind of guessed he might be."

"Why?"

"Cause she said he was older, in his forties, and that he took her to fancy places and expensive restaurants. There aren't too many single men in their forties who Carolyn would date. You know how picky she is. And if they could afford those kinds of places, there'd be women all over them. Most a lot prettier and more sophisticated than Carolyn."

"How did you even find out about him?"

"She came home late one night. Real late. About two in the morning. You were working one of your overnights at the Foundling. Anyway, she knocked on the window and woke me. Not that I was really asleep. I was worried about her. After I let her in, I asked where she'd been all night. I told her I'd tell Mom if she didn't answer me. So, she told me about this guy she's been seeing. But she

53

never said he was married. I only kind of assumed that after I thought about it for a while."

"And you never asked her?"

Peggy shook her head.

"Why not?"

"Maybe I didn't really want to know."

Helen stared at her sister. She didn't know whether she wanted to hug her and assure her everything would be all right, or scream at her for keeping this to herself.

"You should go to bed, Peg. I'll wait up for Carolyn."

Peggy uncurled her legs and walked over to her bed. "You won't tell Carolyn I told you about him, will you?"

"Course not. Go to sleep."

Peggy climbed into bed and pulled the thin sheet up to her chin. "Night, Helen."

"Night."

Helen finished removing her make-up, gave her hair a good brushing, and put on her pajamas. She climbed into bed and opened the book that sat on the night table. She started reading, but when she turned the page, she realized she had no idea what she had just read. She held the book in her lap and thought about Carolyn.

She was always the wildest one of the three of them. Always willing to take a dare, try anything just to see if she could get away with it. Helen remembered the time she spotted Carolyn hanging out with some girls from another neighborhood. They looked like the whores on 42nd Street. Dark mascara and eyeliner, bright red lipstick, too much rouge. And Carolyn matched them, right down to the ponytail tied back with a long chiffon scarf. Helen marched across the street, grabbed Carolyn by the arm, and pulled her away. When one girl ran after them screaming Carolyn had her scarf, Helen ripped it off her sister's head and flung it to the ground. Somehow, she kept herself from giving Carolyn a good beating, but not by much. Carolyn's tears did help wipe the make-up off her face though.

After that came a series of indiscretions. Carolyn getting drunk in the alley behind their tenement. Carolyn twisted around some loser in the backseat of his car. Carolyn smoking cigarettes, and maybe something a little stronger. Although she told Helen she only ever took two drags because she didn't want her teeth and fingers to turn brown like old Mrs. Schmidt. A habit she kept right up to today. All of which Helen hid from their parents.

Carolyn wasn't stupid, but she liked to be pampered and only someone who was making a lot of money could afford to cater to her tastes. Peggy was right about that. But there was always a price to pay, one that usually didn't involve cash.

A loud tap on the window startled Helen and drew her away from the dark thoughts that had crept into her mind.

The prodigal sister was home.

CHAPTER SEVEN

"Thanks," Carolyn said, climbing through the window.

Helen stood in front of her, arms folded across her chest, her lips pulled tight into a slash across her face.

"Where have you been?" she said through gritted teeth. Carolyn froze.

"What?" She looked into Helen's eyes, now steel blue daggers. "Oh, don't be ridiculous," Carolyn said, pushing past her.

Helen reached out and grabbed Carolyn's arm. "You're not putting me off that easily," she hissed. "I saw you tonight at Stillman's and I want to know who that man was."

Carolyn's eyes widened. "You were there?"

"Yes. On a legitimate date. Not sneaking around with a married man, like you."

Carolyn's mouth dropped open, but she said nothing. She pulled her arm away from Helen and strutted over to her bed.

"What I do is none of your business," she said, undressing.

"You couldn't be more wrong."

"Sorry you don't believe me, but it's true."

"What do you think Dad'll do if he finds out you're gallivanting around town with a married man?"

"He won't. Unless you tell him."

"You know I won't do that, but you owe me an explanation. And Peggy."

"Peggy? She doesn't know anything. Unless you blabbed. Couldn't keep this juicy little tidbit to yourself? Just had to tell someone?"

"I didn't need to. She already guessed your dirty little secret."

"What? How?"

"The night you came home at two o'clock. She's not stupid. It didn't take much for her to put two and two together."

"Well, so now she knows," Carolyn said, slipping into her pajamas. "At least now I don't have to keep it a secret anymore. That gets really tiresome."

The slap across her face echoed around the room. Carolyn staggered backwards and grabbed the dresser to stay on her feet. Tears welled in her eyes as her cheek blossomed into a fiery red blotch. She raised her hand to cover it and stared, horrified, at Helen.

"You slut." Helen turned her back on her sister and climbed into bed.

Carolyn never moved as Helen turned out the light, plunging the room into darkness, although she knew she wouldn't sleep that night. Her stomach churned and she swallowed hard, afraid she'd be sick before she could get to the bathroom. She had never hit either of her sisters in anger until tonight. Even after all Carolyn's antics, she always found a reason to forgive. But tonight was different. Something had hit Helen deep in her gut when she saw that ring. She thought about all the bastard babies at the Foundling and the women who left them there because they had no other viable options. Something she didn't like to think about.

Carolyn's behavior went against all the rules Helen had followed her entire life. But Carolyn never played by the rules. She looked for ways to defy them. And now, she had flaunted that defiance in her sister's face. In some strange warped way, in Helen's mind, Carolyn had crossed the line and there was no forgiveness this time.

"Helen?" Carolyn's voice trembled. "Helen, are you still awake? I need to explain."

Helen bolted upright in her bed. "Explain! There's nothing to explain. There's no way you can talk yourself out of this one. I can see now I never should have let you slide all these years. I should have told Mom about all the things you've done and the people you've been with and let her, or Dad, deal with you. I thought you'd grow up and come to your senses. But you're as willful and headstrong as you were when you were twelve years old. I'm done protecting you. You said it yourself the other day. You want men to desire and take care of you. A high-priced prostitute. Seems like you're on the right path, Carolyn. Good luck. You'll need it. Just don't come crawling to me or Peggy asking for help when you wind up in the gutter with the rest of the trash."

Carolyn stood next to Helen's bed, tears streaming down her cheeks. "You don't understand," she whispered.

"Oh, really? Did he tell you his *wife* doesn't understand him? That he's getting separated, or divorced, very soon? That he can't leave right now because of his kids? I didn't think you were naïve enough to fall for any of those lines. Men have one aim in mind when it comes to pretty young women. And I see the results every day when a nurse brings a newborn into the nursery. Is that

59

what you want? If so, you're well on your way. So now, tell me what I don't understand."

Carolyn crumpled onto her bed like a marionette with broken strings.

"I'm all ears," Helen said.

Carolyn looked at her, the defiant glare back in her eyes. "Did anyone ever tell you you're a real bitch?"

Helen smiled. "Frequently." She lay down and pulled up her sheet.

The next morning, the family sat around the kitchen table eating their cereal. Carolyn kept glancing over at Helen, waiting for her to drop the bomb that would expose all her lies. Instead, everyone chattered on as usual, talking about their plans for the day. By the time their mother poured the coffee, Carolyn had broken out in a cold sweat and her hand trembled as she lifted the coffee cup to her mouth.

Aggie noticed that, as a mother would, and asked, "Carolyn, are you sick, love? You're all sweaty and shivering."

"No, Mom, I'm fine." Her mother looked at her with arched eyebrows. "Really. I'm fine."

"You don't seem fine to me." Aggie reached over to put her hand on Carolyn's forehead. But Carolyn pulled away from her touch.

"Now, Aggie," Paddy said, "she's probably just suffering from the too much whiskey she had last night. Am I right, Carolyn?"

Peggy choked on the mouthful of coffee she had just sipped, Carolyn's face turned red, and Helen sat with a smug smirk on her face.

"You could do with some hair of the dog this morning, couldn't you?" he asked.

"No, Dad. I'm fine."

His icy blue eyes stared at her over the rim of his coffee cup. "Well then, since you're so fine, why don't you tell all of us where you were last night and what kept you out till all hours of the morning and why you felt the need to climb up the fire escape instead of using your key and coming in the front door like any civilized person would do?" He slammed his cup down on the saucer, almost shattering the two pieces. "And don't be telling me that's not what you've done. Do you think I'm a simpleton? Well?"

"No, Dad. Of course not."

"Glad to hear that. Well then, we're all waiting to hear your story."

"Paddy," Aggie said, "maybe we should let the girls go get ready for their—"

"NO. We'll all sit here to listen to this lass's tale. And find out who her accomplices are. For this isn't the first time she's been sneaking around like a second story man climbing in windows. Out with it, girl."

All three sisters sat in wide-eyed wonder, but no one said a word.

"Do you three think that just because your mam and I go to bed, we fall asleep while knowing one of you is still out there? We'd be sorry excuses for parents if we could rest easy while you're running around doing God knows what in this foul city." He looked around the table at each of his daughters. Aggie kept her eyes downcast and fiddled with her coffee cup. "Seeing as it's Saturday, I've all day to sit here and wait for an answer, Carolyn."

She looked at each of her sisters, then turned to face her father, her tremors replaced by an iron resolution that hardened her features into plates of steel.

"I was out." She took a sip of her coffee and placed the cup back on the saucer with just the slightest clink.

61

Paddy's hand slammed down on the table, rattling the dishes. All the women jumped in their seats. Aggie blessed herself and mumbled what could have been a prayer.

"Do you think I'll be accepting that as an answer?" Paddy's voice became a roar that filled the tiny kitchen. "Either you tell the whole story, or I swear to God, I'll be locking you in your bedroom and nailing the window shut until you do. And don't be telling me you were out with some other lasses from work, like you always claim." His face turned furnace red and his eyes bulged out of his head.

When Carolyn picked up her coffee cup, it shook so violently that she splashed coffee all over the saucer and tablecloth. Helen reached under the table and squeezed Peggy's hand.

"I had a date," Carolyn whispered, her eyes staring down at the table where Aggie was blotting up the spilled coffee with a napkin.

"A date, is it? And with who?"

"You don't know him. Just someone from work."

Helen and Peggy looked at each other out of the corners of their eyes.

"And why do you think you can date this man without introducing him to your parents?"

"It's just easier to leave right from the office There's no need to come all the way down here so you can *inspect* him. I'm twenty-four years old, not sixteen." Carolyn's defiant tone crept back with each word she spoke. "I should think you'd be happy I have a man interested in me. Not like Helen, who'll probably be an old maid and live here all her life. I certainly don't plan on doing that." She lit a cigarette, hands steady as a rock.

Paddy leaned back in his chair, evaluating his daughter. "Well now, maybe you're right, Carolyn. Maybe

62

you should be able to choose your own man, now that you're such a mature woman."

A smug smile slithered across her face. "Thank you, Dad. I knew you'd see it my way once I explained it to you. And if he turns out to be the—"

Paddy lifted his hand, palm out, towards Carolyn. "Let me finish." He took another sip of coffee. "Since you're so grown-up, I'm thinking you should be out on your own. Somewhere where you wouldn't have to worry about the rules of this house. That seems to be what you want. And then your mam and I could go to sleep not worrying about who you're seeing or what time you're coming home. Why, we wouldn't have to worry about you at all now, would we?"

Carolyn's face paled until there was no color left. But Paddy kept talking.

"You could get into all the mischief you'd want, and we'd never need know. I think that would suit you, would it not, Carolyn?"

"Well... I don't want you to worry about me when I'm out, of course. I can take care of myself. I really can, Dad. And I won't stay out so late anymore either. Promise."

"Don't you worry your head about that," he said. "For I'll not be standing in your way if I don't know where you are, or what you do, or when you come home when you're living on your own, now will I? It's all settled then. You'll start looking for a place of your own today. You should be able to move out by the end of the month, or sooner if you find a place like one of those women's hotels." He took a last sip of coffee. "Aggie, move your chair, love, so I can get up. I've things to do today if no one else in this family does."

"Paddy," Aggie said, "do you not think you're being a bit too harsh on the girl?"

Paddy glared at her. She stood, moved her chair, and watched him stride out of the room.

"Mom, you've got to do something," Carolyn said, grabbing her mother's arm. "Please. The end of the month's only two weeks away. I don't have any money to pay rent on an apartment. If Dad would give me some more time, maybe... or if you could convince him to change his mind . . ." She pleaded with her mother, who looked down at her from where she stood when Paddy left the room. Carolyn's eyes were moist with tears, a tentative smile inching across her face. "Please, Mammy. I promise it won't happen again."

"Now don't you be calling me the name you used when you were a wee babe. You'll not be tugging on my heartstrings doing that. You'll only make me think you're lying through your teeth."

Carolyn's mouth dropped open. Aggie went over to the table and cleared Paddy's dishes. "Helen, can I drop the leaf so's you can get up? If you're finished, that is."

"I am, Mom. Let me help you."

"I'll do the dishes," Carolyn said. She jumped up, scooped hers into the sink, and turned on the water.

"No need, love," Aggie said. "You should get out there and start looking for a place to live. You've not got much time."

Carolyn stood at the sink, dish rag in hand, and stared at her mother. "Aren't you even going to talk to Dad? Tell him I'm sorry? Get him to change his mind?"

Aggie rubbed her hands down the front of her apron. "No, love. He's made his decision and I can't say I disagree. You've always wanted your own way, so now you can have it without having to think of some outrageous lie to tell us in the morning."

"But Mom—"

"No, Carolyn. There'll be no more talk about it. Now, go on and find yourself a newspaper so's you can look at the For Rent ads." She turned and looked at Helen and Peggy, who were standing at the other end of the kitchen. "And I'll be having a word with both of you as soon as she's gone."

The two sisters waited to hear their sentences in this whole fracas.

Aggie looked at Carolyn, who hadn't moved an inch. "What are you waiting for? Get going, lass. Maybe Mr. Callahan, the real estate man down the block, can help you find something quick-like."

"But I don't have any money to pay him," Carolyn wiped away tears from her cheeks.

Aggie sighed. "Maybe those crocodile tears will work on him, love, but they're only aggravating me. Off with you. Now. I want to talk to your sisters."

"Fine." Carolyn threw the dishrag in the sink and stormed out of the kitchen. Aggie poured herself another cup of coffee and waited until she heard the apartment door slam shut before she turned to face Helen and Peggy.

"Well now," she said, pulling out Carolyn's chair. "I think you both owe your da and me an explanation as to why you thought you could lie to protect your sister. And I hope you'll both be going to confession today to tell the priest your sins. God may forgive you with a few Hail Mary's, but it's going to take more than that to get me to forget your trickery." She looked from one to the other. "You'd better sit. We might be here for a while. Best have another coffee too."

Helen went to the stove and brought the percolator back to the table. She poured herself a cup and looked at Peggy, coffee pot raised in her hand. Peggy shook her head, grimaced, and folded her hands in her lap.

"Peggy," Aggie said. "You may as well begin, seeing as how months ago you were the first to be helping your sister down this road of lies and deceit."

"That's not true, Mom," Helen said. "I'm to blame for this mess."

Aggie's eyebrows lifted halfway up her forehead. She took a sip of coffee and said, "Well then, I guess you should start."

Helen gulped some coffee and sat. "I've been covering up for Carolyn for years. And I don't know how many times I let her crawl through the window when it was past her curfew. I guess Peggy watched me do all these things and figured that was the right thing to do. So, she kept doing it even when I wasn't here. Don't blame her, Mom. It's all my fault. I'm the oldest and should have been setting an example, not showing her how to trick you and Dad."

Aggie sat listening and sipped her coffee. After what seemed like an eternity to the two girls, she said, "Why was last night different?"

"What?" Helen asked. "What do you mean 'different'?"

"Helen, your da and I aren't fools and this apartment isn't big enough to keep us from hearing bits and pieces of what goes on in your bedroom. Especially in the middle of the night when the whole world's quiet. And flesh slapping flesh has a sound like no other. So, are you going to tell me what caused you to slap your sister last night? Across the face I'd guess, judging from the raspberry on her cheek this morning. For it surely wasn't just her coming in late and keeping you from your beauty sleep."

Peggy gaped at Helen. "You hit Carolyn?"

"Yes, I hit her. She made me so mad I could have strangled her."

"Helen! You'll not be talking like that about your sister. I won't have it."

"Oh, Mom, you know I don't really mean it. It's just a figure of speech. But you know what she's like. She can be infuriating."

"That she can be, but what tipped you over the edge last night? That's what I'm still waiting to hear."

Helen fidgeted with her coffee cup, took a sip, and breathed a deep sigh. "I really don't want to tell you."

"I know you don't, love. But you have to. If your da's decision to toss her out of here is going to lead to even worse behavior, I have to know. No matter what she's done, she's still my daughter."

"I know, Mom." They could hardly hear Helen over the noise in the street below. She took a deep breath. "The man she's seeing is married."

"That was my worst fear," Aggie said, nodding her head, "and the only one that made sense of you calling her a slut."

"You heard that too?"

"These walls are paper thin, Helen. Or did you forget?"

"I guess I wasn't thinking of anything right then."

"And you, Peggy. Did you not think you should stop your sister before there was a brawl going on?"

"What?" Peggy pulled her eyes away from Helen, who she had been staring at like she was a complete stranger. "I swear, Mom, I never heard a thing."

"She didn't, Mom," Helen said. "She slept through everything. You know her, she'd sleep through an atom bomb."

"You're probably right there. I've never known anyone who could sleep like Peggy. Even as a wee babe." Aggie lips turned up at the corners as she looked at her youngest daughter and shook her head. "But you knew about your sister's foolishness even before Helen, didn't you?"

"Kind of."

"What's that supposed to mean?"

"When she came home so late that night Helen was working, I thought maybe she was seeing a married man, but I wasn't sure. And I didn't ask. I guess I didn't really want to know."

Peggy looked down at her hands still entwined in her lap. Helen reached over and rubbed her arm. Aggie pulled a handkerchief from her apron pocket and swiped it across her face.

"We've got ourselves a mess, for sure," Aggie said, looking at her two daughters. "You've both been dishonest with me, and your da, by not telling us what your sister's been up to. And look where it's got us. Carolyn practically out on the streets, and you two sinning up a storm. Never in my life did I think my girls would turn out like this."

Helen and Peggy looked like two first graders who had been called to the principal's office.

"I'm sorry, Mom," Helen said.

"Me too," Peggy said.

"What can we do to make things right?"

"I don't know as we'll ever be able to make things right after this," Aggie said. "But for now, maybe you'd better go after your sister and see if you can help her find a decent place to live. For I know your da isn't going to change his mind about that. Especially not after I tell him what you've told me."

"Do you have to tell him everything?" Helen asked.

"Aye, love. I do."

Helen and Peggy set off to find Carolyn. They started at Callahan's Real Estate, a storefront in the building next to theirs. But Rory Callahan said he hadn't seen Carolyn.

Not that he could have helped her anyway. He didn't know any decent landlords who would rent to a single woman and all would require the first month's rent, at least. Most would also want a month's security. And if they didn't require that, there was still his fee to pay. Since Carolyn didn't have a reserve fund of ready cash, it seemed impossible that she'd find an apartment.

So, the two women decided that women's residential hotels were Carolyn's only choice. Mr. Callahan pulled the Manhattan Yellow Pages Phone Directory down from the shelf and pointed to an empty desk where they could work. They pulled two chairs over to the desk and flipped through the pages of hotel listings until they came to "Hotels–Residential–Women."

In a few minutes, they had a list of the ones most likely to appeal to Carolyn. They eliminated the ones uptown in Harlem and downtown in the Bowery as being too far removed from her job. That left nine residences, four on the West Side and five on the East Side.

"Girls," Mr. Callahan said, "I don't know what's going on in your household, and I don't want to, but something's got you two in a tizzy. If it'd help, you can use the phone on that desk to call these places and ask whatever it is you're wanting an answer to."

"Really, Mr. Callahan?" Peggy asked. "Gee, that'd be swell."

He stood and reached for his hat that was hanging on the coat rack. "In return, you can watch the store for me while I go have a cup of coffee around the corner at Ed's. If the phone rings, answer it and take a message. If you need me, you know where I'll be."

"Thanks a million, Mr. Callahan," Helen said.

"Oh, one more thing, don't leave until I come back. Or come get me if you feel you have to dash off somewhere."

69

"You got it, Mr. Callahan," Peggy said. "You're swell."

He tipped his hat and strolled down the block.

"Okay," Helen said, "let's get started. We'll call the closest places first and work our way uptown."

Helen dialed the number of the Jeanne d'Arc Residence, only a couple of blocks away. A woman with a heavy French accent answered the phone, but said no one named Carolyn had been in that morning. Peggy checked that one off the list. Helen dialed the next two numbers and got the same response.

"What if she didn't go to any of these places?" Peggy asked.

"I don't know. And right now, I think it's kind of useless making more phone calls. I didn't think of it before, but how could Carolyn find out about all these places and get to them before we did? She certainly didn't keep a list of women's hotels in her pocket."

They stared out the large plate glass window of the real estate agency.

"Helen, do you think Carolyn would've called the man she's seeing?"

Helen's face paled. "She couldn't. She wouldn't. I mean, he's married. She couldn't just call his home. What would his wife say? Carolyn's not that crazy, is she?"

"I don't know. She sounded pretty desperate when she left. And you know her. She always thinks of herself first. She probably wouldn't care if his wife found out. Maybe she even hopes that's what would happen. Then the two of them could get an apartment together."

"That wouldn't happen. They wouldn't be married, and no decent landlord would rent to an unmarried couple."

"I bet there are plenty of landlords who would look the other way if enough money greased their palms. Or

Carolyn could lie and say they were married. Like the couple in the building down the block."

Helen squinted her eyes. "Who? What couple?"

"You know, the airport bus driver who pretends he's a pilot, and his make-believe wife, the stewardess."

"They're not married?"

"Don't tell me you didn't know that. Everyone knows they're not married. Just like everyone knows he's not an airline pilot. He thinks because he wears a uniform like a pilot's with little wings on his breast pocket, he has everyone fooled. But he doesn't. And when Mr. and Mrs. Schmidt went to LaGuardia to pick her sister up, they saw him loading people onto his bus to take them to Grand Central. So that confirmed it."

"How do you know all this?"

"I eavesdrop."

"Peggy, you're terrible." Helen looked at the list again. "I can't believe Carolyn would try to reach the man she's seeing at his home. How would she even know where he lives? And I have to believe she'd never agree to live with a man in that way. She's not that kind of girl."

"Are you sure?"

"She can't be. She just can't."

"Well, I wouldn't put anything past her. We both know she doesn't exactly play by the rules."

Helen placed the phone book back on the shelf. She couldn't believe her sister had changed so much that she would defy everything they were raised to believe. She hoped tonight Carolyn would apologize to their father, and all would be forgiven. When she said this, Peggy looked at her and shook her head.

"You're living in a dream world if you think that's going to happen."

"Probably, but we're not getting anywhere sitting here. I think we should keep this list of hotels and wait for

Carolyn to come home tonight. If she hasn't found a place yet, maybe she could get in touch with one of these. We can't just run all over the city looking for her. That's stupid."

"You're right. Maybe she'll call home and let us know what's going on. Or maybe she went to see Rosemary. She's her best friend."

"Peg," Helen slapped her palm against her forehead, "You're a genius. Why didn't we think of that? Of course. She probably went right to Rosemary's. Come on." Grabbing her purse, she put the list of women's hotels in it, and headed for the door.

"Hold it. We can't leave until Mr. Callahan comes back."

"Damn. Go run around the corner and get him, would you?"

"Why do I have to go?"

"Because you're young and cute and people do anything you ask when you smile nicely. Don't tell me you've never noticed."

"Maybe, a little." She looked up at Helen through her thick brown eyelashes.

"There. That's it. The 'poor girl lost and needs your help' look. Perfect. Now go."

Peggy laughed and ran out the door and down the block. Helen paced the office while she waited and wondered what they could do to find Carolyn if she wasn't at Rosemary's. Or worse, if she didn't come home tonight. Either way, today was turning into a disaster.

"Any suggestions?" Carolyn asked Rosemary.

"Why don't you call him and ask him to meet you? Maybe he'd have some good ideas."

"I couldn't."

"Why not?"

"For starters, his wife knows my voice. She calls the office all the time, and since I'm his secretary, I always answer his phone." Carolyn pounded her cigarette into the ashtray after her usual two puffs. Her eyes darted to the bedroom door again. "You're sure your mother can't hear us?"

"I told you, she's busy baking a cake for Dad's birthday party tonight. Believe me, that will take all her attention for the next couple of hours. Plus, she has the radio on." Rosemary paused and watched Carolyn pull another cigarette out from the half-smoked pack. "We could always go for a walk if you're so worried about Mom."

"No, I guess it's fine. I'm just... I don't know, just... Oh, Rosemary, what am I going to do?" Her hand trembled as she lit her cigarette, the eighth one in the hour she'd been there.

Rosemary put her arm around Carolyn's shoulders and gave her a squeeze. She sympathized with her best friend, but didn't know what she could do to help. She had warned Carolyn that this affair could backfire in her face, but, as usual, Carolyn wouldn't listen to any opinions that differed from hers. Over the years, everyone who knew her had told her that her headstrong attitude would get her into trouble one day, and now it had.

"Can't you just apologize to your dad? Maybe he'll forgive you and let you stay? Of course, you'd have to stop seeing 'Mr. Boss'."

"No. It wouldn't work this time, I'm sure. Besides, I don't want to stop seeing J.P. He's terrific. And he treats me like a queen."

"So you've said. A queen he can only take places where he won't run into people he knows."

"You don't understand." Carolyn smashed her cigarette into the overflowing ashtray.

73

The two women jumped when the downstairs doorbell rang with an insistent buzz, like someone was holding their finger on it.

"Rosemary," her mother called from the kitchen, "could you answer that? I'm up to my elbows in icing."

"Sure, Mom."

"Who could that be?" Carolyn asked. "Are your relatives coming over for your dad's birthday?"

"Not that I know of." Rosemary left the bedroom to buzz in whoever was at the downstairs front door. She went onto the landing to look over the banister and down the staircase. When she saw who was coming, she ran back into her apartment.

"It's your sisters."

"What? What are they doing here?"

"Probably looking for you. What do you want me to tell them?"

"Nothing." She marched to the apartment door and opened it. Helen and Peggy stood there. Helen's fist raised to knock on the door.

"What do you two want?" Carolyn asked.

"Can we talk to you?" Helen asked.

"Mom sent us to find you," Peggy said. "She's worried about you."

"Really? She seemed pretty glad to be rid of me."

"Carolyn," Rosemary said, "maybe they should come in before— "

"Oh, hello girls," Rosemary's mother said. "Are you all going somewhere together today?"

"Yeah, Mom, and we're just leaving."

"Have fun. Don't forget to come back early, Rosemary. I'll need some help with the big celebration."

"Sure, Mom."

Rosemary grabbed her and Carolyn's hats and purses and shooed everyone out and down the stairs. Before they knew it, they were on the sidewalk walking towards Fifth Avenue.

"Hold it," Helen said, stopping the procession. "Where are we going?"

"Who cares," Rosemary said. "We couldn't stay in my apartment. My mom would smell a rat and you don't want that, I'm sure."

"You're right. Okay. Let's go to Madison Square Park. We can sit there and talk things out with some privacy."

The four women walked the few blocks to the park in silence. No one wanted to shout their conversation over the traffic noise, terrified that one of their neighbors would pop out of a store or building and overhear them. News of Carolyn's moving out would be enough to keep tongues wagging for a while. They didn't need to add to it by having a shouting match in the street.

The park was busy when they got there. The warmer weather brought everyone outside and kids ran all over the place. Helen spotted a fairly secluded table, one with a painted checkerboard set up for a game of chess or checkers and benches on either side. Men usually filled all these tables, playing games that lasted the entire day. But today, the women lucked out. As soon as they sat down, Carolyn pulled a cigarette out of the pack and lit it. Her hands were steady now, and a hardness had crept across her face.

"Well, what do you want?" she asked.

"Carolyn, can't you even *try* to be pleasant?" Peggy asked. "We're not the ones who crucified you. You did that all by yourself."

"I don't have to sit here and be criticized by my little sister. I'm leaving." Carolyn threw her cigarette on the ground, crushed it beneath her heel, and stood.

"Sit down, Carolyn," Helen said. "We're not here to fight. Mom wanted us to find you to see what your plans are. She's worried about you."

"Ha. I bet." Carolyn sat back down. "Not worried enough to stand up to Dad though, is she?"

"You know that's not going to happen," Helen said. "But he did give you till the end of the month, so maybe we can help you find something. Something respectable so Mom won't be so worried."

"Oh, sure, let's make sure no one's uncomfortable or feeling guilty about their part in this whole fiasco. No one but me, that is."

"Carolyn," Peggy said, "we're trying to help you, not fight with you, or blame you. It's not our fault that Mom heard you and Helen fighting, or that you snuck in the window last night. But what's done is done, so let's try to solve the problem."

Carolyn looked past them and watched the children play tag. "I don't see how the problem can be solved," she said, tears brimming her eyes.

"There's always a solution," Peggy said. "We just have to find it. Helen, give Carolyn the list we made."

"What list?" Carolyn asked.

"A list of women's residential hotels," Helen said, pulling it out of her purse and handing it to Carolyn. "I've heard of some of them at work."

"Oh great," Carolyn said, "So these are places women go and wait to have their bastards?"

"Carolyn, really," Peggy said. "We're trying to help, remember?"

"And no, it's not like that," Helen said. "Sometimes women from out of town need a place to stay for a while until they can find a job, or an apartment they can share with roommates. Lots of actresses stay in these hotels while they're on Broadway. That way, they don't have to

76

worry about men pestering them or following them home, and most of these places provide breakfast and dinner. So, you wouldn't even have to cook for yourself."

"They don't sound too bad," Rosemary said, who until then hadn't said a word.

"Well... maybe," Carolyn looked down the list. "I have heard of some of them, like the Barbizon."

"Oh, sure," Rosemary said. "That place is famous. Maybe if you stayed there, you'd get to meet some movie stars."

Carolyn grimaced and shook her head. "You read too many of those movie magazines."

"Well, I think that would be exciting," Rosemary mumbled.

"That's neither here nor there," Peggy said. "The point is, you could move into one of these without worrying about the first month's rent and security deposit. Or spend time trying to find a respectable place that would rent to a single woman. There's not many of them, you know."

"I'd have to pay something up front, I'm sure. And I don't have any money."

"Maybe, maybe not. Who knows? And if they do require some advance, maybe we could scrape something together for you. Anyway, you could call them and find out how it works. It's worth a try."

The three women waited while Carolyn fidgeted with the list and lit another cigarette. "Anyone have some dimes I can borrow to call these places?"

Of the nine residential hotels on Helen's list, Carolyn decided to call four of them.

"Why these four?" Peggy asked.

"A couple of reasons. I don't want to be too close to home, so, Jeanne D'Arc is out. It's right on 24th Street, practically next door. Besides, I think it's mostly for French women."

"That's true," Rosemary said. "I see groups of them leaving for work in the morning and they're always speaking French, or at least it sounds like French."

"Same with the Markle Evangeline Residence. Too close to home."

"What's so bad about being close to home?" Peggy asked.

Carolyn's eyebrows shot up and she shook her head. "You're such a child."

"I am not. I just don't understand why you practically have to move to another borough."

"I think Carolyn doesn't want everyone in the neighborhood, including us, knowing what she's doing," Helen said. "Isn't that right, Carolyn?"

"Something like that."

"Oh, I get it," Peggy said. "This way you can date all the married men you want, and Mom and Dad will never know."

"Why don't you go home," Carolyn said, through gritted teeth.

"Girls, let's pull the claws in, shall we?" Rosemary said. "We're all here to find a solution, not fight with each other."

Carolyn let out a deep sigh. "All right, but tell her," she pointed at Peggy, "to shut up if she can't say something useful."

"I'm sitting right here," Peggy said. "You can tell me yourself."

"This is getting us nowhere," Helen said. "The two of you need to stop acting like spoiled brats, and you need to stop right now."

Peggy sat, arms folded across her chest, and glared at Helen. Carolyn tapped her pencil on the table so hard she broke off the tip.

"Damn," she said. "How am I supposed to write anything down now?"

"It's your own fault," Peggy said.

"Enough you two," Helen slammed her fist down. "I've had it. I'm going home." She stood and rummaged through her purse. "Here's another pencil. Try not to break this one too." She slapped it onto the table in front of Carolyn.

"Wait," Carolyn said, "I'm sorry. I'm just upset. I never thought I'd get kicked out of my own home." Tears ran down her cheeks. "I feel lost. Please, don't go, Helen. I need your help."

Helen stood, wavering between believing Carolyn meant what she said or knowing it was simply another ploy in her arsenal of tricks to wheedle her way out of messes.

"I'm sorry too," Peggy said.

Helen sat, not thoroughly convinced either sister was telling the truth, but couldn't abandon Carolyn when she looked so defeated.

"All right, which four places did you choose?"

Carolyn decided to call The Allerton Hotel for Women, The Barbizon, The Webster, and the Brandon Residence for Women. The Martha Washington Hotel was too close to work. Co-workers might spot her going in or out, and she didn't want them to know her business. The St. Agnes Residence, the St. Mary's Residence, and the Sacred Heart Residence sounded too much like convents to suit her. Having decided on her choices, Carolyn left to call them. The three women waited for her to return with either good or bad news.

"It's like waiting for the results of an exam." Peggy stood and paced in front of the table.

Rosemary checked her watch every few minutes and Helen vacillated between clutching the cross that hung around her neck and twisting the Claddagh ring on her finger.

"Here she comes," Peggy said, looking across the park.

"Okay." Carolyn sat at the table. "I have appointments at the Webster and the Brandon for tomorrow afternoon."

"What about the Barbizon and the Allerton?" Helen asked.

"They're too expensive and the rent doesn't include any meals. The other two do, so they'd work out better for me. So, who wants to come with me tomorrow?"

All three women said they wanted to. They fixed a time for Rosemary to come to their apartment, then the four of them would leave together.

CHAPTER EIGHT

The next morning, the four women left to visit the Webster Apartments. Since the residence was on West 34th Street, they saved the subway fare and walked the ten blocks.

Once they arrived there, the administrator on duty took them on a tour of the residence. She explained they allowed no men above the first floor, but there were "beau parlors." These rooms, or cubbies, had no doors, but residents could entertain visitors in them with some privacy. The rent included a hot breakfast and dinner, maid service with linens changed once a week, and use of a large walled-in garden, and a roof deck with views of the Empire State Building. There were 24-hour security guards as well. Each tenant's rent was determined on a sliding scale based on their income.

The private room she showed them was small with a single bed, dresser, chair, and sink. Everyone shared the bathroom at the end of the hall.

Carolyn thanked her and said she'd decide by the end of the day. Then the group hopped on the subway and made their way up to the Brandon Residence for Women on West 85th Street.

Once again, the administrator gave them a tour of the building. The rules here were the same as the Webster. While the Brandon didn't have "beau parlors," there was a large room on the first floor with floor to ceiling windows and groupings of easy chairs and sofas where residents could entertain guests. The administrator said they often held performances there since some residents were music or dance students at the Juilliard School. During these performances, the casual furniture was put off to the side and replaced by rows of folding chairs. There were also some fledgling actresses who performed in Broadway plays and on TV.

There was also a TV/library room and a small room set up for piano practice.

Both the private room Carolyn would occupy, and the other amenities, were the same as the Webster. Located a block off Riverside Park, access to the North River and cool shaded areas would be a bonus during the hot summer months.

As the women toured the building, they noticed the residents ran the gamut in both age and fashion. Some dressed conservatively while others were more bohemian, but they were all friendly. Almost everyone stopped to say hello and tell Carolyn how welcoming and safe they felt living there. The room rate here was fixed, but within Carolyn's budget.

The tour finished, Carolyn told their guide she would be in touch later that day. Then they left and wandered over to Riverside Park.

"Well, what do you think?" Helen asked.

"I'm torn. I like the Webster, but it's awfully close to home."

"It's ten blocks away," Peggy said. "How many of our neighbors do you think you'll run into up there?"

"Peggy's right," Rosemary said. "If it was closer to Macy's or Gimbel's, then maybe. But all the way over on 9th Avenue? There's no reason for anyone to be that far west."

"You're probably right," Carolyn said, "but I think I like the Brandon better anyway. There are so many different types of women living there, and being able to walk to the park is a bonus."

"You can walk to Central Park from there too," Helen said, "but there's not much else around here. It's real residential. No stores or coffee shops or anything."

"I can shop downtown, and I don't need a coffee shop since they include breakfast in my rent. Besides, we really haven't looked around the neighborhood much. Maybe there are places on Broadway, or Columbus, or Amsterdam."

"You're right," Rosemary said. "Why don't we go exploring before you make a final decision?"

"Good idea," Peggy said. "And I'm getting hungry, so maybe we can find a place for lunch."

"Okay, moneybags." Helen threw her arm around her little sister's shoulder. "Is this your treat?"

Peggy opened her mouth to say something, but snapped it shut when she realized she didn't even have enough money to pay for her own lunch. Her face turned rosy, and she looked down at her shoes. "Never mind," she said.

"I'm only teasing," Helen said. "I'll treat. Now, let's go find someplace to eat."

The women walked east to Broadway, found a luncheonette, and settled in to discuss the merits of the two residences they had visited that morning.

After making a list of pros and cons, Carolyn decided to move into the Brandon. Even though it meant taking two trains to get to work every day, one downtown and one across town, she liked the eclectic mix of women who lived there, as opposed to the solid "working girl" roster of the Webster.

"Helen," Carolyn said, "you're awfully quiet. What gives? You're usually more than willing to put your two cents into anyone's opinion of anything."

"I'm just thinking that maybe you're jumping the gun."

"What's that supposed to mean?"

"Look, Dad was angry yesterday and rightfully so."

Carolyn rolled her eyes and lit another cigarette.

"He probably didn't sleep very well Friday night, waiting to hear you sneak in. So, he wasn't in the best of moods. I think you should give him time to reconsider everything. If you move out, he'll never come around and our family will be split up forever. Why don't you wait a week or two, keep your nose clean, come home right after work—"

"Really? Why don't I just enter a convent?"

"Let me finish." Helen crossed her arms and leaned back in the booth. "If not every night, at least most nights. I'm only asking for a week, maybe two, not the rest of your life. Then maybe you can have an intelligent, adult conversation with him about his expectations and your rights as an adult living in his home. Maybe even offer to pay some rent, you know, to establish yourself as a responsible person."

"More like paying for my right to live my own life."

"I wouldn't go that far, but if you move out, you'll just solidify whatever he imagines you're up to, and your move will break Mom's heart. At least think about it before you go off half-cocked and regret your decision in the

84

morning. Besides, you don't even know if there's a vacancy at the Brandon."

Helen's speech burst the bubble of excitement that a minute ago had enveloped the table.

"You have a point about the vacancy. Maybe I'll hold off calling the Webster until I know if the Brandon has a room available. But you know Helen, you're not always right about everything, even though you think you are. Sometimes what I think is best for me really is."

A pall of silence fell across their table. Helen signaled the waitress for their bill before the funereal atmosphere of the group buried them all.

"Let's get out of here," Helen said. "It makes no sense to get upset imagining the worst likely outcome."

"Which would be what?" Carolyn asked. "At this point, I'm not sure what that would be."

"Come on," Rosemary said, "let's go back to the Brandon and see if they have a room for you. Then you can figure out what you want to do,"

On that more positive note, they stood, paid their bill, and walked back to the residence. Carolyn almost sprinted back and the other women had a hard time keeping up with her. Somewhat out of breath when they arrived at the front door, Carolyn pulled out a small mirror from her purse, checked her makeup and hat, and marched up the few steps to the entrance.

"Here goes nothing," she said to them, as she pulled the wooden door open and stepped inside.

Her sisters and best friend stood like sentinels at the curb, eyes fixated on the closed door. Minutes passed like hours and Carolyn hadn't come back.

"Do you think it's a good thing that it's taking so long?" Peggy asked.

"I wish she would give this a little more thought," Helen said. "I don't know if she's really considered everything that's involved here. She'll have to do her own laundry and do they even have a laundry room? Or will she have to lug her stuff to a laundromat? What about a kitchen she could use between meals, or when she gets in late at night and wants something to snack on or a cup of tea? Or who knows what else? What things do we take for granted living at home that won't be available here? Do they have a curfew? Did she even ask about that? There won't be anyone who can open the fire escape window for her here."

"I don't know what to think anymore," Rosemary said. "You make some good points, but you should have seen her when she came to my apartment yesterday. She was so upset. I don't think I've ever seen her like that. You know how she always seems so much in control. But today, it was like someone had cut the strings to a puppet in the middle of a performance. She was like a bag of rags."

Helen and Peggy looked at each other and each took a deep sigh.

"I didn't know she was that upset," Peggy said. "She didn't act like that at home."

"Of course not," Rosemary said. "She'd never let her family think they got the better of her. You know how proud she is."

"You're right, of course," Helen said. "I think she'd rather live on the street than admit she did anything to bring this on herself. But I really hope she considers what I said and rethinks her decision, at least for a little while until everyone cools down."

A minute later, Carolyn bounced down the steps. "Well, that's that."

"What's what?" Peggy asked.

"They have a room and I agreed to rent it."

"You didn't even consider what I said over lunch, did you?" Helen asked.

"I did. And now, we can have the best of both worlds."

"What's that mean?" Rosemary asked.

"The room I rented won't be available for two weeks, so I'll have to stay put until then. So, you see, Helen, this will give your big idea time to work out, or not."

"How do you figure that?" Peggy asked.

"I'll toe the line for a week," Carolyn said, "and see if Dad softens up any. Then if I talk to him and he still refuses to see I'm a grown woman with the right to my own life, well, nobody can say I didn't try."

Helen wanted to smack the smug look right off Carolyn's face.

"And what will happen after the week is up if Dad agrees to let you stay?" Helen asked. "Back to sneaking up the fire escape?"

Carolyn whirled around to face her sister, her eyes blazing and cheeks as red as hot coals.

"I don't know. But I won't have you monitoring my every move for a week. I know that. You may be my older sister, but you don't have the right to boss me around or give me rules about how I live my life. I have no intention of winding up like you—a rule-abiding spinster."

"Carolyn!" Peggy said. "I can't believe you. Helen's trying to make things right and keep peace in our family and all you do is buck her at every turn. You should thank her for even finding this place. And she's not a spinster. Just because she's not willing to go out with every Tom, Dick, and Harry like you are, doesn't mean she's next to being a nun."

"Oh no? What would you call it?"

"I'd call it being sensible, that's what."

87

The two women were toe to toe and looked like they'd be willing to start brawling any minute.

"Stop it. Both of you." Helen said. "My God, I feel like all I've done my whole life is break up fights between you two. I'm sick of it. It's about time you both grew up and stopped acting like schoolchildren. I swear, my kids at the Foundling are better behaved than you are." Helen rubbed her forehead. "I'm going home. And I don't want any company."

She marched down the street, headed for the subway.

"I hope you're happy," Peggy said.

"Me? You started it."

"Me? You were the one who started on Helen and—"

"All right," Rosemary said. "It doesn't matter who started it. It has to end now. Honestly, you're both unbelievable. I don't know how Helen has put up with you all these years."

Carolyn glared at her best friend.

"Don't give me that look, Carolyn. You know damn well none of this would be happening if you hadn't decided to date your boss."

"He's your boss?" Peggy asked. "Oh, that's just great. Good choice, Carolyn." She shook her head and walked away. Rosemary and Carolyn stood rooted to the spot.

When Helen reached the subway station, she was glad she was alone. One more minute of listening to her two sisters scream at each other would have driven her crazy. Although she knew she had no right to tell Carolyn what to do, she couldn't help feeling that her sister was just wrong in so many ways.

But, then again, Carolyn's never cared what anyone thought about what she did or said. Helen couldn't understand such selfishness, and found it even harder to swallow. But this—an affair with a married man—was too much.

How could she? How does she look at herself in the mirror and not feel disgusted? Doesn't she realize she's a homewrecker? And what about his wife and kids? Does he have kids? Does she even care?

Then she thought about Charlie.

How can I explain this to him? He got upset and annoyed about having to meet my parents. How will he react to this bombshell? What will he think of me and my family? A sister, carrying on with a married man, and living out, might be enough for him to walk away. After all, why would he want to get involved with all that? Maybe I shouldn't tell him anything about it. Maybe it will all go away. Maybe Carolyn will start to behave herself and Dad will let her stay at home. Maybe, maybe, maybe. That's not solving the problem of whether I should tell Charlie.

Helen mulled this over as she got on the train headed downtown. The couple sitting behind her were in the middle of an argument and distracted her from thinking about Carolyn for the moment.

"Well, why didn't you just tell me from the beginning?" the man asked.

"I thought the whole thing would blow over," the woman said.

"But it didn't, did it? And now, I'm finding out about it when it's too late to do anything to change it."

"I'm sorry. I should have told you right away, as soon as the problem started, but I didn't want to upset you."

"Well, you've managed to upset me a lot more by keeping this all to yourself."

Their voices faded as they walked to the door and got off the train.

89

That settles it, Helen thought. *I don't know what they were arguing about, but that man was furious. I'm going to tell Charlie the whole story. He has a right to know what's going on in my family, and I have to be honest with him if I want to keep seeing him. And I do.*

I always thought 'love at first sight' was a silly expression. I mean, how can you fall in love that quickly? But with Charlie, I really feel that way. The way he treated Jimmy that first day I met him, and the way he treated me on each of our dates, was so special. I don't want to lose him. I need to be honest with him. Then, if he decides he can't deal with my crazy family, so be it. Better to end it right away than wait until I'm completely head over heels about him. This way, it will only break my heart a little. If I wait, it might destroy me forever.

The decision made, Helen left the train feeling more at peace than she had in days. Until she turned the corner to head up her street. Charlie was sitting on the stoop.

CHAPTER NINE

"Charlie. What brings you here on such a lovely day?" Helen tried to sound cheerful, even though her stomach was flopping around like a newly caught fish on the pier.

"I finished my workout and decided it was too nice a day to spend the rest of it in a smelly old gym. Thought maybe you'd like to go for a walk in the park."

"What a nice idea. But why didn't you go upstairs?"

"I did. Your mom said you went out with your sisters, but that you should be home soon. So, I figured I'd wait down here and get some air."

"I'm glad you did. Just let me run upstairs and tell Mom where I'll be."

"Take your time. I've gotten comfortable here."

Helen laughed. The one thing you could never be comfortable on was a concrete stoop. She hurried up the stairs to her apartment, trying to figure out the simplest explanation for what had happened and why she had come home alone.

"Mom? I'm going for a walk with Charlie. If I'm not going to be home for supper, I'll call, okay?"

"One minute, missy. Where are your sisters? What's going on with Carolyn?"

"Oh, Mom. It's so complicated. I really can't explain it all in a minute. Ask Carolyn when she gets home, or Peggy. Charlie's waiting downstairs for me. I've got to go."

Before her mother could say another word, or ask another question Helen scooted out the door and down the stairs.

"All set, Charlie?"

"I am." He stood and brushed off the seat of his pants. "You look beautiful, by the way." He leaned over and kissed her cheek.

Helen's face colored and she said, "Well, that will give the neighbors something to gossip about for today, and probably tomorrow."

"Good. That way, any guys who have their eye on you will know you're already taken." He grabbed her hand as they walked down the street.

When they were about a block away from her apartment, Helen decided this was the perfect time to tell Charlie about Carolyn's situation.

"Would you like—"

"Charlie, I want to—"

Their words overlapped one another.

"Sorry, you go ahead, Charlie."

"No, no, ladies first."

"This is difficult," Helen said.

"Are you going to say you don't want to see me anymore?"

"Oh, God, no. Just the opposite."

"That's a relief. You scared me for a minute. As long as you don't plan on leaving me, everything else is easy."

"You're such an optimist. I wish it was that easy, but it's not. And I'm afraid you'll be the one waking away after I tell you the whole story."

92

"That bad, huh?" Charlie asked.

"That bad, I'm afraid."

"Well then, let's get it over with."

Helen took a deep breath. "Remember the night we went to see the fight?"

"Sure do. One of the best nights of my life."

Helen gave him a weak smile. "Mine too. But remember how I acted? I think you said I had a fit or something."

"Oh, yeah... Helen... are you sick... or dying... or something?"

Helen burst out laughing. All the tension drained from her body. Charlie, meanwhile, looked like a balloon that had lost most of its air. He stood perfectly still, his shoulders slumped, his head hung.

"Helen, is that it? You're dying? I knew you were too good to be true."

Helen laughed so hard, tears rolled down her cheeks. She wiped them away and shook her head.

"I'm healthy as a horse," she said, between gulps of air. "Oh, Charlie, I didn't realize you could be so dramatic."

"Well, what else could be so terrible?"

Helen took another deep breath before she could continue.

"Let's keep walking," she said.

Charlie took her hand again and waited for Helen to continue her story.

"That night, when I said I thought I saw someone I knew, I had."

"And you were embarrassed to be seen with me. I get it. A lot of people have really bad opinions of boxers."

"No, Charlie. That's not it at all. The person I saw was my sister, Carolyn."

"Is that all? Why didn't you say so? Why didn't you ask her to join us?"

"That's just it. She wasn't alone."

"I wouldn't think so. It would be really strange if a woman came to the fights alone."

"Anyway... and please let me finish. This is hard enough to get out."

Charlie nodded and zipped his fingers across his lips, sealing them shut.

Helen smiled and shook her head. "It turns out, the man she was with is married. I saw his wedding band. That's what made me feel faint. A married man, Charlie. That's unforgiveable."

Helen looked at Charlie for a reaction, but he signaled that his lips were sealed and he would wait until she finished her story.

"That night, I waited up for her and told her I had seen her and her date at the fight. And she didn't even try to deny it. She said she was glad it was out in the open and that she wouldn't have to go sneaking around with him anymore. Can you believe that?"

Charlie shook his head, not willing to break his silence just yet.

"Anyway, we had a big fight, I called her a slut, and slapped her."

Charlie raised his eyebrows, his eyes widened.

"That's right. I slapped her. It was the first time I've ever hit either of my sisters and I felt terrible, but I was so upset. You know?"

Charlie nodded, but let her continue.

"Well, the next morning, Dad asked Carolyn where she had been, why she got home so late, who she was with, and why hadn't she brought him home to meet him and Mom. Like you did, you know?"

Once again, Charlie nodded his answer. Satisfied he was following her story, Helen continued.

"Then she said she didn't think she had to bring her dates to the house 'cause she wasn't sixteen anymore and it was a guy from work, so they left from the office. Dad thought about it for a minute and agreed."

Charlie opened his mouth to speak, but stopped when Helen held her hand up, palm facing him.

"That's not all. Dad agreed, but told her she'd have to get out of the house by the end of the month. So, that's where I've been this morning. Going to look at women's residences with my sisters and Carolyn's friend, Rosemary."

Helen finished and looked at Charlie, tears in her eyes.

"I'll understand if you don't want to get involved with my crazy family, Charlie. Carolyn's a disgrace and before long, she'll be the talk of the neighborhood and everyone will look at Peggy and me in the same way. I'm really sorry, Charlie. I like you a lot and wish it could have worked out, but I'll understand if you walk away."

Charlie unzipped his lips and said, "Is that all?"

"Is that all? Isn't that enough?"

Charlie grabbed Helen in a bear hug and kissed her.

'Charlie, we're in the middle of the street."

"I wouldn't care if we were in the middle of Madison Square Garden. And if you think you're going to pawn me off because your sister's having an affair with a married man, you don't know me very well. Not yet. It'd take a lot more than that for me to leave you, Miss Campbell. I plan on being around for a long, long time."

This time, it was Helen's turn to give Charlie a long lingering kiss.

"Hey," Charlie said, "I have an idea. Why don't we walk over to Gramercy Park? It's a nice secluded place where we can talk."

"But I've heard you need a key to go inside," Helen said.

"You do, but I have friends in high places." Charlie winked. "Then we can grab a bite at Pete's Tavern."

"That sounds wonderful. I'm so glad you stopped by today. I don't know what will happen tonight when Carolyn faces Mom and Dad with her news."

"That she's moving out?"

"That, and where she's moving to. I doubt they'll be thrilled to hear she'll be living in a place with a bunch of actresses and musicians."

"What's wrong with them?"

"Nothing, as far as I'm concerned. But those newspapers they sell at the supermarket always have some sensational story on the first page about an actress or actor. And Mom always has something to say about how they're going straight to hell."

"That doesn't sound good at all. But that's Carolyn's problem to deal with, not yours."

"I guess."

Soon they were at Gramercy Park and Charlie pulled out his key ring and opened the gate. The park was private and secluded. It was hard for Helen to believe such a peaceful place could be found in the middle of the city. It stretched from 20th to 21st Streets and straddled Lexington Avenue between Park Avenue South and 3rd Avenue. Trees lined the fence surrounding the park and buffered the usual street noises. Soon, flowers would fill the large stone urns scattered throughout the grassy areas, as well as the circle around the statue of Edwin Booth that sat in the middle of the park. The two-acre park was an oasis of calm and soothed Helen's frazzled nerves that had been stretched to their limits for two days.

Helen looked at Booth's statue and said, "I wonder why they picked this guy."

"You've never heard of him?"

"Nope."

So, Charlie told her the story of Edwin Booth. How he was a famous Shakespearean actor who, in the 1800s, played the role of Hamlet for one hundred performances, the longest ever for its time.

"He also founded The Players, a private club for actors, other theater professionals, and their benefactors."

While Charlie talked, they wandered over to a nearby bench and sat.

"How do you know so much about this club and Edwin Booth?" Helen asked.

"Part of being a title contender means that you have to go to lots of events and one of them was at The Players. I met some of the members and they gave me a tour and an honorable membership and key to the park. I don't have all the privileges full members have, but this key is enough for me."

"But I thought you said the club was for theater people. You're not in the theater."

"Over the years, they started to include people in the movie and television industry and other types of celebrities. I guess they consider boxing a kind of entertainment that could be included. I don't really care why they included me, I'm just happy they did. It gave us a great place to spend the afternoon."

"Charlie, you continue to amaze me with what you know and who you know."

"It's been a great run and a lot of fun, but I'm getting a little old for this game. I'm thinking of retiring while I still have a name that might open some doors for me."

"Retiring? What would you do?"

"I'm not sure, but I'm meeting with Paul Pilgrim tomorrow and I'll see what he has to say."

"Who's he?"

"The athletic director at the New York Athletic Club. Joe, you remember my trainer, don't you?"

Helen nodded.

"He arranged the meeting. Said maybe I would want to look at a career change."

"Why would he think that?"

"Because he's been in this game for a long time and he's seen fighters hang in after they've hit their prime. It's not a pretty sight."

"Do you think you'd want to work there?"

"I don't know. That's why I'm meeting with Paul tomorrow. I'm curious about what he has in mind. I know one thing. I'm not going to be a lackey for him. Following him around with a clipboard taking notes and making sure there are fresh towels in the showers for all the swells to use after their workouts." Charlie slumped down on the bench, crossed his arms, and looked up at the sky. "I'd rather work on the docks than do that."

In a lot of ways, Helen could understand Charlie's sentiments. She wished she didn't have to take orders from Sister Josephine all the time either, but as a child carer, she had no choice. And she did love working with the children every day.

Charlie pulled himself upright and said, "So, what are your thoughts about Carolyn and her situation? After all, that's what we came here to talk about, not me."

"I don't know. I can't believe her behavior and I just know it won't lead to anything good."

98

"Have to agree with you there. Who is this guy, anyway?"

"Come to think of it, I don't know. I never asked her."

"Maybe you should. He could be a real louse. Someone who just seduces pretty young things then tosses them aside for a new one."

Helen looked at him, wide-eyed.

"Oh God, I hope not. I don't know if Carolyn could take it if he did that. Especially after being tossed out of her home. She acts tough, but I think she's scared to death right now."

"Maybe when you get home, you could ask her about this guy. You know, how they met, what he's like, what his name is. Stuff like that. Then I can nose around and see what I can find out about him."

"Would you, Charlie? That'd be great."

"Course I would. I'd do anything to wipe that worried frown off your face."

Helen looked at him and thought he was the most perfect man she had ever met.

He stood, grabbed her hand, and pulled her up and into his arms so he could give her a proper kiss before they left the seclusion of the park for dinner.

CHAPTER TEN

"I'm home, Mom," Peggy said, walking into her apartment.

"Good. I need to talk to you. Helen was in and out so fast I never got a word in edgewise. Now, sit down and tell me what's going on with Carolyn. And put the kettle on so's we can have a cuppa."

Peggy lit the burner on the stove and set the table for the two of them. Aggie settled in her chair and waited to hear the full story of the morning's events.

"Where's Helen, Mom?"

"Her young man came calling for her and they went for a walk."

"He's becoming a regular fixture around here."

"Never mind about him right now. I want to hear what happened today."

"Well, we went to look at two of the women's hotels this morning."

"And where would these two be?" Aggie asked.

"One is on West 34th Street and the other one is on West 85th Street."

"Och, that's too far away."

"From what Mom? Anyway, Carolyn doesn't think so. In fact, that's the one she's going to move into."

"What? She's already decided? And without talking to me or your da?"

"Seems so. But they won't have a room available for two weeks, so Carolyn will still be home for a while."

"And did you see this place?"

"We did. It's very nice. Clean. Well cared for. Lots of students from the Juilliard School, actresses, musicians, dancers."

"Oh, Lord, bless us. Just the type of bohemians Carolyn doesn't need to get mixed up with. They'll be leading her straight down the road to hell."

"Mom, they're college women, not street walkers."

"And we all know how loose those theater people are. I swear, they've no morals at all."

Peggy munched on one of the cookies she had set out with their tea. Her mother drummed her fingers on the table and stared out the window at the brick wall of the apartment house across the courtyard.

"No. This won't do," Aggie said.

Peggy choked on the sip of tea she had taken.

"What?"

"It won't do. I won't have it. I'll not see one of my girls living in no more than a classy brothel."

"Mom, it's not like that at all. It's a respectable residence. Men aren't allowed past the first floor, and they have to leave by midnight."

"Hmph." Aggie clasped her hands around her teacup. "I'll be wanting to see this place for myself."

"I can't see why Carolyn would object to that."

Actually, I can think of a thousand reasons, but that's her problem.

"So, has she paid the rent for a month?"

102

"I don't know. I didn't ask."

"And why did Helen come home alone? And you too? Where's Carolyn?"

"More tea?" Peggy asked, in an effort to change the subject.

"Don't go trying to distract me. Answer me."

"They had an argument, sort of, and then I yelled at Carolyn and we fought. Helen got disgusted with us and left."

"I don't blame her a bit for leaving, but arguing in the middle of the street, where anyone could see you and hear you. It's a disgrace, it is. You girls have got to stop this constant bickering with each other."

"I know, Mom. But she gets me so angry at times."

"Aye, she knows how to ruffle feathers, she does."

Aggie sipped her tea, a worried frown on her forehead. "Where is Carolyn now?"

"I don't know. Probably back at Rosemary's."

"Call her up and tell her I want to talk to her before her da comes home. Would you do that, love?"

"Sure, Mom."

Peggy walked down the hall to the telephone table that sat near the front door. Rosemary's mother answered the phone and said the girls weren't back yet, so Peggy left a message for Carolyn to come home right away. After telling her mother about the call, she went to her bedroom to catch up on some reading for school. But she soon found that she couldn't concentrate on her books. She kept thinking about everyone's reactions to the events of the day.

Her father—cool and calm on the outside, but she knew how upset he must have been to tell Carolyn she had to move out. And how that must have tortured him. He wasn't a man who was quick to judge or make rash decisions. He had shocked her when he announced his

103

verdict on Carolyn's behavior. Although she said she'd behave for the week, Peggy doubted that promise. If Carolyn was out having fun, she'd be the last to leave the party.

And her mom. Peggy worried about her. She hadn't said much, but Peggy had noticed the trembling hands and worry lines that now seemed embedded in her face. Peggy thought about their mother's insistence on seeing the Brandon Residence. She'd have to make sure Carolyn took their mother there on a weekday when most of the residents would be at school or work. That meant Carolyn would have to take time off work. And since she was dating her boss, and their affair was what caused all this turmoil, Peggy couldn't see how he could object.

Then there was Helen. Helen who always felt it was her responsibility to be the sensible one. The one who was a role model for her sisters. The one who followed the rules and thought everyone else should do the same. Peggy had never seen Helen so angry so often. She was the calm, cool, collected one. But, twice in two days, she had flown off the handle. Even slapped Carolyn. An act that was so out of character for her, it was almost impossible to fathom.

And, last of all, herself. She thought about how all that had happened had affected her. In some ways, it shocked her, but she couldn't honestly say it surprised her. Carolyn had been a wild child all her life. But an affair with a married man was something else. She hated how Carolyn had torn apart the happy family life she knew, but her unconventional behavior was also exciting. So different from her own routine of school and study. She looked at her life as one drab, grey, dull existence. But Carolyn's was all glitter, sparkle, and fun, which would fade in time, she knew. But for now, the anticipation of how this would all play out had her nerve ends tingling.

Over dinner, Carolyn told her parents that she'd be moving out.

A shocked Paddy couldn't believe that she actually took the initiative to go out and find a place on her own. He kept looking over at Peggy while Carolyn told him about the Brandon Residence. Peggy tried to avoid his eyes, but knew that was a losing battle.

"Peggy," he said, "did you, or Helen, have any part in finding Carolyn a place to move to?"

The table exploded.

"What? Why?" she asked.

"Just why do you think I can't find my own place without help?" Carolyn asked.

"Because you've never been responsible enough to do something like this on your own, or take things into your own hands and actually see them through to the end. I smell your sisters' hands in all this."

"Why our hands?" Peggy asked.

"Helen's specifically," he said. "She's the only one in the whole family with a sensible head on her shoulders."

Peggy fiddled with her fork, refusing to look at him.

Aggie let tears roll down her cheeks while Carolyn and Paddy yelled at each other. Finally, Carolyn stormed out. Paddy slammed his napkin on the table and left, and Aggie sat there with her head in her hands.

"What a mess," Peggy said.

She got up from the table, cleared the dishes and washed them. Aggie never moved the whole time.

"Want tea, Mom?" Peggy asked, but Aggie just waved her soaked hankie at her. So, she went to her bedroom to study, leaving her mother alone in the kitchen.

"Do you really think Carolyn will behave for the next week?" Peggy asked, after telling Helen what was said at supper.

Helen gave a little snort. "I doubt it."

"Guess we'll be living in a war zone then."

"Looks like it."

Helen put her shoes away and pulled her slippers out from under her bed.

"I'm going to make myself a cup of tea. Want one?"

"No thanks, but maybe Mom would, now that she's had a little time to recover."

"I'll ask her. Damn. This night is not going the way I hoped it would."

"What were you hoping for?"

"I wanted to see if I could find out the name of Carolyn's... beau? boyfriend? lover?"

"Oh, I know that. It's her boss."

"Her boss! That's just great. Things just keep getting better and better around here."

"That's what I said when Rosemary mentioned him after you left."

"So, Rosemary knew about him the whole time."

"Seems so. But why do you want to know who Carolyn's having this affair with?"

"Charlie said he'd look into him and see what he could find out. Whether he does this kind of thing all the time. Seduce young girls, then toss them away."

"That's just what we need. A broken-hearted sister who'll walk around feeling sorry for herself." Peggy shook her head and turned back to the pile of books stacked on her desk. "I've got to get some reading done."

"I'll leave you alone."

Helen walked to the phone and called Charlie. After a quick conversation in which Charlie said he'd meet her after work the next day, Helen went into the kitchen to make her tea.

Her mother still sat at the table, staring at nothing. Helen put the kettle on and grabbed two cups and saucers from the cabinet.

"Want milk and sugar, Mom?"

"Yes, love," she said, dabbing at her eyes.

"You go into the living room. I'll bring the tea in when it's ready."

"Right, love." Aggie dragged herself out of her chair and trudged down the hall.

Helen watched her go. It was hard to believe that only a few days ago they had been a happy family. In that brief time, Carolyn had managed to enrage their father twice, alienate both sisters, make her mother sit around in tears all day, and split the family apart cleaner than an ax would have.

And all for a man who's nothing more than a louse.

CHAPTER ELEVEN

"There's my girl," Charlie said, as Helen bounced down the front steps of The Foundling Hospital. "I brought Joe along with me today, and filled him in on what's going on with Carolyn. Hope you don't mind."

"Oh, well... "

"If you want me to back out, I will." Joe held his arms up in surrender. "Charlie, here, thought two heads might be better than one in trying to find a solution to your situation. And I'm the soul of discretion."

"No, no. I'm sure he meant well, but... Charlie, next time I'd appreciate it if you asked me before airing the family's dirty laundry."

Charlie shuffled his feet. A rosy color crept up his neck and onto his cheeks, although it was hard to see since he refused to look her in the eye.

"Gee, Helen, I'm sorry. It's just that Joe's like my brother. I share everything with him and he'd know right away if I was hiding something."

"I suppose you're right, and I appreciate your trying to help, Joe. I was just a little surprised. Charlie has a way of taking me off guard."

"Glad to be able to put my two cents in," Joe said. "And it's a pleasure to see you again. And looking so lovely too, I might add. You're a sight for my old eyes."

"Watch yourself, Joe. This one's already spoken for."

"No harm in looking, is there Charlie?"

"None at all, my friend. None at all."

Helen watched while the two men bandied back and forth with each other.

They're like two peas in a pod.

"Let's walk over to the park and find a place away from all the traffic noise where we can talk," Charlie said.

He slipped Helen's hand through his arm and they wound their way over to Central Park to a bench away from the street noise.

Charlie and Joe had devised a plan, of sorts, to find out about Carolyn's boss, a Mr. James (J.P.) Chandler. Since Carolyn didn't know Charlie or Joe, they decided to wait outside her office, then follow her to wherever she was going to meet him. Once they got a look at him, they could easily find out where he stopped for a drink after work and eavesdrop on any conversations with his buddies, or start one with him themselves.

"The only glitch is we don't know what Carolyn looks like either," Charlie said. "So, you'll have to show us a picture or point her out to us when she leaves work. That way, even if they don't leave together—"

"And I'm pretty sure they wouldn't," Joe said.

"Right. We can follow her and wait for lover boy to show up."

"Sounds like you two have done this before," Helen said. "You sure you're really a boxer and trainer, not two spies?"

110

"Sometimes you have to snoop around to get the inside scoop on your opponent," Joe said.

Helen squirmed on the bench and twisted her hands around one another.

"What's the matter?" Charlie asked.

"I don't know. It all seems so dirty, somehow. So underhanded and sneaky."

"Like Carolyn's affair?"

Helen shot Charlie a look that would have turned lesser men into stone, but Charlie didn't blink. Instead, he slumped down on the bench, crossed his arms on his chest, and pulled his cap further down his forehead.

"I'll take a little stroll and let you two hash this out." Joe stood and walked away.

"Maybe I'm the one who should take a stroll to clear my head," Helen said.

"No." Charlie pushed himself upright and his cap back off his forehead. "Yesterday, you seemed anxious for me to find out about this clown. But today, you're not so hot to trot. What gives?"

Helen told him about the conversation at the supper table the night before. And that morning, the family never spoke a word at breakfast. A time that was usually filled with chatter about plans for the day, or dreads about what was to come that day. All day, thoughts of Carolyn going into her boss's office and telling him about moving played different scenarios in her head.

Maybe her boss would decide she was too much trouble and leave her. Maybe he would fire her. Maybe Carolyn would break it off with him. There were too many maybes for Helen to think straight. She stood and paced back and forth until she noticed Joe walking towards her. In some ways, the two men were mirror images of each other. Both were over six feet tall, had barrel chests, light brown hair, although Joe's was starting to turn grey at the temples, and faces that were a little beat up from years in the ring.

Joe smiled. "Have you decided whether or not you'll go along with our plan?"

"I guess I have to. I can't see any other way to find out about this guy. Carolyn never talked about him at home, and now I understand why."

After the three of them discussed the logistics of their scheme, Helen decided to go home for supper. Joe wanted to treat them all to a good meal, but she wanted to be home to quell any further fights that might erupt. She didn't know if her mother could take much more of this turmoil. Carolyn was already breaking her heart by moving out. Helen wouldn't be able to stand it if the fighting spilled over to arguments between her mom and dad.

And it was all due to Carolyn's selfishness. Her belief that she was entitled to more than everyone else. All her life, everyone she met told that she was the beauty of the family. That she didn't belong in Chelsea. That she should be living on the Upper East Side with all the models and swells. And she had come to believe them and consider herself better than everyone else. Anger welled up in Helen's chest on the subway ride home. It had been easy for Carolyn to get what she wanted in life, including jobs. Men fell over themselves trying to please her and win one of her smiles. And she played them for everything she could get. But this time, Carolyn's plot to get whatever it was she wanted from this man, had affected her whole family. And she didn't seem to care one little bit.

The next day, Helen waited outside Carolyn's office building on Madison Avenue. She readjusted her hat and pulled at her gloves for the hundredth time. A nervous sweat ran between her breasts. As people passed, she imagined they stared at her, knowing she was there on a nefarious mission. Her thoughts drifted to war spies and she wondered how any of them had kept their cool under those harrowing conditions. She could barely maintain her composure now, and she was only meeting her sister. She glanced across the street at the two men who were supposed to be watching and waiting for her to approach Carolyn. But they seemed to be in deep conversation with each other.

Are they even paying attention?

Helen paced in front of the building, but stopped when she realized she could easily miss Carolyn when her back was turned. She took up her post by the lamppost again.

All at once, the building's doors burst open disgorging workers by the dozens. Helen hadn't expected to see such a surge of humanity all at once. She tried to scan all the faces, but realized that was an impossible task. Instead, she forced herself to remember what Carolyn had worn at breakfast. The scene at the kitchen table flashed before her and she visualized Carolyn's lilac blouse and brown pencil skirt. Now she just had to focus on colors. A flash of purple caught her eye, but it was too vibrant. Another mass of workers streamed through the doors and Helen spotted the lilac blouse and her sister's blonde hair.

"Carolyn," she yelled, over the cacophony of voices and honking horns.

Carolyn stopped and looked around, a frown creasing her forehead. She spotted Helen making her way through the people headed in the opposite direction.

"Helen, what are you doing here? Is everything all right at home? Is it Mom or Dad? Did something happen to them? Why didn't you call?"

"Stop." Helen held her hand up, palm facing Carolyn. "They're both fine. Although I didn't think you really

113

cared about them very much, considering how you've been acting the past few days, or maybe months."

"Oh, please. Stop throwing the Irish guilties on me, would you? What are you doing here?"

"I wanted to know if you've thought any more about keeping your promise that you'd behave for the next week. It didn't seem that way last night. I don't know what time you got home, but I know it was after I fell asleep, so it had to be pretty late."

"I don't know why this is any of your business."

"Carolyn, you agreed to keep your nose clean and then maybe Dad'll let you stay at home. You know you're breaking Mom's heart by moving out. Not that having an affair with a married man didn't already do that."

"Keep your voice down." Carolyn pulled Helen over to the curb. "I don't need you screaming my business from the rooftops."

"Well, then, maybe you shouldn't be doing something you're ashamed of."

"Little Miss Perfect. This is so typical of you, Helen. Don't you ever want to break out and do something exciting and adventurous? No, guess not. That would soil your perfect image."

"I'm just trying to prevent you from making a mistake that could ruin your life."

"According to you, I've already done that. Or at least that's what our family thinks. But I'm having fun. Remember fun, Helen? He takes me to the best restaurants, and cocktail lounges, and nightclubs. We dance and laugh and have fun together, which is more than you do with your life."

"And then does he take you to some hotel where you have to hide while he rents a room, then sneak upstairs when the desk clerk is busy?"

114

Carolyn's face turned red as a radish. "I don't have to listen to you. I have an appointment to keep."

"I wonder who you could be meeting?"

Carolyn bared her teeth at Helen, her lips curled into a snarl, and stomped away. Helen looked across the street. Charlie touched the brim of his cap and the two men followed Carolyn down the block.

Helen walked to the subway, wondering if she was doing the right thing. This was an invasion of Carolyn's privacy, and Helen believed people should decide, for themselves, how they wanted to live their lives. But Carolyn's actions had disrupted everyone's life. That was something Helen couldn't ignore, and if she could do anything to restore harmony in her family, she would. The further she walked, the more she justified her actions, at least to herself.

She waited for the light to change so she could cross the street and realized she had walked all the way to 23rd Street. Right past her own block. Her aching feet reminded her that high heels weren't meant for long distance treks. She pulled a token from her change purse and waited for the crosstown bus. It was a bit of a luxury for such a short ride, but her feet needed the rest.

She spotted an empty seat, grabbed it, and wondered what Charlie and Joe would report back to her.

You must have some real feelings for this girl," Joe said, as they tracked Carolyn from across the street.

"It's funny, Joe. From the minute I met her, I felt she was the girl for me. You should have seen her with her kids. A perfect combination of gentleness and caring but with a firm hand. And I could tell they all loved her. I don't know what it is, Joe. I just know I feel better about everything when I'm with her. She makes me feel like anything is possible."

115

"You've got it bad, kid. But I'm happy for you. She seems like a great gal, and she's not hard to look at either."

"That she is not, my friend."

"Hold on. Looks like our filly is stopping here." Joe jerked his chin in the direction of a hotel across the street.

"Oh great," Charlie said. "If she gets a room we're done."

"C'mon, let's get over there. Maybe she's going to the bar."

The two men hurried across the street ignoring the taxi cabs' blaring horns. Once through the door, they took a quick look around the lobby. Carolyn had disappeared.

"I'll check the bar," Joe said. "You look in the dining room."

They split up to continue their search. Charlie scanned the almost empty dining room, then poked his head in a small gift shop that stocked the toiletries often forgotten on trips. But no Carolyn. When he returned to the lobby, Joe wasn't there. Hoping that was good news, he walked into the bar.

Joe sat on a bar stool, a full pilsner glass of beer in front of him.

"I assume she's here and that you're not just thirsty," Charlie said.

"Yup, over in the far corner."

Charlie signaled for the bartender, ordered a beer, and looked around like a typical tourist might do. The bar was impressive. Oak walls and high-backed booths, tables placed discreetly apart. Waiters in long white aprons stood next to a prep table loaded with clean tablecloths and sparkling glassware, all ready to dash over and take your order at the slightest signal.

"Quite a place," Charlie said. "Must cost a pretty penny to drink here."

116

"It does," Joe said, fingering his change on the bar. "Remind me not to run a tab here, or I'll be washing dishes till the cows come home."

"Nurse your beer and we'll leave as soon as lover boy shows up and we get a good look at him."

They didn't have to wait long. A tall sophisticated well-dressed man with specks of grey hair at his temples strode across the room like he owned it. He reached Carolyn's table and bent to kiss her before sitting down.

"That suit probably cost more than I made in my last fight," Charlie said.

"I'm sure it did. I guess if you're going to have a sugar daddy, you may as well go for one who can take you to places like this without batting an eye."

Joe picked up his glass. "I'm going to have a closer look."

Before Charlie could react, Joe slid off his bar stool, beer in hand, and walked over to Carolyn's table.

"I don't believe it." Joe's voice boomed around the room, which was starting to fill up with an after-work crowd of executives. "Tom, isn't it? I never forget a face, but sometimes names aren't my strong suit."

He stuck his hand out and J.P. automatically shook it, pushing his chair back and trying to stand at the same time.

"We met at the insurance agents' convention in Chicago last summer. Don't tell me you've forgotten your old pal, Buddy. We had a few wild nights out there, didn't we, Tom? But I guess I shouldn't mention them in front of the missus, hey?" Joe winked at "Tom" and nudged him with his elbow. "How'd ya do, Missus. I'm Buddy Griffin." He extended his hand to Carolyn, who took it, her lips curled in a tentative smile.

"I'm afraid there's been a mistake, Mr. Griffin," J.P. said. "My name isn't Tom and I'm not in the insurance business. Now, if you'll excuse us."

"You're not Tom? You're a dead ringer for him. I'm sorry. I feel like a fool, but you know what they say, no fool like an old fool. Well, no harm done. You two enjoy your evening. Nice to meet you, missus."

He walked away, shaking his head and muttering. When he got to the bar, he sat next to Charlie and pointed to the couple, still shaking his head.

"You should go on the stage," Charlie said. "That was quite a performance."

"Like it, did you?"

"Thoroughly entertaining." Charlie drained his glass and signaled for two more from the bartender. Joe raised his eyebrows. "On me," Charlie said.

He looked in the mirror behind the bar and watched the couple's reflections. They both drank martinis, heads close together, hands clasped around each other.

"He's a cool one," Joe said. "Doesn't ruffle easily, although she seemed a little flustered by the whole thing."

"Yeah, I noticed that too. Maybe he doesn't care if people know he's carrying on with her, but she looked more scared than just taken off guard."

"I agree. I wonder why."

Helen sat at the telephone table waiting for the phone to ring. Her fingers danced a jig on the wooden surface.

"You'll leave a dent there if you don't stop soon," Peggy said.

"I can't help it. I'm waiting for Charlie to call and tell me what he found out about Carolyn's... I don't even know what to call him. Boyfriend sounds too much like a high school teenage romance, which this certainly is not."

118

"You can say that again."

"Ring, damn it. Ring." Helen shouted at the phone.

"That's useful." Peggy shook her head and headed for their bedroom. "I've got studying to do. Let me know what he says when he calls."

Helen nodded and went back to staring at the phone. Instead of the phone, the doorbell rang. Helen jumped at the noise, her nerves frayed raw. She buzzed back to open the downstairs door, went into the hall, and looked over the banister to see who came in.

"Charlie! This is a surprise."

"Want to go for a walk?" he asked.

"Sure, just let me grab my hat and purse."

She went back into her bedroom to get her things.

"Thought you were waiting for Charlie to call," Peggy said.

"He's here. We're going for a walk. Mom," she called down the hall, "I'm going out for a while. I won't be late."

Before her mother could answer, she was out the door and down a flight of stairs. When she landed on the first floor, Charlie gave her a kiss on the cheek, grabbed her hand, and pulled her outside.

"Can't let all your nosy neighbors gossip about you making out with your beau in the vestibule," he said. "I'll give you a proper kiss as soon as we find a secluded doorway."

Helen slapped his arm.

"You're terrible." But her smile gave away what she really thought.

They rounded the corner and Charlie, true to his word, pulled her into the shoe store's blackened doorway. He clasped his arms around her waist and held her close. Helen threw her arms around his neck and they kissed with a passion she didn't realize she was capable of.

"Charlie Sanders, you take my breath away."

"And I'd say you do the same to me."

Still holding each other in a tight embrace, she asked, "What happened today with Carolyn?"

Charlie told her about the hotel and described the man who met her there.

"He sounds like the same guy I saw at Stillman's Gym."

"Gosh, I hope so. I don't want to have to keep following her around to track down a whole line-up of lover boys."

She looked at him wide-eyed. "You don't think she has more than one, do you?"

Charlie laughed. "No. I'm sure she only indulges in one at a time."

"Do you think she's done this before?"

"I don't know. I've only just met your family, remember?" Charlie thought for a minute. "How many jobs has Carolyn had since high school?"

"Let me think." She leaned back against the pane glass window. "Two others, I think."

"So, this is her third job in how many years?"

"Six. Why? Does that seem like a lot?"

"Think about it. How many jobs have you had?"

"One," Helen said with hesitation.

"And why did she say she left the other jobs?"

"She said she didn't get along with her boss."

"Uh huh."

"What? What's 'uh huh' mean?"

"I'm thinking," he said, pulling her onto the sidewalk, "that she probably flirted with them to get the job, but when they wanted something more for their troubles, she ran. Or was fired."

Helen walked next to him, not speaking.

"Did she ever say she was fired, or laid off, or anything like that?"

120

"Not that I remember. But she always got another job so quickly I never thought about why she left the one she had."

"Sure. All she had to do was bat those baby blues, hitch her skirt up a little when she sat down, and the men didn't stand a chance."

"Charlie! Carolyn's not like that. I mean... we weren't raised like that. How would she even know how to do that?"

"It doesn't take a genius to figure it out. I think flirting is something women are born knowing."

"That's ridiculous."

"Maybe so, but you can't tell me you've never turned a man's head around by just a look."

She thought back to the day at the real estate agency when she told Peggy to smile nicely and convince Mr. Callahan to come back to his office so they could look for Carolyn.

"Well... maybe—"

"I knew it. I swear you're all born with it."

Charlie looked very smug as he swung Helen's arm and picked up their pace.

"That doesn't prove anything," Helen said.

"No, but I think I know how Carolyn's mind works now."

"Oh really? How?"

"Well, the way I figure it is... Wait a minute. Can we get a beer while I explain? Did you eat yet?"

"I ate, and yes, we can get a beer."

"Great, cause I'm starving. I wasn't about to pay the prices at that fancy hotel for a burger. so I came right here. No supper. There's a pub on the next block. Let's go there."

They walked one more block to McCauley's, a neighborhood pub filled with local people. They walked

121

past the bar to the tables in the back. Charlie ordered a burger, fries, a beer for himself and one for Helen.

"Now explain your theory to me."

He told her how he had watched various women get what they wanted by playing men. How the women would flirt and tease while the men pursued them buying them dinners, drinks, jewelry, some high rollers even went so far as to give their ladies fur coats. But at a certain point, the men expected their rewards to be more than just a beautiful lady on their arms. Unfortunately, for a lot of these women, when they balked, they earned a black eye, or worse. Of course, Charlie explained, he was speaking of the men he had met in the boxing world, not successful business executives like Carolyn was dealing with. They would probably just fire her and hope she learned her lesson that way. And people like Carolyn did learn. Only what she learned was to look for a bigger fish to land. One that could provide her with more expensive trinkets than her last conquest, before she walked away or vice versa. And since they were all respectable businessmen, she wasn't worried about getting beaten up in some dark alley when she refused their more aggressive advances.

"I'm afraid your sister is what is commonly referred to, in my social circles, as a gold digger."

Charlie had been chomping away on his burger the entire time he expounded on his theory. Now he looked at Helen who sat staring at him, shaking her head.

"You can't be right, Charlie. I don't believe, I *can't* believe, that my sister is that money hungry."

"Helen, I don't mean to hurt you, but it's easy for men like good ole J.P. to turn young girls' heads. They take them to an innocent lunch one day, at a very fancy restaurant, then make up some pretense that causes them to meet for a drink after work. That starts the intimacy. Next you know, they give them a small, not showy but expensive, piece of jewelry. Usually for a birthday, a Christmas present, any occasion or excuse will do. And little by little, they break down the girl's defenses. Sometimes, she doesn't even realize it's happening. And my guess is that's exactly what happened with Carolyn's first job. But when she refused the final proposition, she got fired."

Charlie signaled for two more beers. While they waited, Helen thought back to the conversation she and Peggy had with Carolyn about getting what she wanted from men, without marrying them. A queasy feeling was working its way through her gut. She would have to speak to Peggy about this new twist. She knew this could only get worse and Carolyn could find herself in real trouble. Businessman or not, no one likes to be played for a fool. Carolyn was playing a dangerous game.

"After that, Carolyn realized she could wheedle almost anything out of a man if she played her cards right. Maybe she even quit her second job when she realized her boss was getting too chummy. But this one... I don't know about this one. When Joe went over to talk to them—"

"Joe talked to them?" Helen almost screamed the question.

"Oh, that's right. I didn't tell you about that. This is rich." He waited while the waiter landed their beers, and scooped up Charlie's empty plate.

He told her about Joe's routine at the table. He imitated Joe to a tee and had her laughing at the absurdity of the situation.

"But one thing neither of us could figure out was why Carolyn looked scared."

"Neither can I. It's not like the family would be in such a fancy place, and besides, we all know about him. In a way."

123

They thought about this puzzle while they finished their beers.

Back at the apartment, Helen and Peggy put their heads together to try to figure out why Carolyn would be scared to be seen with J.P.

"It doesn't make any sense," Peggy said. "She's always so cocky. I can't imagine her being scared of anyone. I've seen her talk her way out of some really sticky situations. Why would she be scared of some random guy?"

"That's what doesn't make sense. Do you think she recognized Joe?"

"From where? You didn't even know him until a little while ago."

"Maybe that's it. Maybe she saw him at the fights. Maybe she put two and two together and thinks Joe is a wise guy who wanted to get a good look at her."

"Why? Oh God." Peggy cradled her head in her hands. "This just gets better and better."

The two women sat lost in their own thoughts until their mother popped her head into their room to say goodnight. And Carolyn still wasn't home.

The next morning, Helen shot out of bed as soon as the alarm rang. Her two sisters mumbled and rolled over, not willing to get up just yet.

"C'mon sleepyheads." Helen stood between their two twin beds and shook their shoulders. "Work and school today. No dawdling."

As Peggy and Carolyn begrudgingly rubbed their eyes and sat up, Helen headed for the bathroom.

"Don't take all day in there," Carolyn yelled after her. "I have to get ready too, you know."

"You're one to talk. You hog up that mirror like you own it."

"As I've said before, beauty can't be rushed. Besides, soon, you won't have to put up with me anymore."

Peggy grimaced and shook her head. "How many women will be sharing the bathroom in your new place? Better get yourself an old-fashioned wash basin, pitcher, and mirror."

Carolyn charged out of the room, marched down the hall, and banged on the bathroom door. Helen pulled the door open, toothbrush in her mouth.

"Can I, at least, finish brushing my teeth?" she asked.

Carolyn stood in the open doorway tapping her foot on the wooden floor. After rinsing her mouth out, Helen looked at her.

"Thought you were going to behave for the next week."

"Changed my mind. I was having too much fun."

Helen pulled her sister into the bathroom and sat on the closed toilet lid.

"Listen. When you move into that Brandon place, they're not going to put up with you and your shenanigans. They'll boot you out of there so fast it'll make you head spin. Why don't you do yourself a favor and get used to a curfew while you're still living here? Who knows, maybe showing a little respect for Mom and Dad will soften him up and you won't have to leave. It certainly couldn't hurt. But now, you're just throwing fuel on the fire. It's like a slap in the face to them when you come home so late."

"I wouldn't know anything about slaps in faces. That's your department." She reached down and grabbed Helen's arm. "Now, get out of here so I can get ready for work." She shoved Helen out the door and slammed it behind her.

125

"Girls! What's all that racket about?" Their mother stood at the entrance to the kitchen, wiping her hands on a dish towel. "If you girls don't get a move on it, you'll all be late for work. And you, Missy," she pointed at Peggy, "have classes to go to. Am I not right?"

"Yes, Mom," they both said.

Inside their room, Peggy asked Helen what was going on with Carolyn. As they dressed, the two sisters tried to devise a plan to keep Carolyn on a somewhat straight and narrow path, at least until the end of the month. But how to accomplish this herculean task still hung over their heads like a thunder cloud as they sat down to breakfast.

Carolyn breezed into the kitchen a few minutes later acting like they were the happiest family in New York City, even though the tension in the room zipped around the table like live wires brought down after a storm.

"Will you all be home for supper?" Aggie asked, pouring coffee for everyone.

"And where else would I be going, love," Paddy said.

"I will," Peggy said.

"Me too," Helen said.

Everyone stared at Carolyn, who sat eating her cereal ignoring the rest of her family.

"Carolyn," Paddy said, "you'll answer your mam. You're still a member of this household and you'll show her some respect."

Carolyn looked up from her cereal bowl and with stone-cold eyes stared at her father. "I don't know."

"Aggie, we'll take that as a no. Prepare no dinner for the trollop. She can eat elsewhere tonight."

"I didn't say no, Dad. I—"

"I did. You'll not be eating supper here tonight. I don't care where you do eat your meal, but it won't be here."

126

With that, Paddy gulped down the rest of his coffee, gave his wife a kiss on the cheek, grabbed his lunch pail from the top of the fridge, and slammed the front door shut.

Aggie stood, staring down at her middle child. "Are you happy now you've got your da all upset before his day even begins? I swear some days I truly believe the wee folks switched you for a changeling years ago."

"Really, Mom? Not that old country malarky again. It's the twentieth century, not the twelfth. Times change. Customs change. Women have more freedoms now. I shouldn't have to be at your, or Dad's, beck and call every day. I'll let you know later if I'll be home for supper."

"Don't even think about it. Your da's already decided you won't be. So, don't plan on eating here. You and your gentleman friend can go have a bite any place you like. Just not here."

"But what if he has other commitments for tonight?"

"I'm sure you'll manage on your own then."

"But Mom, it's not very respectable for a woman to eat out alone and it costs money."

"Now we're worrying about being respectable? That's a laugh. And there're plenty of places that're cheap enough. And there's always the Automat."

"The Automat! I wouldn't be seen dead in there."

"That's your choice, love. Now, girls, it's getting late. Best you all be off for work and school. Grab your lunch bags before you go. I didn't make one up for you, Carolyn. Seeing as you're so high and mighty now, I didn't want to embarrass you at work."

"Fine." Carolyn's face was red as hot coals and her eyes shot daggers around the room. She threw her napkin on the table and stormed out of the apartment.

"Seems Carolyn forgot to put her dishes in the sink," Aggie said, clearing Carolyn's place.

Helen and Peggy sat at the table like two proper school girls. Neither said a word, or moved an inch.

"Have you two turned to stone?" Aggie asked.

"No, Mom."

"Sorry, Mom."

They scooped up their empty cereal bowls and coffee cups and stacked them in the sink. Then they each grabbed a lunch bag from the top of the fridge, gave Aggie a peck on the cheek, grabbed jackets, purses, hats, and gloves, and headed downstairs. Outside, Peggy waited for Helen.

"That was uncomfortable."

"To say the least."

"I feel like we're in a war zone. What happened to Carolyn toeing the line for a week to see if Dad would let her stay?"

"I guess that's not going to happen while she's having fun, as she says."

"Great. That's just swell. I may have to move in with Joanne until all this blows over. I can't take this constant fighting and concentrate on my school work."

"Don't you dare. You're not leaving me all alone. You've got to help me figure out a way to end these battles every day. Either that or I think Mom will have a nervous breakdown."

"I'm worried about her too."

They trudged to the corner; the morning's breakfast battle fresh in their minds.

CHAPTER TWELVE

Over the next few days, an unspoken truce settled over the Campbell household. No more morning melees and Carolyn's empty chair at dinner became the norm rather than the exception. Peggy studied in peace, Helen spoke with Charlie over the phone when she didn't see him in the evenings, Aggie and Paddy watched TV shows like *Dragnet*, or *The Jack Benny Show*, and, of course, *The Lawrence Welk Show*, which everyone in the neighborhood seemed to enjoy. Carolyn usually came home early enough to use the front door, not the window. The whole apartment seemed to breathe a sigh of relief.

One Sunday night, while the family watched *The Ed Sullivan Show*, Aggie said, "Carolyn, I'd like to go see this place you'll be living at. I thought tomorrow morning would suit."

Carolyn's jaw dropped open. "But... but Mom, I have to go to work in the morning."

"We'll go early then, before your normal leaving time. I'm sure your man won't mind if you're a little late.

And you can always telephone if we're not done by nine o'clock."

"But, Mom, I might have to call them and make an appointment or something."

"Nonsense. You've already agreed to rent a room there, so I can't believe they wouldn't let your own mam have a look at one. And this way, maybe I'll get to see the kind of women who live there."

"But, Mom—"

"No more buts about it. It's settled. We'll leave here at seven tomorrow morning. That should give you enough time. Paddy, girls, you can manage breakfast on your own, can't you?"

"Sure, we'll be fine," Paddy said.

"I'll make up your lunches for you before I leave, so's you won't have to worry about that."

"That'll be grand," Paddy said. "Right girls?"

"Yes, Dad," Peggy and Helen said.

With a nod of her head, Aggie went back to enjoying the show on TV. Helen looked at Peggy, her eyebrows raised halfway to her hairline. No one spoke for the rest of the show. As soon as it was over, Helen said she was going for a walk. Peggy and Carolyn both agreed that was a great idea and the three sisters grabbed hats, gloves, and purses and made a beeline for the door before their mother could stop them. Outside, Helen headed down the street at a quick clip, her high heels tapping away on the sidewalk.

"Did either of you know about Mom's scheme?" Carolyn asked, her face flushed.

"Not me."

"Me neither."

"What's she trying to pull?" Carolyn asked.

"Beats me," Peggy said. "Maybe it's just what she said. She wants to see the place and the type of women who live there."

"Swell. Just swell. With my luck, there'll be out of work actresses lounging all over the place in satin kimonos, smoking, and flipping through movie magazines. Just the type of bohemians, as Mom would say, who'll corrupt me even more than she already thinks I am."

"Carolyn, I think you're exaggerating," Helen said. "I'm sure if there are any out of work actresses, they'll be dressed and leaving to try to find auditions or whatever they do to look for work."

"That's right," Peggy said. "And I bet a lot of the residents there go to school. So, they'll be leaving for classes. You're getting all worked up over nothing."

"Maybe," Carolyn said, stopping to grind her cigarette out on the pavement. "I just don't like the way she sprung it on me. Why couldn't she ask me what would be a good time to go there? Why does she feel she has the right to dictate this visit to me?"

"Because she's our mom and that's the way she is," Peggy said.

"Doesn't mean I have to like it."

"No, you don't, Carolyn," Helen said. "But can I give you a piece of advice? I think you should act thrilled to show her your new home. If you act like there's something you don't want her to see, she'll scour over every inch of the place until she finds something unacceptable. Then she'll harp about it until you wind up getting thrown out. Maybe they won't even want to rent a room to you if she creates a scene."

Carolyn stopped dead. "They can't do that. I've already paid them a week's rent."

Helen and Peggy leaned against a car parked at the curb.

"They can give it back to you and tell you you're unsuitable." Helen looked over at Peggy who shrugged her shoulders. "And where did you get a week's rent?"

"That's none of your business." Carolyn lit another cigarette and paced to the corner and back. "I could scream," she said as she passed them. On her next lap, she stopped in front of them. "Do you think that's what she plans to do? Create a scene? Why? Surely, she doesn't want me to be without a place to stay. And I can't stay at home. Dad made that quite clear."

"I don't know what she wants. Maybe Peggy's right. Maybe she just wants to see the place to ease her mind."

"Why does everything have to become such a big deal?"

Carolyn continued to pace, puffing furiously on her cigarette for her two drags, then replacing it with a fresh one.

"Keep going through cigarettes at that rate and you won't have enough money for next week's rent," Peggy said. "Unless, of course, you're not really the one paying the rent."

"Oh, shut up. You know, this whole mess is your fault, Helen."

"My fault?" Helen slammed her open hand on her chest, eyes bulging. "How in God's name did this become my fault?"

"If you hadn't argued with me and slapped me, Mom never would have known about J.P. and I wouldn't be in this situation."

"You're amazing." Helen shook her head. "Did it ever occur to you that if you kept your nose clean and didn't decide to have an affair with your boss that you *also* wouldn't be in this situation? Or is that too much for your feeble brain to grasp?"

Carolyn threw her purse to the ground and headed for Helen ready to claw her eyes out. Helen pulled off her gloves and stuffed them in her pocket. Peggy jumped between the two women and held her hands up towards their chests, palms out. "Stop it. Both of you. Do you really mean to have a fist fight right here in the street? What's gotten into you two? We're sisters. We're supposed to stick together. Not behave like alley cats. Honestly, you both disgust me."

Carolyn and Helen backed down. Carolyn retrieved her purse and lit another cigarette, her hands trembling. Helen tugged her gloves back on, leaned against the car and looked up at the darkening sky.

"Sorry, Peg."

"Me too."

"Don't apologize to me. But you'd better work things out between the two of you. I have an idea we're all going to need each other a lot more than you realize in the coming weeks."

They both looked at her quizzically, but she just shook her head and walked away.

"What do you suppose she meant by that?" Helen asked.

"Who knows. Maybe she's trying to be mysterious."

"Peggy? Mysterious? That's not like her at all. She's all facts and logical thinking. Certainly not someone who weaves a spell of intrigue around herself," Helen said, waving her hands and fingers in front of her.

"Whatever she meant, it distracted us."

"So, I guess she achieved her purpose."

They walked back to their apartment, their high heels and Carolyn's cigarette puffing the only sounds on the silent street.

Carolyn grabbed Helen's arm when they reached their stoop. "Thanks for the advice about Mom. I'm sure

133

you're right. I'll try to seem happy that she's taking in interest in my welfare."

"You'd better do more than put on a show. She can see right through any phony baloney we try to pull on her."

Carolyn sighed and walked up the steps to the front door.

"Hey," Helen said, "want me to go with you tomorrow? I could be a kind of buffer between you two."

Carolyn spun around. "Could you?" Her eyes glistened with unshed tears. "That would be great. I'll owe you for this one. And I promise I'll pay you back somehow."

"Let's not worry about that now. I'll feel better if I know you're settled in a decent place. And you're going early enough that I'm sure I can get to work on time. If I'm a little late, I'll blame it on a subway delay."

Carolyn rushed back down the stoop to the sidewalk and hugged Helen. "You're terrific. Best big sister ever."

"Yeah, yeah. Remember that the next time you want to rip my throat open."

Carolyn's face turned red. "I'm sorry about that. I guess I'm a little crazy what with everything that's been going on the past few days, or weeks, or whatever it's been."

"Me too. This has been tough for all of us. After all, it's the first time we'll be living in different places."

"It's not like I'm moving to Alaska or something."

"I know, but it's still strange."

"Let's make a pact that we'll all meet for lunch or dinner or a drink at least once a week."

"I'd like that but I don't know if Peggy can afford it."

"We'll find a cheap place and you and I can cover her meal. How about it?"

Helen thought for a minute and extended her hand. "It's a deal."

The two women shook hands and headed up the stairs arm in arm. They reached their apartment and yelled "We're home" before heading to the bedroom to change into pajamas and get ready for bed. Tomorrow would be an early start and they wanted to be on their toes for any of their mother's tricks. They knew she could be the most devious person they had ever met when she decided on a course of action to reach her goal.

Peggy watched and listened to their chatter and decided they had made peace with each other. So, she closed her book and stowed it and her notebooks in the satchel she took with her every day. That night, the women's mundane nightly routines only contributed to the tense nervousness that crackled around the room.

"So, this is it?" Aggie asked, looking up at the Brandon Residence. "Looks decent enough from the outside, at least."

Both sisters breathed a sigh of relief.

"Passed the first test," Helen whispered to Carolyn as they climbed the steps to the front door.

At the reception desk, Carolyn reintroduced herself to the switchboard operator/receptionist and asked to see the manager. They walked into the main visiting room, which was meant to impress with its floor to ceiling windows and intimate groupings of upholstered chairs and sofas. And judging by Aggie's wide-eyed expression, and the way she pulled herself up to her full height, the two young women knew it had accomplished its purpose. They chose chairs by one of the windows that looked out onto the garden in the back of the property. They only sat for a few minutes before the manager breezed into the room.

135

"Miss Campbell, how nice to see you again," she said. "Is there something I can do for you? Haven't changed your mind about living here, have you?"

"Oh no, nothing like that." Carolyn introduced her mother and sister. "We were wondering if we could see my future room, or a comparable one. Although I've described everything to my mom, she'd like to see it for herself."

"I'm sure you understand," Aggie said. "I don't like to think my daughter's staying somewhere unsuitable. I'll sleep better knowing she's in a decent place."

"I can assure you, Mrs. Campbell, we hold this residence, and all the women who live her, to the highest standards." The manager stood ramrod straight in front of Aggie, color creeping up her neck and face. "If you'll follow me, please."

She stopped at the front desk and said a few words to the receptionist, then led them through the TV/library room, the piano practice room, and the dining hall. Back at the receptionist's desk, she picked up a key and led them to the elevator.

"Mary, our receptionist, called one of our residents and asked if we could view her room. Please don't touch anything or open the closet. That is all personal property and I ask that you respect her privacy."

"As if I would be prying into other people's things" Aggie said. "The very idea." She slapped her gloves against the palm of her hand. "I never."

"She has to say that, Mom," Carolyn said. "There are probably people who would go snooping into closets and dressers just to be nosy."

The elevator doors opened and they stepped in.

"Well, I just hope she doesn't think I'm one of those people," Aggie said.

"Of course not, Mom. She just has to be sure." Carolyn looked at Helen and rolled her eyes.

"The room's very adequate," Helen said.

"I'll be the judge of that," Aggie said. "That's why I've come all this way uptown, isn't it?"

"Yes, Mom."

The elevator stopped and the manager walked down the hall to one of the doors lining both sides of the hallway. She knocked before using her key. Then she stepped aside so Carolyn and Aggie could enter the small room. It was a carbon copy of the one Carolyn had seen with a single bed, chair, dresser, and nightstand. But this resident had added her own touches.

Floral print curtains fluttered in the light breeze that came through the partially opened window. Framed landscape pictures adorned the walls, and small personal items and family photos covered the tops of the nightstand and dresser. She had also added a small bookcase that overflowed with books and binders. A bedspread in the same pattern as the curtains completed the room's transformation from a dreary cell-like cubicle to a welcoming refuge.

"Nothing to write home about, is it now?" Aggie said. "More like a hotel than a home."

"Mom, you know I can't afford a whole apartment. Not in a decent place anyway. This will work out fine. And I think it looks very nice what with the pictures on the walls, and the curtains and bespread. It's cheerful and cozy. A real homey feel."

"Hmph. If you say so. After all, it's you who'll be living here, not me."

Helen heard her mother's tone and stuck her head in before Carolyn said something she'd later regret. "How cute. This room is lovely, don't you agree, Mom? And Carolyn, think of what fun we'll have decorating yours.

137

Have you thought about what you'll buy? What colors? Pictures for the walls?"

"Well, no. I haven't given it any thought at all. I didn't realize I'd be able to decorate. This'll be fun, Helen. Maybe we could go to Macy's or Gimbel's together and look at what they have. When can we go?"

"Gee, I'm not sure. I'll have to check my schedule and see when they have me working next week."

"Speaking of which," Aggie said, "shouldn't you two be going off to work?"

"You're right, Mom," Carolyn said. "I got so caught up in decorating ideas that I forgot I still have to get to the office."

"Well, let's go then. Thank you for showing me around," Aggie said to the manager, who had been watching and listening to this exchange with interest. "I'll be heading back home now girls and you get yourselves off to work."

"We will, Mom," Helen said. "Do you want me to take you back to the subway stop, or can you find it by yourself?"

"I got myself here from Ireland, didn't I? I think I can find a subway station."

Aggie nodded at the manager and Carolyn and Helen thanked her for her time. The three women headed to the elevator while the manager locked up the room. Back on the first floor, they walked to the front door. When they reached the sidewalk, Aggie told them she was going to sit in the park for a while to wait out the rush hour crowds on the trains. So, Helen and Carolyn left her there and walked towards Broadway.

"That went well," Helen said, once they were out of earshot.

"Thank God. I was terrified that some of the women would be lounging around in their skivvies."

138

"I doubt that's allowed. That manager doesn't look like she'd tolerate any such behavior."

"I agree, but you know what I mean."

"I do. And I'm glad for your sake that no one was around. At least now Mom can't badmouth some poor innocent woman."

A block later, Carolyn said, "Helen? Did you mean it about going shopping with me?"

"Sure, unless you don't want me to."

"Oh no, I do. You're much better at decorating than I am. I only seem to be good at fashion and hair styles. Anything that even smells of domesticity escapes me."

"A left-handed compliment if ever I heard one."

"Gosh, I didn't mean it that way." Carolyn stopped and grabbed Helen's arm. "I'm sorry. I... I guess that came out all wrong."

"Forget it. You are better at fashion. I'm going to miss borrowing your clothes whenever I really want to look stylish."

The two of them laughed and headed to the nearest subway stop.

"You're late," J.P. said when Carolyn sauntered into his office, closing the door behind her.

"That's not the greeting I expected," Carolyn said, walking around his desk. She leaned over for her usual morning kiss, but got the top of his head instead. "Oh, come on, you can't be that mad at me for being a little late. I had to take my mother uptown to show her where I'll be living. She wanted to make sure it wasn't some kind of brothel."

"I have a lot to do today, Carolyn. The client meeting for the ad campaign I'm working on is in three days. I don't have time to listen to your family problems." He shuffled through the papers on his desk, never lifting his eyes to look at her.

"My family... ?" She almost shrieked with incredulity. "My family problems? You mean our problem, don't you?"

"Keep your voice down. Do you want the whole office to know we're sleeping together?"

"I have an idea they already assume that. We're not terribly discreet, you know."

"That's exactly the problem. *You're* not discreet. I think you enjoy flaunting the fact that you're having an affair with your boss in front of the other secretaries." He looked up into her shocked face. "Don't you?"

"No, of course not. Why?... How could you say that?" She perched on the corner of his desk.

"And please get off my desk. If you feel you must sit, sit in one of the chairs." He continued to go through his morning's mail, ignoring Carolyn.

"J.P. what's going on?" she asked, moving to the chair in front of his desk. "Why are you acting like this? Why are you treating me like someone you don't love?"

"I never said I loved you, Carolyn."

"What? Of course, you did. Maybe not in those exact words, but you said it in so many other ways."

J.P. leaned back in his chair and stared at her. "What ways, Carolyn?"

"Every way," she sputtered. She twisted her hands around one another, suddenly terrified about where this conversation was headed. "The way you look at me. The way you, usually, greet me every morning. The way you take me to the finest restaurants, and spend money on me. The way you make love to me."

"Did you ever think I spend money on you so that I can take you to bed? And that's the only reason I do so."

"No... no. I don't believe you." Her stomach rolled and sweat seeped down between her breasts. "No one

140

could put on that good an act. I know you love me. What about the talks we've had about getting an apartment together, so we won't have to sneak around in hotel rooms? Making a place just for the two of us?"

"As I recall, those were always your pipe dreams, not mine."

Carolyn stared at the man she loved. She couldn't believe he was transforming into this cold, hard, cruel person before her eyes. This wasn't her J.P. This was a man she didn't know.

"Look, Carolyn, you came into this ad agency as randy as I've ever seen a pretty young thing be. You were hot to trot, as they say. And I thought, why not? You have to agree it didn't take much to get you into bed. A few nice dinners. Some champagne. A couple of trinkets. A lavish hotel room. And you couldn't wait to show me just how much you appreciated being treated to things you could never afford. You liked the lifestyle I showed you and you were willing to do anything I asked to experience it. Isn't that true?"

"Of course, I liked it. What girl wouldn't? But you never would have treated me to all that if you didn't love me and want to be with me." She took a deep breath. "You know, I never planned on falling in love with anyone. But I did. With you. But it seems I was nothing but a diversion for you, wasn't I?"

J.P. shook his head. "You really are a child in so many ways. Of course, I desired you. You're young, beautiful, easily impressed, and so inexperienced in the ways of the world I've lived in all my life, it almost wasn't fair to seduce you. But you were fresh, like a deep breath of clean air. You appreciated any little trifle from me and never really expected anything. Certainly refreshing, considering the materialistic, status seeking women I

141

usually encounter in my social circles. Yes, you were fun. But it can't go on."

"What do you mean? Are you breaking up with me?"

"Carolyn, really? Breaking up? Isn't that a high school term? Look, we've had our fun but it's over. I should have realized from the beginning you'd turn this simple crush you had on me into something more and blow it all out of proportion. You expected a great romance when all I wanted was a few laughs."

"I don't believe you." Tears finally crested the rims of her eyes and rolled down her cheeks. "There's another reason, isn't there? Another woman who's caught your eye? A new secretary? There has to be something else going on. Tell me there's something else, J.P., please."

"Afraid not, Carolyn. But don't worry, I said I'd help you out with the rent for that place you're living in now—"

"I'm not living there yet."

"Well, you will be soon," he said, waving her objection off, "and I said I'd help you, so I won't renege on that deal."

He opened his desk drawer, pulled out an envelope, and slid it to her. "Here's six months' rent. That should give you enough breathing room to tide you over until you find another job."

Carolyn's jaw dropped. She wiped the tears off her cheeks and stood, staring at the man she thought she knew. "You're firing me, as well?"

"It's best this way. You can't really expect to continue to work here after the end of our affair."

Her face heated up as she picked up the envelope, shoved it into her pocket, and walked around his desk to stand in front of him.

"You're a real bastard," she said, and slapped him hard across the face. She stormed out of his office, ignoring the stares of the other secretaries on the floor, gathered her things, and left the building.

J.P. rubbed his cheek where she had hit him and watched her leave. He shook his head and smiled.

In a lot of ways, I'll miss that girl. She's got spunk.

A minute later, he picked up his phone and dialed the extension for the office of the president of the ad agency.

"It's over. She's gone," he said.

"Good. Honestly, J.P., what were you thinking taking your mistress to The Pierre? You might as well have put your affair on the front page of the *New York Times*. Try to be more discerning in the future or your career in advertising, or anywhere else in the communications field, will be over," his father-in-law said.

J.P. sighed and hung up the phone.

CHAPTER THIRTEEN

Carolyn walked over to Fifth Avenue and headed uptown to Central Park. She thought its calmness might quiet the screams in her mind. She wondered about what had just happened. *How could J.P. do this to me? After all I've given him. And all the promises he made. And the plans we had for the future. What happened to that J.P.? Where was the man I fell in love with? He certainly wasn't in his office this morning. Now what am I going to do? I don't know if I can even afford the rent in the Brandon Residence once the money he gave me is gone. And I don't know if I really want to live there now. I did all this just so I could be with him, now what? No J.P. No family home. A desolate lonely life living among women who are all on their way someplace else while I'll be stuck there living like an old lonely spinster.*

What have I done?

She walked into the park entrance on 59th Street at the Artist's Gate and wandered the paths, finally stopping at the pond. She plunked down on a bench and watched the ducks paddling around. The mother ducks swimming toward an unknown destination, their ducklings following along, trusting her completely to lead them somewhere safe. Carolyn wondered why we, as humans, couldn't be so trusting in our parents' advice and leadership. She thought back to how her father had reacted when she told him about her involvement with J.P.

Why didn't I rethink my relationship then? How could I have been so naïve and trusting?

Pushing herself to a standing position like an old lady riddled with rheumatism, Carolyn continued her walk through the park. Since it was Monday, the paths were almost deserted. Meandering aimlessly, she passed the Chess and Checkers House, a few men mesmerized by the game in front of them, and the carousel with its riderless horses racing in their endless circle. Images of children urging their noble steeds to go faster reminded her of something Helen said about meeting her current boyfriend in the park. Something about bringing her little charges here. Now Carolyn regretted how little attention she paid to Helen's and Peggy's prattling about their daily lives. If only she could talk to Helen, things would be so much better. Helen, always the clear-headed logical person in a crisis, would know exactly what to do. She thought she might go to the Foundling and talk to her, but she also knew how angry *she* would be if one of her sisters barged into the office to discuss personal problems with her.

No chance that'll happen now.

As she continued wandering through the park, she heard children's voices. She followed the sounds hoping against hope they were Helen's charges.

Extremely doubtful, considering how my day is going so far.

Suddenly, one of the children yelled, "Miss Helen, Bobby won't get off the swings and it's my turn."

146

It is Helen's group! Thank God. Maybe she can help me figure out what to do.

Carolyn quickened her pace and soon spotted the small group of children. Her sister sat on a nearby bench, watching them.

"Helen," Carolyn called, waving her arm.

"Carolyn?"

Carolyn almost sprinted the remaining distance between them and plopped down next to her.

"What are you doing here? Why aren't you at work?"

"That's a really short story. I got fired."

"What! No. Why?"

"He decided I was getting too attached to him and that he had to end our relationship."

"Well, that's a lousy thing to do, especially after all the brouhaha at home over him. Did you tell him you had to move out because of him?"

"I think that's what started his cold feet."

"Why? I don't understand."

"Well, we had talked about us getting a place together. Maybe here in the city or up in Riverdale closer to his home in Westchester. That way, he could probably spend some time with me on weekends too. So, when I told him about moving into Brandon Residence, I also mentioned how now it would be easier for us to get our own place since I wouldn't have to explain moving out to my family."

"That's true, although you'd still have to justify an apartment, especially in Riverdale. It's expensive up there."

Carolyn sighed. "Guess it doesn't matter now anyway. He said that all the talk about a place together was my pipe dream, not his. That he never said anything about that."

"No. How could he? You didn't let him get away with that, did you?"

"What was I supposed to do? I didn't exactly have a recording of what he said."

"All right. Don't get all huffy on me. So, he broke up with you, but why did you get fired? You didn't cause a scene or anything, did you?"

"Of course not." Carolyn threw her cigarette on the ground and stomped on it. "He said I couldn't continue to work for him now that our circumstances had changed."

"That's ridiculous. I bet there are plenty of office romances that end and no one gets fired."

"Maybe. But they may also be between two single people."

"You could have a point there."

Both women stared off into the distance, not saying a word.

"So, what now?" Helen asked.

"I don't know."

"Are you still going to move out?"

"I don't know about that either. Do you think Dad will let me stay now that I'm not out carousing every night?"

"Maybe. But what do you think will happen if you start seeing someone new? You can't expect him to let you slide again."

"Guess not. Maybe I *am* better off making a clean break and moving out. Then I won't have Dad's rules hanging over my head every time I have a date."

"No, just the Brandon Residence curfews. And no fire escape or willing accomplice, like Peggy, or me, to help you get in past curfew."

"Oh, don't blame her. She thought it was all a wild adventure, like in one of those spy novels she's always

148

reading when she doesn't have her head buried in textbooks."

"It's time that girl grew up and faced the real world. Not everything's the stuff of novels."

"Wait until she finishes medical school and faces a bunch of men leering at her. That'll wake her up to the real world."

"Guess you're right about that."

"It's mine," a tiny voice said.

"Is not."

"I saw it first."

Helen heard the squabble and scanned the area to find the two quarreling children.

"Bobby, John, come over here now."

Two boys stopped their arguing on a dime and walked over, heads drooping to their chests.

"What are you two raising a ruckus about?"

"I found it first," Bobby yelled, his bravado resurfacing, "and John says it's his and he only put it down for a minute, but he's a liar."

"Bobby! We don't call our friends liars. You know that."

"Yes, Miss Helen."

"John, what do you have that Bobby says is his?"

John opened his hand. A dirty cat's-eye marble rested in his palm.

"I did find it first, Miss Helen. Honest."

"No you didn't," Bobby said. "I did." Tears threatened to overflow the rims of his eyes. "It's mine. I found it and when I showed it to John, he grabbed it out of my hand and said it was his and that he found it first and put it on the ground so he could go on the swings."

Helen looked at John, one eyebrow raised. "Why would you put it on the ground and not in your pocket, John?"

"Cause."

"Cause is not an answer."

"I was afraid it would fall out when I was on the swings. Cause I go real high and tilt back."

"Yes, I know. Another thing we have to talk about. Why didn't you ask someone to hold it for you? Or give it to me?"

John scuffed his foot across the dirt, hands shoved into his pants' pockets, chin resting on his chest. He shrugged his shoulders.

"I don't know."

Helen barely heard his mumble.

"Hmm," she said. "I'll have to think about this." Bobby glared at John, fists clenched. "But for now, two minutes on the bench for both of you for arguing. One at each end." Helen pointed to the bench next to her. "Go."

The two combatants scrambled over to claim their end of the detention spot, both scowling at each other.

"Quite a problem," Carolyn said. "How are you going to fix it?"

"I don't know. Usually, after a minute on the bench, they're distracted by a game some of the other kids are playing, and all they want is to get off the bench and join in. Marble long forgotten. But I'll put it in my purse and see who's the most persistent about getting it back."

"If only we could all be so easily distracted when something we think is ours is claimed by someone else."

Helen smirked. "J.P. wasn't yours first, you know."

"That your morning news bulletin?"

Helen opened her eyes wide, stared at Carolyn, eyebrows raised, and shook her head.

"I'm sorry. I shouldn't be so sarcastic. I know you're right. I'm just hurt. And I don't know if I want to cry or go back there and knock his lights out instead of the slap I gave him."

150

"You slapped him?"

"Right across the face. Good and hard. Wonder how he'll explain the red welt that's bound to appear."

"Good for you," Helen said. A minute later, she started to laugh. "Bet he never expected that."

Carolyn felt a giggle rise up in her chest. "Don't mess with a Campbell girl, right?" Then she started laughing. In another minute, the two women sat clutching their sides, roaring laughter. The children stopped playing to stare at them.

A while later, Carolyn walked back to the Foundling with Helen and her tiny crew.

"What are you going to do now?" Helen asked.

"I don't know. Guess I'll buy a newspaper and start scouring the help wanted ads. I'm dreading going home and telling our parents I got fired."

Helen thought about that for a minute, then said, "Don't."

"Don't what?"

"Don't tell them. Not yet. Get up and dressed everyday like you're going to work. And come right home after what would be your normal work day. Meanwhile, you can go to the library and check out all the morning papers for jobs. Maybe even go to some of the ad agencies and fill out job applications at their personnel offices. That way, they won't know you got fired and it'll buy you some time. At least for a little while."

"You think I could pull it off?"

"Sure. Let's face it. They want to believe you're trying to live by their rules. And maybe Dad'll change his mind about you leaving home."

They walked along in silence, Helen keeping her eye on her young charges, Carolyn in deep thought.

"There's only one glitch that I can see," Carolyn said.

"What's that?"

"If there is a job available, how can personnel get in touch with me? They always call to set up an interview."

"I hadn't thought about that. Give me a minute."

After another block or so, Helen said, "I know. Tell Mom and Dad you decided to look around for a better job, or maybe just a different one. That you don't feel comfortable working with a man you're dating. You're afraid of the possible office gossip. So, you might be getting phone calls from other places."

"You think Mom'll buy that?"

"Not really, but she'll go along with it for a while. Might be enough breathing room for you to actually get another job."

"Well, it's a plan and better than anything I've got since I don't have one at all."

"Great. And don't tell Peggy you got fired either. That girl can't lie to save her soul and Mom knows that. She'll hone in on Peg and ask her what she knows about the whole situation. Better she knows nothing. That way she won't have to lie."

"Good idea. You're right. Mom'd have the true story out of her in about a minute."

"So, we have a deal?"

"We do."

They had arrived at the Foundling. "Got to leave you here," Helen said. "Take the day off. Go shopping, or browsing. Don't buy stuff or you'll have to explain to Mom how you had so much time on your hands."

"Right. Think I'll wander around for a while, then hit the library. May as well start the job search right away."

"That's the spirit. Have fun today."

"Oh yeah. It'll be a real blast cooped up in a library all day." Carolyn sighed and shook her head. "Thanks, Helen. Take care of these little brats. See you at home later." She strutted off down the street. A new determination in her stride.

Helen watched her go, and shook her head.

I hope she can bounce back from this. She's a lot more fragile that she lets on.

"Come on, everyone. Let's get inside. Time for morning snacks and naps." Helen herded her charges up the steps and through the door.

Carolyn's outward confidence belied the inner turmoil she felt. She had always been the one to dump her boyfriends. She didn't like being on the other end of the stick. At the moment, her emotions ran the gamut from wanting to lunge a knife into J.P.'s chest to running to him asking to be taken back. She loved and hated him at the same time. She still couldn't make sense of his sudden change of affection. Just last week, when they were discussing her move to Brandon Residence, he had said that arrangement probably wouldn't work. That he'd have to find a place where he didn't have to leave her at the front door. A more "relationship friendly" place, as he phrased it.

Well, I won't have to worry about that now.

Once again, she recalled the past few days trying to find a reason for J.P.'s change of heart. She went over every little thing they'd done together, the places they'd been, the people they'd seen . . .

The people!

She stopped dead in the street and smacked her forehead, "Of course." People bumped into her, looked at her, and hurried away.

Now everyone thinks I'm one of those crazy people roaming around talking to themselves. But that's it. It has to be.

153

She recalled the man who came to their table when they were at The Pierre. J.P. didn't know him and neither did she. At the time, she thought there was something fishy about him. He definitely wasn't dressed well enough to be a regular Pierre customer. His suit was cheap and his manner coarse.

I bet he was some kind of private detective J.P.'s wife hired to spy on him. That would explain his sudden attitude change.

Her stride became more purposeful as she concocted a plan to get J.P. back. She ducked into the first drug store she passed and checked to see if she had enough coins in her wallet. Satisfied with what she saw, she squeezed into the phone booth, shut the door, and dialed J.P.'s office.

"Mr. Chandler's office," a woman said.

"This is Mrs. Chandler," Carolyn said in her best imitation of J.P.'s wife. "Put my husband on the phone."

Her imperious manner had always irritated Carolyn, but now she found she could use it to her advantage.

"Good morning, dear. Anything wrong?" J.P. asked.

"Nothing that can't be fixed with a kiss," she said.

"Carolyn? Are you all right?"

"I'm fine, but I need to talk to you. I figured it all out."

"Carolyn, I don't know what you think you figured out. There's nothing to figure out. It's over, Carolyn. It was fun, but it's over."

"No, J.P. I realize what happened. Look, tell whoever's sitting at my desk that you have to leave for a few minutes. I'll be waiting in the coffee shop around the corner on 53rd Street."

"Carolyn, you're being unreasonable. It's over. Just accept that fact."

"No. I won't. I can't. Either you meet me in ten minutes, or I'll come up there and create a scene. Your choice."

154

She waited for an answer.

"Five cents for the next ten minutes," the operator said.

Plunking a nickel into the coin slot, she said, "I'm waiting," once the connection was reopened.

J.P. sighed. "I'll be there." The phone clicked. Now all Carolyn heard was a dial tone.

A smug smile on her face, she strode out of the drug store and marched down Madison Avenue to 53rd Street.

If he thought I was buying that whole "It's over" deal, he has another think coming. I can play the game a lot better than his silver spoon wife. And I know how to play dirty.

Glowing with self-approbation, she attracted the eyes of every man she passed. But she was oblivious to their stares. She had her sights set on one target, and one target only.

Hang on to your hat, J.P. You're not going to know what hit you.

Settling herself in a back booth in the nearly empty coffee shop, Carolyn kept her eye on the door. She didn't want to give J.P. a chance to say he didn't see her and left.

Right after the waitress landed Carolyn's coffee and Danish on the table, J.P. walked in. she waved and he headed over to her.

"All right, I'm here. What's this all about? This is very inconvenient. I have meetings to prepare for, you know. The campaign for our biggest client is well underway and I have to go over everything before the presentation in three days."

His cold indifference made her skin crawl.

"I don't care about that. How can you even think about an ad campaign when our lives have been shattered?"

155

J.P. sighed and leaned back against the padded booth.

"What can I get you?" the waitress asked, magically appearing at his side, offering an instant reprieve from Carolyn's probing eyes.

"He'll have coffee, black, and a cheese Danish," Carolyn answered for him.

The waitress raised her eyebrows and looked over at J.P., pencil poised above her order pad.

"That's fine," he said, waving her away. As soon as she was out of earshot, J.P. turned to Carolyn. "Look, there's no reason to drag this out or make it more difficult than it has to be. Let's just make a clean break and be done with the whole affair. You're not a child. It was fun, but it's over. Accept that fact."

"No. I won't accept it. You don't make love to me one minute then tell me it's all over the next. That doesn't even make sense."

"Maybe not, but that's the situation."

"No, J.P. I figured it all out. That man. The man who came over to our table at The Pierre. I figured out he was some kind of detective your wife hired to follow you. I don't know what you did to make her suspicious, but, somehow, she got the idea you were seeing someone and had you followed. I mean, he certainly didn't belong in The Pierre. His suit was cheap and he—"

"Stop, Carolyn. It wasn't—"

"Here you go, hon," the waitress said, landing the coffee and Danish in front of him.

"Thank you." J.P. stirred sugar into his cup and stared at the swirling black liquid.

"You were saying?" Carolyn asked.

"Where was I? Oh yes. The man at The Pierre. He had nothing to do with this, or my wife. Simply a case of mistaken identity."

"No. I'm sure you're wrong. He caused this whole kerfuffle. I know it. So, all we have to do—"

"Stop. Please, Carolyn. Stop." J.P. covered his face with his hands for a moment and took a deep breath. "I didn't want to have to tell you this, but I see now I have no choice. My father-in-law called me first thing this morning before you arrived. Late, as I recall."

Carolyn brushed that comment aside with a sweep of her hand.

"Anyway, he said a colleague of his had seen us at The Pierre and felt it was his duty to tell my father-in-law before we became an item on Page Six of *The Daily News*."

"That's ridiculous. Why would the society column care about us?"

"Because, as you might remember, my wife is an extremely wealthy society lady. And her father, my father-in-law, owns J. Walter Thompson, where I work and you used to work. He let me know, in no uncertain terms, that unless I ended the affair and severed all association with you, I'd be out of work and divorced faster than I ever realized possible. He also told me I'd never work in advertising or any related field ever again. I'd also never see my children again. And his tentacles stretch far and wide. I'm sorry, Carolyn, I can't, and won't, give up my whole life for you,"

Tears ran down Carolyn's cheeks, her mind numb with these revelations.

"You never really did love me, did you? It was all a little dalliance on the side. That's all I ever meant to you. Maybe an excursion into the seedier part of life in New York City. A diversion from your high society friends and affairs. Or maybe that's a poor word choice. You took advantage of me, dazzling me with gifts, fine dinners, cocktails at The Pierre and other high-faluting places you

157

knew people from my side of the tracks never get to frequent. How many other young women have you seduced into your bed that way? I bet you've got a myriad of notches on your belt. Then, after you've had your fill, you take them to a very public place where you know someone from your social set will see you, someplace like The Pierre, your wife's daddy is notified, and you get to end the affair with clean hands."

Carolyn put her hand against her chest and raised her eyes to the ceiling. "'Daddy-in-law is forcing me to do this. It's not my choice'. Isn't that your usual game? A way for you to bow out through no fault of your own?"

"It's not like that, Carolyn. Believe me, I never meant—"

"Never meant what? For the affair to last this long? For me to fall in love with you? For daddy-in-law to find out? You're more of a bastard than I thought you were." Carolyn slid to the end of the booth, slipped her gloves on, and stepped into the aisle. "Don't worry, J.P. I won't bother you anymore. Just one parting memento so you'll always remember me."

She picked up her almost full coffee cup, took a sip, and poured the rest of it into his lap.

J.P. gasped.

"Bye, sweetie," she said and blew him a kiss as she swept out of the shop.

J.P. heard the waitresses laughing. His face turned crimson as he grabbed a handful of paper napkins and tried to blot up the brown stain soaking through his grey suit pants.

"Anything else?" the waitress asked, smirking at him. "More coffee? Or did you have your fill for today?"

J.P. scowled at her. "Check."

Carolyn left the coffee shop with a new attitude.

158

Never again will I let myself fall in love with an unavailable man, no matter what he promises for the future. From now on, I'll be the one in charge. I ceded all my power to J.P. It won't happen again..

Later that day, Carolyn watched as Helen finished fixing her hair and reached for her lipstick.

"What are you getting all gussied up for?"

"Charlie's taking me to dinner."

"He's still in the picture?"

"Of course. Why?"

"I don't know. I just figured he was long gone. I haven't heard you mention him lately."

"Then you haven't been listening. Peg says I never shut up about him."

"Oh. Guess I've been too busy worrying about me."

"What? Carolyn worrying only about Carolyn? I'm shocked."

"Oh, shut up," Carolyn said, throwing a pillow across the room at Helen.

"Hey! You'll mess up my hair that I've just spent a half hour trying to tame into place."

"You look great. Besides, you'll have a hat on, so that will keep it in place."

Helen shook her head, pressed her lips together to seal her lipstick, and reached for her tan crescent hat on the closet shelf. She fished through the top dresser drawer for matching tan wrist-length gloves.

"There. All set." She checked her wristwatch. "He should be here any minute now."

"You mean I'll finally get to meet this guy? You're sure he's not a figment of your imagination?"

"He's very much a real person. If you came home early more often, you'd have met him already."

159

"No more worries about that since I'll be home for dinner every night now. At least Dad backed up on that."

As if on cue, the buzzer rang for the downstairs door.

"I'll get it," Helen called down the hallway. "It's probably Charlie."

She buzzed him in and went out to look down the staircase.

"Is it him?" Carolyn asked, coming up next to her.

"Yep." Helen grinned as Charlie turned the corner for the last flight of stairs.

"There's my girl," he said, standing at the bottom of the staircase, hands on his hips, looking up at Helen. "Beautiful as always."

"Charlie, stop. You're embarrassing me."

He took the last flight of steps, two at a time and grabbed Helen around the waist, picked her up and whirled her around, finally setting her down before he kissed her.

"Quite an entrance," Carolyn said.

Charlie, with Helen still in his arms, looked over at her. "You must be the elusive sister who's never home."

"That sounds like me," Carolyn said, a smirk stealing across her face. "But elusive no more, I'm afraid."

Charlie stuck his hand out. "I'm Charlie Sanders. Nice to meet you."

"Charlie, this is my sister Carolyn. The middle one of the three of us."

As Carolyn shook his hand, she peered at him. "You look familiar. Have we met before?"

"Not that I know of."

She couldn't possibly remember me from that day at the hotel bar, could she? I tried to avoid facing her way. And I don't think she even looked at me at Stillman's. Too low class for her.

160

"Guess I have one of those ordinary faces that everyone thinks they've seen before."

"Maybe," Carolyn said, but she didn't look convinced.

"Where's the scholar tonight?" Charlie asked.

"Library. Studying. Said she needed to get away from the family crises."

"Right. Should we get going?"

"Come in and say hello to my parents while I get my hat and bag."

"After you, m'ladies," he bowed deep and swept his arm out towards the open door.

"You are such a clown," Helen said. They walked into the apartment and Helen headed to the bedroom while Carolyn and Charlie walked down the hall to the living room. He greeted her parents and, of course, her father asked him to stay for dinner.

"There's plenty," he said. Helen held the hat pin in her hand waiting for Charlie's answer.

"I appreciate the offer, but I've made plans for tonight and it's too late to cancel them now."

"Oh, well, another time then," her father said.

Helen secured her hat in place, grabbed her gloves and bag and went to rescue Charlie.

"Ready?" she asked.

"Ready. I won't keep her out too late. Work tomorrow, I know."

"Have fun you two," Carolyn said.

Their father was already settled back in his chair, newspaper in hand.

"Still don't know if I trust that lad," he mumbled. A minute later he cried, "Hah! Look here, love," he called over to Aggie, slapping a page of *The Irish Echo*. "It seems Ireland is going to be admitted into the United Nations. That should show those Brits that the rest of the world

161

acknowledges Ireland as its own country, even if they still think it's theirs."

"That's wonderful news, Paddy. We can only pray it brings some jobs to them and gets rid of some of the hard times over there."

"Aye, love. Let's hope. And now maybe we can keep England out of Ireland."

Out on the sidewalk, Charlie took Helen's arm. "It's a beautiful evening. Want to walk over to Pete's Tavern?"

"I'd love to. The food is great there, but why not just go to the pub around the corner?"

"Not good enough for a celebration."

"Are we celebrating something?"

"Let's save that for dinner. Meanwhile tell me about your day and your little urchins."

"Where to start? They do keep me on my toes." Helen regaled Charlie with all the children's antics on their walk across town.

CHAPTER FOURTEEN

Their meal ordered, Helen asked, "So, what are we celebrating?"

"Oh, yeah, that," Charlie said. "Well... I've accepted a job as Boxing Coach at the New York Athletic Club."

"What? I didn't realize you were *serious* about looking for a job."

"That's just it. I wasn't. This all came as a complete shock to me. When Joe first talked to me about the idea, I thought he was crazy. I mean, I'm so close to a title bout. I'm the Number One contender. But Joe pointed out that I'm also ten years older than the present champ and not getting any younger."

"But, Charlie, is this really something you want to do? You love boxing."

"I do, Helen. I always will, but this job will keep me in the game, in a way, and I'll still have time to work with the kids down at the Settlement House. *And* I won't be tramping all over the country, staying in hotels, eating lousy food, and working out in some of the worst gyms I've ever seen. Let's face it, sooner or later, I'll have to quit and this way, I get to leave with a great record. My name's still known all around the boxing world, and I'm respected by other boxers. I don't want to be like one of those guys I see at Stillman's, punch drunk has-beens who stayed in the game too long and are now pitied by all the up-and-coming young boxers." Charlie shook his head, and looked down at his hands, kneading them together as he spoke. "I'm better off getting out now, while I can still hold my head up high."

"You're sure?" Helen reached across the table and placed her hand on top of Charlie's knotted fists.

"I'm sure." He lifted his head and smiled at her, then slid one hand out from under hers and lay it on top of their clasped ones. "And now I'll have more time to spend with you."

Helen laughed. "Charlie, I see you almost every day. How much more time can we spend together?"

"Well... I was thinking about maybe every night too."

"Every night?" Helen's eyebrows squished together; her head tilted to one side.

"Listen, Helen, I've been around for quite a few years more than you—"

"Only thirteen."

"Long enough. And I've realized that when you find a good thing, you go for it, grab it, and hold on for dear life. And you are the best woman I've ever met. I don't want to lose you." Charlie held each of Helen's hands in one of his. "What I'm trying to say, and making a real mess of it, is will you marry me?"

"Chicken cacciatore," the waiter said, holding the dish over their clasped hands.

"Oh, yes. Thank you," Helen said.

"And lasagna for you," the waiter said, placing the steaming plate in front of Charlie.

"His timing stinks," Charlie said, looking at the waiter's retreating back. "Or maybe mine does." He reached across the table, and took hold of Helen's hand again. "Will you? Will you marry me?"

Helen's eyes glistened with tears that brimmed the rims. "Yes, Charlie. I'll marry you. You're the best, most wonderful man in the world, how could I ever say no?" The tears cascaded over her eyes' rims and flowed down her cheeks.

Charlie jumped up from his side of the booth, squeezed in next to her, and kissed her. A long lingering kiss. The two of them oblivious to the stares of the other diners.

When they separated, Charlie dug into his pocket, pulled out a handkerchief, and wiped away Helen's tears.

"I hope those are tears of joy," he said.

"What else would they be?"

They sat, staring into each other's eyes, dinners forgotten, until Helen's stomach growled loudly and made them both laugh.

"Guess we should eat," she said, never taking her eyes away from Charlie.

"Guess so." He ran his thumb beneath her eye, flicking away the last of her tears before sliding his plate across the table so he could stay next to her. "Have enough room?"

"Of course. I don't want an inch of space between us."

"Me neither."

Somehow, between grabbing for each other's hands, and stealing quick kisses, they managed to finish their dinners.

"Dessert? Coffee?" the waiter asked, whisking their plates away.

"I think I'd rather go for a walk," Helen said, looking at Charlie.

165

"You know," he said, "you're actually glowing. I think you'll light up the whole city tonight."

The waiter coughed and brought them back to reality.

"Oh, just the check, I guess," Charlie said. He paid the bill and they left, arms around one another.

"Since we're right here," Charlie said, "let's go sit in Gramercy Park for a minute."

"Seems we have the place all to ourselves tonight," he said, unlocking the gate.

"It's like our own lovely private garden."

"Well, I think it's a nicer place to give you this instead of a noisy place like Pete's." He slipped his hand into his pocket and pulled out a small box. "I hope you like it," he said, opening the top to reveal a diamond ring, its center stone surrounded by tiny sapphires. "I know you like blue."

Helen gasped. "It's the most beautiful ring I've ever seen."

Charlie slipped it on her finger. "If it doesn't fit, we can get it resized."

"It fits perfectly. I'm never going to take it off. Oh, Charlie." She threw her arms around his neck and kissed him with a passion that even surprised her. Their tongues explored each other's mouths while their hands explored each other's bodies. They were totally lost in their ecstasy. The rest of the world dissolved around them.

"Oh my God. It's gorgeous," Peggy squealed, holding Helen's hand. "Carolyn, did you see this? Isn't it the most beautiful engagement ring you've ever seen?"

"It's very pretty," Carolyn said, changing into her pajamas. "All the best, Helen."

166

"You don't seem very excited for her," Peggy said. "Or is that a little jealousy creeping in?"

"Absolutely not. I've already told the two of you, if that's the path you choose, I'm happy for you. I just can't see what's so wonderful about being married, tied down to one man, cooking, cleaning, and having his babies. I want a lot more than that out of life."

"That's right. I forgot," Peggy said. "You're going to be the belle of the ball. Best restaurants. Best furs. Best jewelry. Best apartment. Best men in the city."

"That's right."

"And just how do you plan on accomplishing all that? Or maybe all your Prince Charmings will saunter down here from their Park Avenue penthouses and sweep you away? Is that your plan?"

"Girls, stop," Helen said. "This has been the most wonderful night of my life and I don't want it to end with you two fighting."

"You're right," Carolyn said. "I really am happy for you, Helen. I could see tonight how much you two love each other, even if this has been a whirlwind courtship."

"It has been that," Helen said. "But I think I knew he was the man I wanted to marry from the minute I met him, as silly and cliched as that may sound."

"It's not silly at all," Peggy said. "It's very romantic."

Carolyn rolled her eyes and pulled down her bedspread. "I'm going to bed."

"Helen?" Peggy asked, "Have you told mom and dad yet?"

"No, they were already in their bedroom when I got home. I'll tell them at breakfast. Why?"

"Just wondered what they said, that's all."

"Well, it doesn't really matter to me. I'm going to marry Charlie, no matter what."

167

"My, my," Carolyn said, "suddenly got a spine, did you?"

"Oh, shut up and go to sleep," Helen said. "Something we'd all better do. Night, ladies."

Helen turned off the light and climbed into bed. She lay in the darkened room for a few minutes staring at her ring, barely visible in the feeble light from the streetlamps below. She couldn't believe what had happened that night. To think a wonderful man like Charlie wanted to spend the rest of his life with her was amazing. She snuggled under the sheet and thought about their future.

They had already decided they would rent an apartment in the same neighborhood where they both lived now. That way, their parents could easily visit, especially after they had children. Helen knew her mother would want to see her grandchildren as often as possible. Maybe someday they could buy a little house in Queens or Brooklyn, or maybe even on Long Island, but that was too far in the future to even think about. For now, Helen was just happy to set up a life for them in a little one-bedroom place. A private world for them alone. Those thoughts warmed her very soul. She fell asleep thinking she was the luckiest and happiest girl in the world.

"And what would that be on your finger?" her mother asked the next morning when Helen stepped into the kitchen.

Mom doesn't miss a trick.

"Oh, Mom, it's so wonderful. Last night, Charlie asked me to marry him. And I said yes."

"Blessed be. I knew you cared about him, but do you really love him? It's not been that long that the two of you have been seeing each other."

"Mom, I knew he was the one the day I met him."

168

"Ah, love at first sight, was it? That's a lovely notion, but I'd be thinking about it a little more seriously if you plan on spending the rest of your life with him. Have you thought this through enough?"

"I have, Mom. And I know this is the right thing for me to do."

"Ah well, I can see I'd just be talking through my hat if I tried to change your mind, so I'll give you my best wishes for a happy life, love." She held Helen by the shoulders and kissed her cheek. A lone tear escaped her mother's eye and ran down her face.

"Mom, are you crying?"

"A tear of joy, that's all. My first born about to go off on her own. Hard for me to believe."

"Well, you'll have a little time to get used to the idea. It's not like we're getting married tomorrow."

"I know love. I know. You'll understand when it happens to you."

"What will she understand?" Helen's father asked, as he strode into the kitchen.

"Our Helen's about to get married, Paddy."

"Married? To that boxer fellow?"

"His name's Charlie, Dad, as you well know."

"Of course, I know his name, but he's a boxer, am I not right?"

"Actually, he's given that up."

"So now he's out of work?" Paddy asked, eyebrows raised.

"No, Dad," Helen said, laughing. "He's taken a job as Boxing Coach at the New York Athletic Club."

"What? Teaching a bunch of toffs boxing? What do they want with that?"

"Well, they're not going to go out and compete. It's just another type of exercise for them."

169

"Another way for them to waste their money," Paddy mumbled. "But, I guess, if they're going to throw their money away, you may as well benefit from their foolishness."

"That's certainly one way to look at it."

"Paddy," Aggie said, "are you not going to wish our girl well?"

"Of course, I am. All the best to you, pet."

Like Aggie, he leaned over and kissed Helen's cheek.

"Thanks, Dad. Did you see the ring Charlie gave me?" Helen stuck her hand out for her parents to admire.

Paddy let out a low whistle. "Looks like Helen's Charlie has money to burn, Aggie."

"It's lovely," Aggie said. "The very best to you."

"Isn't it gorgeous?" Peggy said, bounding into the kitchen. "It's so exciting."

"Yes, yes, but could we please sit down and eat breakfast before I'm late for work," Paddy said. "Where's Carolyn?"

"Right here, Dad," she said, walking into the kitchen.

Silence settled around the table as everyone ate and had their coffee while Helen dreamed about what her future home would look like. The thoughts of furnishing her own place loomed in front of her like her own personal Mount Everest. Suddenly, what she envisioned as their cozy little retreat became an obstacle that scared the wits out of her.

How am I going to do this? Can we afford to do this? I need to talk to Charlie today. Has he even thought about what all this will cost?

By the end of breakfast, Helen's wave of happiness had transformed into a sea of anxiety.

"So, decided to bite the bullet, did you?"

170

"I did do that, Joe. And I couldn't be happier," Charlie said.

"Well then I'm glad for you and Helen both. I don't know, Charlie, between getting married and taking a regular job, you're dangerously close to becoming a respectable citizen."

Charlie punched Joe's arm. "Hey, I was always respectable."

Joe laughed. "Respectable, maybe, disreputable, always."

"Well, you taught me everything I know, so . . ."

They both laughed at that remark while Joe signaled the bartender for two more beers.

"But to be serious for a minute, Joe. I know you arranged the interview at the Club for me, so I'm sure you wanted me to get the job, but what are *you* going to do now? You can't be a manager to someone who's not on the circuit anymore."

"No, that's true enough. Believe me, Charlie, I thought about this a lot before I even put your name forward for that job. I'm getting a little too old for all this tromping around the world to boxing matches. Of course, if you said you didn't want to retire, I would have stuck with you. You know I'd never walk out on you, but I was almost relieved when you told me you accepted the job."

"Joe, I never knew you felt that way. Why didn't you say something before now? I never would have made you stick with me if your heart wasn't in it. You know that, don't you?"

"Course I do. And that's just it. I haven't lost my love for the game. It's just that my body's telling me it's time to call it quits. So, since we've been back in the city, I've been nosing around to see what I could do other than live out of a suitcase."

"You sly old dog, you. And? Find anything?"

171

"I think so. Actually, there are two possibilities. They're pretty much the same, so I just have to decide which one appeals to me more."

"Well, c'mon, give. I'm all ears."

"I've been offered jobs at Stillman's Gym and Sunnyside Gardens in Queens."

"Doing what?"

"Arranging bouts. Finding new talent. Promoting events. Means a lot of hanging around saloons, like this one, where the boxing crowd is. Picking up on the gossip about raw talent. Some training, if they need it. Talking to managers. Letting all the bartenders know what I'm doing so they can fill me in on the latest hot up-and-comers. That kind of thing."

"Sounds perfect for you. You love talking to all those guys and with your rep, you'll have people banging down your door with their protégées."

"That's the only part that worries me a little. I'm not going to be forced into putting just anyone in the ring. They'll have to prove they're ready for a bout before I'll book them. And I'll have to get the word out that any fight I schedule will be a clean one. I'm way too old to start dealing with the mob."

"I don't think you'll have to worry about that. Everyone knows you run a clean operation. Your reps too big for anyone to mess with."

"Yeah, well the bent nose crew doesn't always care about someone's rep. They make their own rules. You know that."

"Yeah, I remember. But we didn't put up with them in the past, so I think they know you're not someone they can bribe."

"Hope so, but I'm not going to worry about that now. I'll deal with it when, and if, it happens."

172

The men sipped their beers, each thinking about their futures and how their lives had changed in such a short amount of time.

Charlie asked Joe for all the pros and cons of each offer. Since the salaries were almost identical, that wasn't an issue.

"So, what's the one thing that will sway you?" Charlie asked.

"Location. I know Sunnyside has some great bouts and is on TV, but I just feel like I'd be a little out of the action if I went there."

"I know what you mean. And you'd have the Irish mafia to deal with there. I really don't even know their bad guys, do you?"

"One or two. Thing is, with them, you never know if the person you're talking to is one of them. I mean, those guys all dress like regular working men. Not like the wops. They're all flash and always have an entourage of yes men at their heels. The micks—they travel alone in worn out plaid shirts and dirty trousers. Sneaky little bastards. You never know who you're dealing with until it's too late."

"Then maybe you're better off staying here, in the city, with the devil you know."

"I'm thinking you may be right." Joe stared into his beer.

"Say," Charlie said, "how about we all go out for a celebratory dinner?"

"Who's all?"

"You, me, and Helen."

"Nah, I'd feel like a third wheel You two kids go paint the town."

"Aw, c'mon Joe. It wouldn't be a real celebration without you. After all, you're celebrating too."

Joe shrugged and finished his beer.

173

"This round's on me," Charlie said, pointing his empty glass at the bartender. "I know. I'll ask Helen to bring her sisters. They're both real pretty and you can have one on each arm. Really make a splash in the club."

Joe thought about waltzing into one of the classiest clubs in town with two beauties hanging on to him.

"Wouldn't that be a scene?" he said, roaring laughing. "no one would believe they'd do that without being paid. Not with this mug."

"Who cares? We'll have fun. A big night before we get down to becoming respectable citizens. C'mon Joe. Please?"

"Why the hell not. I'm in."

"Great." Charlie slapped Joe on the back. "I'll arrange everything. Limos, club, the whole nine yards. How's Friday night for you?"

"I've got nothing but time right now. But you'd better check with the girls and find out when they're free."

"Oh, right. I'll talk to Helen tonight and get everything set up. This'll be great. Just like one of our old nights out when we were on the road."

"You might not want to bring that up when you're with Helen. I don't think she'd want to know what a ladies man you were."

"All in the past, my friend. All in the past."

Joe raised one eyebrow and shook his head. "I hope so."

Since Helen had to work the morning shift on Saturday, they moved the celebration to Saturday night.

"Please say you'll come," Helen said to her sisters. "Charlie really wants all of us to be there. He wants to get to know both of you and so does Joe, his manager, or I should say his former manager. It'll be fun. I promise. And if you're not having a good time, you can always leave.

174

Charlie's hired a limousine for the whole night, so the driver can take you home and come back for us if that's what you want."

Peggy and Caroline looked at each other.

"I'll go if Carolyn agrees to go too. I don't want to be stuck talking to someone I don't even know while you two lovebirds make moony eyes at each other."

Carolyn shrugged half-heartedly. "Oh, why not? I don't have anything better to do since Dad decided not to evict me. Now all I do is come home every day and be a 'good girl' just to prove I can. How boring!"

"Thank you," Helen said, clapping her hands and bouncing on her toes. "This will be so much fun. I can't remember the last time the three of us went out for a night on the town."

"Probably because it never happened," Carolyn said, brushing imaginary lint off her sleeve.

"I hope you're not going to have that puss on your face all night," Peggy said.

"Don't worry about me. I can put on as good an act as any actress can."

"I'm sure you won't have to," Helen said. "Charlie's a lot of fun and Joe's a real gentleman."

"And probably an old prude," Carolyn said under her breath.

"I heard that and he's not, I just meant that you won't have to worry about him trying any funny stuff with you."

Carolyn raised her eyebrow and huffed.

Helen stood by the window looking down at the street. She gasped when a long black limousine stopped in front of her building.

"They're here," she said, "and the car is enormous."

175

"Let me see." Peggy pushed Helen to the side so she could peer out the window. "Oh, my God. It's gigantic. Carolyn, look at this thing."

"I've seen limos before. Why don't you two come away from the window and stop acting like you just came into town on a turnip truck. Really!"

"Oh, she's so so sophisticated," Peggy said, placing her hand on her hip and sticking her nose in the air. "Yas, dahling," she said in her best imitation of a Park Avenue matron, "do let's act nonchalant. After all, I wouldn't be seen dead in any other form of transportation."

Helen gave Peggy's arm a light punch. "Come on. Get your bags and let's go downstairs. We don't want to keep the boys waiting."

"Heaven forbid," Carolyn said, pressing her hand against her chest.

They gathered their evening bags, checked their hair and makeup in the primping mirror next to the door one last time, and left the apartment. Their cocktail dresses matched the accessories their friends had loaned them to complete their outfits.

Helen opened the building's front door just as Charlie bounded up the stoop. He whistled low and long.

"I don't think I've ever seen so many beautiful women in one place before. Except maybe in the Miss American pageant."

"Oh, Charlie, stop," Helen said, her face turning a rosy color. "You boys look pretty handsome too."

Joe stood to the side of the open limo door. Both men were dressed to the nines in tuxedos and polished patent leather dress shoes. Carolyn stood on the top step and stared at Joe.

"I know you," she said. "You're the guy from the bar at The Pierre. What's going on? What kind of scam is he trying to pull this time?" she asked Helen.

"This isn't the time or place for that now," Helen said, turning her head to whisper into Carolyn's ear. "We'll talk about it later. DO NOT ruin this night for me or Charlie or Joe."

"Joe? Is that the name he's using tonight?"

"Carolyn, I'm warning you."

Carolyn glared at her sister. "I'm only going along with this charade for Peggy's sake. I know she won't go without me and she needs a night out. But you owe me an explanation."

"Later. Not now. Right now, put on a smile and act like you've never met him before tonight. Do you understand?"

"Perfectly." True to her boast about her acting ability, Carolyn smiled her winningest smile. An act that any Broadway star would envy.

"C'mon you guys," Peggy called from the back seat of the limo. "Let's get this party started."

"Coming," Carolyn said.

Charlie had retreated to the sidewalk when he realized the two sisters were arguing. Now he stepped onto the first step and extended one arm to each of the women. "Ladies," he said.

"I can manage on my own," Carolyn snapped. "But thank you," she added, seeing Helen's eyes shoot daggers at her.

Carolyn waltzed over to Joe. "Was that ruse at The Pierre simply a way to meet me?" she whispered to him. "Well, it didn't work then and it won't work now. You're not my type."

Helen came down the stairs and took Charlie's arm. "This will be an interesting evening, I'm afraid."

Charlie leaned over and kissed her cheek. "It won't be boring anyway."

During the ride uptown, Joe tried to be pleasant to both women, but Carolyn didn't want anything to do with him. When he asked a question, she just sneered at him and stared out the window. Joe sighed, thinking this was a bad idea after all. However, Peggy was only too glad to tell him all about her studies and her upcoming summer semester working in a hospital. When she started to tell them about a recent excursion to the operating room, Helen shushed her.

"Peggy, take a breath," Helen said. "Not everyone is as enthused about medical procedures as you are. Poor Joe can't get a word in edgewise."

"It's all right, Helen. I enjoy hearing about Peggy's experiences. Medicine's always fascinated me."

"Better you than me," Charlie said. "I'd never have the patience to listen to all those gory details."

"Then it's a good thing you chose the sister who has nothing exciting going on in her life," Carolyn said, casting her eyes out the window.

"Carolyn," Peggy said, "you're being deliberately rude. And here Helen is trying to make this night special for all of us. Is this how you show your gratitude? I'm beginning to think I made a mistake insisting you come tonight."

"Oh Peggy, come off your high horse. Helen knows I didn't mean anything by it. I've got a lot on my mind."

Helen leaned over and whispered in her ear, "I told you that you have to keep a civil tongue in your head if you want to join the celebration tonight. That hasn't changed. If you're going to spend the night criticizing everyone, you're mistaken. So, stop your nonsense now or go home."

Carolyn's face boiled red.

Inside the Copacabana, the maître d' greeted them. "Mr. Sanders, Mr. Hayes, how nice to see you again. Dining room or lounge?"

"We'll be having supper so you can seat us wherever you think is best," Joe said.

"Very good. Right this way."

Joe and Peggy followed him to a large corner table in the dining room, but Helen grabbed Carolyn's arm when she started down the aisle after them.

"What have you decided? Because I swear by all the saints if you do anything to destroy tonight's celebration, I'll pick you up and throw you out of here myself. I'm done being polite. If you're going to act like a child, I'll treat you like one."

"Let go of me." Carolyn pulled her arm away from Helen's grasp.

"I mean it, Carolyn."

"And I'll be there to back her up the whole way," Charlie said.

"Yes, I imagine that's your style, Charlie. After all, you do love smacking people around, don't you?"

"That's enough, Carolyn," Helen said. "You've made your position clear. You can either leave on your own, or have me create a scene and remove you."

"Charlie!" a voice boomed behind him. "Doesn't seem fair that you have two lovely ladies and I'm all alone."

Charlie turned to face an old nemesis. "Just what you deserve, I think."

"That's not very polite, pal. Aren't you going to introduce me?"

"I'd sooner put them in a pit with man eating tigers."

The two men stood eye to eye and toe to toe and glowered at each other.

"I'm Carolyn," she said, extending her hand. She looked the man over from head to toe. His diamond cufflinks sparkled as he took her hand and kissed it.

"A lovely name to suit a lovely lady," he said. "Why don't you join *me*? I'm sure I'll be better company than this punch-drunk has-been."

Charlie had his fist in the air before the other man realized it, but Helen had anticipated the reaction and pulled his arm back.

"No, Charlie, it's not worth ruining tonight for either of them." She stepped in front of him and put her hand on his face.

Charlie's unfocused eyes slowly registered her, his breathing slowed, and the color receded from his cheeks. "You're right. Maybe they deserve each other." He took Helen's arm and led her to the table where Joe and Peggy sat talking, oblivious to the near melee that Helen had averted.

"Who is that?" she asked. "Quick, tell me before we sit."

"His name's Gino Fiori, and he heads up a group of unscrupulous bookies, even though he says he imports religious statues from Italy."

"Oh no. We can't leave Carolyn with him."

"She made her choice. She's a big girl. It's up to her to decide what she wants to do with her life."

"But she doesn't know anything about him. She could be in real trouble before the night's out."

"That she could. That she could."

"Are you two going to join us or stand in the aisle talking all night?" Joe asked.

"I was just debating that in my head. 'Should I sit with this big ugly bloke and his lovely lady, or should I snatch Helen away to a more *private* situation?' That's what I was thinking, Joe."

180

"Since we know you don't have a brain in that head of yours, I'll make the decision for you, as always. Get your ass over here and sit down."

Charlie's roaring laughter attracted the attention of the neighboring tables. "Guess we have no choice," he said, pulling out a chair for Helen.

"Charlie, you're incorrigible."

"I hope that's something good. I'd hate to think my own fiancée is berating me, and in front of other people too."

"Sit down before I knock you down," Helen said.

"Now that I'd pay to see," Joe said.

"Where's Carolyn?" Peggy asked.

"She decided not to join us after all," Helen said.

"You should become a diplomat," Charlie whispered in her ear and gave her cheek a kiss.

"All right, you lovebirds," Joe said, "that's enough of that. Champagne for everyone?" He looked around the table and everyone nodded. "A toast and then something to eat. How does that sound, Peggy?"

"Perfect, Joe, but no more than a toast. I have to be up early tomorrow for Mass."

"A toast, some food, and a little brandy to wash it down, then home. All right?"

"Yes, Joe. But I'm still concerned about Carolyn. Did you put her in the limo, Helen? Is she all right?"

"She's fine, Peggy. We can talk about it when we get home."

Peggy frowned.

The champagne arrived and Joe and Peggy toasted the newly engaged couple and wished them long and happy lives. Moments later the waiter asked if they were ready to order their meal.

"I'm afraid Carolyn has ruined our evening," Helen said. "Now I'm sorry I insisted she join us."

181

"Not at all," Joe said. "While we wait for our dinners, we'll talk about something pleasant."

"And what would that be?" Charlie asked.

"I thought I'd tell you about my new apartment."

"An apartment? How exciting," Peggy said.

"And you didn't say a word about this before now? Helen, I think Joe is becoming very secretive."

"No, no secrets. I only heard about the place this morning. And when I did, I rushed over to see it and signed the lease before anyone else could grab it."

The waiter arrived with their meals, giving everyone time to absorb Joe's news.

"Joe," Helen said, as soon as the waiter left, "I'm thrilled for you, of course, but did you look at it carefully? You didn't need to rent a place out of desperation. Once Charlie and I are married you know you'd always be welcomed there."

Charlie reached over and squeezed Helen's hand. "She's right you know, Joe. We wouldn't let you tramp about the streets with no place to go. You didn't have to rush into signing a lease."

"Just what two newlyweds need—an old man puttering about interfering with your honeymoon year."

"No, Joe," they protested together.

"Listen to me, the two of you. I've lived too long on my own, doing things my way, coming and going as I please, even having a beer or two too many from time to time, to start living on someone else's schedule, or adjust to their habits. My bad habits are my own and I'd like to keep them tucked away in my own private sanctuary. I appreciate your offer, but believe me when I say I'm a confirmed bachelor and would like to live alone with my eccentricities."

"So, Joe, don't keep us in suspense," Helen said. "Tell us about this apartment."

182

"It's a new six-story building on the West Side. I can walk to my job at Stillman's from there. A nice brisk walk to start my morning. And on bad weather days, I can always grab a cab. My apartment's on the fifth floor away from the street noise, and there's an elevator, so no stairs for this old man. It has a living room, bedroom, bath, and kitchenette. All I need."

"Sounds great," Charlie said.

"It sounds perfect," Peggy said. She looked at Joe with starry eyes. Her admiration of this new acquaintance grew with every word he spoke.

If only I could have a place of my own with no one to tell me when to be home for supper, or how late I can stay out, or what to eat, or wear. If I could rule my own life, I'd be the happiest woman in the world.

"Peggy?" Helen broke into her thoughts.

"Wha . . ."

"Off with the faeries," Joe said, winking at her. "Or at least that's what my Granny used to call it."

"Joe asked if you'd like an after-dinner brandy to toast his new home," Helen said.

"I don't think I've ever had one."

"Well then, it's high time you did," Joe said. He signaled for the waiter and ordered coffee and brandy for everyone.

When the drinks came, Peggy took a sip and started coughing.

"Whew, that's strong," she said.

"Here, let me put a little water in it. That'll cut it a bit." Joe added a splash of water to the snifter and handed it to Peggy.

She took a tiny sip. "That's much better. Thank you." She smiled up at Joe who was beaming as if he'd just performed the perfect feat of magic.

183

The band started playing and Charlie and Joe asked the girls to dance. One dance turned into a whole evening of dancing. Helen couldn't stop smiling and when she looked over at Peggy, she seemed just as happy in Joe's arms.

"I don't know when I've had a better time," Helen said, sitting back at their table. The band was on a short break, which gave the couples time to relax and rest.

Helen slipped her shoes off and rubbed her feet under the table where she hoped no one could see her. "I hate to break up the party, but I'm afraid I've just about had it. It's been a long day and it's getting late. Charlie, would you mind if we left?"

"Whatever you want to do," he said, finishing off his brandy.

"Joe, I'm sorry to be the party-pooper, but I'm exhausted."

"I think we're all ready to leave, Helen. Unless you'd like to stay for a little while longer, Peggy? I can grab a cab and see Peggy home so you two can head out, if that's all right with you, Peggy?"

"Sounds perfect to me," Peggy said.

Helen looked at her sister, her eyebrow raised. Peggy gave her a little nod.

"All right. Thank you, Joe. Charlie? Are you ready to leave?"

"I am. Joe, I'll come by your hotel tomorrow morning."

"Good. Plan on having breakfast with me."

"I will."

"Good night, Joe. Thanks for making it a lovely evening."

"Anytime, Helen. Thank *you* for providing such a lovely dining companion for me. Certainly beats having to eat with this old bruiser all the time."

"Old bruiser, huh? You come down to the club anytime and I'll show you who's an old bruiser."

Joe laughed and said, "Get out of here, you two. See you at breakfast, Charlie."

Outside, Charlie signaled for the limo. Once they were settled in, he said, "Now I'd like that kiss I've been waiting for all evening."

Helen melted into his arms and forgot all about Peggy, or Carolyn, or anything outside the little world they occupied at that moment.

Joe and Peggy finished their drinks and decided to move to the lounge. On their way, a number of gentlemen greeted Joe. One, in particular, stood blocking their way.

"Join me for a quick one, Joe?" he asked, his eyes focused on Peggy. "That is, if your lady friend would agree to join us."

"Peggy, another brandy or a sherry?" Joe asked.

"If you'd like one, Joe," she said, emboldened by the drink she'd already had.

"That's settled then," the stranger said. He turned towards the lounge where the maître d' led them to a small round table for two. He pulled over another chair and held it for Peggy.

"This is cozy," she said.

"Peggy, this is Tim Hanratty. One of the best boxers I know," Joe said. "Tim, Miss Peggy Campbell."

"Miss Campbell, a pleasure," Tim said, enveloping her hand in his massive paw.

"Mr. Hanratty."

"Peggy, you can have a coffee if you prefer," Joe said.

"I think maybe another brandy, with some water, the way you fixed it at the table."

Tim ordered the drinks and they settled into a companionable conversation. The Copa, as it was called,

185

was a favorite stop for current and former celebrities from all the entertainment fields, including boxing, and everyone connected to that sport seemed to know Joe, judging by the number of men who stopped by the table to say hello and inquire about Joe's future plans. Word had spread throughout the boxing world of Charlie's retirement from the ring and there were dozens of boxers and promoters who wanted Joe to take over their training, or manage their protégés. Peggy was impressed, and amazed, by the high regard they all held for both Charlie and Joe.

"Peggy," Joe said, "I think when you finish your drink, I should be getting you home."

"No need, Joe," Tim said. "I'm sure you need your sleep, being such an old man, but the night is young. And so is Miss Campbell, much too young for you. Maybe I should take over from here for tonight. I can see Miss Campbell home after we catch the late show over at the Stork Club."

"Sorry, Tim, but I promised Charlie and Peggy's sister that I'd see her home, and I'm not about to go back on my word."

"Let's leave it to Miss Campbell, then. Do you really want to go home?"

"I've enjoyed our conversation, Mr. Hanratty, but, yes, I should be going. Thank you for the drink."

Joe rose from his chair, shook hands with Tim, and whisked Peggy away before Tim created a scene they would all regret in the morning.

Settling into a cab, Joe asked, "Did you enjoy yourself tonight, Peggy?"

"I had a wonderful time. And you know so many people. I'm quite intimidated to be with such a celebrity."

"Believe me, I'm not that at all. I've been around the fight game for a long time, made a lot of friends, and this place attracts all sorts of sports people. That's all."

"You're too modest, Joe. I heard the way those men sought your advice and wanted you as their trainer. You're a celebrity whether you want to be or not."

"Let's forget about me for a minute. I never got to know a lot about you tonight. I know you're studying medicine, but that's about it. Do you actually plan on becoming a practicing doctor?"

"Of course, I do. Why else would I be studying medicine now?"

"I just wondered since it seems to me it's not a profession many women aspire to."

"Actually, there are a few other women in my class. More than I expected, despite the prejudices we have to fight against every day."

The cab stopped. "We're here," she said. Joe jumped out of the cab, helped Peggy out, and escorted her up the stoop.

"I feel like I barely got to know you," Joe said. "And I'd love to hear more about your classes, and future plans. Could we have dinner Monday night? I'd say tomorrow, but I think I'd like to move some things into the apartment. Of course, if you're too busy studying, I understand."

"I would love to have dinner with you, Joe. I'm scheduled to be at the hospital on Monday until six o'clock. Can I meet you after that?"

"Why don't I call for you here at seven-thirty? Would that give you enough time?"

"It would... But I prefer it if you could meet me at the hospital. Is that possible? Or can I meet you at the restaurant?"

"I'll come to the hospital—St. Vincent's, I presume?"

"No, why would you think that?"

"I've taken my share of boxers there after their turn in the ring. I just assumed you'd be studying there."

"Unfortunately, they don't allow women physicians to practice there—yet. No, I'm at New York University and Bellevue Hospital. It's pretty far from where you are. That's why I suggested meeting you at the restaurant."

"No need for that. It'll be nice to get away from where I work."

"If you say so."

"Then I'll see you at six o'clock Monday. Good night, Peggy." He gave her a little salute and went down the steps to the waiting cab.

Peggy let herself in the front door and floated up the hall stairs to her apartment.

CHAPTER FIFTEEN

Sunday morning, Helen woke early. The first thing she noticed was Carolyn's bed. It hadn't been slept in.

Oh no. What did that girl do now? Just as Mom and Dad are starting to trust her again, she goes off and does something stupid like stay out all night. When is she ever going to learn her lesson?

"Peggy." Helen shook her sister awake. "Did you see Carolyn last night after Charlie and I left?"

"Wha... oow, my head hurts."

"It's just a hangover. It'll pass. Well, did you?"

"Did I what?" Peggy rubbed the sleep out of her eyes.

"See Carolyn. After I left?"

"Why would I see Carolyn? You put her in the limo and sent her home, didn't you?" Now fully awake, Peggy sat on the edge of her bed. "You told me you did."

Helen rummaged around in the dresser pulling out clothes to wear to Mass that morning.

"Helen? You did, didn't you?"

"Not exactly."

"Either you did or you didn't. Which is it?"

Helen wasn't used to being interrogated by her younger sister and refused to look at her. Peggy walked over to Helen, grabbed her arm, and spun her around so they were face to face. Helen, still refusing to look up, stared at the floor.

"You didn't. You lied to me."

"I didn't want to spoil the night for everyone."

Peggy folded her arms across her chest and tapped her foot. "I think you just wanted to celebrate your engagement and didn't care where Carolyn went, as long as she didn't ruin your night. Right?"

"Probably a little of that is the truth," Helen said, her face turning scarlet. "But that's not the whole story." So, she told Peggy about the argument she had with Carolyn and about Gino Fiori.

"What! You left her with a gangster? Helen, she's your sister. How could you?"

"I'm not proud of that... now. But last night, she got me so mad I didn't care where she went or with whom. Besides, we don't know if she left with him or not. Maybe she realized the type of man he is and left by herself. Maybe she grabbed a cab and went—"

"Went where? Not home. So, where do you think she might be?"

Helen went back to rummaging around in the dresser drawer, but Peggy wasn't going to let her slide.

"ANSWER ME."

"I don't know," Helen said, crumpling onto the floor. She covered her face with her hands and tears ran down her cheeks between her fingers. Peggy slumped down next to her.

"Maybe it's not as bad as we think. Maybe she went to Rosemary's."

Helen's puffy red eyes looked over at Peggy. "Do you really believe that?"

"I don't know. But we have to start looking for her somewhere. So, we may as well start there."

Peggy stood and stared down at Helen. "Get up and go wash your face. If Mom sees you looking like that, it'll be the third degree, for sure. Maybe we can sneak out before they get up."

The kettle's harsh whistle shrilled through the quiet apartment. The girls looked at each other.

"Too late for that," Helen said.

"Maybe we can just tell them that she went to spend the night at Rosemary's. We can say she left early 'cause she wasn't having a good time, but didn't want to come home and answer a lot of questions."

"You're going to tell Mom that she asks too many questions? Are you crazy?"

"Well, we've got to cover for her somehow. You have any better ideas?"

"Not really," Helen said, still sitting on the floor.

"Well then, get your ass off the floor and get dressed. We still have to go to Sunday Mass. Let's just hope Rosemary isn't there."

"Oh, God. If she is we're doomed."

"Don't be so melodramatic," Peggy said. "Now get up and wash your face."

Helen got up with all the energy of a ninety-year-old woman. She dragged herself to the bathroom and stared into the mirror.

God, I look wretched. Hopefully makeup will cover most of this.

A short while later, they were dressed and ready to leave. As they passed the front door, Peggy grabbed Helen's arm. "Mom," she called down the hall, "we'll meet you and Dad at church."

"What?" Aggie asked, standing in the kitchen doorway. "Come have your coffee."

191

"That's okay, Mom. We'll have some after Mass."

Before Aggie could say another word, the two were out the door and down the stairs.

"Now what are those girls up to?" Aggie asked, under her breath.

"That was quick thinking, Peg," Helen said, once they hit the street.

"A sudden flash of inspiration. Maybe if Rosemary *is* at Mass, we can corral her before Mom does."

"You're thinking awfully clearly for a girl with a hangover."

"That disappeared the minute you told me Carolyn never came home. But I'm really only delaying the inevitable. Mom's going to realize Carolyn isn't at Mass and then there'll be hell to pay for both of us. You know how she feels about lying."

"We haven't lied... yet. We didn't say Carolyn was with us. We can't help it if she assumed that."

"A very fine line, my dear. Not one I'm sure our mother would agree with."

"I know. I just don't know what to do. This is all my fault. I left her with that Gino guy. I never should have done that. At best, I should have put her in the limo and sent her home."

"Oh yeah, like she would have willingly let you do that. This is some mess."

The family got through Mass without incident. Carolyn wasn't at the church and neither was Rosemary. Helen took that as a good sign. Maybe they *were* together. Maybe Carolyn went home when the rest of the family was out, changed her clothes, and would be sitting having tea when they got back.

Yeah! And maybe Santa Claus is real. But I can still hope this will all end well.

192

Mass over, the girls scooted out of church and hurried home before their parents finished socializing with some friends. Helen kept her fingers crossed that Carolyn would be there. Carolyn?" Helen called as soon as she opened the door.

Silence. Her face crumpled and she looked on the verge of tears again.

"Helen, pull yourself together. Mom and Dad will be here any minute. I'm going to call Rosemary." Peggy dialed her number. "Oh, hi Mrs. Burns, is Rosemary there?... Thanks... she's calling her," she said to Helen. "Rose, it's Peggy. Is Carolyn with you?" She shook her head and pulled her lips together. "Okay, thanks. If you see her, could you tell her I want to talk to her?"

She hung up the receiver and looked at Helen. But before she could say a word, a key turned in the lock and their parents came into the apartment.

They ate breakfast much like monks did. In silence. Helen could barely manage to keep a slice of toast down. Peggy didn't fare much better. Finishing the last of his coffee, Paddy pushed his chair back from the table.

"Aggie, I think you have something you want to talk over with our girls. Do you not?"

"That I do, Paddy."

"Well then, I'll leave you to it. I'm off to Gaelic Park to watch the game." He leaned over and kissed Aggie on the cheek.

"Have a good day, love."

"Girls."

"Bye, Dad," they said.

"Well, that's done. Now. Who's going to tell me where Carolyn is, and who she's with?" Aggie stared at her two daughters, both fiddling with their coffee cups. "I've not got all day, you know."

193

Helen and Peggy looked at each other. "Okay," Helen said. "I'll tell you what I know, but it's probably not the whole picture." She told her mother everything she knew about the previous evening's encounter with Gino Fiori.

"She went off with him, you say? And you did nothing to stop her?"

"What could I do, Mom? She's a grown woman. She's not a little girl who I can order around."

"You could have pulled her away from that hooligan. That's what you could have done."

"And caused a riot in the place? Do you think Charlie would have just sat there if I went over and started to make a scene? He would have been up in a minute, with Joe right behind him. Mom, this man had a whole entourage with him. There must have been four or five that I could see. Who knows how many others were there inside or outside? It would have been a slaughter. And this Gino person would have snuck out with Carolyn in the midst of the brannigan anyway."

"Maybe, maybe not. But it was your duty as the eldest to try to stop her."

"Mom, there's no way I could have done that and you know it. You know what Carolyn's like. She gets an idea in her head and no one is going to change her mind. Even if she didn't really want to leave with him, which I don't believe, she would have out of spite if I tried to stop her."

Aggie pulled a handkerchief from her apron pocket and dabbed at the corners of her eyes.

"And what did you do?" she asked, staring at Peggy.

"Me? I didn't even know what was going on. Joe and I had already gone to the table. When Helen and Charlie arrived, they told me Carolyn had decided to leave."

"Is that the truth, Helen?"

"Yes, Mom. I didn't see any reason to ruin Peggy's night out."

194

Aggie stared off, seeing nothing. "What are we going to do now?" she mumbled so low that Helen had difficulty hearing her.

"I don't know. If I talk to Charlie, he'll want to go looking for this Gino and there'll be a confrontation that can only end with one, or both, in a hospital or dead. I'm sorry, Mom, maybe I'm being selfish but I'm not about to get Charlie mixed up in this to save Carolyn's honor. What little of it might be left."

"I've a good mind to smack your mouth for that last remark. Your sister might be in trouble. You don't know for certain that she went with this man of her own free will, do you?"

"No, I guess not. But he wasn't dragging her to his table by her hair, or anything like that."

"Maybe, maybe not. I can't believe she's gone that far astray from all she's been taught her whole life."

Helen sighed. "Mom, Carolyn likes being pampered. She likes men spending money on her, taking her to the best places, being on the arm of a handsome, well-dressed man."

"Handsome, is he? You think a hooligan like him can be handsome? With all the sins on his soul? They show, you know. You can see the evil in their eyes and the malice in their hearts. Men like that are never handsome, no matter how fine they dress. You know what they say about making a silk purse out of a sow's ear. It can't be done. Handsome indeed!"

"Mom, I only meant that he's the type Carolyn's attracted to. Flashy. Throws money around to dazzle women. Things like that impress her. That's why she took up with her boss. He's wealthy. She told me he took her to the finest places, to shows, restaurants—"

"Hotels."

"I guess. What I'm trying to say is that I don't think it would do any good to try to find her. It will only make her more determined to stay with him, if that's where she is. If we leave her alone, maybe she'll realize he's not the type of man who will provide a good life for her and leave him. But if we go after her, she'll dig in her heels and stay with him, whether or not she really wants to."

Aggie sat, breathing heavily, occasionally wiping at her eyes.

I wish she'd say something. Anything.

"What if she's hurt? In hospital? Or in a gutter somewhere?"

"We can go to the police station and inquire. Would you like to do that?"

"Have you any idea where he might have taken her?"

"No, but from what Charlie told me, the police will know who he is and where to look for him."

"Aye, that they will, I'm sure."

They sat in silence a while longer.

Aggie stood and brushed off her apron. "We should talk to Hank."

"He should be easy enough to find. Our god ole local beat cop is never far from Moran's bar. Maybe he can snoop around for us."

"That's a good idea," Peggy said. "I'll go with you."

"Go now. In fact, I'll go too," Aggie pulled off her apron and looped it over a nail inside the broom closet. "I'd like some answers before you da comes home."

As they walked down the street, Aggie spotted Hank. She waved to him, and he walked toward the women.

"You're a sight for sore eyes, you are, Hank. And just the man who could do me a good turn."

"Aggie, Helen, Peggy" he said, giving them a little salute. "With what can I help you today?"

196

"It's a matter of some delicacy," Aggie said.

"That's me specialty. You know I always thought I'd make a grand detective. Like to keep things close to me vest, so to speak. The soul of discretion, I am. Should we speak here, or should I come upstairs where it's more private like?"

"Ah sure, the neighbors will be gossiping about it either way, so you may as well come in and have a cuppa."

"Nothing would please me more," he said.

They climbed the stairs to the apartment and once there, Helen put the kettle on. Aggie put some cookies on a platter while Hank made himself comfortable.

"Would you care for a little sweetener in your tea, or maybe on the side?" Aggie asked, holding up a whiskey bottle.

"Maybe just a touch to sweeten the tea," he said.

Aggie half-filled his cup with the brown liquid.

"That's grand." He took a sip while the kettle heated up. "Ah, warms me up, that does. I see Paddy is a man of taste."

"He doesn't indulge too often, you know, but on that rare occasion, he likes to have the best on hand."

"And a fine policy that is. Ah, here's our tea. You can pour it right in here, love," he said to Helen pointing to his half-filled cup and winking at her. "Adds a little flavor to the cuppa." He took a healthy swig of the tea this time. "Lovely, lovely." Reaching for a cookie, he said, "Now, what can I do for you fine ladies?"

"Helen, it's your story to tell, for I don't know all the particulars like you do."

Helen sat and told Hank about last night's events. He made some notations in his notebook and asked a few questions during her narrative.

197

"We're all thinking that maybe something happened to Carolyn. Something bad. Maybe she's in a hospital, or... or something."

Hank rubbed his chin. "She always was a bit of a wildcat that one. I remember when she was just a wee girl, how many times I chased her home. Her being where she shouldn't be and doing what she shouldn't be doing."

"And you never thought you should say something to me or Paddy? Hank, I should throttle you, I should."

"Now, Aggie, we both know you knew what was going on. I kept my eye on her. I'd not let anything happen to her. I hope you know that."

"Aye, that I do."

"No one's to blame, Aggie. She was born with that wildness in her. Back home we would say the banshees got to her before the wee folk could, that's all." He reached over and patted Aggie's hand.

"Aye, you're right, Hank," she said, dabbing at her eyes with a handkerchief. "But I'm worried about her now. This is more than a few puffs on a cigarette or a sip out of a pint."

"That it is, Aggie. I know a little about this Gino fellow. Seen him down by the docks from time to time. I'll ask around at the station house, quiet like, and see what I can find out." He paused and took a healthy slurp of his tea. "Would I be right in thinking you'd rather Paddy knows nothing of this?"

"He doesn't know the whole story, but he knows something's not right. It's better I tell him what we know than keep it from him. I've never in my whole married life kept anything from him." She walked over to the pantry and took down the whiskey bottle. "More tea?"

"Maybe one more, Aggie."

She busied herself fixing his tea, then said, "I'll talk to him tonight when he comes home."

"Grand, grand. Then I'll feel free to come to you whenever I get some answers. Is that right?"

"Aye."

He took a sip of the replenished tea. "Lovely."

He drained the rest of his cup and said, "I'd best be getting back downstairs. It wouldn't do to have the Sergeant come looking for me and not see me out on me beat. I'll let you know as soon as I hear anything, Aggie. Meanwhile, try not to worry. Carolyn's not a stupid girl. She can take care of herself."

"Thank you, Hank."

"Thank you for the tea and biscuits, Helen."

"You're welcome."

He retrieved his cap from the top of the refrigerator and headed downstairs.

"He's a good man," Aggie said. "If anyone can find out about Carolyn, he can." She took a sip of her tea and said no more.

"I know I said I wouldn't, but maybe I *should* call Charlie and see if he can help too," Helen said. "He knows this guy, Gino, so maybe he knows where he lives or something."

"All right, love," Aggie said. "I feel like I haven't the energy to do a thing today."

Helen and Peggy looked at each other. It was true. Aggie had no color in her face and her hand trembled when she picked up her teacup. She looked more like an old sock doll than the robust "take charge" woman they were used to seeing.

"Mom," Peggy said, "why don't you have a little rest? Helen and I'll make supper."

"Good idea. And I'll call Charlie now," Helen said.

"Goodness knows, my old nerves could use a rest. All me insides are still jumping up and down."

"Then you need to lie down."

199

"Aye, maybe I do at that. Nothing fancy for dinner, girls. Your da likes his meat and potatoes, you know."

"I know, Mom," Peggy said, as Helen walked back into the kitchen. "Maybe meatloaf and mashed potatoes?"

"Aye, that'll suit. And you could use the practice, Helen. Since you'll be cooking for your own husband soon enough. What did Charlie say?"

"He'll be right over. He didn't want to talk on the phone."

"Maybe I should wait for him and see what he has to say."

Helen rolled her eyes. "Go lie down."

Aggie went down the hall to her bedroom, mumbling the whole way, but neither girl could make out what she was saying.

Helen fixed the meatloaf, and Peggy peeled the potatoes. They had just put the makings of dinner in the fridge when there was a knock at the door.

Maybe that's Carolyn. But why didn't she use her key?

Helen started down the hall, but Peggy was already at the door. She opened it to find Hank standing there, hat in hand.

"Hank, come in. Do you have news about Carolyn already?"

"I do," he said, still standing by the door. "When I left here, I went down to the docks to see if that Gino fellow was around. I told you I sometimes see him down there."

"Yes. Go on," Helen said, walking towards them.

"He was there all right. Big as life and twice as brazen, he was. And who do you think was on his arm?"

"Carolyn."

"Aye, love. Carolyn it was. Hanging all over him like some two-bit... forget I said that."

200

"Yes, yes. Go on."

"Well, I went over to them, I did, and asked Carolyn if I could speak to her, private like. She looked at me with a sneer on her face and told me I could say whatever I wanted in front of Gino, as he was her boyfriend and she had no secrets from him. Her boyfriend! You could have knocked me over with a feather, you could have. Well, anyway, I told her you girls and your mam were looking for her, and were worried about her." He stopped, fiddled with his hat, and brushed some imaginary lint off his jacket.

"What did she say?" Helen asked stone-faced.

"She said, and you'll forgive me for speaking so plainly. 'I don't give a damn about them. If my mother was so worried about my welfare, she wouldn't have let Dad throw me out of the house a while ago.' Those were her words exactly."

Helen drew in a sharp breath and shook her head.

"Now I don't know what she was talking about with this throwing her out business, and it's not any of my concern what went on, but those were her exact words."

"Anything else?"

Hank shuffled from foot to foot and looked down at the floor.

"What is it, Hank?"

He looked at Helen, and said, "That Gino character said she was his concern from now on, and he didn't appreciate me prying into his business."

"Oh Lord." Helen covered her mouth with her hand and shook her head. "It seems we've lost her for good this time."

"Aye, so it does."

The three of them stood in the hall. Helen wiped her hands over and over on a dishtowel she had carried with

201

her from the kitchen. Peggy stared at the floor. and sighed. Hank twiddled with his hat.

"I best be getting back to me beat, girls. I'll keep me eye out for the two of them and let your mam know if I see them again."

"Thank you, Hank. Mom's always said you're a good man and you are."

"Helen? Is someone here? I thought I heard—Hank. You're back, are you?" Aggie stood still as a granite column when she saw him. "Is it bad? Is she hurt... or dead?"

"No, Aggie, she's well and healthy, in a manner of speaking."

"I'll tell Mom what you had to say. We don't want to keep you."

"Thank you, Helen."

He gave a quick nod of his head to them and left. Aggie rushed down the rest of the hall, looked at Helen's face, and tears rolled down her cheeks.

"It's bad, isn't it, love?"

"I'm afraid so, Mom." Helen told her everything about Hank's encounter with Carolyn and Gino. Aggie listened, her tears flowing freely.

"That's that, then," she said, blowing her nose and wiping her face. "She's gone to the devil's side, for sure. Maybe if your da hadn't thrown her out . . ."

"Mom, don't even think like that. Carolyn gave him no choice. Dad gave her a chance to leave that relationship, but she refused. She liked the idea of being taken care of. And when it all fell apart, she became bitter. Now this Gino is probably promising her money, fancy clothes, fancy restaurants. That's the life she wants and nothing we say or do will change her."

"And when he sees a new pretty young thing, he'll toss her in the gutter. Then what will she do? Become a common street whore? Is that what her life will be? I can't even think about it."

Mom's right. What will happen to Carolyn if this Gino throws her out? Oh, little sister, you may have outsmarted yourself this time.

"Maybe Charlie'll have an idea when he gets here."

CHAPTER SIXTEEN

"Joe, you came too? I'm so glad," Peggy said when she opened the door.

"I hope you don't mind, Helen." Charlie looked down the hall to where Helen stood, dishtowel still in her fists.

"Of course not. I feel like he's one of the family already."

Charlie smiled, walked down the hall, and kissed her cheek. "Hi, Mrs. Campbell. How are you today?"

"About as well as a mother can be when she's just found out her daughter has taken to a life on the streets."

Charlie looked at Helen, eyebrows raised, a question in his eyes.

"Mom," Helen said, "they don't know what's going on. Why don't I fill them in and you can go lie down again?"

"Yeah, Mom. Maybe get rid of those puffy eyes before Dad comes home," Peggy said.

"Like I should be some kind of beauty while I tell him our Carolyn has taken to the streets?"

"No, Mom," Peggy said. "And we don't know that. Or at least it hasn't happened yet, and maybe we can stop it from ever happening. Now, go lie down. Doctor's orders."

"You're not one yet, missy. And don't think you can order me around like you are."

Peggy sighed and shook her head. "Yes, Mom. But would you please go lie down. I think this may be a late night."

"Hmph." Aggie dragged herself down the hall and closed her bedroom door.

"Now how about you two fill us in on why we're here," Joe said, settling himself at the kitchen table.

"Joe, you know how last night Helen said Carolyn had decided not to join us?" Peggy asked.

"Yeah. I thought that sounded strange, but I didn't want to question her."

"I thought that too, and I could swear I heard Carolyn's laugh a little while later. It turns out we were both right."

Peggy told Joe the whole story about Carolyn's encounter with Gino Fiori the night before.

"And when she never came home last night, Mom suggested we ask Hank, he's our local cop, if he could help find her, or at least find out something."

Joe sat still as a stone except for the frown on his forehead that deepened as Peggy related the story. Charlie held onto Helen's hand to stop it from shaking.

"Gino's a bad character, Peggy," Joe said. "I won't try to hide it from you. He's a gangster, plain and simple. I took Charlie on the road to get him away from him and his henchmen. After Charlie refused to throw a fight, a decision I encouraged, I knew Gino would be furious. A man like that isn't used to hearing the word, 'No.' Every day, I expected a few of his thugs to show up to beat Charlie, and me, to bloody pulps, or kill us outright. I have

206

to say, my intentions weren't totally altruistic in getting Charlie away from New York. I saved my own hide as well."

"Do you think you're still in danger?"

"No. We're both out of the fight game now. We're no more important to Gino than the roaches he surrounds himself with."

"I don't like to hear about Carolyn getting mixed up with him," Charlie said. "That can't come to any good."

"What do you mean?" Helen asked.

"I've known other women who got involved with him and none of them came out of the relationship better than when they went in. Some never came out."

"He killed them?" Helen asked.

"Let's say they disappeared under questionable circumstances."

"Joe," Peggy said, "we have to find her. We have to get her away from him before it's too late."

Joe leaned over and grabbed Peggy's hand. "Peggy, I know you don't want to hear this, but I don't think that's something we can do."

"Are you afraid of what Gino might do to you?"

"To me, Charlie, you, and your whole family. Peggy, you don't understand. This man is ruthless. He'd do away with his own mother if she stood in his way. Not that *he* would actually do anything. He'd have his lackeys do it. And he's got an army of them. Along with half the New York City Police Department, so he'll never be arrested for anything he does."

"The police?"

"Sometimes I forget how young you are," he said, squeezing her hand. "Haven't you ever heard of corruption?"

"I have, but I thought that only concerned politicians, not the police."

207

Joe shook his head. "Don't ever lose your innocence, Peggy. It's something I really like about you."

"I am *not* innocent. You should see what I see every day at that hospital. I'm far from innocent."

"Whatever you say."

The kitchen went quiet. Everyone absorbed in their own thoughts.

There must be a way to let Carolyn know what this Gino person is like, Peggy thought. *But how? I don't even know where she is. Maybe one of the bars he goes to. Maybe Helen and I could find out, go there and wait for them to show up. Yes. That's what we'll do. But we can't tell Joe or Charlie. They'd stop us, I'm sure. Helen'll have to think of a way to get away from Charlie for a night, or two. Oh, this is getting complicated.*

"What are you thinking about?" Joe asked.

"Nothing in particular."

"Yes, you are. I can tell. I've had years of reading boxer's faces. So, what is it? I don't want either of you girls taking things into your own hands, thinking you can solve this."

Peggy looked at him with her mouth agape, eyes blinking furiously. "What?"

"Joe's right," Charlie said. "This isn't a game. We'll figure something out, but you two stay out of it. You're no match for Gino and his crew."

"You can't expect us to sit and do nothing," Helen said. "This is our sister we're talking about. Not some floozy Gino picked up off the street."

"Calm down," Charlie said. "I know that. I'd just rather attend *our* wedding than *your* funeral."

"You're being dramatic."

"No. I'm really not, Helen. Believe me. I'm not. Now give Joe and me a chance to ask around, figure a few things out, and we'll get back to you. Promise me you won't do anything stupid before that. Promise?"

Helen looked down at her knotted hands and nodded.

"Uh uh. You need to say it out loud. Promise?"

"I promise," she said, so softly Charlie had to lean down to hear her.

"You too, Peggy," Joe said. "I'm just getting to know you. I'd rather our next time together wasn't at your grave."

Peggy let out a loud sigh. "Fine. I promise."

"You don't have your fingers crossed under that apron, do you?" Joe asked.

Peggy put both hands flat on the table and said, "I promise."

"Glad that's settled."

"Now, Joe," Charlie said, "how about we nose around and see what we can scare up?"

"Can we come too?" Helen asked.

"No," Charlie and Joe both said.

"Why not?" Peggy asked.

"Because some of the places we plan on going aren't suitable for ladies," Joe said.

"Like where?" Peggy asked.

"Like maybe some whore houses," Joe said.

"Oh." Peggy's cheeks turned red as the radishes she had been cutting up for their salad.

Charlie's eyebrows pulled together and he shook his head at Joe.

"What? I'm being honest with her."

"Maybe a little too honest," Charlie mumbled.

"No, Charlie," Helen said. "Joe's right. We'd only get in the way. You two go and find out what you can. Neither of us plan on going anywhere tonight. So, I want to know anything you learn. It doesn't matter how late it is. Either call or come by. I'll wait up."

"Okay," Charlie said. Giving her a kiss, the two men left.

"It's all we can do, Peg."

"I know. It just doesn't feel like enough."

"Nothing we do ever will. Unless it brings Carolyn back home."

Joe and Charlie spent the rest of the day wandering around the docks looking for one of Gino's lackeys. One who could be *persuaded* to tell them where or when they could talk to Carolyn alone. Then they spotted Mario, inside one of the warehouse sheds, leaning against the wall, taking bets on the daily numbers.

Joe poked Charlie in the ribs. "There's Mario. One of the lowest on Gino's totem pole. He'll talk."

"He probably will, but I doubt he knows anything. Like you said, he's one of the bottom feeders."

"Yeah, well, we've got nothing so far. I say we try him and see what happens."

"Nothing ventured . . ."

Absorbed in his chits, Mario never looked up as they sidled up on either side of him. "Be right with you, guys. Just straightening out my—"

"No rush." Charlie pinned Mario's shoulder up against the wall. Joe did the same on the other side. Mario's eyes opened wide, darting from one to the other. Sweat beaded up on his forehead and he dropped his pencil onto the wooden floor.

"Who are you? What do you want from me? I ain't got no money, if that's what you're looking for."

"Not money," Joe said. "Just some answers."

"Answers? I don't know nothing, I swear."

"Mario," Charlie said, "we haven't even asked you anything yet. Maybe you know more than you think you know. After all, word on the street is you're a pretty smart guy."

"One of Gino's best men," Joe said.

"Well... yeah. I mean, he's real good to me and everything."

"Bet he treats you better than a lot of the lowlifes who work for him, doesn't he?"

"Sure, sure. He counts on me to keep those micks, or anybody else, from horning in on the action here."

"And you do a great job for him, don't you?"

"Course I do. I'd do anything for him."

"See, Joe, I told you Mario's our man. He's got Gino's ear, don't you?"

"Sure."

"Well then, my friend," Joe said, brushing dust off the shoulder he had pinned to the wall, "maybe you could help us do a favor for Gino."

"Sure, sure," Mario said, rolling his shoulders back and standing straighter now that he had been released. "What'd Gino want me to do?"

"Not what *he* wants you to do," Joe said. "It's what *you* could do for *him*. And you wouldn't ever have to tell him you did it. Just count it as one of those little things you can keep in your vest pocket in case you ever need it. Capisce?"

"Oh, I get it. A little insurance, maybe."

"See, Charlie, I told you he was smart."

"And you were right, Joe. I never should've doubted you."

Mario smiled, his head turning side to side to follow their conversation.

"Okay, Mario, we're going to trust you to keep this between the three of us, got it?"

211

"Sure, sure. Shoot."

"We heard Gino's got a new lady friend."

"Sure does. And she's some looker. And classy too. Not like some of the other dames he usually hangs around with. The first night he showed up with her on his arm, everybody in the club stopped whatever they were doing just to look at her. She's swell." Mario's eyes drifted off, remembering the first time he saw Carolyn.

"Yeah, well, she's got some baggage that Gino might not know about."

Mario's attention snapped back to the two men. "Baggage? What kinda baggage? She don't got a kid or something like that, does she? That'd kill Gino."

"Nah," Joe said. "She's not that stupid. But she's got a debt she's got to pay. You know how ditzy these babes can be. Bet once she caught Gino's eye she forgot all about it. We'd just like to remind her."

"Yeah," Charlie said, "so we were thinking, if we could talk to her private like, without Gino around, we could settle this and he'd never have to know. You wouldn't want anything to happen to Gino, would you, Mario?"

"No. No. I'd do anything for him. He's like a big brother to me."

"See, Joe, I told you Mario'd help us out. Now all we need from you is a time and place where we could talk to this babe, without Gino knowing anything about it. And you'd be doing a big favor for him."

"Even though it would be anonymous."

"Anonymous, huh? That mean it wouldn't cost me nuttin'?"

"Something like that," Joe said.

Mario looked up at the warehouse ceiling and pulled his lips together.

"Got it. Gino goes to the barber shop every Wednesday at one o'clock. And he's always there about two or three hours. I don't know what he does all that time, but you could set your watch by him. I heard him telling her that she could go shopping while he did that, and maybe go to the beauty parlor too. He said his driver would drop her off wherever she wanted, then she could call the club and tell them to send him to pick her up when she's finished. He even gave her a roll of cash to spend."

"Did he?" Charlie opened his eyes wide. "How much you think?"

"I don't know, but I saw a few hundreds in the roll before she tucked it away."

Joe whistled. "Must really like this one, huh?"

"He's over the moon about her. I can tell. I ain't never seen him like this with any other dame."

"Mario, you're a prince among men," Charlie said.

Mario beamed. "Like I said, I'd do anything for Gino."

"Just one more thing," Joe said. "We need to know what store she's going to. How else are we going to find her and have our little chat?"

"Right," Mario said, rubbing his chin. Joe and Charlie looked at each other over the top of Mario's head. Joe closed his eyes and shook his head.

"I know," Mario shouted, "I'll talk to her tonight at Gino's place. I'll ask her what store she's going to and tell her my girl wants to get some new things, classy things, like what she wears. I'll tell her I want to buy a gift but don't know where to go. How's that sound?"

"You're a genius, Mario," Charlie said, slapping his back. "Meet us here tomorrow at ten o'clock to tell us what she said. Capisce?"

"Sure, sure. Thanks, guys. I won't let you down."

"We're sure you won't," Joe said, patting the side of his jacket. "Capisce?"

Mario swallowed hard and nodded his head.

"Ten o'clock," Charlie said, as they walked away.

"I'll be here," Mario yelled after them.

Charlie and Joe crossed the street and headed up the block. When they got to the corner, Joe said, "He's a real brain trust, that one."

Charlie started to laugh and, in a minute, the two men were roaring with laughter.

"I need a beer after that act," Charlie said.

"You and me both, my friend. You and me both."

Charlie took a long swig of his beer. "Guess I should report back to Helen."

"I think you'd better before she sends a search party out to find you."

"Be right back." Charlie headed for the phone booth at the front of the bar. A few minutes later, he returned, rubbing his hand up and down his face.

"What's wrong?" Joe asked, as Charlie gulped down the rest of his beer and signaled the bartender for another.

"The girls want to come with us."

"What? I hope you told them no."

"You've never tried to argue with a Campbell girl. Obviously. Helen said she knew what Carolyn would want to buy and that she'd be better able to talk to her in the lingerie department than we would. And in the dressing rooms."

"I can't argue with her there, but doesn't she have to go to work? And Peggy has to be at the hospital."

"Helen said she could take a sick day on Wednesday."

"And Peggy?"

214

"She said she'd talk to you about it tomorrow night over dinner." Charlie said, eyebrows raised. "Did you know you were having dinner with her tomorrow?"

"Of course, I knew. I asked her." Joe shook his head and rolled his eyes.

"Sorry. You never said."

"Amazingly enough, I sometimes do things I don't tell you about."

"So it seems. First, the apartment, and now a dinner date with my fiancée's sister."

"Don't make a big deal out of it. We started talking about her going to medical school and didn't finish the conversation, so I suggested dinner."

"Uh huh." Charlie grinned, a twinkle in his eye. "You are a sly old dog."

"Shut up before I wipe that silly grin off your face," Joe said, his cheeks blazing red.

"So, tell me. How are you going to convince Peggy not to join us? I'll defer to your age and wisdom."

"Keep it up. In about two minutes, you'll be wearing that beer."

Charlie laughed and shook his head. "Okay, enough horse play. Really. Any ideas?"

"Well... they're not going to be able to tell Carolyn what Gino's really like. We're the only ones who can do that. And put the fear of God in her."

"True. True."

The men sat nursing their beers, lost in their own thoughts. Charlie munched on stale pretzels from one of the bowls the bartender had put out.

"I think we need to speak to them in person to make our case," Charlie said. "And then, it'll be two of us against two of them. A fair fight."

"Maybe we should look at this more as a negotiation, not a fight."

"All right, a negotiation. Let me call Helen and ask them to meet us."

"Where?"

"Where." Charlie's eyes drifted to the ceiling and he let out a long sigh. A few pretzels later, he clapped his hands. "Madison Square Park. It's not far from where they live."

"It's not exactly pretty, either, but I guess it'll have to do. At least it's neutral territory."

"And you said this wasn't a fight. Hah!" Once again, Charlie walked to the phone booth.

"We can't stay too long," Helen said, giving Charlie a peck on the lips. "I want to get home before Dad, and we promised Mom we'd make dinner tonight."

"Just wanted to get things straight about Wednesday," Charlie said, "before you both wind up in trouble for skipping work."

"It's not a problem," Helen said. "I have sick days I can use and tomorrow I'll see if I can switch shifts with someone. If not, they'll still have time to call someone in to sub for me."

"That may be fine, but Peggy doesn't have sick days, do you?" Joe looked at Peggy.

"Well... no... not really."

"Then that's settled," he said. "You'll go to the hospital, as usual."

"And just who do you think you are to order me around?" Peggy asked, hands on her hips, eyes blazing.

"I didn't mean it as an order. There's just no reason for you to skip a day of learning what you really want to when it's not necessary. Charlie and I can meet you two that night and tell you everything that happened."

"I don't know. Helen?"

"Look," Charlie said, "we may not be comfortable in the ladies' unmentionables department, but she's not going to stay there all afternoon. And Joe and I *know* Gino. We know what he's like, what he's capable of. You ladies don't, and there's no reason you need to hear what we'll say to Carolyn."

"You already gave us a pretty clear picture of Gino," Helen said.

"But, Carolyn didn't hear that and, I bet, she wouldn't believe it if you told her. But, she might if Joe and I do. We've dealt with him before."

The two women stood there, facing off the men, as worthy a pair of opponents as any Charlie had met in the ring.

"Don't you have to go to work too?" Helen asked. "What about your new job, or yours, Joe?"

"I don't start for another couple of weeks," Charlie said.

"And I pretty much make my own schedule."

"Must be nice." Helen's eye caught some children playing in the dirt and focused on them while she thought things over.

"All right," she finally said. "You go alone, but you have to tell us everything that happens. Wednesday night. No excuses. Deal?"

"Deal," Charlie said.

"Joe?"

"Deal. Cross my heart and hope to die."

"Don't be so dramatic, you big jerk," Peggy said, slapping his arm.

Joe burst out laughing and took her arm to walk her home, Charlie and Helen behind them.

"And just where did you two traipse off to?" Aggie asked Helen and Peggy when they came home.

217

"Charlie and Joe asked us to meet them. They worked out a plan to see Carolyn and wanted to tell us about it."

"And what plan would that be?"

Helen told her mother the men's plan. When she finished, Aggie argued that she wanted to go with the men. When Helen reiterated all the reasons they had given *her* for not tagging along, Aggie wasn't happy about it, but she accepted their decision.

That settled, the girls told Aggie to go watch TV, or work on the sweater she was knitting while they put dinner together. Peggy pulled flour and other ingredients needed to make biscuits from the cupboard while Helen shooed their mother down the hall to the living room. They had just finished all the prep work for dinner when their father came home.

"Paddy?" Aggie called down the hall, "I need to talk with you."

He looked at his daughters, unspoken questions in his eyes. They shrugged their shoulders and looked away.

"Coming, love."

The two women tiptoed down the hall and stopped outside the living room entrance. They eavesdropped on Aggie telling Paddy about Carolyn's latest escapade and all they had done to get more information about her and her whereabouts.

"Maybe I should go with the two lads," Paddy said. "Just in case there's trouble."

"I don't think they'd appreciate that," Aggie said. "They seem to think they can handle this on their own. It seems they've had dealings with this Gino fellow before."

"Aye. I could believe that. The fight game's a dirty business. All kinds of gangsters and other hooligans with their fingers in the pie, so to speak. I'm glad this young man of Helen's is well out of it. I don't know as how I could give my blessing to her marriage if he wasn't. I wouldn't want her to get mixed up in that life."

Peggy stared at Helen who sucked in a deep breath and silently mouthed, *"What!"* Peggy shook her head, her eyes closed, and squeezed Helen's arm.

Their parents were so quiet after that statement that the two eavesdroppers were afraid to move. Afraid every step would sound like a hammer pounding nails into the floor. Helen slipped out of her shoes and motioned for Peggy to do the same before they tiptoed back to the kitchen.

Once there, Helen lit the oven, slipped the meat loaf in, then lit the burner under the pot filled with cut up potatoes. With the table set, biscuits on a baking sheet, ready for the oven, and broccoli in a water filled pot, ready to go, there was nothing left for them to do but wait. They each plopped into a chair.

"I don't know about you," Peggy hissed at Helen, "But I can't sit her doing nothing for forty-five minutes."

"It won't be that long. I have to put the biscuits in the oven in about a half-hour and —"

"Don't be ridiculous. You know what I mean."

The whispers flew back and forth, the tension in the room becoming a living, breathing entity.

"How are we supposed to go about our normal lives with Carolyn's fate hanging over us like Damocles' sword?" Peggy asked.

"I don't know. But we'll have to. For Mom and Dad's sake. We can't fall apart or become another knife in their hearts. That would definitely kill them."

"You're right, I know. But everything inside me is flip-flopping around like Mexican Jumping Beans. I don't think I can eat a thing tonight."

"Well," Helen said, "tell your insides to settle down, at least through dinner. Please. Don't give Mom another

219

thing to worry about, like you not eating. You know how she is about finishing your meal."

"I'll try, but I'm not guaranteeing anything."

"You'd better try harder than that."

Helen went to the stove and stuck a fork into one of the potato pieces. "Still hard as a rock." She plopped back down in the chair.

"They've only been on about ten minutes. What did you expect? That they'd be done?"

"I don't know what I was thinking. You're not the only one who's upset, you know. I blame myself for everything that's happened. Mom's right. I never should have let Carolyn go off with him."

"Helen." Peggy reached across the table and grabbed her sister's arm. "You couldn't have done anything to stop her and you know it."

Helen put both elbows on the table and let her head sink into her hands. "Maybe, but I should have tried harder." Her words muffled beneath her fingers.

Hearing footsteps on the wooden floor, Helen wiped her eyes on a dishtowel and, once again, went to check on the potatoes.

"I hear you two are in charge of dinner tonight," Paddy said, striding into the kitchen.

"Yes, Dad," they said at the same time.

"That's good of you, giving your mam a break. Nothing too fancy I'm hoping. Not like you're used to getting in those fine restaurants your young man takes you to."

"Meatloaf, mashed potatoes, broccoli, and a salad. How's that sound, Dad?"

"That's grand. Now, I'll just be getting a little something to settle your mam before dinner." He reached into the cabinet above the broom closet and pulled down a bottle of port wine. Helen and Peggy looked at him, slack

220

jawed. That bottle only came out for holidays and special occasions.

"Good for the digestion, they say." He got two small wine glasses from the cupboard and filled them to the brim. "Some for you two? There's plenty," he said, holding the bottle up to the light.

"None for me, thanks," Helen said.

"Me neither. I don't like port."

"Ah... well then, back it goes." He put the bottle away and returned to the living room.

"That's a first," Helen said. Peggy nodded, her mouth hanging open.

CHAPTER SEVENTEEN

Peggy came out of Bellevue's main entrance and saw Joe leaning against a parked car, reading a newspaper.

"Anything interesting?" she asked.

"Oh, here you are. No, just catching up on yesterday's sports. Nothing earth shattering going on."

Joe walked over to a trash can near the hospital's entrance and tossed the paper. He looked at his hands and frowned. "Damn newsprint. Looks like I've been digging coal all day."

"Want to go inside and wash your hands?"

"That's okay. I'll hit the gents when we get to the restaurant. Hungry?"

"Of course. I'm always hungry."

"Good. Thought we'd go to Molly Malone's. It's not far from here and the food's good. Nothing special, but good."

"Sounds perfect."

Joe raised his hand to hail a cab, but Peggy grabbed his arm and pulled it down.

"I'd rather walk, if you don't mind. I need to get the hospital smell out of my nose."

"Sure." Joe took her elbow and led her across town. "I just thought you'd want to get off your feet."

"So, where is this Molly's?" she asked, changing the subject.

"Not far. About four, maybe five, blocks away."

"Oh, that's nothing. And you wanted to take a cab. Shame on you."

"I was thinking of your poor weary feet."

"Sure you were. Bet you don't walk anywhere. You and Charlie probably personally support the New York City cabbies."

"I don't know if I'd go that far. But," he held up his hands like he was being robbed, "I surrender. We do take a lot of cabs."

"I knew it. God forbid you two should get on a subway or bus."

"I have to admit, I don't like them very much. We're here," Joe said, pointing to the pub just ahead of them.

"I can't believe I've never been here. It's not far from home or work."

"It is close to the hospital, but it's all the way across town from your apartment. Hope you like it."

"I'm sure I will. What's not to like about a good ole Irish pub?"

Joe held the door open. "After you," he said, tipping his hat.

As soon as they were inside, the bartender waved. "Hi, Joe."

"Pete. We're going to the back for something to eat."

"Enjoy yourselves."

It took a minute for their eyes to adjust to the dark interior after being outside in the daylight. A bar stretched along the right side of the room, already filled with men and women enjoying an evening cocktail. On the left were a few booths for anyone who didn't want to sit at the bar. At the end of the bar, the room opened up a little for the small dining room, chopped up to accommodate columns that covered pipes bringing heat to the apartments upstairs. Tables were squeezed into every available nook and cranny, making the arrangement haphazard, at best. Joe picked a table against the wall that offered a modicum of privacy and after sticking a match book under one foot of the center post to steady it, looked at the menu.

"Any suggestions?" Peggy asked. "Any favorites?"

"I've never had a bad meal here, and I think I've ordered everything they serve."

"Hi, Joe," the waitress said. "Your usual?"

"Sure, Rita. This is my friend, Peggy."

"Nice to meet ya," the waitress said. "Same for you?"

"I don't know. What's Joe's usual?"

"A pint of Harps."

"Sure. That sounds fine."

"Know what you want to order?"

"Everything sounds good, but maybe the Shepherd's Pie," Peggy said.

"Good choice. Had it for lunch myself today. It's good. Joe?"

"Beef stew, I think."

"You got it. Be back in a sec with your beers."

"Guess you do come here a lot." Peggy said.

Joe nodded. "I like it here. Everyone's friendly and it gets me away from boxing for a while. I can sit here, have a beer and a meal, read the paper, and relax. And it's usually not crowded, except for weekends. If I come here then, I come early and leave before the dinner crowd shows up."

"Must be nice, to have your time to yourself and be able to come and go as you please. I wish I could. Right now, I feel like I'm tied to a clock, between classes, hospital shifts, and being on time for dinner or whatever my mom plans. I can't wait to be able to be out on my own with my own schedule, or none at all."

"You're always going to have responsibilities, Peggy. Especially being a doctor. You'll have patients and hospital rounds, and who knows what else. Maybe even a family someday."

"I guess." Peggy sighed and looked away from Joe.

"Here you go. Enjoy." Rita landed the beers on the table, just in time to break the somber mood that had invaded Peggy's mind.

"Cheers," Joe said, lifting his glass. "To our first dinner together."

"Cheers." Peggy clinked her glass against his.

Our first dinner? Will there be more? Do I want there to be more?

All these thoughts ran through Peggy's mind as she sipped the tangy beer.

"Ah," Joe said, "that hits the spot."

"It is good. I've never had Harps before."

Joe shook his head. "Seems to me you've lived a much too sheltered life. No Harps, no brandy till the other night. I have my work cut out for me, I see."

"Oh? And what would that be?"

"Exposing you to all the world's vices before you finish school and go out into the wonderful world that doctors occupy. The country clubs, nightclubs, cocktail parties galore."

"Funny, I haven't heard any of the doctors mention any of those things. Most of them are so tired after their shifts that all they want to do is pick up a pizza, go home, and go to bed."

"Just wait. You'll see."

"Here we go. The plates are hot, so be careful."

"Thanks, Rita. Two more beers, please."

"Comin' right up."

Peggy and Joe dug into their food, both quiet for a minute.

"This is delicious," Peggy said.

"Glad you like it," Rita said, landing the beers on the table and taking away their empty glasses. "I'll tell the cook."

"Please do," Peggy said.

"Ditto from me," Joe said.

Rita smiled and patted Joe's shoulder as she left the table.

"You two are pretty chummy," Peggy said.

"Yep, you get to know each other pretty well when you eat here as often as I do."

"That all it is?"

Joe looked at Peggy and shook his head, smiling. "Pete, the bartender, is Rita's husband."

"Oh." Peggy's face flamed red but thanks to the dim lighting, Joe never noticed.

"So, you were going to tell me about your school and what you're doing at the hospital. Or anything else you want to tell me about yourself. I feel like I've gotten to know Helen pretty well, but I know nothing about you."

"There's not much to know, Joe. I'm afraid I haven't lived an exciting life like you have. I've never been anywhere except this little part of Manhattan. You've been all over the world. I must seem very unsophisticated to you after all the famous people you've met."

"You are one of the most interesting women I've ever met. I've never known anyone brave enough to pursue her dreams the way you're doing, Peggy. I can't imagine how much courage it must take every day to walk into your school, or hospital, knowing you'll be surrounded by men

227

who think you should be home raising babies. I have enormous respect for you."

I don't know what to say. He respects me? Me?

She could feel her face getting hot and tried to hide it by patting her lips with her napkin.

"Now, tell me why you decided to become a doctor."

"I guess I've always been drawn to it. I used to see Doctor Gerrity visiting the sick people on our block. When they recovered, they were so grateful to him. And you could see how pleased he felt."

"Sounds like someone committed to their profession. Is this Doctor Gerrity still around?"

"Oh, yes. He's still treats everyone in the neighborhood although he's getting a little old to make his way up to the fifth-floor apartments. I don't think he'll stop until he dies."

"Probably not. Did you follow him around when you were a little girl?"

Peggy thought for a minute then said, "I did. Isn't it funny you should ask that? I haven't thought about that in ages. I guess I adored him. He became a real miracle worker in my eyes. I'd watch him bandage up cuts, and give shots and medicine that seem to instantly cure people, but I'm sure a lot of my memory is distorted. Needless to say, I worshiped him and wanted to be exactly like him. I remember practicing on my sisters, always trying to bandage up one of them. Helen had infinite patience with me. She let me practice all kinds of treatments. Carolyn, on the other hand, was Carolyn. She could never stay still long enough for me to tie one bandage on her much less the five or six I had deemed necessary for her survival. Always in a hurry, she had to be off doing something, running somewhere, usually getting into trouble."

228

Seems not much has changed. She's still running into disasters.

"I think you'll be a wonderful doctor. I don't know when I've heard someone speak with so much heartfelt meaning about their work. You're a very special lady, Peggy."

Peggy blushed and sipped her beer.

I need to say something before I burst. I can't believe he thinks I'm special.

"I've been chattering away and never gave you a chance to tell me about your position at Stillman's. I want to know everything about it. Helen seemed to know the place, and apparently Carolyn's been there too. I'm the only one who doesn't know anything about it. What's it like? What will you be doing there?"

"Oh, it's nothing special. Not anything as grand as being a doctor. It's a gym that's put out some of the best boxers in the city and owned by an old friend."

"That sounds interesting. Tell me all about it."

Joe swallowed the last of his dinner and said, "I think I'll need to fortify myself for that. I'm going to have a brandy and a coffee, I think. What would you like, Peggy?"

"I don't know if I should have any more."

"You wouldn't let me drink alone, would you?"

"Oh, I don't mean to insult you or anything."

Joe laughed and said, "No, you'd never do that. It's pretty hard to insult an old codger like me."

"You're not old, Joe."

"I'm not in my prime anymore."

"You're just right—mature, not silly like some of the men I'm training with."

Joe shook his head, "You are a treat, Peggy. Now what will you have to drink?"

"I think I'd like the same."

"Coming right up," he said and signaled to Rita.

He's the one who's special, not me.

When Rita returned with two coffees and brandies, Joe added a little water to Peggy's glass.

He remembered the way I like it. How sweet.

Then he told her all about Stillman's and what he would be doing there. It was a world Peggy knew nothing about so she asked dozens of questions. By the time they finished their drinks, she felt she knew quite a lot about boxing, Joe, and Stillman's.

Finished with their drinks, they left to walk crosstown to Peggy's home. On the way, they talked about Joe's new apartment and Peggy's wish that she could find a place like that for herself.

"Thank you, Joe, for everything tonight." On tiptoes, she placed a light kiss on his lips, and hurried inside. Before the door closed, she heard Joe say, "Well, I'll be damned."

CHAPTER EIGHTEEN

"Any expectations for today?" Joe asked Charlie as they waited outside Saks Fifth Avenue.

"None," Charlie said. "Just keep your eyes peeled for her. I wish there was only one door."

"That would make things too easy."

The men stood between the entrance doors and swiveled their heads back and forth watching for Carolyn.

"You've got to say she's got good taste. This is one of the more expensive department stores in the city."

"It's easy to pick the best when it's not your own money you're spending."

"She's here," Joe said, pointing to a woman getting out of a black car that had pulled up to the curb.

"Let her get inside for a minute. I want to make sure Gino didn't send one of his goons to stick with her."

Carolyn went in one entrance and Joe and Charlie went in the other door. They watched her stroll through the first floor. No one seemed to be with her, but they kept their distance to be sure she was alone. When she got on the escalator, they waited for a few other people to step on before they followed her upstairs. She headed for the lingerie section. The two men's worst nightmare. They both pulled their hats further down their foreheads and plowed ahead.

"Now do you wish you'd brought Helen?" Joe asked.

Charlie gave him a glassy stare. "No."

Carolyn stopped at a rack holding long flowing negligees.

"No time like the present," Charlie said. He sauntered over to Carolyn and said, "Where's your guinea wise guy today?"

Carolyn drew her breath in and clutched her chest with one hand. Her face became as red as the negligee she was holding and her eyes darted around looking for a place to hide, or an escape route away from Charlie's furious glare.

He stood in front of her, legs planted wide apart, his arms across his chest.

Carolyn recovered her composure somewhat and said, "Maybe we should go have a cup of coffee."

"Do you think I won't start a fuss in a public place? It makes no difference to me where we are. If you feel you need a coffee, we'll go get one. But you're going to listen to me before you leave today."

She stood up straighter and looked him in the eye. "Why do you think you have any right to question anything I do? Or who I see? Or where I go? I'm not your girlfriend. You can't order me around."

"No, I'll leave that to Gino. That's his specialty. Ordering people around. I'm just trying to get some answers for Helen, your sister. You remember her, don't you? The person who's so worried about you she can't think straight."

"It's none of her business," she whispered.

232

"And that's where you're wrong. What you do goes back to your whole family. If you want to be a slut you need to get far away from here and go off and do what you want without any one of the Campbells knowing where you are or what you're doing."

Carolyn had started to cry softly. She rummaged through her purse looking for a hanky

"Here." Charlie thrust his handkerchief at her.

"I'm not a slut," she mumbled, her words muffled by the wadded up cloth. "Just because he's different than you doesn't mean I can't fall in love with him."

"What! Are you listening to yourself? What do you even know about him? All you want is the lifestyle you think he can give you." Charlie's arms flailed about. His booming rage started to attract the attention of the salesgirls who scurried back and forth between the counters.

Snorting like a bull ready to charge, he fought to get himself under control. Carolyn had retreated to the side of the lingerie department and huddled there like an abandoned waif.

"Listen to me," he said, breathing deeply and rubbing his face with both hands. "I plan on marrying Helen—"

"I know and I think that's wonderful."

"Listen! She said you're disgracing the whole family and she doesn't know how my family would even want to meet her when they find out her sister's a gangster's girlfriend, or lover, or whatever you call yourself now. *Your* parents won't be able to walk about without shame. And you would do all this to your family because you think you're in love." Charlie stopped to catch his breath.

"You make it sound so cheap, Charlie. It's not like that. We love each other."

"Oh, so I guess he wants to marry you? Is that right? Since he's not married, which I know for a positive fact,

233

you've got an open playing field. Not like your last affair. So, are you two getting married or what?"

"Oh, *I don't know*. You've got me all confused. I'm just not explaining it right to you."

She slumped down onto the floor. All her bravado and recklessness were gone. In its place stood a defeated twenty-four-year-old girl whimpering under Charlie's stern gaze.

"How do you think you'll end up, Carolyn?" Charlie asked more gently, seeing she felt crushed by their conversation. "Where do you think you'll be in a few years? Gino's not known for keeping women around for very long. How long will it be before he starts looking for a new plaything? Have you thought about that? Have you thought for one minute about your family? Are you willing to walk away from them for this man? Because if you stay with him, that's what you'll have to do. No self-respecting person is going to want to be associated with a gangster's lover, which is what you are, Carolyn Campbell, make no doubt about that. It'll mean never being able to go back home, not like last time. This will be permanent. And then where will you be? A lot to think over."

"I don't think I can walk away from my family forever," Carolyn mumbled.

"Well, you'll have to. They'll want nothing to do with you. You mark my words on that."

Charlie watched Carolyn's face. He could see her mentally going over all the scenarios he had presented.

"C'mon," he said. "We'll go somewhere a little more private to continue this conversation." He reached down, grabbed her arm, and pulled her to her feet.

Carolyn tried to pull her arm away, but he had it in an iron grip.

They marched along in silence to the door of a restaurant down the block. Once inside, he led her to a

234

booth in the back and Joe pulled up a chair to sit at the end of the table.

"You're the rudest man I know," Carolyn said through gritted teeth.

"I might be," he said with a smile. "I'm glad we got that all straightened out. Now I don't even need to pretend to be civil to you."

Joe signaled for the waitress and ordered coffee and roast beef sandwiches for all of them.

"Have you given some thought to what I said?" Charlie asked, taking a bite of his sandwich.

"Yes, I have. And let me tell you something. Maybe you don't remember what it was like growing up the way we did—poor. You've been living the life of Riley too long. You don't remember making a pound of chop meat stretch to feed five people, or a can of tuna fish. Or putting cardboard in your school uniform shoes in March because there are holes in the soles and your parents can't afford to buy new ones that won't fit when the next term starts. Or never having new clothes and always having to wear Helen's hand-me-downs. Or maybe you never experienced any of that.

"Whatever the case, I don't intend to spend my adult life scrimping and saving and watching every penny I spend because I'm afraid I won't be able to pay the next month's rent. Gino treats me like a queen. And I learned enough from my last relationship to see the end coming. This time, I'll be sure I have another sucker lined up before he can dump me. I'll be the one dumping him. So, it gives me great pleasure to tell you that I will *not* be ending my relationship with Gino, and if that means Helen will never marry you, that's her choice." She took a large bite of her sandwich and stared at him as she chewed.

235

Charlie wiped his fingers and mouth with his napkin and put it back on his lap. He leaned back, folded his arms across his chest, and glared at her through narrowed eyes. "You know, you're a real bitch," he said. His voice barely above a whisper.

Carolyn choked on the bite of food she had in her mouth and started to cough. A few people looked their way, but no one approached the table.

"How dare you call me that," she said when, at last, able to speak.

"I could call you a lot worse, but we *are* in a public place."

"Why should I give up my happiness so you can have yours?"

"And like I said, what's going to happen to you when he gets tired of you? He's no dope, you know. He won't give you a chance to get to know another man until after he dumps you. That'll be a sad day for you, Carolyn. If he's willing to let you leave, that is. Most of his other girls have simply disappeared. Never to be seen or heard from again."

He took another bite of his sandwich and watched her face change from defiant to confused.

"That won't happen," she said in a whisper.

"You think not? You think I've never seen this play out with men I've known? And I don't expect anything different from him. But don't you have any self-respect left at all?"

"Yesterday, Gino told me he wants to buy me my own apartment, uptown, on the East Side. What do you think of that?"

Charlie stared across the table at Carolyn.

"There! You think you know everything. Guess I shocked you with that little bit of news. See how much Gino loves me?"

236

"How sweet," Joe said, who until this time had remained silent. "A little love nest. Isn't that sweet, Charlie?"

"An apartment? Uptown? So sweet, Joe, it makes my teeth ache."

"Yes," Carolyn said.

"I guess that's far enough away that we can tell everyone you died and no one will run across you."

Carolyn's coffee sprayed out of her mouth. "What? You'd tell people I died?"

"We certainly couldn't tell them you're living in sin in a fine apartment your gangster boyfriend bought for you, could we now? No, it's better everyone thinks you're dead, for you will be to your family and mine. It's good we had this chat, Carolyn, and you told me what you'll be doing with the rest of your life. Now, tonight I can tell your parents and sisters why you won't be at our wedding, and why they won't have to worry about you and your future. It'll do their hearts good to know you're *so* well provided for in your new life as a whore. I hope you enjoy it. Goodbye, Carolyn."

Charlie and Joe stood, threw some bills on the table, and walked away.

"Charlie, wait!"

He turned and said, "There's nothing more to say. You've made your choice to be a kept woman. Helen and I will have no part of it, or you."

Before she could say another word, Charlie made his way up the aisle and out the door leaving everyone in the restaurant staring at her, especially some men who now had lecherous looks on their faces.

That evening, the Campbell's living room was silent. The only sound being the ticking of the grandfather clock. Charlie and Joe had just finished recounting their

237

conversation with Carolyn that afternoon. Helen, perched on the arm of Charlie's chair, squeezed his hand. A hint of a smile lifted the corner of her mouth the tiniest bit possible. Aggie and Paddy sat next to each other on the sofa, silent tears creeping their way down Aggie's cheeks. Peggy had pulled two kitchen chairs into the room and sat next to Joe, her hands clasped in her lap.

"Well, Aggie, that's it, I guess. We've lost her for good. You see, lads," Paddy said, looking at Charlie and Joe, "she'd always been... reckless, as they say. Always looking for some excitement. But Aggie and I thought she'd outgrown all that. Once she started working, we thought she'd be more responsible. We didn't think we'd have to watch all her comings and goings. When she said she was going to spend the night with girls from work, we were happy she'd made some new friends. Respectable-like lasses. We trusted her. I see now we never should have done that. For who knows what mischief she was up to the whole time."

"Now Paddy, don't go blaming yourself," Aggie said. "I was no better. As her mam, I should have seen where she was headed. I should have seen the devil in her."

"No, love, it's meself I'm blaming for this mess. I know more of what men are like than you. And I should have known she'd find trouble, if it was there to find. She's always wanted more, and always will. Why can't she accept her station in life? Why does she think she has the right to be better than everyone else? But if she's willing to give up her family and all the things we've taught her, she's made her pact with the devil, and she's lost her immortal soul."

"Paddy, do you really think that she's completely lost to us?"

"I do, love. It's best we stop worrying about her and be grateful for the two lasses we still have."

Aggie wiped away her tears and nodded.

Both men shifted in their chairs and glanced quickly at Paddy, then looked away.

"I don't know about anyone else," Helen said, "but I'd like to get some air."

Both men and Peggy replied as one.

"Great idea."

"Me too."

"Sounds good to me."

"Mom? Dad? Want to join us?"

"No, love," Aggie said. "I think your da and I are fine. You young folks go have a walk. Tea, Paddy?"

"I could go for a cuppa."

"Well then, off you go," Aggie waved the two couples out of the living room. "I've got to get your da his tea."

The women collected their hats, gloves, and purses and joined the men who waited in the hall for them. Once they were out of the building, Charlie took Helen's arm.

"I don't know about anyone else, but I could sure use a drink," Helen said.

"Hear, hear," Joe said. "Peggy?"

"Oh, definitely. I feel like I've been through the wringer."

"You do?" Helen said. "Imagine how these two feel. C'mon. Let's get away from here. Let's go someplace lively. All the bars around here will be filled with working men drowning their sorrows. I want to hear some laughter."

"And I know just the place," Joe said. He hailed a cab and they piled in. Joe gave the driver an address downtown, but refused to say where he was taking them.

It wasn't long before the cab stopped in front of a place with red and white barbershop-style columns out front and illuminated signs that read, "Your Father's

239

Moustache" with a cut-out of a huge handlebar moustache hanging below.

"If this place doesn't bring a smile to your faces, I don't know what will," Joe said as he paid the cabbie.

As soon as they opened the door, Peggy and Helen started laughing. A Dixieland band was playing upbeat music that everyone sang along to. All the band members, waiters, and bartenders wore red and white striped vests and garters on the sleeves of their white shirts. The bartender also had a straw boater on his head. They looked like they had just stepped out of the 1890s.

"Oh, Joe, it's perfect," Peggy said. "How did you ever find this place?"

"At my age, you get to know all kinds of places for all different occasions."

"And if you don't stop calling yourself old, I'm going to leave and never see you again."

Joe smiled. "We wouldn't want that to happen."

Peggy gave his arm a squeeze as they followed the host to a table. Charlie and Helen were behind them and had watched their interchange. Even though the music was too loud for them to hear the conversation, they looked at each other. Charlie lifted his eyebrows, shrugged his shoulders, and shook his head. Helen sighed. Was this another new romance, she wondered?

The two couples squeezed onto the wooden bench's empty spaces at a long table filled with other revelers.

"It's certainly cozy here," Charlie said, his lips right next to Helen's ear. It was the only way he could be heard over the music.

"Yes, maybe a little too cozy," Helen said, pointing to her sister who had cuddled up next to Joe, practically in his lap.

"Well," Charlie said, "you can't leave room for the Holy Ghost if you're going to have a conversation in here.

Between the music and the singing, this place is deafening."

"Maybe we should have stayed with the working men's bar."

"Nah. This'll be fun." Charlie put his arm round Helen's shoulder and pulled her in close."

The waiter landed a pitcher of beer, which Joe had ordered, and four glasses on the table. He filled each glass and they lifted them to clink a silent toast to the night. Before long, they were singing along with everyone else, on their second pitcher of beer, and feeling much better than they had when they left the apartment.

CHAPTER NINETEEN

"Joe? What ... Is everything all right? Is someone sick or hurt? Or... dead?" Peggy whispered the last word, her eyes filling with tears.

"Oh God, no. No. Nothing like that," Joe said. He put his arm around her shoulder and pulled her close. Handing her his handkerchief, he said, "I just didn't feel like eating alone. So, I thought, since I haven't seen you in about a week, you might be willing to spend some time with me. If you're not sick of me, that is. And maybe let me take you to dinner. How about it?"

"I'd love to have dinner with you," Peggy said, dabbing her eyes dry. "And I don't think I'd ever get sick of you, you silly goose." She wrapped one arm across his chest and squeezed him.

Joe grinned like the cat that ate the canary and kissed her forehead.

"Well then, let's go." He reached for her hand and they walked towards the street corner.

"Oh, wait. I should call home and let Mom know I won't be there for dinner. Give me a minute." Peggy ran back to the hospital and disappeared through the double doors while Joe paced the street from corner to corner. Minutes later, Peggy hurried up to him, took his hand again, and asked, "Molly's?"

"Want to try a different place?"

"Sure. What did you have in mind?"

"How about the Jaeger House? It's uptown at 85th and Lex. Willing to give German food a try?"

"Why not?"

Joe stepped off the curb to hail a cab, but Peggy pulled his arm down. "Can't we grab a bus or take the train?"

"What do you have against cabs?"

"Nothing. It just seems like such a waste of money. And the subway's probably faster anyway."

Joe threw his hands up in surrender. "I give up. But I have no idea what train to take. I really don't like them very much. They're crowded and noisy, and—"

"Leave it to me." Peggy looped her arm through his and led him across the street and west to the Lexington Avenue subway. "This'll take us right to 86th and Lex. Close enough?"

"Whatever you say." Joe patted her hand, then followed her down the stairs into the caverns of the New York City subway system.

Peggy reached for her purse to get a token, but Joe stopped her. "My treat." Since it was rush hour, the train was packed with commuters going home from work. At every stop, the car disgorged numbers of commuters while others pushed their way in to fill the empty spaces. By the time they reached 86th Street, there was actually breathing room, but, of course, it was also their stop. Once on the sidewalk, Joe took a deep breath.

"Next time, it's a cab. God. I don't know how people do that every day."

Peggy laughed. "You get used to it. Don't you remember doing it when you were beginning your career?"

"Not really. I think I walked most places. Or maybe there just weren't so many people. Or maybe it was too long ago to remember."

"Don't start on the age thing again or I'll go right back down there and jump on a train home."

"Oh no you won't. You made me suffer through that torture, you'll have to suffer through dinner with me."

Joe took her hand and with his other arm pointed to the restaurant's sign a block away. They walked down the street, Peggy's head swiveling around to catch a glimpse of all the unusual butchers, bakeries, and restaurants on the block.

"It's like a whole other world up here," she said.

"It's Yorkville. You've never been here?"

"No. I guess there was never a need to come this far uptown. I've been to Central Park and the Metropolitan Museum of Art, of course, but they're over on Fifth. I've never been over here. It's like being in Germany or Austria."

"Yep. It's Germantown up here for sure. Just like Chinatown or Little Italy, you can get almost anything you want here that's German. Newspapers, meats, pastries, all kinds of things."

"I'm amazed."

"Here we are." Joe held the door for her and they stepped inside giving their eyes a minute to adjust to the dark interior after the sunshine outside.

A passing waiter led them to an empty table and gave them menus. Another waiter came over for their drink orders.

"A beer?" Joe asked Peggy, "or a cocktail?"

"Beer is fine. Whatever you're having."

245

Joe ordered two Lowenbrau's and the waiter nodded, left, and returned a few minutes later with two large steins of beer.

"Wow, that's a lot of beer," Peggy said. "I'm used to a glass, not a big mug."

"It's called a stein here," Joe said, "and it's a little stronger and more bitter than American beer, so I'm not sure you'll like it."

Peggy took a sip. "Not bad."

"Want something else?"

"No. I'll struggle through." She smiled and took a larger drink, then asked Joe about some of the dishes on the menu. Most of them, she had never heard of before. They both agreed that she might like the sauerbraten and Joe ordered the knockwurst for himself. When their dinners came, Peggy was thrilled with her selection and teased Joe about having a giant hot dog for dinner. He tried to convince her there was a major difference between knockwurst and dirty water hot dogs, but even after she tasted a piece Joe cut for her, she wasn't convinced. Although, she did admit the knockwurst had more flavor.

Over dinner, Peggy asked Joe about all the places he'd been to when he and Charlie were on their boxing tours. She was amazed at how much travel was involved. They toured all across the country and some cities in Europe as well.

"Gosh, I feel like a country bumpkin. I've never even been up here, in my own city, and you've traveled all over the world."

"Mostly gyms and hotels. It's not like I've seen the sights in all those places. Everyone thinks travel is so exciting and exotic. It's not. Not when it's business travel, like this was. It's just a string of, mostly, seedy hotels, bad food, smelly gyms, and crowded arenas. Try keeping a boxer in shape under those conditions." Joe shook his head. "I'm glad to be done with it."

"Are you sure? Don't you think you'll get bored being stuck in one place?"

"Not at all. At least, not while I can count on having you as my lovely dinner companion."

Peggy's face heated up and she lowered her eyes to her plate.

"Can I? Count on you as a dinner companion?"

She looked at Joe and saw only love and tenderness in his eyes and realized that she felt the same way towards him. It was so sudden, her chest hitched.

"Every day, if you'd like."

"I'd like that very much." Joe reached across the table and held her hand.

"Coffee, dessert?" the waiter asked, scooping up their empty dinner plates.

"You must try the apple strudel," Joe said. "It's wonderful." Turning to the waiter, he said, "Two of those please, and two coffees."

The waiter nodded and left. Joe looked across the table and smacked his forehead. "I'm an idiot. I never asked if that was okay with you."

"Perfectly okay."

Joe shook his head. "You're too good to believe, and beautiful to boot."

She could feel her face becoming as hot as the radiators in winter and she couldn't stop smiling at the wonderful man sitting opposite her. Joe made her feel so special, so different than she felt with any other man she had dated. She wanted to feel like this for the rest of her life.

"Joe, how is it that women aren't fighting over you every day? Are you sure you've never been married? How can that be? You're too wonderful to be out there single all this time."

"Oh ho, so now who's calling me old?" Joe chuckled. "No, Peg. No one's been breaking down my door trying to put a ring on my finger. At least, no one I've cared about enough to let that happen. But you, my dear, are in a class all by yourself."

The waiter landed their desserts and coffees and cut short their conversation.

Peggy cut a piece of strudel and as soon as it passed her lips, she closed her eyes and leaned back in her chair. "Sheer heaven," she said, swallowing the delicacy. "I never knew apples could taste this good."

"Sometimes I think I only eat dinner here so I can enjoy the strudel afterwards."

They savored their desserts and finished their coffees. After Joe paid the check, he said, "How about a little walk to work off dinner?"

"That would be lovely."

"Carl Schurz Park isn't too far from here, if you're up for a walk to the East River."

"Sounds perfect."

They strolled across town on 86th Street, Joe pointing out various restaurants and other places they might like to explore in the future. When they reached the park, they sat on one of the benches along the waterfront and watched the ships and boats glide along the East River. Joe put his arm around Peggy's shoulder and she nestled in to a spot that felt like it was specifically designed for her.

CHAPTER TWENTY

A week later, Peggy left the hospital and saw Joe leaning against a lamppost reading a newspaper.

"Fancy meeting you here, Mr. Hayes."

He folded the paper in half and leaned down to kiss her. "Did I forget to tell you I'd be waiting for you?"

"Were you planning to take me to Molly's for dinner?"

"Unless you want to go somewhere else."

"A fellow med student told me about a place up on 72nd Street. The Ruc. It sounds interesting. I think it's German or Czechoslovakian. Something like that. Anyway, he said there's a neat garden in the back of the restaurant and since it's such a mild night, I thought it might be fun to eat outside."

"Is that what he suggested when he asked you out to dinner?"

Peggy's face blushed. "Well... uh . . ."

Joe laughed. "Peggy, I'm sure you'll get plenty of dinner invitations from handsome medical students and doctors for the rest of your life. In fact, I'm amazed you made it through college without being whisked away by some young up and coming executive. Were they all blind to what an intelligent, and beautiful, woman you are?"

"No, just silly boys who don't know how to treat a woman. I much prefer an older man, like you. Not that you're old. I don't mean that. I mean more mature."

Joe roared laughing. "Oh, Peggy. Please don't think you're offending me by calling me old. I am. I'm always afraid I'm *too* old for you. That one day you'll turn around and tell me you've fallen in love with a young handsome doctor and that it's been fun, but . . ."

Peggy stopped walking and spun Joe around to face her. "Is that what you think? Why do you think I look forward to seeing you every day? Just to have a dinner companion? I could go home and have dinner with my family, you know. I'm happy to see you every day because I love you, you big dope."

"You do?"

"Yes, I do. I thought maybe you had figured that out already," she whispered, lowering her eyes so she didn't have to see his reaction.

"And seeing you every day makes me ridiculously happy."

Peggy looked up into his face. "Does it, Joe?"

"Yes, love. Seeing you come through those doors is the best part of every day for me. And when I walk you to work in the morning, seeing you go into that building is the worst part of that day, for I know it'll be hours before I can be with you again."

"I feel the same way. If I didn't love what I'm doing so much, I'd leave it right now so I could be with you all the time."

"I'd never ask you to do that. I know becoming a doctor is your dream and I won't take that away from you.

250

But do you think you could ever consider sharing that life with me? I know you'd have plenty of duties here at the hospital and in your own practice, but would you consider spending all the rest of your time with an old curmudgeon?"

"Joe, what exactly are you asking?"

"I guess I'm asking you to marry me."

"You guess?"

"No, I *am* asking you to marry me. Would you give it some thought?"

"I don't need to think it over. The answer is yes, yes, a thousand times yes." Peggy's face glowed. Joe pulled her tight against him for a minute, then lifted her face to his and kissed her. Peggy felt her knees shake and her legs grow wobbly.

When Joe finally pulled away, he looked down into two eyes so filled with adoration he thought his heart would burst. Peggy saw her feelings mirrored in Joe. As they reentered the reality around them, Joe noticed several women casting disapproving looks at their public display of affection.

"I'm afraid I've compromised your good name in the hospital," he said. "It seems we've crossed the line of acceptable behavior."

"Who cares. I don't. I'm so happy I could start dancing right here in the street. Now that would attract a few stares, wouldn't it?"

Joe laughed and slipped her arm through his. "Let's get away from here before we attract a whole mob of morally offended women."

They walked down the street absorbed in each other, ignoring the glares from people they brushed against.

I don't think I'll ever be as happy again as I am right now. I can't wait to tell Helen.

"Maybe I should show you where I work now that you're going to be sharing that part of my life with me."

"Oh, Joe, I've been terrible. I spend all our time together talking about my work and never ask you about yours."

"Yours is much more interesting. My days in the rough and tumble world of boxing and saloons is not a world for the likes of you, Peggy, but I'd like you to see it once anyway."

"I want to see it, and I want to be a part of it the way you're a part of mine. Believe me, there are plenty of rough characters, men and women, at the hospital every day. I imagine some of your boxers don't get beaten up as much as some of the women who come to us for help."

"You're probably right, although it sickens me to think that men can abuse women that way. At least in boxing there are rules and if you violate them, you're thrown out. It's too bad there aren't rules like that in real life."

"There are some laws, but most times the women won't even talk to the police. They need their husband's income and know they'll wind up on the street if he goes to jail. So, we patch them up and they go right back to their private hells until the next time we see them."

"That's terrible. There should be a way for these women to live without being beaten up on a regular basis."

"If only there were, but there's no place for them to go. They can't go to work, they have children to take care of, and any kind of work they could do at home doesn't pay enough to feed them and pay rent. I can't see a ready solution for them, not right now. Maybe someone will come up with an idea in the future, but for now there's no answer."

They walked along in silence each absorbed in their own thoughts.

"We'll give it some thought, Peggy, but right now this is too glorious a day to be marred by their plight."

"You're right. So, I'm finally going to see the infamous Stillman's. I can't wait. Will Mr. Stillman be there? Can I meet him too? Helen says he's awfully nice."

"She did, did she? And have you two sisters been talking about me behind my back?"

"Of course. That's what sisters do, discuss beaus, dreams, plans for the future."

"Wait a minute. When did I become a beau?"

"The first night I met you."

"What?"

"I think I fell a little in love with you then, and a little more each time I saw you."

"And you never let on? You're a scamp, Peggy Campbell."

"It wouldn't do for me to say something first, would it? Even though that's just what I did. When did you start to like me?"

Joe's face reddened. He tugged at his hat and looked around. "We should get a cab."

"Joe Hayes, I'm waiting for an answer."

"What? Oh, well . . ."

"Well, what?"

"The first night I met you too," he said, his face now the color of ripe apples.

"And it took you this long to ask me to marry you?" Peggy asked, playfully punching his arm. "You are exasperating. We could have been married by now."

"I never thought you'd be interested in me. I'm an old man. I figured you'd have lots of young men vying for your affection, and I wouldn't stand a chance against them."

"As I keep telling you, those young men are all foolish, self-centered idiots who I have no time for. I prefer a mature man, like you, who knows how to treat women properly."

"Peggy, you're a delight," he said, running his fingers down the side of her face. "Now, let's get a cab."

Once they were settled inside, Peggy turned to him. "Out of curiosity, how old are you?"

Joe laughed so heartily that the driver looked back at them. Calming himself, Joe wiped his eyes and said, "Forty-five. Want to reconsider your betrothal?"

"Absolutely not. I think forty-five is the perfect age for a man to be. And that is the last discussion we will have about age. Agreed?"

"Whatever you say, my dear," he said, pulling her to him and kissing her again. Peggy curled into his arms and hoped the cab ride would never end.

"Here we are, my love. Stillman's Gym," Joe said as the cab stopped in front of a run-down building.

"Couldn't we just keep riding around and never leave this cab?"

"I'm afraid not. Besides I thought you wanted to see where I work."

"I do, just not right now." She looked into his eyes, her desire overwhelming him.

"We'll take a longer ride later," Joe promised in a husky voice. "But now, let's get inside and have you meet Lou." Joe paid the driver and led her upstairs. Once inside, Peggy stood flabbergasted at the enormity of Stillman's.

"I thought this was a little gym. It's gigantic."

"I guess it is big. I'm so used to it I don't even notice it anymore."

Peggy looked around, amazed at all the different sections: boxing rings, weight areas, an overhead track for running or rope jumping, a section with speed bags, heavy bags, and more.

"Let me see if Lou's around," Joe said. "Have a seat. I'll be right back." He led her over to some chairs set against the wall.

"And make sure you get all that shit cleaned up before opening time," Lou said, standing in the doorway that led to the locker room.

"Yes, Mr. Lou," a young boy's voice said.

Turning away from the door and striding into the room, Lou came to a quick stop. "Damn," he muttered under his breath. "Excuse me, miss. I didn't see you there. If I had, I would have cleaned up my language. I apologize."

"No apology necessary. You must be Mr. Stillman. Joe's gone looking for you."

"Joe? Joe Hayes? Then you must be the young doctor—Peggy, isn't it? —who he's always talking about."

"He talks about me?"

"We can hardly get him to talk about anything else."

"I see Lou found you all by himself," Joe said.

"And why have you kept this pretty young lady under wraps, Joe? Afraid I'd steal her away?" Lou winked at Peggy.

"I enjoy her company too much to share it with the likes of you, old man."

"How do you like that? Insulting me in my own gym. I should take you in the ring and teach you—"

"Mr. Lou, Mr. Joe, Mickey's hurt. Come quick." The boy Peggy had heard before now sounded panicked.

Lou and Joe hurried to the locker room, Peggy right behind them. When she stepped over the threshold, the reek of sweat assaulted her senses. She recoiled a step then plowed ahead to catch up to the men whose pace had quickened.

255

"It's nuttin' I tell ya. I can still fight tonight. Why I could beat that bum with one hand anyways."

"Shut up and let me see what you've done to yourself," Lou said. "Damn. You were the main event for tomorrow night, you stupid ass. Didn't you think about that before slamming your fist into whatever you slammed it into?"

"It ain't nuttin', Mr. Lou. Mr. Joe here can bandage me up and I'll be fine. Right, Mr. Joe?"

"I have to look at it first," Joe said. "Now sit down on the table and let's see the damage."

"I can stand right here. It's not like I'm goin' faint or somethin'."

"SIT DOWN." Peggy's command cast a sepulchral silence over the room. "Right here." She pointed to the edge of the table.

Mickey lumbered over to the spot Peggy indicated and boosted himself onto the table, looking like a little boy who has been reprimanded by Sister Mary Teresa.

"Give me your hand," Peggy said.

"Peggy," Joe said, "maybe you should—"

"I'm a doctor. This is what I do, Joe. Your hand, Mickey."

Mickey produced a mangled fist that showed signs of previous damage. Peggy winced when she saw it.

Why does anyone want to be in a profession where you deliberately abuse your body this way?

She felt along the tips of each finger watching Mickey's face for signs of pain. When she placed her hand on his knuckles, he inhaled a sharp deep breath.

"See, nuttin' wrong."

"Be quiet. You've done some real damage to your knuckles, Mickey, and maybe your wrist as well. What did you hit?"

"Aw, just the locker over there."

256

They all looked where he pointed and saw a sizable dent in one of the metal cabinets that stood against the wall.

"They're steel, man," Lou said. "What did you think you were going to accomplish doing that?"

"I don't know. I was mad, is all. My girl said she don' wanna see me no more. She made me mad, is all."

"And you thought driving your fist through a steel cabinet would change that, did you? You're dumber than a box of rocks." Lou raked his fingers through his hair. "Now what am I supposed to do for a headliner tomorrow? And you," he said, pointing at the man cowering at the far end of the room. "You're supposed to be his trainer. How could you let this happen? Useless, the two of you."

Lou stormed out of the room, cursing and swearing under his breath the whole time.

"Joe," Peggy said, "Mickey needs to go to the hospital. I don't have what I need here to patch him up. We can take him to Bellevue. They know me there and I can get a doctor to look at him right away."

"Oh no, I ain't goin' to no crazy hospital."

Peggy knew that over the years, Bellevue's psychiatric ward had become so well known that most people believed the hospital only treated psychiatric patients.

"You'll do exactly what I tell you to do. Is that understood?"

"Yes, ma'am," Mickey said, shrinking under her baleful stare.

"Can you get a cab, Joe?"

"Frankie," Joe said to the boy who stood staring wide-eyed at the scene, "run and get a cab for us."

"Yes, Mr. Joe."

257

"Mickey," Peggy said, "try to stand. Your system's had a shock and you may be a little wobbly."

"This ain't nuttin' ma'am. You shoulda seen what I looked like after the McCrory fight."

"Yes, well, I'm glad I didn't. Now, stand up."

Mickey jumped off the table and swayed a little.

"Joe, grab his arm."

"I'm okay, Mr. Joe."

"Sure you are, Mickey. Mac," he called to the trainer, "get on his other side. You're coming with us. I don't intend to spend my night at the hospital."

"Sure, Joe, sure." Mac hurried over to Mickey's side.

"Cab's here, Mr. Joe," Frankie called from the doorway.

"Let's go, Mickey. Nice and easy."

The entourage made their way out to the cab and piled in. It didn't take long for them to reach the hospital and Peggy ushered them into an examination room. She ordered a series of X-rays for his wrist and hand and told the doctor on duty what happened. The orderlies wheeled Mickey away and Mac and Joe went to the waiting room. Peggy went with Mickey to make sure he didn't cause any problems for the other doctors or nurses. As soon as the X-rays were taken, Peggy left him in the hands of the orderlies who were used to violent patients and prepared to handle any outburst from Mickey.

"It'll be a while before the doctor can see the X-rays, but I can almost guarantee that he's broken a few fingers, cracked his knuckles, and maybe splintered the bones in his wrist."

"That bad, huh?" Joe asked. "Well Mac, looks like your boy will be out of the fight game for a while. Maybe this time he'll learn to keep that temper under control."

"I doubt it, Joe. He's a hothead. Always has been and, I'm afraid, always will be."

"Then I wish you luck with him. Ready Peggy?"

"Yes, Joe. Mac, he's going to need to see a doctor when he leaves here. Make sure he does or he'll lose the use of that arm for good."

"I'll see to it, miss. Thank you."

Peggy took Joe's arm and they walked out into a darkened street.

"I didn't realize we had been in there so long," Peggy said. "What time is it?"

Joe looked at his watch. "Past nine. Not exactly what I had planned for our engagement night."

Peggy smiled at him and patted his arm. "It's only one night." She lowered her head and wrung her hands, lost in thought.

"What's wrong?" Joe asked.

"Well, now you see that I can be called at any time to help someone or even go back to the hospital in an emergency. Are you sure you want a wife who might not always come home at the end of her workday? Or be pulled away in the middle of the night?"

"If she doesn't come home for dinner, then I'll pick up some food and bring it to her so she isn't starving all night."

"But... what about a family? Do you want children? We've never talked about that."

"I'd love to have children. Do you want a family?"

"Oh, yes. I do, Joe. But I'm not willing to sacrifice my profession for it. Can you understand that?"

"Of course, my love. You keep doctoring and I'll be the family man at home. Or we could hire a nanny. We'll work it out." He kissed her on the forehead.

"Joe, you really are remarkable. I was so worried you'd make me choose. And I can't."

"Well, your worries are over. I fully intend to be both the husband of a brilliant doctor and the father of as many children as you would like."

Peggy threw her arms around his neck and gave him a very long, loving kiss.

When she pulled back, he took a deep breath, kissed her forehead and hailed a cab. "Hungry?"

"Starving for lots of things, but right now, a meal."

They climbed into the cab and Joe gave the driver an address. Peggy snuggled next to
him, lost in dreams of their future.

CHAPTER TWENTY-ONE

"I'm sorry, miss, no women allowed," the clerk at the front desk said when Helen walked into the New York Athletic Club.

"I'm here to see Mr. Sanders. Would you send for him, please?"

"Yes, miss, but I'm not sure he's here."

"If he's not, I'll speak to Mr. Pilgrim."

"Yes, miss." The clerk left to search for one of the two men.

Not here? Where would he be? He couldn't be at Stillman's, could he?

"Helen, sweetheart. What brings you down here?" Charlie's voice boomed across the wide foyer. "Wait a minute. Shouldn't you be at work? Everyone at home all right?"

"I took a couple of hours off. Everyone's fine. Except me. I'm furious. Where were you last night? And don't even think about making something up."

Charlie looked around, embarrassed at Helen's outburst. "Helen, this isn't the place to be discussing our private affairs," he whispered in her ear, but the glare in her eyes told him she wouldn't settle for waiting until the evening for an answer. "Let me see if there's an empty room we can use." He turned to the desk clerk and said, "Larry, is there an office available?"

"Yes, Mr. Sanders. You can use the one over there," he pointed to a small room where prospective members could complete the club's application form.

Charlie took Helen's arm and steered her to the empty room. Once inside, he closed the door and stood against it, arms across his chest. "What's going on? I don't appreciate you coming to my work and scolding me like I'm a schoolboy. What I did or where I went last night could wait until tonight when I see you."

"Oh? *Are* you going to see me tonight? Or will you be at Stillman's again for another fight?"

Charlie's jaw dropped and he pulled at the towel wrapped around his neck.

"I thought so," she said. "Why, Charlie? Why? You told me you were through with boxing, and now you've gone back on your word. You lied to me."

"How did you find out I was at Stillman's last night?"

"Does that matter? Would you have told me the truth tonight if I hadn't found out? Or would you have made up some excuse?"

"Sit down, and let me explain."

"I'm not sure you can explain this away, Charlie. I think I know what happened. Lou's fighter for last night injured himself, Lou thought you could fill in, and you jumped at the chance to be back in the ring. Am I close?"

"Very close. But you're wrong about two things. I didn't 'jump at the chance,' as you say. And I didn't jump into the ring. Joe called to tell me about Mickey and asked if I'd be willing to substitute for him. That much is true, although I don't know how you... Peggy. It was Peggy told

262

you. Of course. That's who Lou was going on about. Your sister." He looked off, lost in his own thoughts for a minute. "I should have known when he said Joe and his lady friend. Damn. Joe and Peggy, at Stillman's. Why did he bring—"

"Could we get back to what happened with you?"

"Sorry, it's just now got me thinking... but we can talk about all that later. Lou did ask me to fill in, but I made a promise and I wouldn't break my word to you. If I ever want to go back to boxing, I'd talk to you about it first, but I doubt that will ever happen. I'm happy here. I get to keep my hand in, so to speak, but without all the bruising."

"So, why *were* you at Stillman's last night?"

"Because Joe called. Lou was in a fix and I thought I had a way out for him. I've already told you about Sean, the young boy I've been working with at the Settlement House. Anyway, I thought maybe Lou would be willing to give him a try, but I couldn't explain all that on the phone to your mom, so I just told her I had to cancel. Then I picked Sean up and the two of us went to talk to Lou. He agreed to let Sean substitute for Mickey. And, well, you know the rest."

"Charlie Sanders, I could—"

Before she could say another word, Charlie pulled her into his arms and kissed her.

When he released her, she told him about Peggy and Joe getting engaged.

"What!"

"Oh! Excuse me. Mr. Sanders, you've a telephone call," the young clerk said, bursting into the room.

"A telephone call? I'd better take that. See you tonight?"

"You'd better."

263

He gave her a quick kiss and they left the room together. Charlie headed for the phone room and Helen for the door.

"Hello?" Charlie said.

"Charlie? That you? Speak up. These damned pay phones aren't the greatest. It's Tex. Tex Hardiman here."

"Tex. Sure, I know you. We met once in New Orleans."

"Could be. Could be. I travel a lot. Got this number from Lou Stillman. Saw your boy, Sean, fight last night. He's good, Charlie. Raw, but good."

"I agree with you there. Needs training."

"He does, but I'm willing to take a chance on him. When can we meet to discuss setting up a tour?"

"A tour? You'd stake him? That's great. I'll track him down and let him know."

"No need to do that. I already spoke to him, but he says he won't sign anything or go anywhere without you."

"Me? What's the boy want with an old brawler like me?"

"Says you're the one taught him everything he knows and he won't go anywhere unless you go too."

"He's crazy. I'll talk to him tonight at Stillman's. You'll be there?"

"I will, but this offer doesn't last forever, Charlie."

"I know that."

The phone went dead in his hand.

Now what am I supposed to do about this predicament? I've just told Helen I've washed my hands of the fight game, and here comes the opportunity of a lifetime for young Sean. How can I let the boy down? On the other hand, how can I let the love of my life down? You've got yourself in a fine pickle, you have, Charlie Sanders. Maybe Joe can help out here, if I can find him, that is.

264

Charlie sat in the phone room and ran his hands through his hair.

"Everything all right, Charlie?"

"Paul!"

Paul Pilgrim stood in the doorway of the small room a worried expression on his face. "I heard you got a phone call. Family all right? Helen?"

"Everyone's fine, Paul, thanks for asking. I've a different kind of problem to deal with."

Charlie told him about Sean and the call from Tex Hardiman.

"Tex, the big fight promoter?"

"That's the one."

"What an opportunity for Sean."

"It is, but the catch is that he wants me to go with him."

"Aren't you getting married soon?"

"I am. And I just finished telling Helen that I'm done with the fight game. That I'm happy with the little bit of sparring I do here and working with the boys at the Settlement House. And I am. But I have to tell you, I never saw this coming."

Paul leaned against the door jamb and considered Charlie's problem. "I think you need to get away from here for the rest of the day, Charlie. You're no use to me all tied up in knots thinking about what you're going to do. You'll either knock out one of the pompous asses who tries to best you, or you'll get knocked out yourself for not watching what they're doing. Either way, it's not good for the club. Go clear your head. Talk to Joe. He's been around long enough to know the game well."

"He has. The trick is finding him."

"Well, you won't do it by standing here. Get yourself changed and go look for him. Maybe he's at Stillman's."

"He could be, what with the fight tonight and all the people Lou invited. Thanks, Paul. I'll do that. I'll go to Stillman's."

"If he shows up here, I'll tell him you went there."

Charlie trotted off to the dressing room to change into his street clothes.

Now I've two things to talk to Joe about. Sean and Peggy. I think it was easier getting my head bashed in every day than dealing with all these problems outside the ring.

Half an hour later, Charlie walked into Stillman's. "Is Joe Hayes here?" he asked the doorkeeper.

"I think he's setting up."

Charlie walked through the doors to the exhibition area. Joe was directing a small army of men who were setting up chairs and benches for the night's event.

"Joe," he called.

"Charlie. What are you doing here in the middle of the day? You didn't get canned, did you?"

"No, nothing like that. I've a little problem I want to discuss with you if you've got a minute."

"Sure, sure, these boys know what they have to do. Would you like a beer?"

"I could use one."

"Fine, I'll meet you at the pub around the corner."

Charlie walked to the pub and chose a table away from the bar. He ordered two beers and as he took his first sip, Joe strode across the room.

"So, what's this 'little problem' you have? You do something to make Helen mad at you?"

"Not yet, but I might manage that yet today."

"Are you trying to sabotage your wedding?"

"Speaking of weddings . . ." Charlie hesitated, "when's yours?"

"Heard about that already, did you?"

266

"Did you plan on telling me, or is this to be a well-guarded secret?"

"I planned on telling you tonight at the fight. I knew you'd be there, since your boy, Sean, is the main event. I suppose you heard it from Helen."

"Yep, she came to see me today. All in a fuss because she thought *I* fought last night. Seems your Peggy told her about being there, and Mickey, and since I had sent a message saying I couldn't see her last night, well, she drew her own conclusions. Loaded for bear. Stormed into the club ready to dress me down for lying about giving up boxing. That girl has some temper." Charlie shook his head remembering how her steely eyes bored through him as he walked across the club's foyer. "After I sorted all that out, she told me about you and Peggy. You're a sly one, Joe. Never said a word to me about your intentions."

"Don't think I knew them myself until yesterday. I mean I had thought about it, but something about Peggy yesterday, the way she looked at me. Before I knew it, I had asked her to marry me and she had said yes. I'll be honest with you Charlie, I don't know if I was more shocked that I actually proposed or that she accepted."

Charlie's roar bounced off the walls. "Oh, Joe, you're well caught," he said, wiping the tears away from his eyes. "Confirmed bachelor, my ass." He shook his head and took another gulp of his beer. "So, when's it to be?"

"I don't know. I guess that will be up to Peggy. She's still got a year or two of school before she can apply for a license. She might want to wait until after that."

"I wouldn't count on that long a reprieve. She'll have you all wrapped up before the summers out if I know the Campbell girls. And I think I might know a little more about them than you do."

"I'll grant you that. We'll see. Whatever she wants is fine with me."

267

"She *does* have you wrapped around her little finger, doesn't she?"

Joe's face was turning bright red just as the waiter approached and asked if they'd like another beer. "I think we might," Charlie said, "if you don't think you'll be in trouble for it later today."

"Two more," Joe said to the waiter. Turning to Charlie, he said, "And you can go to hell."

Charlie burst into uproarious laughter again.

"Aside from annoying the hell out of me, why did you come here today?"

"I'm having so much fun, I almost forgot." Charlie told Joe about the call from Tex Hardiman an hour ago.

"Tex, huh? He's big time, Charlie. Your boy can't do much better than him."

"I agree with you there, but I'm no trainer or manager. I wouldn't know one end of a contract from the next. You always took care of those things for me. I wouldn't be doing the boy any good if I was to take over his career."

Joe sipped at his beer and leaned back in his chair.

"I agree with you about Sean. He needs someone to look out for his interests. Tex may see some talent in him, but, as long as the money is lining Tex's pocket, he doesn't care if the boy makes money or not. And if he doesn't turn out to be as good as Tex thinks he may be, he'll drop him like a hot potato and abandon him wherever they are. That poor kid will be walking back to Chelsea with nothing to show for his time away but some bruises, if he's lucky. You're right. You're not the person Sean needs right now, but you're the person he wants in his corner and that counts for a lot."

"You're not making this any easier for me. Are you saying I should agree to go on the road with him? Is that what you're trying to tell me?"

268

"I'm not telling you anything, Charlie. These are your decisions to make. I am saying Sean needs someone who knows how to look out for him financially. Aside from that, well, I don't know."

The two men sat in silence while they finished their beers.

"Charlie, what made you want me as your manager and trainer?"

"I trusted you."

"Exactly. That's how Sean feels about you. He's only a boy. He's never been away from home, I'm sure, and never been offered an opportunity like you gave him last night, or what's happened since then. He's scared, Charlie, and he trusts you. Right now, you're the only person he knows in this game. You're a big name to him. He looks up to you. He sees how people respect you, your opinions. He knows he never would have been able to get on the card tonight if it hadn't been for you. It's only natural he wants you to stay with him.

"Now, whether or not you decide to go on a tour with him is entirely up to you, but you need to talk to Sean about the necessity of bringing someone on board who knows the business end of boxing. And if you decide to go with him, you'd better talk to Helen about it before you get married. You owe her that much. Let her decide if she wants to go through with the marriage knowing you'll be on the road for years. Don't dump that decision in her lap after you tie the knot. She'll hate you for the deceit, and I guarantee, you'll hate yourself as well.

"I should go see if those men finished everything for tonight. You all right?"

"I am. One more question, Joe. I know this is as bad a time for you as for me, what with your upcoming nuptials and all, but would *you* be willing to be the boy's manager?"

269

"No, Charlie. I'm done with living the life of the vagabond. And now I have Peggy to think about. Believe it or not, she means the world to me and I wouldn't hurt her for all the tea in China. She's expecting a home and a full-time husband. And I'm ready to give her that, and to give myself the luxury of a nice easy chair, slippers, and the newspaper at the end of the day. That's my future, Charlie. You have to decide what you want yours to be. See you tonight." He patted Charlie on the shoulder and walked back to the gym.

Charlie sat at the table for a while longer.

Joe's a lucky man. He doesn't have to look Sean in the eye tonight and make a decision that will change the boy's life forever.

"Another beer, sir?"

"No, just the check."

Charlie left the pub and walked downtown. Lost in his own thoughts, he found himself in front of the Settlement House.

I didn't realize I'd walked so far. What do I say to the boy? Either way I go, it'll break someone's heart. But which way will break mine?

Joe waited for Peggy outside Bellevue, as usual. He watched her as she skipped down the steps and hurried toward him.

"Peggy, you're a marvel," Joe said, patting her hand. "I don't know how you have such energy after the hours you put in on your feet. Now tell me about your day."

They strolled, arm in arm, downtown, then across town to Peggy's apartment.

"We're here. This is where I live, remember?"

"I do. Why don't I come upstairs with you, say hello to your parents, before I take you to dinner? It might be a

270

good idea for them to get used to me, a little at a time, before we get married."

"You don't think they'll have any objections to you, do you?"

"Well... I'm closer to your father's age than yours. And that might be a problem. Or, at least, raise a few eyebrows."

"Really? Do you think your age will bother them? It doesn't bother me."

"Even so... maybe we'd better keep this under wraps for a while."

"Okay. If you think that's best." Peggy bounded up the stairs to her apartment.

"Mom, Dad, look who's here," she said as Joe came in behind her. "You remember Joe Hayes, don't you?"

"Of course, we do," Aggie said. "We're not that far gone, you know."

"Joe, good to see you," Paddy said, rising to shake his hand. "And what would be bringing you down here?"

"I met Peggy after work and we wound up talking and found ourselves here."

"Anyway," Peggy said, "Joe wants to take me to dinner. He's anxious to hear about my day. Is it all right?"

Aggie looked at Paddy. Unspoken questions filled the air between them.

"It's kind of you to take an interest in our Peggy, I'm sure," Paddy said. "She'll talk your ear off though, she will. Once she gets started on all that hospital mumbo-jumbo, she forgets that not everyone finds it the fascinating place she does. Is that not right, Aggie love?"

"Aye. Maybe a night out will do her some good. It's too caught up she is with all that. Now you two go off and have a wee bit of fun for a change. Have you your key, love? That way, I'll not have to wait up for you to come home."

271

"I do, Mom. Thank you, Dad."

"I won't keep her out too late," Joe said.

"Och, go enjoy yourselves," Paddy said. "It's good to see the young folks having a bit of fun, is it not, Aggie? I remember when we were young and enjoyed a night in town once in a while."

"Do you remember that far back?" Aggie asked. "It's been an age since I thought about the dancing and the music back home."

Peggy looked at Joe and silently mouthed, "Let's go."

"Good to see you both," Joe said. "Ready, Peggy?" He shook Paddy's hand and nodded his head to Aggie.

Once outside, Peggy said, "Well done, Joe. Once they start talking about 'back home' they can go on for hours."

"I know. My parents were the same way. Now, how about we try that place your young admirer wanted to take you?"

"The Ruc?"

"That's it. I couldn't remember the name. The Ruc it is." Joe hailed a cab and they headed uptown.

The cab stopped in front of a building with a wine-colored awning that extended from the townhouse wall to the curb, "The Ruc," emblazoned on the side in bright white letters.

Joe bounded down the few steps to the door and held it open. "After you."

Peggy led the way into a brightly lit room. The closely packed tables were covered with bright floral tablecloths and candles burned in red globed lamps on each one.

"I can help you?" The maître d' asked a heavy Germanic accent giving his ancestry away.

"May we sit in the garden?" Peggy asked

"Ja, this way please." He led them through the dining room and out into a backyard fantasy land. There were three dining tiers. Placed on the ground in front of each tier were flower boxes that spread across the garden with only a narrow space in the middle for access. Trees throughout the yard provided shade and lanterns hung from the branches. At the back of the garden was a platform set with music stands and chairs. The maître d' led them to the middle tier and stopped at the table set under a large elm tree. "This is good, no?"

"This is lovely," Peggy said. "Thank you."

He pulled out a chair for her.

"Joe, this is breathtaking. It's like being in the country."

They looked over the menus the maître d' had left with them. and ordered dinner.

While they waited for their food, Peggy asked, "So, what did you do today?"

"It's a long story. Let's start with last night. While you were taking care of that idiot, Mickey, I thought about Lou and the bind he was in. I thought maybe Charlie could fill in for Mickey last night. So, I gave him a call."

"I remember you told me you called Charlie."

"But... what I didn't tell you was that Charlie had a better idea. He suggested substituting a young man, Sean, he's been working with at the Settlement House. He's good but he still needs some training. I've watched him once or twice. Reminds me a lot of Charlie at his age, all fisticuffs, no style, no discipline. I agreed that maybe a real boxing match would be good for him. See if he means to stay in the game or not. If it worked out, he could headline tonight. Give him some exposure.

"I didn't know how it went last night until I talked to Charlie today. Turns out, a big fight promoter offered to sponsor him and Lou agreed to put him on tonight's card, so I've spent the day getting trainers and managers to come and take a look at him. It could be the opportunity of a lifetime for the boy. Up-and-coming star, so to speak.

273

"Today, Charlie told me Sean was terrific last night. According to Charlie, 'Danced around the other guy for the first two rounds, just like I told him to. Got to give the folks a bit of a show, I told him. It won't do to knock him out too soon, I told him. And he listened. Took a few punches, but nothing he couldn't shake off. Bided his time. Then when he saw the other guy starting to drop his defenses, he went in for the final blow. Knocked him out clean as could be.' Charlie was awfully proud of him.

"I was planning to take you to Stillman's tonight to see Sean fight the main event. Lou likes the boy, and he's invited some newspaper men to come see him. Now wouldn't it be great if Sean could get started in a whole new career all because of Mickey being an ass, if you'll forgive the expression."

"You love the 'game,' as you call it, don't you?"

"I do. I'll never lie to you about that."

"And do you miss not being a part of it anymore?"

"No, love. I'm getting a bit too old to be tramping all over the country, and Europe, again. It was fun when I started out, but that was long ago. No, it was taking me too long to recover from long bus and train rides, and there were too many aches every morning getting out of bed. It's time for me to settle down for good. And I still get a taste of it with this job. I can find new talent and still give these youngsters a few tips. I can usually see them winding up for the roundhouse punch long before it comes. They haven't learned the fine art of faking and feinting yet. If I can show them a few tricks then I'm happy with what I'm doing here. It's great seeing the young ones, like Sean, take an interest in working hard to get somewhere. I truly enjoy that. But, if we're going to see him in action, we'd better get moving."

Joe signaled the waiter for the check and they left for Stillman's.

Across town, Helen and Charlie waited for a cab.

"I didn't know we were going to Stillman's tonight. You never told me this morning."

"I didn't because I didn't know it myself until that telephone call. Ah, great, here's a cab." Once they were settled inside, he said, "You remember, don't you? Just before you left—"

"I remember, now get on with it."

"The call was from Tex Hardiman." He told her the whole story, including his conversation with Joe. "There it is, sweetheart. What do you think?"

Aside from fidgeting with her purse, Helen hadn't moved a muscle since they entered the cab.

I knew it. I knew this whole dream of mine was too good to be true. He lights up whenever he talks about boxing. That's his first love. I'll always only be second. Why did I ever let myself believe that he'd be happy outside the boxing ring?

"Sweetheart? No opinion?"

Helen gave him a resigned smile. "It sounds like a wonderful opportunity for Sean. He's a very lucky boy."

"A talented boy. There's no such thing as luck when you're standing in front of a guy who wants nothing more than to beat you to a pulp. But what do you think I should say to him?"

"This is your decision to make. I won't tell you what to do. You have to decide for yourself."

Then I'll have to decide whether or not I still want to marry you.

The cab stopped at Stillman's. "Come on, sweetheart. I'll get you settled, then go find Sean."

"Okay, Charlie."

What is he going to do? Why won't he say anything?

275

Helen had barely sat down when the gym door opened and Joe and Peggy breezed in. Peggy babbling away about something and Joe absorbed in every word.

They really are in love. I can see it in Joe's eyes and Peggy's glowing face. I didn't see that look in Charlie's eyes tonight. Maybe I haven't for a while. Maybe I'm fooling myself in thinking he wants to be married as much as I do. I don't know if I can stay here tonight. I feel like I'm waiting for the executioner to appear and tell me it's time.

"Helen," Peggy cried from across the room. She rushed over to her sister. "Joe didn't tell me you and Charlie would be here."

"Charlie's protégé, Sean, is fighting tonight, again."

"Joe told me. What an opportunity for him. He must be thrilled."

Helen gave her sister a weak smile. "I'm sure he is."

"Helen, what's the matter? Something's not right."

"It's nothing, Peggy," she said, patting her sister's hand. "Nothing at all."

"Well then, you two ladies have a little chat while I go find Sean and Charlie. One of us will come get you seated up front when it's time for the fight."

"Joe, tell Charlie, I want to go home." Helen stood and grabbed her purse and gloves.

"What?! Don't you want to meet Sean, at least?"

"No, I... I . . ." Helen started to cry, and ran to the ladies' washroom.

"I'll see to her," Peggy said. "You go do whatever you have to right now. I won't let her leave before Charlie has a chance to talk to her again."

"Thanks, Peggy. I'll be back in a minute." He headed for the lockers.

"Helen, what's all this about?" Peggy asked.

276

"It's Charlie. I think he's going to go on the road with Sean. And he swore he wouldn't."

"You *think?* All this hysteria because you *think* he's going on the road?"

"He was talking about it in the cab on the way down here. He lied to me."

"Did he actually tell you he was going on the tour with Sean?"

"I'm... I'm not sure. I was so upset. I don't think I was listening very carefully."

Peggy folded her arms across her chest and tapped her foot on the floor. "I thought Carolyn was the drama queen, but you take the cake. At the very least, you need to talk to him and let him explain the whole situation. Do you think you can do that?"

Helen blew her nose, wiped her eyes, and looked at Peggy who stood there with eyebrows raised and mouth drawn in a tight line.

"I guess."

"Good. About time you started acting sensible again. Let's get outside."

Joe burst into the dressing room, "Where's Charlie?"

"I don't know," Sean said. "He said he had some things to take care of and he'd see me in a few minutes."

Joe ran his fingers through his hair and paced across the room.

"Is something wrong?"

"It seems Helen's not feeling well and he's got to take her home."

"And miss my fight?" Sean asked. He began to tremble all over. "I don't think I can go out there without him."

"Without who?" Charlie asked, coming into the room.

277

"You."

"Can't you just put her in a cab or something? I need you in my corner, Charlie."

Joe told Charlie about Helen feeling ill and wanting to go home.

Charlie looked hard at Sean.

"Sean, you know I think you can handle yourself in the ring. You do know that, don't you?"

"Yeah."

"Well then, you can do it whether or not I'm there. Listen to me. I may have shown you a few tricks, but where Tex wants to take you is far beyond what I can teach you."

"I don't understand."

"Here, give me your hands and let's get you wrapped up while we talk." Charlie grabbed the cloth strips and began wrapping Sean's hands. "It's like this, Sean, I'd be doing you a disservice if I was to go on the road with you."

"No, Charlie, you wouldn't."

"Let me finish. It's all well and good for me to go down to the Settlement House and teach you boys a bit of how to defend yourself, or throw a proper uppercut, but that's about as far as my talents go. Tex wants to put you into a world of boxing that I only dreamed about."

"You were a champ, Charlie."

"In my own head only, Sean. I never did get to fight for the title. I guess, truth be told, I was never ready, never quite good enough. Almost, but not there. Maybe I didn't work hard enough for it. I don't know. But that's in the past. What we're talking about is *your* future. You've got the makings of a champ, Sean. I can see the hunger in your eyes, and the power in your punch. And with Tex behind you, you'll be the main event on every card in no time."

"And you'll be there with me, right, Charlie?"

278

"This is what I'm coming to, Sean. I can't take you there. You need a real trainer now. Someone who knows how to make you great. That's not me."

"But—"

"Not another word until I've had my say. A real trainer can spot the mistakes you're *going* to make before you make them, and he can tell you what to do so you don't do it again. I can't do that. I can *see* what you're doing wrong, but I can't see *why* you keep doing it. A real trainer can. And you need a manager. I don't know my ass from my elbow about contracts. Joe always saw to them. I just signed where he told me to. Now, I'm not saying Tex is a shyster or anything like that, but he'll look out for his own interests before yours. So, you need a good manager to look over this agreement he's offering before you sign anything. Believe me, Sean, I'd love to be with you on this tour, for I know in my heart and soul, you'll be a great success. But I wouldn't be doing you any good."

Charlie finished wrapping Sean's hands, not daring to look into the boy's face where silent tears rolled down his cheeks.

"I'm scared, Charlie."

Charlie finally looked at him. "Not of that overweight punch-drunk clod you're fighting tonight, are you? And look at you. You're sweating so much, it's running down your face." He wiped Sean's face with a towel. "I'll bet that brawler won't be standing after the third round."

"The second," Sean said, and they both laughed.

"Now, I spoke with Joe today, and I think he may have some trainers and managers in mind for you. Would you speak to him about them?"

"If that's what you want me to do."

"It is."

"Okay, Joe, Sean's ready to talk to you about getting a real trainer and manager."

279

"That's fine, Sean. I got in touch with some friends of mine and after the bout, they're going to come back here and talk to you. So, you'd better give them a good show tonight."

"I will, Joe. I won't let you, or Charlie, down."

"Great. Now, Joe, could you put Sean's gloves on? I don't know what the problem is with Helen, but I need to see her."

"Sure, go ahead. I'll see to Sean, and we'll see you at ringside?"

"I'll be there."

Charlie rushed back to the main room. Peggy and Helen sat, heads together, talking quietly.

At least she's talking, not crying from what I can see. I don't know what came over the girl. I'll probably never understand her, but I'm going to spend the rest of my life trying.

"There you are, sweetheart. Feeling better?" Helen looked at Charlie with such despair that his heart almost split in two. "What is it, sweetheart? I'm beginning to think boxing doesn't agree with you."

"It's not boxing, Charlie. It's you."

"Me?" Charlie's heart pounded and his skin turned clammy. In barely a whisper, he asked, "Are you saying you don't love me?"

"No, Charlie. I love you more than anything, but you don't seem to love me. At least not enough to walk away from Sean, and Stillman's, and all they represent. I don't want to be the second love in your life. I want to be the first love in someone's life. I thought I was, but after tonight, I can see I'm not. So, I release you from your promise to me. You can go on tour with Sean and not have to think about me, or what will happen when you come back, if you ever do. Now, if you'll get a cab for me, I'll go home."

280

Helen had not looked at Charlie once while she spoke. Now, when she looked up, she saw a smile twitching at the corners of his mouth. "Oh, sweetheart, you gave me quite a scare," he said and burst into a roar of laughter. He stood and pulled her up into his arms. "Now, don't pull a stunt like that on me again, do you hear me? I thought for a minute you were serious. You near gave me a heart attack."

"I am serious, Charlie."

"Oh sweetheart, sometimes you still act like a silly little girl who didn't get her way and is going to stand around with her bottom lip puffed out pouting like a spoiled child." He shook his head and sat Helen back in her chair. "Listen to me, sweetheart, for I'm not going to go over this every time you get it in your head that I'm choosing something over you. You are my first and only love. I've loved you since the day we met. I don't know why, but there it is, and I can't see that changing for the rest of my life."

"But you love boxing more."

"No, sweetheart. I love boxing. I do. But I love it like I love lemon cake or stew. But boxing can't love me back, and believe me, it hasn't, but I still love it. There's nothing wrong with that. It doesn't mean I don't love you. When are you going to get that through that thick Irish skull of yours?"

"But Sean, and his tour."

"He'll be going with a real trainer and manager. I had a long talk with him tonight. I won't say he's totally happy with my decision, but he's young. He'll see some day that I'm right." Charlie put a finger under Helen's chin and lifted her face to look at him. "Did you think I'd give you up to go on tour with Sean, sweetheart? Is that what this was all about?"

281

"Yes, Charlie. When you told me about Sean, you didn't sound very sure about which way you wanted to go, with him or with me. I figured if you were that confused, then you must love boxing more than me, and if that was the case, then I decided to break our engagement even though it broke my heart."

"Oh, sweetheart, I'm sorry. I never meant for it to sound that way. I was only telling you what had gone on so you'd know why we were here tonight. I wanted you to tell me how I could let Sean know I wouldn't be going with him, but you didn't hear that, did you?"

"No."

"You were too busy drawing conclusions about me wanting to be back on the road to really listen to what I was saying."

"Maybe."

"What am I going to do with you, sweetheart?" Charlie sighed and ran his fingers through his hair.

"Mr. Charlie," a young boy called from the doorway to the locker room, "Mr. Joe's waiting for you."

"Tell him I'll be right there." He turned back to Helen. "Will you come ringside and watch Sean with me, or are you going to sit here against the wall all night and pout?"

Helen looked up and saw a familiar mischievous twinkle in Charlie's eyes. "I'll come with you, you big... you big... oh, whatever you are."

Charlie's booming laugh filled the room.

"Gentlemen," Lou said, "and ladies." He nodded his head to the two seated at ringside. "Tonight, we have a repeat performance by young Sean Cassidy. If you were here last night, you witnessed a champ in the making. He's captured the eye of none other than Tex Hardiman. Tex, get up here and let the crowd see you."

Tex bounded through the ropes and walked around the ring, waving to the audience whose hoots and cheers became a deafening roar.

"Who's that?" Peggy yelled in Helen's ear.

"He's a big fight promoter."

"And we have sports writers from our finest newspapers here tonight too, folks," Lou continued after Tex left the ring. "This is going to be an eventful night. So, without any further ado, let's get these two pugilists up here."

The two fighters entered the ring. Lou introduced each one and they took their turn around the canvas. From the minute the bell rang, Sean was on offense. He sized up his opponent with flutter punches, but never let the other man touch him. Between rounds Charlie and Joe gave him instructions and pointed out his opponent's weaknesses. Contrary to Sean's prediction, but true to Charlie's, the other fighter lay on his back, out for the count, in the third round.

Charlie glowed with pride when he came over to Helen. "Did you see him, sweetheart? Wasn't it a work of art? The way he took his time, countered every jab, until he had him right where he wanted him, then pow, the final blow. The boy's going places, that's for sure. It was a thing of beauty."

"Yes, Charlie," Helen said. "I watched it very carefully. You trained him well. You should be proud of him, and yourself."

"That I am, sweetheart. Proud as punch." Charlie couldn't stop grinning as he accepted congratulations from the men in the hall. "I just have to get Sean settled with some of the trainers who have come to see him."

"I'll take care of the ladies," Lou Stillman said, jumping down from the ring. "You go see to your boy, Charlie. I'll make sure they have whatever they need."

283

"Thanks, Lou. Would that be all right, sweetheart?"

"Yes, Charlie, go see to Sean. Thank you, Lou."

"My pleasure. It's not every day I get to spend time with two lovely ladies like yourselves. I have to take advantage of the opportunity. It's a privilege for me to have ladies come to a boxing match, so I want to make sure you enjoy every minute of your time here." They chatted for a few minutes, then Lou said he had to see to the men in the locker room.

"What a nice man," Peggy said. "I'm so happy Joe's working here. When I think of how grumpy some men can be, well . . ."

"Sean seems to be all set," Charlie said, plopping into the chair next to Helen. "Joe here did a great job of finding the best trainer and manager for him. They hit it right off."

"And I, for one, was glad to see that," Joe said. "You never know if two people are going to be able to work well together or not. But those two blended like cream in my coffee. You won't have to worry about Sean any longer. Gus'll take good care of him."

"I'm sure he will. I have to say, it's taken a weight off my mind. The boy was none too keen on me leaving him, you know. But that's all over and done with now. You have my thanks, Joe."

Joe smiled at his friend. "How did you ladies enjoy the fight?"

"It was wonderful, Joe," Peggy said, pulling her chair closer to his. "I could see how Sean listened to every word you said. You must be a wonderful trainer. But I'm glad it ended when it did. I wondered if I'd have to step in to care for the wounded. Joe, *is* a doctor standing by somewhere?"

"There is," Joe said. "But he's getting old, and he told me the other day that he's thinking he'd like to retire and go live in the country."

284

"What will you do if he does that?"

"I don't know, my love. We'll have to find someone to replace him."

"I think Peggy would be a great candidate," Charlie said.

"Me? Why me?"

"From what Joe told me about the way you handled Mickey the other day, I think you'd be able to hold your own with these bruisers. And they wouldn't be as likely to push you away when they need medical attention the way they do to the doc now."

"That's not a bad idea, Charlie. I'd have to run it by Lou, of course. But I don't think he'd object."

"Excuse me," Peggy said, "aren't you forgetting one teensy detail?"

The two men stared at her; their blank expressions mirrored their confusion.

"Does it matter at all, what *I* think of this idea? Do I get to have a say?"

"Of course, my love, of course you do. I just thought... well, I guess I didn't think, did I?"

"No, Joe, you didn't. Honestly. The two of you sit there and talk about me and my future like I'm not even here, or that it doesn't matter whether or not I *am* here. *You're* going to decide what's right for me. If you think I'm going to be the kind of wife who sits around like a toadstool and never utters my opinion, then you'd better think again. I thought you already knew that, Joe."

"I did. I made a mistake, Peggy. Forgive me. I would never presume to tell you what you should do with your doctoring. You know that. I got caught up in Charlie's idea and ran with it. I guess in one way, I pictured the two of us working here together and that made it seem like a wonderful idea. Forgive me?"

285

Joe held Peggy's hand between his two sausage fingered ones, and looked so abashed that only someone with a stone-cold heart could refuse his plea. Peggy did *not* qualify as that type of person.

"Sometimes you say the most inane things. And sometimes you say the most endearing things ever. Of course, I forgive you, you big buffoon."

Joe's smile lit up the entire room. He leaned over and gave Peggy a kiss on her forehead. "It won't happen again, my love."

For Joe and Peggy, the rest of the room disappeared. They sat entranced by each other. Charlie coughed.

"Oh right," Joe said, "we'd like you two to join us tonight. I planned on us going out for some champagne to toast our engagement."

"We'd love to. Right, Charlie?"

"Absolutely."

"It's settled then," Joe said. "We'll all go to the Copa. Do you remember that place, my love?"

"It's where we first met," Peggy said.

Joe beamed and patted her hand. "I think we'll need two cabs," he said.

CHAPTER TWENTY-TWO

Days later, Charlie and Helen sat on what had become their usual bench in Gramercy Park.

"It's so peaceful here," she said. "I can almost forget all my worries about Carolyn."

"How are your parents taking the whole mess?"

"Hard to tell with Dad. He still goes about his normal routine. You know, work, newspaper, occasional stop at the bar. Mom seems quieter these days, but at least now I don't see a tear or two rolling down her cheeks every time she sets the table."

"That's an improvement, I guess."

Helen stood and reached for Charlie's hand. "Let's walk around the park. Thinking about Carolyn has made me restless. I can't believe there's nothing we can do to get her away from that gangster."

He took her hand and they walked to the path that encircled the park. Many of the flowers were already blooming, so the grounds were a riot of colors.

"Say, I have an idea," he said. "Maybe this will take everyone's mind off Carolyn for a while. Why don't I take both our parents to dinner to celebrate our engagement? They've never met, and you haven't met my parents either. It would be a relaxed way for everyone to get to know each other before the wedding."

"That's a great idea, Charlie. Where and when?"

"How about the Old Homestead? It's not too far from where either of them lives. Let's invite Joe and Peggy too. They can fill in any awkward moments. They all know Joe and he's always good for a story or two."

"Perfect. Now, when?"

"How about a week from Saturday?"

"A week from this coming Saturday?"

"Why not? It's not like they need time to get ready."

"Right. It's just a casual dinner, and Dad likes to go watch the games in Gaelic Park on Sundays, so you never know what time he'll be home or what mood he'll be in depending on which team won."

"Then next Saturday it is."

"Terrific. Maybe this dinner will turn things around and get everyone out of their doldrums."

"Let's hope so."

They continued to stroll through the park, Helen in a much lighter mood than before. They started to talk about plans for their wedding. She knew they would have to see a priest at St. Columba's to arrange for their marriage banns to be announced at least three weeks before the ceremony, so she wanted to fix a date not too far in the future.

But the more they talked about it, the more problems and questions popped up. They had to think about how many people they could afford to invite to a reception, and where that would be. And, most importantly, where would they live after they were married?

Charlie said he'd be willing to go apartment hunting. He already had a few leads from some people at the

Settlement House where he still volunteered training kids who wanted to learn to box.

"But," Helen said, "I want to see the place."

"Don't worry. I won't sign anything until you say okay. But I can look, can't I?"

"That'd be great, but what if you find a place and they want us to take it right away?"

"Then we will. And I'll live there alone until we're married. In fact, that would work out even better. You can decorate and get it all fixed up the way you want before we move in together."

"I guess." Her hesitation put a frown on Charlie's face.

"You don't like the idea."

"It's just that I thought it'd be fun doing it together."

"It still will be. We *will* do it together. It's just that I'll be sleeping there, *alone* I might add, until we get married. Then... well . . ."

Helen's face turned beet red.

"Charlie, stop."

He pulled her close and kissed her. "You don't want me to sleep there alone forever, do you?"

"No, Charlie. Not at all."

CHAPTER TWENTY-THREE

Peggy watched Helen change her outfit for the third time since she'd come home from work. "You'll have to decide soon. Charlie and Joe will be here any minute."

"I just can't decide. I'm so nervous. What if his parents don't like me?"

"Of course, they'll like you. Everyone who meets you likes you. You're being ridiculous."

The doorbell rang and Helen jumped.

"I'll get it," Peggy yelled down the hall to her parents. "You look beautiful. Stop worrying."

Helen heard the two men at the door and smoothed down her skirt. She gave one final look in the mirror and left the bedroom.

"Gosh," Charlie said, "you look radiant. I'm some lucky man."

"That you are," Joe said. "Should we get this show on the road? Charlie, your parents are probably there already and we don't want them waiting for too long."

"I'm ready," Helen said.

"Give me a minute to grab my things," Peggy said.

The family started down the stairs while Joe waited on the landing for Peggy. After she locked the door behind her, he looked around to make sure no one could see them and gave Peggy a peck on her lips. She threw her arms around his neck and gave him a longer kiss back.

"There. That's better," she said, smiling up at him.

"You'd better get down those stairs young lady before I kidnap you and take you far away."

Laughing, she bounced down the three flights of stairs and out onto the sidewalk. The rest of the family had already started to walk down the street.

"Hey, Joe," Charlie called back to him, "I think we need two cabs."

"Right. You go with Helen and her parents. Peggy and I'll grab another one and be right behind you."

"Don't get lost."

The two cabs arrived at the restaurant within seconds of each other, so they all entered together. Charlie stopped at the podium, gave his name, and they followed the maître d' to the table where Charlie's parents were waiting, sipping their cocktails.

"Mom, Dad, this is Helen and her parents, Paddy and Aggie Campbell, and her sister, Peggy. You already know Joe."

Charlie's father stood and extended his hand to Paddy. "Good to meet you, mate. Please, call me Gilbert or Gil is fine too."

Paddy automatically shook his hand, but his mouth hung open. "You're a Brit."

"I am. We both are or at least we were before we became US citizens. Well, Rose," he said, looking down at his wife, "I guess I still don't sound like a real American."

"Aggie," Paddy said, "you can put your gloves back on. We won't be staying. Girls, you'll be coming with us. And Helen, we'll talk when we get home."

292

"Dad," Helen said, "what are you talking about?" She looked at him, her eyes wide, her forehead furrowed. Her mother had already started back up the aisle. Peggy just shrugged, equally puzzled by the sudden turn of events.

"Mr. Campbell," Charlie said, "I think you owe me and my parents an explanation."

"You certainly do, Dad. Mom come back here. Let's sit. We're creating a scene."

Aggie stood in the center of the room, clearly not knowing what to do.

"Dad, please," Helen said. "Sit." She pulled out a chair and glared at him. He shook his head. "Please." The word became an order, not a plea.

He lowered himself into the chair and Helen waved her mother back to the table. The rest of their group seated themselves in the empty spaces. Raised eyebrows, shrugged shoulders, heads shaking on all of them.

"Now," Helen said, "an explanation for your rude behavior." She stared at her father, then glanced around the table for a clue to his actions. But she met blank stares from everyone.

Paddy gave a long sigh. He looked at Charlie. "First off, I wish you had asked for her hand private like so we wouldn't have to discuss this in front of everyone. But you've chosen this path, so now I'll have my say."

Helen's heart sank. She knew her dad well, and he didn't say much unless he felt strongly about something. Then his words were, more often than not, ones of disapproval.

Please, Dad, don't ruin this night for me.

"I don't see how I can give this marriage my blessing. Since Helen's birth, I promised her, and Aggie, that I would protect her, keep her safe so to speak, and give her the best life I could. I can't see how being your wife will do that."

293

"But, Mr. Campbell—"

"Let me finish, Charlie. So far, you've lived a life of traveling and excitement. You've no home, and I don't think you'd be content staying in one place for long. My brother, Thomas, and I have worked with men who used to box, not at your level, but box they did. Now they're married and settled with wee ones at home and a regular job with wages coming in every week. And all they talk about are the fights they had. It's the only time there's a light in their eyes. The rest of their life they're only passing time. Now, I'm not saying they don't love their families, it's just their lives they don't love. They're restless, misplaced, so to speak. Do you see what I'm getting at, Charlie? I can't see you being happy joining me and my brother as a mason, and if you're not happy, Helen won't be either. That's one reason that's been on my mind ever since you've come calling on Helen. But now, there's another reason that's an even bigger impediment and it's one that you can't change. I'll not have a daughter of mine marrying a Brit."

"Dad! Charlie's an American. The same as me and Peggy and Joe. What are you talking about?"

Paddy looked at Helen, her face white, her eyes bright with tears. Aggie sat with her head bowed, hands folded in her lap. Paddy rested his forearms on the table and stared across it into Gil's eyes. "It wasn't that long ago that the likes of Mr. Sanders here and his mates, as he calls them, were killing my brother and cousins. Your uncle and cousins, Helen."

"Dad, what are you talking about? Mom, do you understand any of this?"

"I'm afraid I do, love. Your da's talking about the Rising."

"The what? The rising? What's that supposed to mean."

294

Gil leaned back in his chair and blew out a breath. Rose rubbed her forehead. "I had no part in that," he said. "In fact, I thought it was despicable."

"On whose part? Yours or ours?"

Gil shook his head. "We should go Rose and let these people eat their dinner in peace." He stood and reached for the back of her chair.

"Sit down, Dad," Charlie said. "No one's going anywhere until we get this ironed out. Mr. Campbell, it might interest you to know that at the time of the Easter Rising, which is what I believe you're referring to, my parents were already living here in New York. I'm a bit older than Helen, you know, and so they're just that much older than you. But you probably never gave that a thought, did you? You just stand behind an old worn-out prejudice against anyone and anything you consider British. Did you ever think that maybe my family lost relatives in that fight? Probably not. That wouldn't fit in with your perception of who was right and who was wrong. I'm not your enemy and neither are my parents. Ireland's been independent since 1922. Isn't it time to move on and stop bringing up old grievances?"

"Not for me, lad. Not when I watched my brother killed, and my uncles wounded. It'll never be time to move on until all of Ireland is free of the Brits and out from under their heel. And for that reason, I'll have to say no to your marriage. Let's go, Aggie. I thank you for the offer of dinner, Charlie, but I won't break bread with a Brit."

After their speeches, everyone at the table sat frozen, their eyes glued on the two men.

Paddy pushed his chair back and stood, waiting for Aggie.

No, no, this can't be happening. Why is Dad doing this? Mom, why don't you say something?

295

"Mr. Campbell," Charlie said, "I listened to you, and now I'd like you to do me the courtesy of hearing me out."

"That's fair," Paddy said, sitting back down.

"You said you wanted to protect Helen, to give her the best life you could. And you've done that. Now, I want to take over that job. I love her with all my heart. All I want is her happiness and I'll do everything in my power to give her that. If she had refused my proposal, I'd have walked away. I'd be a broken man for the rest of my life, but if that's what she wanted, I'd give it to her. But it's not what she wants. She wants to marry me as much as I do her. As far as the boxing goes, why Joe here will tell you, I'm getting a little long in the tooth for that. It's a young man's game. I always said if I wasn't ready for a title bout by the time I was forty, I'd quit the game. But then I thought about Helen." Charlie reached out and held onto her hand. "The first day I saw Helen in the park, I knew she was the one I wanted to spend the rest of my life with."

"And what do you plan on doing with your life now?" Paddy asked.

"You know, sometimes luck even comes to someone like me. I've accepted a position as Boxing Coach of the New York Athletic Club."

"Helen told us that and that's all to the good," Paddy said, "but I wonder if you won't be getting itchy feet and be wanting to get out on the road and back in the ring before too long."

"I wouldn't do anything that would make Helen lonely or unhappy. Can't you see? This is the best of all worlds. I'll be teaching young men how to box. Getting in a few jabs myself, now and then. Keeping up with all the latest techniques. And, most important of all, I'll have Helen to go home to every night. And I've spoken to the director of the Hudson Guild Settlement House and told him I'd like to continue my work with some of the young kids there. In my free time, that is."

"And you'll not be missing the excitement?"

"Ah, that. Let me share a little secret with you, Mr. Campbell. If it wasn't for the money I've been able to put aside, I would've quit a long time ago. There's no excitement in traveling from town to town, staying in rundown hotels, eating terrible food, and finding time to train from dawn to dusk. Is there, Joe?"

"I'll agree with you there, Charlie. Life on the road is hard and not for the faint of heart. I'll be glad to settle down now and live out the rest of my life in one place."

Charlie smiled at his best friend. "That's what I'm looking forward to myself. With Helen by my side the whole time. She's as precious to me as my very soul."

Paddy stared down at the table and fiddled with his teaspoon. Everyone else held their breath waiting for him to speak.

Dad, say something, Helen thought. *I can't stand this waiting.* She looked over to her mother, her eyes pleading for her to say something. But Aggie never looked up.

"Dad, please say yes. I love Charlie. He's thought of everything. He has a steady job now, and just before we got here, he told me he found an apartment for us."

Everyone's head snapped up at that news.

"An apartment?" Aggie asked.

"Yes, Mom. On 12th Street. We're going to go look at it tomorrow. Isn't that wonderful? I won't be so far away that I can't walk over to visit and have a cup of tea with you. And you can help me pick out curtains and furniture and everything. You too, Mrs. Sanders."

"Slow down, girl. I haven't said yes yet," her father said. The overwhelming tension at the table made everyone uncomfortable. Charlie squeezed Helen's hand.

297

Rose folded and unfolded her napkin. Gil sat, hands clasped on the table, eyes fixed on Paddy. Aggie reached out to rub her hand over Paddy's fists. Joe looked around at the other diners.

If he doesn't say something soon, I think Charlie will break into a thousand pieces, or break the table into a thousand pieces. "Dad?"

Paddy looked at Helen. "Is this truly what you want, girl?"

"It is, with all my heart."

"I need to think this over a bit. I'll not say yes to you right now, Charlie. I'll consider all you've said. *But* I'll say this to you right now, if I do decide to give my blessing there's one fact I want you to know. If you ever do anything to cause her a day of worry, or make her unhappy, it will be your last day on this earth."

"Don't worry yourself about that, Mr. Campbell. For that day will never come." Charlie lifted Helen's hand to his lips and kissed it.

"Aggie, get your things. We'll be leaving now."

Aggie leaned over to kiss Helen on the cheek. "I'll speak to him when we get home, love," she whispered in her ear.

"Aggie."

"I'm *coming*, Paddy. Just saying goodbye to Helen."

The couple left the restaurant, but no one else moved an inch, except for Charlie and Helen. She dabbed at the corner of her eyes and sniffled, while he rapped his knuckles on the table so furiously, she thought he'd break it in half. She reached over and placed her hand over his. "Mom's going to talk to him. It'll all work out, Charlie."

"Personally, I don't give a shit whether or not he gives us his blessing."

"Charles Sanders, your language," Rose said.

298

"You're not in the gym with your other boxing mates, Charles," Gil said. "Apologize to your mother, Peggy, and Helen."

Charlie mumbled an apology, then said, "Helen, as far as I'm concerned, we pledged ourselves to each other the day you agreed to marry me, and I'm holding you to that promise unless you tell me right now that you've changed your mind. You're a grown woman who should be able to choose a husband for herself, not wait and let her father decide who's best for her. So, I'm asking you again, do you want to marry me or not? If you say no, I'll leave here and never bother you again. But I'm not going to let one man's fool ideas about my future plans and his prejudices stand in the way. What do you say, sweetheart?"

Helen sat staring at Charlie. "I think I've spent my whole life waiting to meet someone like you, Charlie. And my happiest day was when you asked me to marry you. I've also spent my life obeying my father. Now I have to choose between you." She looked away and bit down on her lower lip. The knuckles on Charlie's clenched fists were as white as the tablecloth. Helen looked back at Charlie, "And I know what I want the rest of my life to be. I made my promise then, and I won't take it back now. Yes, Charlie. I will marry you with or without Dad's blessing."

The tension at the table burst like a pricked balloon,

"I think we'll be leaving too," Gil said. "I can't say I feel much differently about this marriage than Mr. Campbell does. When someone's as prejudiced against the English as he is, he'll never accept you into the family and he'll make your lives a living hell. And as nice a young lady as Helen seems to be, I can't believe she hasn't been infected with at least some of the same feelings."

299

"But Dad, you've barely spoken to Helen, much less gotten to know her."

"Helen," Gil said, "did you even know Charles was a Brit before today?"

"No, I didn't. But I don't see what difference it makes. I love him and he loves me. I don't care what country his ancestors came from. Charlie's an American and so am I."

"Your parents don't seem to think the same way. Charles, I'm afraid marriage is out of the question."

"Dad, you're being unfair to Helen and to me. Mom? Don't you have something to say?"

"I think your father's right, Charles," Rose said. "I'm sure you'll find someone else somewhere down the road After all it doesn't look like this marriage will ever happen. And maybe that's all for the best."

Charlie clenched his fists and his face turned red. "I don't plan on meeting someone else somewhere down the road. I love Helen and I'm going to marry her come hell or high water. And we'll do it whether her parents approve or you two or anyone else on this planet."

Gil stood. "I'm sorry to hear you feel that way. It's never a good idea to divorce your families just to take on a new one. Ready Rose?"

Rose nodded. Together, they looked at Charlie, sorrow etched on their faces.

Everyone watched them leave. No one spoke. Charlie's face went from red to ash grey.

"I can't believe them. They're just as pigheaded as your dad," he said, looking at Helen.

"They'll all come around. I'm sure of it," Helen said, rubbing his arm.

Charlie shook his head, "I doubt it."

CHAPTER TWENTY-FOUR

"Well, Paddy, have you had a chance to think things over on the way home?" Aggie asked as she climbed the stairs to their apartment.

"Aye, I have."

"And?"

"I don't know, Aggie. I just don't know."

"Hmph. You don't know," she said as she unlocked the door and walked into their apartment. "But you're willing to sacrifice our Helen's happiness because you think that maybe, just maybe, Charlie isn't ready to settle down. Is that what you're telling me?"

"Well . . ."

"Don't you 'well' me, Paddy Campbell. For that's exactly what you're doing." Aggie slammed the kettle down onto the stove so hard Paddy jumped in his chair

"I'll tell you something now I've never told you before." Aggie tied on her apron and slapped plates and cups onto the kitchen table causing Paddy to wince with each collision. "When I knew for sure you were going to ask to marry me, I asked my mam if da would say yes. I can tell you right now, it's shocked I was when she sighed and said, 'He won't agree to the match'."

"What? He agreed right off, he did, with never a moment's hesitation. Are you telling me a tale, Aggie?"

Hands on her hips, she threw down the tea towel she had been holding and said, "When have I ever told you a tale? After all our years together, do you think I'm about to start now?"

Paddy looked down at the table and mumbled, "Go on then."

"As I was saying, my da didn't approve of your ideas about going off to America. He thought you had big pipe dreams of finding your fortune here and when that didn't come true, as he was sure it wouldn't, you'd climb into the bottle leaving me and whatever wee ones we had to fend for ourselves. He was convinced I'd be better off marrying one of the local lads who was content to stay on the farm and wasn't always off dreaming of situations above his station in life." Aggie poured the brewed tea into their cups. She turned back to the stove, cracked some eggs into a frying pan, scrambled them up, looked over her shoulder to Paddy, and said, "Is all this sounding familiar to you? Or is there no sense left in your head at all?"

Elbows on the table, Paddy covered his face with his hands.

"If you want your eggs, you're going to have to move your elbows off the table."

Paddy straightened in his chair while Aggie ladled out their impromptu dinner. She sat down opposite him, grabbed a slice of bread from the loaf on the table, and pounded a wad of butter onto it.

"Why have you never told me this before?" he asked so softly she almost didn't hear him.

"And what good would that have done? You'd have spent our days together determined to prove my da wrong, the whole time feeling angry and misjudged. Instead, we've had a fine life. Raised three good lasses, even if one of them has gone astray a little, and we've not wanted for food on the table or a place to lay our heads. Why would I have wanted you to keep thinking you should be doing more if only to show my da, long gone now, that he was wrong about you? No, Paddy, that would have been no way to live our lives together. And you wouldn't have known to this day if you weren't being so pigheaded about Charlie."

She chomped down on her bread and shoveled a forkful of eggs into her mouth. "Are you going to be eating your dinner, or did I make it only to waste my time?"

Paddy put a bit of egg onto his fork, but stopped halfway to his mouth. He lowered the fork back to his plate. "Even if he believes he's given up the boxing for good, he's still a Brit. I don't think I can get over that."

"There is that. But don't you think it might be time to bury the dead and get on with life. Letting this eat your insides up isn't doing anyone any good. You heard Charlie. His parents weren't even in England when the Rising was going on. And our girls are Americans. They don't hold the same feelings for the Brits that we do. We raised them not to. We never talked about it and there's no reason for any one of them not to fall in love with a boy whose family happened to be born in England."

Paddy stared out the window and sipped on his tea. "I don't know Aggie. I just don't know."

"I'll tell you what I do know. If you keep up with your stubborn ways, you'll chase Helen away from us. For there's no way she can choose between Charlie and us, and seeing the way she looks at him, we're not going to be her choice. Then she'll be left with no family to turn to when things don't go right. And mark my words, there will

303

be those times ahead, for no married couple escapes them."

She thought back on their first days in America when they were staying with Paddy's brother, Thomas, and his wife, Kathleen.

"What are you thinking of?" Paddy asked.

"Just remembering the night you told me about the first apartment you rented for us."

"Aye, things didn't go right for us that night, I remember."

"If it hadn't been for Kathleen, I don't think we'd be sitting here together today."

Paddy picked up his cup of tea and sat staring into it.

"So, are you going to tell me what it is you're thinking about this marriage now?"

"Same as I was thinking at the restaurant when I said my piece."

"About his boxing? He told you he's given it up. Taken a position at the New York Athletic Club. Going to work with some of the young lads who come to the settlement house. He's even found an apartment for him and Helen."

"Aye, he did. And maybe he'll be content for a while, but I'm worried that won't last. Before long, he'll tire of teaching the toffs at that club how to box. For they're not serious about it anyway. It's just sport to them, like playing golf, or any of the other silly games they fill their time with. Then he'll be looking for some real excitement. He'll think about his boxing and be sorry he walked away from it. And if he doesn't go back in the ring, he'll lose his spirit, what little might be left in him. If he does go back, where will our Helen be? Will she be traveling around the country with him? Maybe with a wee one in tow? Or will she stay home, alone, never knowing when, or if, he'll come back? And when he realizes he's old and washed up, what kind of man will he be then? A useless, broken-down failure. No good to anyone. Is that what we want for our Helen? And I still don't know if I can get over him being a Brit. It goes against every fiber of my soul. And when I think about my own brother, lying there in the street, his life bleeding out of him, I don't know how I can accept a Brit in our family. I don't think I can agree to this marriage at all."

"What if they've already been to see the priest, Paddy."

"They've not said their vows, have they? Then it's not too late."

"Paddy Campbell, I don't know why you feel ruining our Helen's life will somehow avenge your brother's death, but I'll not have you taking away the happiness I saw on her face when she told me about this marriage."

She looked over at Paddy's plate and saw he hadn't eaten a bite. "Give me your plate and I'll heat those eggs back up for you. Or should I take this perfectly good food and toss it in the trash?"

"No, I'll eat. Thank you, love," he said, handing her his plate.

"Don't go thinking I'm going to do this every day for you. You'll eat the food when it's given or you'll eat it cold. Do you hear me?"

"Aye, and it's right you are."

"It's only that it's a sin to waste good food."

Paddy smiled a little at Aggie's back, and was still smiling when she turned around to put his re-warmed eggs on the table.

"What's that silly grin for?"

"For the woman I love who's kept me out of my own trouble all these years. You're a wonder, Aggie."

305

"Go on with you. Now eat those eggs before they're as useless as your arguments against Charlie. It's only the thought of losing our Helen that's got you into this state. But the girls are all grown up now, Paddy. And they have to make their own lives whether or not we like it. For sure, they'll make their mistakes, and we'll be there for them when they do, but we have to let them make those mistakes. We can't keep protecting them from everything. They won't put up with it. We agreed, long ago, to let them have their own minds and make their own choices. And now that they do, you don't like it. Well, get used to it, for it's too late to change them now."

Paddy ate the last of his eggs, took a sip of his tea, and said, "It's right you are, Aggie. I wanted them to stand on their own, and now that they do, I'm thinking I don't like it very much."

"A bit late for that kind of thinking, love. Once the horses have left the barn . . ."

"Aye."

They sat at the table, not talking, for a while longer.

Aggie took their empty plates to the sink and turned to face Paddy. "I don't want to talk about this anymore right now. Tonight, think over what you're doing to our daughter and we can talk about it tomorrow, if you still have your doubts. But I'll tell you this, Paddy Campbell, I've lost one daughter already. I've no intention of losing another. For as sure as I'm standing here, Helen *will* marry Charlie with or without your blessing. And I for one, will be at her wedding."

Paddy stared at her, mouth agape, eyes wide for a few seconds before Aggie stormed down the hall to their bedroom.

CHAPTER TWENTY-FIVE

After both sets of parents left, the waiter asked if they'd like to order dinner.

"I'd rather have a drink than dinner," Helen said. "My stomach feels like it's doing somersaults."

"Drinks are an excellent idea," Charlie said and Peggy and Joe agreed. "Here or somewhere else?"

"Let's walk down to the White Horse," Joe said. "It's a good ole hard core drinking saloon."

"Sounds dangerous," Peggy said, wiggling her eyebrows up and down, a twinkle in her eyes.

Joe stared at her. "Hmm. Maybe you don't need to have a drink."

She slapped his shoulder. "Only teasing. C'mon, let's go."

"Soon as we pay the check, m'dear," Joe said.

"Oh right. I forgot about that little detail."

The check called for and paid, they left for the White Horse. Walking down Hudson Street, Helen pulled on Charlie's arm to slow him down.

"Let them get a little ahead of us. I want to talk to you."

Charlie frowned, but Helen raised her finger to her lips. They paused at a shop admiring the artwork displayed in the window and let Peggy and Joe get about a block away before resuming their walk.

"I thought it might be better if Peggy doesn't hear my idea since she can't seem to keep secrets from our mother,"

"What are you up to, Helen?"

"Just this. We want to get married, right?"

"Right."

"Okay. Then what are we waiting for? My father is never going to agree to it. I could see that as soon as he started talking about the Rising. He hates the British and he'll never change his mind. He's one of the men who proudly marches up Fifth Avenue on St. Pat's Day holding an 'England Get Out of Ireland' banner."

Charlie shook his head.

"But I really don't care about that or how he feels about your family. The only person I care about is you and our happiness. So... I've been thinking—"

"I could smell the wood burning."

"Anyway... here goes nothing." She looked to the sky and exhaled a long breath. "I want us to elope."

Charlie stopped dead in his tracks, and almost knocked Helen off her feet since her arm was looped through his.

"Elope? But... but . . ."

"Before you tell me to get lost, hear me out."

"Go ahead."

They started walking again, much slower now.

"You once said you have a friend with a car. Maybe he'd let you borrow it tomorrow and we can drive up to

308

Rhode Island. It's not that far. We'll track down a Justice of the Peace, get married, then drive home."

"No priest? I thought you always said if we don't get married by a priest, it's like not really being married at all."

"Well... I've changed my mind. Think of all the couples who aren't Catholic. They didn't have a priest marry them."

"True, but they're not Catholic."

"We can always have a priest marry us after the civil ceremony. In fact, that's a great idea. We'll go right to the nearest rectory and ask the priest to marry us. How about that?"

Charlie walked along debating all the pros and cons of her scheme in his head.

"Helen, have you thought this through? I mean, this goes against all your rules. It defies your father and everything you've been brought up to believe. If we do this, it might mean you'll be disowned by your family. You might not ever see your mother or father again. Is that what you really want?"

"I can't say it's the best of all worlds, but my father created this situation. If it means choosing between them and you, I'll always choose you, Charlie. Once we're married, you'll be my family. Make no mistake about that. And I don't believe my mother will walk away from me, or us. If she does, then that's her choice, not mine. As far as my father's concerned, I can't live my life according to his prejudices. If he wants to live in the past, let him. I won't let the past control my future."

"You're full of surprises. And I do love you. But since you're committed to the idea, why can't we get married here? Why do we have to drive to Rhode Island? Why two ceremonies?"

"In New York, after we apply for a marriage license, we have to wait for a day or two before we can get married. But there's no waiting time in Rhode Island. And we need a Justice of the Peace because, as a state official, he can give us a license. The priest can't."

Charlie stopped again and stared at her open-mouthed. "Helen Campbell, how long have you been plotting this out?"

Helen looked down the street and pulled at her gloves. "I had a feeling my father didn't approve of you. I could never understand why, but it was there. Something in my gut that told me he just didn't like you, or trust you, or something. And tonight, he proved me right. He never liked the fact that you were a boxer. I overheard him tell mom that fact the day you guys told us about your plan to meet up with Carolyn. He just doesn't believe you've given it up for good. The fact that your parents are English was just the icing on the cake."

He looked at her out of the corner of his eye. "I think it was more than that. Were you looking at him when he was speaking? I think if he could have, he'd have killed all of us Sanders right then and there."

Helen started walking again. "He was pretty worked up. I don't think I've ever seen him that angry, or heard him talk that much."

They walked the next block in silence. Helen was terrified that Charlie would squash her plans and she'd lose him forever, so she kept her mouth closed and gave him time to think. They stopped at the corner to let a car drive past and a smile crept along the corners of his mouth.

"Let's do it," he said. "I'm thrilled I have such a sneaky fiancée." She threw her arms around his neck and kissed him. "But now I know I'll have to keep my eye on you, you sly devil. Now we definitely have to have that drink to celebrate. But I think we need a better plan. Here's what I think we should do."

Charlie's plan was a bit more detailed than Helen's had been. Since he had told the landlady they'd be over to look at the apartment the next day, Helen agreed they should do that.

"After all, we'll need a place to live," he said. "Then, if you like the place, we can start buying furniture. We don't have to furnish the whole place all at once. Maybe just a sofa, table and chairs, and a bed for starters. Then we won't even have to go to Rhode Island. We can get a license here on Monday and we can get married as soon as the apartment is ready. How does that sound?" He put his arms around her waist and pulled her close.

"It sounds wonderful."

Charlie kissed her to "seal the deal."

"I'll meet you after Mass tomorrow, outside the church, and we'll go look at the apartment."

"I can't wait."

They walked into the bar grinning like two Cheshire cats.

"Good afternoon, Mr. Sanders," Mrs. Lynch said, opening the vestibule door. "Is this your intended?"

"It is indeed. Helen, this is Mrs. Lynch, hopefully, our future landlady. Mrs. Lynch, Miss Helen Campbell." The usual pleasantries were exchanged, then Charlie said, "I hope we haven't come at a bad time for you. It's such a beautiful day I thought you might be out enjoying a stroll through the park."

"That would be lovely, but a landlady's work is never done. And since Mr. Lynch passed on, it all falls on my shoulders." She lowered her eyes, lifted her shoulders, and heaved a heavy sigh.

311

Charlie and Helen looked at each other, not knowing what to say. After a minute, he said, "We were wondering if Helen could take a peek at the apartment today. That is, if it's not too much trouble."

"Oh, of course, of course. When I start thinking about Mr. Lynch, I lose all track of things. You'd have liked him, Mr. Sanders. A big man, like you. Built like a bull, as they say. And handy. He could fix most anything. Now I have to rely on handymen to do those jobs and half the time they make a bigger mess than they came to clean up. Are you handy around the house, Mr. Sanders?"

"I don't really know. I've spent most of my life on the road, in hotels, so I've never had to worry my head about such things."

"I see," she said, a frown creasing her forehead.

"He was a boxer, Mrs. Lynch," Helen said.

"Ah, I should have known what with those great broad shoulders and all. But now you're working at the New York Athletic Club you said?"

"I am. No more road traveling for me."

"That's good. I wouldn't want to think about this pretty little thing sitting up there all alone night after night."

The three of them stood in the hall looking at each other.

"The apartment, Mrs. Lynch?" Charlie reminded her.

"Where is my head? Of course. Come right this way, dear," she said, taking Helen by the arm. The landlady chatted away for the whole time it took them to reach the third floor, asking, what seemed to Charlie, every question under the sun.

I can see we'll have no peace until Mrs. Lynch knows our whole life histories and maybe even those of our parents and grandparents.

"The Byrnes family lived here before and were a fine tenant. Paid the rent on time. Always kept the place neat and tidy, not like some of the others in the building. Now, you take Mr. and Mrs. Schmidt on the second floor. Lovely lady, but I don't know how she puts up with that husband of hers. Why I don't think I've ever spoken to him when he wasn't three sheets to the wind. Of course, I'm having your apartment repainted, but I may need to clean up a bit after the painters finish."

"I'm sure it will be fine," Helen said. "We won't be too long. I'd just like to get a look at it so I know what I'll need to furnish it."

"You know, I might have some things in the basement. Why, it would curl your hair to hear some of the reasons people give me for wanting to store their things. Other times, though, people just leave dressers, or tables, or chairs they don't want any more when they move, like they're going to disappear on their own. The only thing that disappears is their security deposit when I have to have their things moved. Or, they put them down there to make room for more beds, then forget about them. I'd be happy to let you look at everything, if you want."

"That would be wonderful, wouldn't it, Charlie? You know my mother told me that's how she and dad got most of the furniture for their apartment when they arrived here."

"Arrived here from where, dear?"

Helen, I think you've opened the door to a tale that has no end.

"From Ireland."

"Oh! Well, we'll have to have a cup of tea so you can tell me all about what county they came from and when they came over—"

"That would be lovely, Mrs. Lynch," Charlie said. "But today, we've so much to do that I'm afraid I'm going to have to steal Helen away from you."

"Oh... of course." Mrs. Lynch opened the door wider and led Helen on a tour of the apartment. "Here, let me point out some of the features. This is a lovely apartment. It faces the street, so you'll get lots of air and light." Mrs. Lynch took her arm and dragged her from one room to the next. "The kitchen has a nice deep sink, a range, refrigerator, dish cabinets, shelves, everything you need. The bedrooms have closets and plenty of room. One looks out onto the street, and the other one onto the courtyard. And here we are back in the living room. As you can see, it's almost completely freshly painted. Any questions?"

"It looks great. And how much is the rent?"

"Only $60 per month."

"Sixty," Helen said. "It's lovely, and so big. How will we ever fill it, Charlie? And so much light comes in through these front windows. I'm glad we face the street, not the courtyard. It's perfect, Charlie."

The smile on her face and the sparkle in her eyes reassured him that he had made the right choice. He watched as she spun back into the kitchen to check the range and the cabinets again, nodding her approval and signaling for him to join her so she could tell him what her plans were for the space.

"And, of course, there's the extra bedroom for any little ones that come along," Mrs. Lynch said.

Helen's face turned scarlet at the landlady's implication.

"We don't want to get ahead of ourselves on that count," Charlie said. "Right now, we'll just worry about settling in. Isn't that right, sweetheart?"

"Yes... um, yes."

314

Charlie looked around again at the spacious living room. The sun poured in the front windows and glistened off the polished mahogany mantle. He looked at Helen and she nodded. "We'll take it," he said.

"That's wonderful, Mr. Sanders. Come downstairs with me and sign the lease, and we'll be all set for you to move in whenever you're ready."

Mrs. Lynch led them out and back downstairs to her apartment. "Have a seat. I'll get the lease for you to sign. You know you have to pay the first month's rent, and a security deposit today."

"Yes, I've come prepared to do that."

"Good. I'll be right back."

As soon as Mrs. Lynch left the room, Charlie pulled a wad of bills out of his pocket.

Let's see, that's sixty for rent, sixty for security, and how much for Mrs. Lynch? Better give her sixty too. That way, I can be sure the apartment will be clean when we move in.

"Here we are," Mrs. Lynch said, as she bustled into the living room. "It's your usual apartment lease, but feel free to read it all. Why don't I make us a cup of coffee while you look it over?"

"That would be terrific," Charlie said.

She hustled back to the kitchen, and Charlie settled in to read the lease. "Lots of legal mumbo-jumbo," he said to Helen. "I'll just make sure there's nothing sneaky in it. Some of these landlords are pretty sly."

Mrs. Lynch returned with coffee and a plate of cookies. She sat quietly eating and drinking while Charlie read.

"This seems to be in order," Charlie said. "If you give me a pen, I'll sign my life away."

"You're a card, Mr. Sanders. There's a pen on the table, next to the plate of cookies."

315

"So there is. Didn't even see it hiding there."

Charlie picked up the pen, signed the lease with a flourish, and finished his coffee. "There you are, Mrs. Lynch, a pleasure doing business with you. I assume I can get the keys today?"

"I've got them right here for you."

"Great. I'll just pay you what's due, and we'll be on our way."

Charlie reached into his pocket and took out the bills he had separated from the rest of his wad. "Here's sixty for rent, sixty for security, and sixty for your time and help."

"Oh, that's too much, Mr. Sanders."

"I insist, Mrs. Lynch. It's only right that you get paid for your time. Like you said, there's still some cleaning to be done. Am I right?"

"Well, when you put it that way. . ." she stuffed the bills in her pocket and began to tell Helen all about what went on in the building and the neighborhood.

Jumping in when Mrs. Lynch paused for a breath, Charlie said, "Come on, love. We still have a lot to do today."

"Yes, Charlie. I'm ready."

"Thank you, Mrs. Lynch, for taking the time to show Helen the apartment."

"Yes, thank you, Mrs. Lynch," Helen said. "I enjoyed meeting you. I can't wait to see what treasures you might have in the basement. Would it be all right if we came back some day this week to look through them?"

"When would that be, dear?"

"I'll have to check my schedule at work to be sure."

"I'm sure it'll be fine. I'll give you my phone number so you can call and remind me." she scribbled her number down on a pad kept near the phone.

"I will. Thank you again for today."

316

"You're welcome. See you this week," she called down the hall after them. A head poked out from one of the apartments. "Just saying goodbye to my new tenants. Did you happen to see them? Such a lovely couple. She seems very refined, and he is certainly handsome."

"I thought we'd never get out of there," Charlie said when they reached the sidewalk.

Helen laughed and squeezed his arm. "She does like to talk. I guess it's because she's all alone. I'm sure it's been hard on her."

Charlie looked at her and shook his head. "I can see that she'll make herself at home in our apartment. You with your sympathetic ear and all."

"Don't you worry about that. I'll shoo her out when I have to."

"Not you, love. I'll have to do it when I get home from work each night."

Helen smiled and a faint blush colored her cheeks.

"And that's one of the many reasons I love you so much," he said, lifting her hand up and kissing it. "Now let's get something to eat." He whistled for a cab and when it stopped, helped Helen in, then climbed in after her and gave the driver an address. "In a few days, we'll be a married couple," he said, leaning over to kiss her.

CHAPTER TWENTY-SIX

Helen found it hard to concentrate on her group of children on Monday. She kept looking at the clock willing the hands to move faster. She knew it would be a close call to get to the city clerk's office by five o'clock, but she was sure they could make it if the subway didn't have too many delays. Then they could get their marriage license. After that, whatever way they decided to get married, priest or judge, would be up to them.

She had arranged to get Thursday off and planned on going back to the apartment to scavenge thorough Mrs. Lynch's basement for usable furniture. Charlie wanted them to buy everything new but Helen said there would be so many other expenses that this was one area where they could save some money. Her mind whirled with all the purchases they'd have to make. She slipped her list out from her pocket. Dishes, pots and pans, glasses, linens, silverware. The list grew longer every time she looked it over. And she hadn't even started adding all the grocery staples they'd need. She shoved the scrap of paper away when Sister Josephine entered the playroom.

"How are the children today?" she asked.

"Fine, but a little restless. I'm thinking about taking them to the park for a little exercise before lunch."

"Good idea. The fresh air will do them a world of good. You have a watch with you? I don't want them to be late for lunch. It upsets the kitchen too much when they have to hold the meal over."

"We'll be back in plenty of time."

"Well then, enjoy yourself." Sister Josephine swept out of the room, the rosary beads that hung from her belt tinkling all the way down the hall.

Helen gathered her charges together and inspected their pockets for any hidden toys. She didn't want a reoccurrence of the incident with Jimmy and his concealed ball. Although that had led to meeting Charlie. She smiled at the memory.

Satisfied there was no contraband, she led them out of the Foundling and headed for Central Park. But before they reached the corner, a well-dressed woman stepped in her path. Distracted by the children, Helen hardly gave the woman a passing glance.

"Not even a hello?" a familiar voice asked.

Helen peered at the woman. "Carolyn? Carolyn, is it you? Oh, oh . . ." she hugged her sister. "Let me look at you. I almost didn't recognize you with your new hairdo and fancy clothes. You look like one of those Park Avenue ladies who have tea at The Plaza."

Carolyn giggled. "I have charge accounts at all the best stores, so I can buy whatever clothes I want and I have my hair done every week. And I do sometimes have tea at The Plaza. Or I did, at least one time. It was wonderful but I wished you and Peggy were with me. I actually was headed into the hospital to see if you could have lunch with me. But I didn't expect to take this whole mob. Where are you off to?"

"The park. Want to join us? Do you have time? I'm afraid I eat lunch with these guys and only get about a half hour to myself which I usually spend in the hospital cafeteria. Not exactly a great lunch spot."

"God no. But I'll walk to the park with you. I have nothing but time most days. Gino has business to take care of during the day, and I usually don't see him until dinner."

"Great. At least we'll have time to catch up."

Helen looped her arm through Carolyn's and the group continued across town. Once they were settled in the playground area, Helen led Carolyn to a bench where she could keep an eye on the children, but be far enough away from the other mothers and nannies for privacy.

"So, what's doing?" Helen asked. "And don't tell me you just wanted to say hi because I won't believe you. What's the matter?"

Carolyn's chest heaved with a great sigh. "I'm pregnant."

Helen shook her head. "I was afraid that's what you were going to say. How could you let that happen? I thought you were smarter than that."

"Oh, don't start scolding me like I'm one of your charges. I don't know how it happened. I'm always very careful about using a sheath for protection, but... I don't know. Guess nothing is one hundred percent infallible."

"Are you absolutely sure?"

"Absolutely. I got the verdict from the doctor this morning. That's why I came looking for you. What am I going to do?" Carolyn's hands twisted around each other and a few silent tears filled her eyes.

"I'm assuming Gino doesn't know?"

Carolyn shook her head.

"Do you think if you told him he'd marry you?"

"I doubt it very much. And I don't want to get married anyway. Besides, Gino likes to have a beautiful, young, fashionable woman at his side, not a big fat pregnant one. He loves showing me off. That's why he doesn't care how much I spend on clothes. As long as I 'look good and classy' as he says. I don't think maternity clothes would fit the bill."

"Probably not, but maybe he'd like to have kids. Lots of Italians like big families. You never know."

Carolyn gaped at Helen, one eyebrow raised, her head cocked to the side. "That would be just dandy. I can see it all now. A little house in some remote area of Brooklyn or Staten Island. Me at the stove cooking spaghetti for a bunch of his kids, and him going out every night with some young beauty on his arm. I'd wind up shopping from the Sears Roebuck catalog while she had the run of all the stores I've grown to love." She shook her head. "That may be the life you dream about, but no, that is definitely not the life I envision for myself. Which is why I've come to see you."

"Me? What can I do?"

"You work in the orphanage wing of the hospital. You must know someone who could help me take care of this little problem."

Helen stared at Carolyn, her mouth hanging open. "You can't be talking about an abortion," she whispered.

"That's exactly what I'm talking about."

"Carolyn, not only is that so very wrong, it's also illegal."

"I know that. And I don't want to go to some butcher in a back alley somewhere. That's why I came to you. There must be some doctor or nurse who does them. You know, picks up some extra money on the side."

"Carolyn! How can you even think such a thing? They've taken an oath to help heal people, not kill them."

322

"I'm not killing anyone. I simply need to end this problem sooner rather than later, and I thought you could help me. Guess I thought wrong." She folded her arms against her chest, her crossed leg swinging rapidly. "Maybe Peggy'd know someone from medical school."

"Oh no you don't. Don't go getting her involved in your criminal activities."

"Criminal activities? Really, Helen. A bit dramatic. Even for you."

"And since they are criminal activities, maybe your gangster boyfriend could help you out. That's his field after all, isn't it?"

"I wouldn't know. I don't question him about his business." Carolyn stood and straightened her skirt. "I should have known it would be a mistake to ask you for help. God forbid you break one of your rules, but I didn't know where else to go. I'm sorry to have bothered you. Goodbye, Helen."

"Wait." she stood and grabbed Carolyn's arm. "I'll ask around and see if I can get any information for you. Give me a couple of days, all right? How can I reach you?"

"Thanks, Helen. But I'll get in touch with you. Can I meet you after work on Thursday?"

"No, I'm off on Thursday. Wednesday?"

"All right. Wednesday. We'll go for a drink."

Carolyn gave her a hug and walked away. As Helen watched her leave, she thought about the mess her younger sister had already made of her life.

That afternoon, Helen trudged down the Foundling's front steps, the cloud of Carolyn's news overshadowing all other thoughts.

"You don't look like a happy bride-to-be," Charlie said, bounding off the car parked at the curb to greet her. "More like someone who's just lost her best friend."

323

"Charlie. Oh gosh, I forgot. We have to get to the city clerk's office." She looked at her watch. "I hope we make it before they close."

"No need to worry about that," Charlie said. "I went there this morning to see if I could get the forms we'll need to fill out. I figured maybe we could knock them off on our way downtown. And it turns out, the office closes at four o'clock. So, no rush now. How about we get the forms done and go there first thing Thursday morning, before we scavenge through Mrs. Lynch's basement? That way we can get married any day we want after the two day waiting period."

"Okay then. Thursday it is." Helen fidgeted with her purse and stared at the ground.

"What's wrong?" Charlie put his finger under her chin and lifted her face up so he could look into her eyes. "If you have second thoughts about marrying me, I'd appreciate it if you tell me now, not six months from now after we're husband and wife."

Helens' eyes widened and almost bulged out of her head. "Charlie, how could you even think such a thing? There's not a hint of doubt in any fiber of my being about us getting married. I've never been more sure of anything or wanted anything more in my life."

"Well then, what's bothering you? Because something is. Usually I, at least, get a peck on the cheek when I meet you. Today, you won't even look me straight in the eye."

"Oh, Charlie." she threw her arms around his neck and cried.

He rubbed his hands up and down her back and waited for her to regain her composure. "Feel better?" he asked after the sobs turned to deep breaths and sniffles.

"It's Carolyn."

"Thought she was a lost cause."

"Maybe more lost than either you or I realized." Helen pulled away from his embrace, took his hand, and walked him to the corner. "Can we go to the park?"

"Sure. Maybe we'll even recreate our first date and grab a hot dog."

A wisp of a smile didn't take away the frowns digging deeper into her face. On their walk across town, Helen told Charlie about Carolyn's visit that morning. He let out a low whistle and shook his head.

"She gets herself into more and more trouble every day, doesn't she?"

"And now she wants my help."

"To do what?"

They reached the park entrance and stopped at the hot dog stand. Charlie ordered for both of them, then led Helen to a nearby bench.

"Does she expect you to go with her when she tells Gino?"

Helen took a bite of her hot dog, swallowed it, and said, "She's not going to tell him."

Charlie coughed, gagging on his food. Gulping his soda to help him swallow, he wiped his eyes. "Doesn't she think he'll notice in a couple of months?"

"Don't be so dense. She plans on having an abortion."

His mouth dropped open and he stared wide-eyed at Helen.

"I know. That's how I felt too when she told me. And she wants my help."

"How?"

"She wants me to find a doctor or nurse who'll do it."

"Oh, sweetie." Charlie put his arm around her shoulders and pulled her in close, his chin resting on top of her head. "No wonder you're so upset. And I made you feel worse thinking you didn't want to marry me." He kissed the top of her head. "Why would she think a perfectly respectable professional, like the ones you know at the Foundling, would get involved in something illegal?"

"I don't know. And why she thinks I can just go around asking people if they do something like that is a mystery to me. She knows we have a whole ward just for single pregnant girls who come, stay, have their babies, then put them up for adoption. Certainly, if there was someone willing to perform abortions, that ward wouldn't be full all the time. I don't know what to do."

Charlie unwrapped his arm from her, took the cold hot dog from her hand, walked to the nearest trash can and threw both of the dogs away. He came back and pulled her up from the bench. "A nice brisk walk will do you a world of good." Looping her arm through his, they started down the path that would lead them to the boathouse. He hoped someone would have a model boat in the water to distract her for a while.

While they walked, he thought about Carolyn's problem. He was furious she had put Helen in the middle of the situation. He could feel the tug-of-war that was going on in her mind between wanting to help her sister and taking part in an illegal operation. He knew Helen couldn't, and wouldn't, dare approach anyone at the hospital for help. But maybe between his contacts and Joe's, they could find someone who wouldn't butcher up the foolish girl and ruin any prospects of future children for the rest of her life. It would cost plenty, he was sure, but that wasn't his problem. Carolyn would just have to get the money somehow without telling Gino why she needed it. He had no doubts she could manage that. Even though he wanted to find her and tell her exactly where she and her wise guy boyfriend could go, he calmed himself before he tried talking to Helen. She didn't deserve any of this. And she didn't need to see how angry he was. He took a deep breath.

"Helen, you don't need to get involved in this."

"But I promised Carolyn."

"What I mean is, you can't go around the hospital asking if someone performs illegal operations on the side. You'd be fired before you could blink, if not arrested."

"But—"

"Stop." He held his hand up, palm out. "Listen to me for a minute. Boxing has a very dirty side, as I'm sure you've heard. I've steered clear of most of it, but you can't be in the game for as long as I was without hearing some of the sordid details of other guy's escapades. Between me and Joe, we might be able to come up with a name. I'm not sure if we can do it by Wednesday, but we'll try. How about I call Joe now and the three of us can go to dinner and talk it over?"

"That's a terrific idea. I feel like a giant weight has been lifted off my shoulders."

The smile she gave him made his heart jump. He knew he would move heaven and earth to keep her that happy forever.

"Peg!" Helen said, "what are you doing here?"

"Gee, what a warm welcome. Joe and I had plans for dinner tonight, so when Charlie asked him to join you two, he asked if I'd mind and I said it would be fine. Why? Is there a problem?"

Helen looked at Charlie then rubbed her temples. "I didn't want you to get involved in this mess."

"What mess?" Peggy looked at Joe, but he shrugged his shoulders and shook his head. "Should I leave?"

Everyone looked at Helen. She took a deep breath, eyes cast to the ceiling. "I guess not. Carolyn'll just go to you if we can't come up with a solution, so you may as well stay."

"Carolyn?"

"Please sit," Helen said, "and I'll fill you in."

Charlie took her hand and rubbed his thumb across the back of it. She took another deep breath and told them about Carolyn's visit that morning. Halfway through her story, their waiter came to the table to take their dinner orders. Charlie gave his and the others said they'd have the same.

"Go on, Helen," Joe said.

She ended by telling them that Carolyn would stop back for a name on Wednesday and that if she didn't have one, she planned on asking Peggy to find someone.

"Otherwise," Peggy said, "I guess I'd be kept in the dark. Why do both of you think you have to shield me from everything? Do you really think I'm so innocent I have no idea what's going on between Carolyn and Gino? Or that I didn't think this was a real possibility? I just assumed that if it did happen, they'd get married. I guess that was childish thinking on my part. But, being realistic, I guess if she's going to hang around with a criminal, she may as well become one herself."

"Peggy, that's a terrible thing to say about your own sister," Helen said. "And that's not why I didn't plan on telling you."

"Then why all the secrecy?"

Helen squirmed in her seat and looked around the dining room before she said, "Because you have a terrible habit of telling Mom everything. You never could hide anything from her. One look at your face, and she knows something's up. Then all she has to do is stand there with her hands on the hips, tap her foot, and say, 'Out with it,' and you blab everything to her."

Peggy's face turned red. "That's not true."

"Yes, it is and you know it." Helen reached across the table and grabbed Peggy's hand. "You're just too honest. There's nothing wrong with that, but sometimes I wish you could conceal things. Mom doesn't always have to know everything about us."

Peggy couldn't look at Helen. She knew she was right. She wasn't sure if it was because her mother put the fear of God in her or because she wanted her to know what her two older sisters were up to. They always seemed to think she was too young to understand anything, even thought there was only a year's age difference between all of them. And she resented being treated like a baby.

The tension at the table was palpable. Joe's eyes wandered around the room. Charlie took tiny sip after tiny sip of his beer. Helen held onto Peggy's hand and wished her sister would look at her.

"Well," Peggy said, raising her head and staring into Helen's eyes, "this is one time Mom won't find out what's going on from me. I'm not going to be the one who gives her a nervous breakdown or puts my sister in jail. Carolyn'll have to find a way to do that by herself. And if she keeps up with what she's doing now, that probably won't be too far down the road."

Helen had never seen this steely look of determination and resolve that came over Peggy's face. She looked at her sister with newfound respect. This was a side of her that Helen realized Peggy kept hidden from her family. For this was the part of Peggy that got her through all the discrimination she faced in college and medical school from her male counterparts. She had underestimated her little sister. Peggy was the strongest one of the three of them. She had a steel will that wouldn't bend when she needed or wanted it, and this was one time she would use it.

"I believe you, Peg," Helen said. "And I apologize for not giving you the credit or respect you deserve for so many things. I promise not to treat you like my innocent little sister anymore."

"Thanks. Now, I guess we'd better get some kind of plan together to get Carolyn out of her latest jam."

There was almost a collective sigh of relief as everyone relaxed. Tight shoulders loosened. Charlie downed the rest of his beer in one gulp. Joe smiled at Peggy. And Helen released her grip on her sister's hand.

With perfect timing, the waiter appeared and set their dinners on the table.

"Another round of drinks, please," Charlie said.

Over dinner, Charlie and Joe bandied names and situations back and forth trying to narrow down the possibilities of reliable sources. By the time everyone had cleaned their plates, they had settled on three people who could probably give them a doctor's name.

"I think we should talk to these guys together," Joe said. "Gives our... um, request a little more weight."

"Agreed. When and where?"

"Meet me at Stillman's tomorrow. Ten o'clock. That will give us two days to get this done, and get a name to Helen before Carolyn shows up."

"Thank you both," Helen said.

"Yes, thanks," Peggy said. "I guess every occupation has it's seedy side, even the lofty world of medicine."

"Unfortunately, that's true," Joe said. "But sometimes these charlatans can actually wind up doing something good for someone who needs a break. I'm not totally convinced that's the case with Carolyn, but I'm willing to give her the benefit of the doubt if only for the reason that it'll ease both your minds."

"I know I'll feel better thinking she'll be going to someone who's not doing this on the kitchen table in some filthy tenement," Peggy said.

"Does that really go on?" Helen asked, her eyes widened and she raised her hand to her mouth.

Peggy shook her head, her lips drawn into a tight line. "Now who's the innocent? You wouldn't believe some of the butchery and horror stories we hear in the emergency room at the hospital. Believe me, if I was ever an innocent, I'm not now."

"I never realized."

"And hopefully, you'll never have to witness anything like it."

"I think we could all use a brandy," Joe said, signaling the waiter.

When the drinks came, Joe reached over and poured a little water into Peggy's glass.

The mood was considerably lighter now, even though there had been a major realignment of Helen's and Peggy's relationship. They looked across the table at each other and, in that moment, they knew they had moved on to a more equal standing, a friendship that went beyond, and was deeper than, just being sisters.

By the second day, the men had the name of a doctor in Brooklyn who agreed to see Carolyn that Sunday at eleven o'clock. When Carolyn showed up at the Foundling, she found Charlie leaning against a parked car.

"Charlie? What are *you* doing here?"

He looked her over from head to toe. "Seems like you learned how to spend Gino's money pretty quickly. That outfit probably costs more than you used to make in a week."

331

"What of it? Gino expects me to look my best all the time." She tried to look down her nose at Charlie, but since he was a good head taller, she only looked foolish.

"Nice to see he's getting his money's worth."

Before they could start an all-out brawl, Helen opened the hospital's front door and bounced down the steps. "You're both here. Great."

Charlie pulled a piece of paper out of his pocket. "Here's the name, address, and phone number you asked for, and your appointment time on Sunday."

"Sunday? I don't know if I can make it on Sunday. And I prefer to make my own doctor appointments."

"Suit yourself, but that's the only day he's willing to do abortions," Charlie said.

Carolyn and Helen both winced at the word.

"The rest of the week, he sees legitimate patients. Ones who don't ask him to commit a crime. So, it's up to you. You can call and cancel if you want. I gave you his phone number. Oh, and he said to bring five hundred dollars. Cash."

"That's outrageous. How am I supposed to come up with that much money by Sunday?" Carolyn asked.

Charlie glowered at her. "You're asking the man to perform an illegal operation. If he gets caught, he could go to jail, lose his license, and never be able to ever practice medicine again. I'd call it a bargain. Ready, Helen?" He took her hand and started to walk away.

"Wait a minute," Helen said, tugging on his arm. "Carolyn, Charlie and Joe spent two days trying to find a doctor for you. The least you can do is thank him. How you get the money to pay for this is none of our business, but showing some gratitude would be nice."

Carolyn stared at the slip of paper in her hand. "Thank you, Charlie. And thank Joe for me too. Helen?"

332

She looked at her sister. "Would you come with me? I don't want to be alone."

Helen sighed. "I don't know. If anyone finds out, I'll lose my job."

Carolyn stood slumped and defeated, all bravado evaporated. "Please. I'm scared."

Helen looked at Charlie, but he shrugged his shoulders. "I'll give you two a minute." He walked down the street and waited at the corner.

Carolyn grabbed Helen's arm. "Please. I don't think I can do this on my own. And what if something goes wrong?"

Helen took a deep breath. "You know this goes against everything I believe in." Carolyn waited for an answer while Helen paced the sidewalk for a couple of minutes. "Meet me after Mass at Ed's coffee shop."

"Thank you." Carolyn hugged her and kissed her cheek. "You're a good sister and a good person. See you Sunday." She gave her another quick hug and left.

Charlie shook his head as Helen joined him. "You're a pushover, you know that?"

"She's my sister."

He took her hand. "What do you want to do tonight?"

They wandered the streets talking about their plans for tomorrow. They'd go to the city clerk's office first thing and get their marriage license. Then, Helen wanted to go to their new apartment and rummage through the basement for furniture they could use.

"I still think we should buy new stuff," Charlie said. "Nothing down there will be any good. That's why people left it."

"You never know. Maybe someone died and the family didn't need their stuff. So, they put it down there until they could figure out what to do with it, then forgot all about it. Some of it might be okay for now. There are

333

still so many things we have to buy. This will just save us a little money. And we won't have to spend the time shopping. We can always replace the pieces. Little by little."

"I can see I'm not going to change your mind, but if I go with you, I might keep you from taking everything upstairs."

"That would be perfect. This is exciting. We're really going to be married and living there soon."

"Next week."

"Really? That soon?"

"When's your day off next week?"

"Thursday, again."

"Then Thursday it is. We'll go down to the city clerk's office and get married."

"I can't believe this is happening. Oh, Charlie, you've made me the happiest woman alive." She threw her arms around his neck and kissed him.

"Keep this up and I won't wait till Thursday," he said, kissing her again.

"I guess we should behave. We are on a public street."

"You're making it very difficult for me to do that, but I'll try." He pulled away from her but didn't let go of her hand. "Want to go see a movie? We can sit in the last row and act like teenagers." He wiggled his eyebrows up and down.

Helen slapped his arm. "You're terrible." They walked a few more steps and she said, "What's playing?"

Charlie roared laughing. "Who cares?"

They stopped at the first movie theater they passed and spent the next couple of hours enjoying the last row and the dark privacy of the theater, blissfully ignorant of whatever was playing on the screen.

On Thursday morning, Helen and Charlie were first in line for their marriage license. They handed the clerk their completed forms and birth certificates, and paid the fee. In return, the clerk handed them their license.

"That was easy enough," Charlie said. "Now let's see about making an appointment to get married."

"Look Charlie, it says here that we don't need an appointment. Just our license and an ID, and... a witness. That could be a problem."

"Why?"

"How can we ask someone to be a witness when we don't want anyone to know we're getting married?"

"We won't tell our witness why we want him, or her, to meet us until that day. Once we're married, they can put it on the front page of *The New York Times*, for all I care. It's only till then that we don't want to tell anyone."

"You're right. I don't know what I was thinking."

"And as soon as we're married here, we can go to the rectory at Elizabeth Seton Chapel down at the Battery and have a priest there marry us again."

"Do you think he will? Without banns or any of the other requirements?"

"They don't have a regular congregation, so I'm sure a healthy donation will grease the wheels. And I'll get Joe to be our witness, okay?"

"Perfect."

"Oh, and by the way, I asked him to meet us at the apartment to help carry any furniture you like upstairs."

"Oh no. Don't tell him about our plans yet. He'll want to tell Peggy."

They took the subway uptown and when they got to their building. Joe was already there, reading the newspaper.

"Hope you haven't been waiting too long," Helen said.

335

"Nope. Just enough time to read the sports section."

Charlie unlocked the front door, and rang the landlady's bell. After finding out who Joe was and how long they knew him, Mrs. Lynch took them downstairs to the storage room. Charlie looked at Joe, shrugged, and rolled his eyes. Joe chuckled.

"Now, are all these items available?" Helen asked.

"All except the ones in that little cubby," Mrs. Lynch pointed to a small room off the main storage area. "Those things belong to people still living here."

"Well then, let's get started." Helen roamed among the furniture piled willy nilly in the basement. "Charlie, how about that table and chairs, and the dresser over there?"

"Whatever you want. You pick it out, we'll haul it upstairs."

"Let's start with them and I'll keep looking around." In the end, Helen found another dresser for the second bedroom, a coffee table, and two matching end tables. While the men lugged everything upstairs, Helen went to the apartment to see about arranging her "new" furniture. She expected it to look barren, but was shocked when she entered the bedroom. A bed, dresser, and two night tables were already set in place.

When the men came in with their load of furniture, Helen threw her arms around Charlie's neck. "Aren't you full of surprises. When did you manage to buy a bedroom suite and get it delivered?"

"Oh, I have my ways."

"Well, I guess we won't be needing that second dresser, after all. We can put one in the second bedroom though. Maybe the smaller one."

The men nodded and trekked downstairs to continue moving furniture. A couple of hours later, they were done and Charlie decided they deserved lunch and a few beers for their efforts. They left after saying goodbye to their landlady and assuring her they had locked everything up tight.

They found a pub a block away and slid into a booth, glad to be out of the dusty and damp basement.

While they ate, Joe told them about his new job and how it was interesting looking at the new up and coming talent. Charlie talked about the kids at the Settlement.

"I just wish we had more equipment for them to use. Maybe once I start my job, in earnest, I can get some of those Wall Street guys to finance some. Right now, I'm just going in to the club on my own time. Paul wants me to get used to the place and the men, and for them to get used to me. He thinks that will prevent any one of them from trying to prove himself to me and cause a problem."

"You'll probably be able to get them to finance something. They're usually a pretty generous lot," Joe said, ordering two more beers and a coffee for Helen.

CHAPTER TWENTY-SEVEN

"Are you sure this is the right address?" Helen asked Carolyn, as they got out of the cab.

"Well, it's the one your boyfriend gave me," Carolyn said, flashing the crumpled slip of paper in Helen's face. "He might enjoy sending *me* into this seedy Brooklyn neighborhood, but he'd never put you in any danger."

The two women looked up at the dilapidated building. The wooden front door with its peeling brown paint and one broken glass pane was sandwiched between a pawn shop and a diner. The stench of grease and rotting garbage caused both of them to cover their noses with handkerchiefs. They stepped inside and scanned the mailboxes for the doctor's name.

"Here it is," Carolyn said. "Dr. Nicholsonn, 3A."

They climbed the stairs, littered with debris and pieces of broken toys to the third floor. When they entered the doctor's office/apartment, the conditions weren't much better. A woman sat behind a desk in what would normally be a living room. A few metal chairs with cracked and split padded seats, the stuffing spilling out, completed the room's furnishings. No tables. No pictures on the walls. No outdated magazines to read. Only the bare essentials.

"You must be the eleven o'clock. Right?" she asked.

"Yes. I guess so," Carolyn said.

"Did you bring the money?" The woman walked toward Carolyn, hand stretched out to accept the payment.

"Yes." Carolyn reached into her purse and pulled out five one-hundred-dollar bills, which the woman counted twice.

"It's all there," Carolyn said, pulling her gloves off and stuffing them into her purse.

"Just wanted to make sure they're not fakes," the woman said. "I'll tell the doc you're here."

She disappeared through a doorway off the back righthand side of the room. Carolyn wiped the sweat off her forehead.

"Carolyn, are you sure you want to go through with this? This place is disgusting. It's filthy and that woman is... I don't know what to say about her."

"I don't have much of a choice, do I? Charlie said this was the best one he could find."

"But surely—"

"C'mon," the woman called from the open door, "the doc here don't got all day, ya know."

"Give me your purse," Helen said, "and your hat."

Carolyn pulled her hat off and flung both items at Helen. Inside the procedure room, Carolyn stared at the metal table in the center of the floor. Off to one side was a rolling cart with a variety of surgical instruments on it. Another cart held an assortment of towels and other cloths.

Outside, Helen paced the room, wrung her hands, and wiped the sweat off her forehead and neck. Dull

340

murmurs came from behind the closed door. She heard Carolyn yelp a few times, but knew there was nothing she could do to help her. She had made her decision and that was that. The best Helen could do was be there for her when the procedure was over. Then Carolyn would need a friend, not an antagonist.

Carolyn staggered out of the room a little while later, her face ashen. Helen rushed to her side and led her to a chair.

"Sit before you fall down," Helen said.

"I just want to get out of here," Carolyn wailed.

"I know, but take a minute to get yourself together, all right?"

Carolyn closed her eyes and leaned her head back against the wall.

"You can't stay here," the nurse/receptionist said, emerging from the procedure room. "The doc's got another appointment and he don't want anyone hanging around after they're done. You gotta go now."

"Can't you give her a minute?"

"No doll, I can't. Now go. This ain't no hotel."

"It's all right, Helen. I'd rather leave anyway."

Helen helped her stand, wondering how she was going to get her down three flights of stairs and where she could take her to recuperate. In the cab on their way back to Manhattan, Helen realized the only place she could take Carolyn was a hotel.

After the women checked in at the small midtown hotel, Carolyn slept for a while. When she woke, she showered and left to meet Gino. Still a little weak and groggy, she insisted she was well enough to go home.

"Carolyn," Helen said, "don't you think it might be time to reconsider your relationship with Gino? How many more times are you going to have to go through an

341

abortion to keep your figure and keep him interested in you? You could do some real damage to yourself. Ruin any possibility of having kids in the future."

"I've already told you. I don't ever want to have kids. Your dream of a house with a white picket fence and a swing set in the back yard is not for me. I want a luxurious apartment uptown with all the trappings, and furs, and jewelry, and everything else that goes with that lifestyle. That's my dream. Gino's just a stepping stone. I'll use him for everything I can get, then get rid of him, and move on to richer pastures."

Helen shook her head. "I find it hard to believe that you've changed so much, abandoned all the values we were taught."

"Well, get used to it. I got tired of penny-pinching my way through life. Through some weird roll of the dice, I was born gorgeous and I intend to cash in on that and use it to get even more than I deserve."

"Good luck. I doubt that will happen, but I guess you'll die trying."

"Thanks for today," Carolyn said, as she swept out of the room.

Helen sat there for a minute, then went down to the lobby and called Charlie to tell him the procedure was done and where she was. He told her to stay there and arrived a little while later to find her waiting for him.

"How was it?" he asked.

"Terrible. I don't know how she went through with it." Helen shivered just thinking about that morning. "I wonder when I'll see her again."

"The next time she needs you for something."

"Charlie. That's heartless."

"But true." He took her hand and they walked out of the hotel and headed downtown. "Where to?"

342

"I could use a drink and some dinner."

"Done and done." Charlie hailed a cab and gave the driver the cross streets of their destination. Then he leaned back and put his arm around Helen. She nestled in next to him, happy for his unquestioning acceptance of the day's events. She didn't want to relive the nightmare of that day.

The cab stopped in front of a tiny restaurant on the first floor of a brownstone in Greenwich Village. The hostess showed them to a table by the fireplace where a huge fire roared filling the small dining room with a comforting aroma of burning cedar and birch. The deep burgundy walls, low lighting, and candles on each table gave the room a cozy feel. Photos of old New York covered the walls and the subdued atmosphere transported diners back in time. As if not to break the spell, conversations were held to little more than a whisper, and the clink of cutlery against plates sounded almost musical.

"This place is lovely. I feel like I'm in someone's home back in the early 1900s," Helen said.

"It does have a real soothing quality to it. I always come here when I want a quiet place to think, relax, and eat great food. Speaking of which, I recommend the chicken pot pie. I don't know how they do it, but the crust is like a popover. I've never had anything like it anywhere else, and it's delicious."

"Pot pie it is then, And I think I'd like some wine tonight."

"We'll get a bottle."

"A whole bottle?"

"Helen, that's about two glasses each. So yes. A whole bottle."

Charlie ordered a bottle of merlot and two pot pies as soon as their waiter appeared. A few minutes later, he

343

returned with the wine, two glasses, and a platter filled with liver pate, crackers, and celery sticks.

Charlie lifted his glass and said, "To us, and a long life together."

"To us," Helen said. They clinked glasses and took a sip. "That's lovely and just what I needed. As is this restaurant. Charlie, you always seem to know exactly what to do to make me feel special."

"Because you are special and I love you."

"And I love you."

Charlie reached across the table and held her hand. "Wonder what I did today?"

"Uh oh. I'm not sure I want to know."

"I decided to cut down on some of the things you feel you have to do, so, I bought a set of pots and pans, a whole bunch of utensils, dishes, and glasses. If you don't like them, we can take them back, but I thought it would, at least, get us started."

"You're wonderful. Can I see them tonight? After dinner? I know it's getting late, but that's so exciting. I can't believe you did that."

"I know you were worried about not having all those things, so, I decided to take care of a few items on your list. You don't mind, do you?"

"I'm thrilled. It's certainly more than I expected. You're full of surprises. You know that, don't you? No wonder I love you."

Charlie's smile reached up to his eyes, which glistened with joy and reflected the firelight.

Their dinners arrived and were as delicious as Charlie had said they would be. Helen closed her eyes and savored the thick creamy gravy of the filling and the rich light airiness of the popover crust. Coupled with the dry red wine, it was a feast that she knew she would remember for a long time. Helen allowed these warm feeling to reach her innermost being and erase the horrors of the day.

After dinner, they walked over to their new apartment. Charlie opened the door and Helen stood at the threshold astounded by the number of boxes and bags on the kitchen table.

"A few things? I don't know where to begin." She walked around the table mesmerized. The reality of their plan hit her like a mac truck. Until this moment, their plans hadn't materialized in her mind. They were fantastical wannabes. But seeing all the necessities of a domestic life together turned her dreams into a sharp reality.

"Charlie, do you think we're rushing into this?"

Charlie stopped opening boxes and stared at her.

"What?"

"I mean, maybe we should take some more time before we elope. Maybe time to talk to our parents and try to convince them that this is the right decision we've made. And that it's time to give up old feuds that happened back in Europe."

Charlie rubbed his hand up and down his face. "Look, Helen, if you're having second thoughts about marrying me, just say so."

"No. No. It's not that. I want to marry you. More than anything else in the world. But I hate thinking my parents will cut me out of their lives forever."

"That won't happen. I know your father talks tough, but look what happened with Carolyn. He took her back in after she stopped seeing her married lover."

Helen winced at the term.

"I know, but once we get married, there's no changing that. It's not like I'm going to go home after a week or so and tell them I'm not seeing you anymore, and beg his forgiveness."

"I sure as hell hope not."

Charlie pulled out a chair and sat down. He pushed another one out with his foot. "Have a seat."

Helen sat.

"I understand what you're saying, Helen. But you have to decide which is more important to you. Us or your parents."

Helen kept her eyes downcast and twisted her hands around one another.

"Think about it this way," Charlie said. "If you went home tonight and your father said he forbid you to see me again, what would you say? Or do?"

Helen looked at him, eyes widened in terror. "I couldn't do that. I couldn't agree to that."

"Because I think that's exactly what's going to happen. In fact, I'm sure he'll tell you that you have to break off our engagement and stop seeing me. I'm amazed he hasn't done so already."

"If my father makes me choose between my parents and you, I want you to know I'll always choose you. Never doubt that for a minute."

Charlie pulled her out of her chair and held her so close she thought her ribs might break. Their passionate embrace lasted a long time. Their kisses setting them aflame with desire.

"Maybe we should elope tonight," Helen said.

"Maybe we should. Want me to see if I can get my friend's car? We could drive to Rhode Island, wake the Justice of the Peace, and surprise everyone. Or we could make believe we did that, move to the bedroom, and break in the bed."

346

Helen shook her head. "As tempting as that sounds, let's keep the plans we've made. It'll only be a little bit longer."

"Whatever you say, sweetheart."

"Now," she pushed Charlie away and turned to the treasures that filled the table. "Let's see what you bought for us. This is better than Christmas."

The two of them unwrapped all the goodies Charlie bought. Eight place settings of dishes in a blue willow pattern, which Helen loved. Two boxes of everyday glasses in different sizes. Boxes of pots and pans. A box of wine glasses. Cutlery for eight, plus serving pieces. And an assortment of utensils: can openers, spatulas, various types of large spoons, carving knives, and everything else needed in a kitchen.

"Where did you find all this stuff? You must have been shopping for hours."

"It was actually very easy. I bought the dishes, silverware, and pots and pans at Klein's. Then I went over to the Bridge. It's a restaurant supply place in the East 50s, and bought everything else."

"You're amazing. But now, we have to wash all these things before we can put them away. You didn't think to buy dish rags, or sponges, or dish towels, or soap, did you?"

Charlie looked at the ceiling. "Uhh . . ."

"I thought not. I'll pick some up tomorrow after work, And I'll have to buy a silverware tray for the drawer to keep everything in place. And—"

"Not tonight, sweetheart. It's time I took you home. It's late. I don't need giving your father any additional reasons to dislike me."

"How could anyone dislike you? You're wonderful." Helen kissed him and once again felt transported from life's everyday cares.

"Let's go," Charlie said in a husky voice, "before I decide not to let you go at all."

Only a few more days before I never have to leave him again.

CHAPTER TWENTY-EIGHT

It's Thursday. Finally. My wedding day.

Helen opened her eyes and smiled. Although one part of her regretted the fact that her family wouldn't be with her to share her big day, another part was overjoyed and celebrated her decision. Terrified that her father would, somehow, have uncovered her plans and prevent her from leaving the apartment, Helen was determined to leave before her parents woke.

Tiptoeing around the room in the dark, she reached under her bed and pulled out the hidden box that contained the new pale blue suit she had bought for today. She dressed, fixed her new floral hat on her head, and held onto her beige high heels as she snuck through the apartment and down the stairs. When she reached the front door, she saw Charlie standing at the curb dressed in a navy-blue suit, a small white rose in his lapel, and a bouquet of white roses in his hand. Her body tingled. She ran down the stoop into his arms. He gave her a long passion filled kiss.

"You look beautiful. I've never seen you looking so radiant."

"Oh, Charlie. I think my heart's going to burst. And you look so handsome."

They stood in an embrace, not able to take their eyes off each other. Only a car's honking was able to bring them back to reality.

"Almost forgot," Charlie said. "I brought these for you."

He handed her the bouquet.

"They're beautiful. Thank you. That was so sweet of you."

"Couldn't let my girl get married without a bouquet, could I? Isn't that something every bride is supposed to have?"

"I don't know if it's a requirement, but it's awfully nice."

"Shall we?" Charlie extended his arm. Helen slipped her hand through and they walked to the corner where he hailed a cab. He gave the driver an address downtown near the city clerk's office.

"I thought we could have breakfast beforehand, and it's also a place to wait for Joe."

"Will they be open? It's awfully early."

"They're open twenty-four hours a day. I guess they cater to some night workers in the area."

"You've thought of everything, as usual. I just hope I can keep breakfast down. My stomach's jumping around like crazy."

"Pre-wedding jitters?"

"I guess."

"Any regrets before we go through with this?"

"None. Not a one."

"Good."

The cab stopped in front of a brightly lit coffee shop amid all the darkened buildings on the street. They were the only customers. A lone waitress sat at the counter smoking a cigarette, and rummaging through the paper. The cook, all in white, leaned on the counter looking over her shoulder.

"Anywhere?" Charlie asked.

"Sure, hon," she said, never looking up. The cook whispered something to her that caused her head to snap up from the paper and twirl the stool around to look at them. She let out a low whistle.

"Well, don't you two look swell. I don't think we've ever had such a cute couple of newlyweds in here before. Have we, Hank?"

"I think you're right, Bernie. I'll have to make something special for them."

"Oh, we're not married yet," Helen said.

"But you will be soon as the clerk's office opens, right?" Hank asked.

"We sure will," Charlie said, reaching across the table for Helen's hand.

"Well then, we can still celebrate." Bernie walked around the counter, grabbed two cups and saucers and a pot of coffee. "Just brewed this," she said, pouring it. "Don't worry about ordering. If I know Hank, he won't listen to you anyway. He's determined to make you a special breakfast and when he gets that look in his eyes, nothing you say can stop him. So, sit back and relax for a while."

"I'm not sure I can keep anything down," Helen said.

"Don't worry, sweetheart," Charlie said. "I'm sure he's seen nervous brides before and he'll make something you won't be able to resist."

As they talked about their plans for that day after the ceremony, Helen's stomach settled. A radio played soft

351

music in the background and the aromas from the kitchen carried her back to unhurried holiday breakfasts. But before the sun's rays shone through the large plate glass windows, or people walked by on their way to work, or the world began another busy business day, Hank delivered his wedding day breakfast. One that you would expect to see at the Waldorf-Astoria Hotel, not a downtown coffee shop.

"Here we are," he said, placing the plates in front of them, a wide grin on his face. "Strawberry shortcake French toast sprinkled with some confectionary sugar and a side of bacon. And, just to make sure you don't leave here hungry, I made some banana and blueberry mini-muffins that you can have now, or take with you for later." He winked at Helen. "Enjoy."

Helen and Charlie stared at the feast in front of them. Hank had concocted a tower of English muffin French toast separated by layers of fresh strawberries and whipped cream and topped with more berries and cream. On a separate plate, he had stacked a pyramid of mini-muffins, still warm from the oven.

"It's magnificent," Helen said, looking up at Hank. "You could be a chef in a fancy restaurant."

"I used to be," Hank said. "But I gave it all up when I decided to open this place, and I've never been happier. Now, eat before all the cream melts."

Helen and Charlie dug into their breakfast and for a while contented sighs became the only sounds in the little store.

"I'll wrap these muffins for you," Bernie said, "unless you want to eat them now."

"I don't think I could eat one more mouthful," Helen said.

"Me neither. Tell Hank that was probably the most delicious breakfast I've ever had."

"I will. More coffee?"

"Please."

Just as Bernie left their table, the door opened and Joe strode in.

"Well, don't you two look nice." He slid into the booth next to Charlie. "You eat yet?"

"We had the most amazing breakfast ever," Helen said.

"Think I'll have time to grab something before we set off for wherever we're going?"

"We've got plenty of time. It's only seven and they don't open till eight-thirty. And we're only going across the street."

Bernie placed the box of muffins on the table, refilled Helen's and Charlie's cups and landed an empty one in front of Joe. "Coffee?"

"Absolutely, and scrambled eggs, bacon, toast, home fries, the whole magillicuddy."

"You got it."

"What's in the box?" Joe asked.

"Part of our breakfast that we couldn't finish," Helen said. "Banana and blueberry muffins."

"If I'd known that," Joe said, "I wouldn't have ordered anything."

"Oh no," Charlie said. "Hank made these special for us. You're not getting your mitts on them."

"Okay, okay. So, now that you've dragged me down here in the middle of the night, you going to tell me why?"

"It's not exactly the middle of the night and we want you to be our witness."

"Here you go, hon." Bernie put Joe's breakfast in front of him. "I'll be back with more coffee."

"Witness to what?" Joe asked, shoveling some eggs into his mouth.

"Our marriage," Charlie said.

353

Joe coughed and almost spit out his eggs. He took a gulp of coffee.

"Your marriage?" he stared wide-eyed at the two of them, his mouth hanging open.

"We're getting married this morning," Helen said.

Joe leaned back in the booth and kept looking back and forth at them.

"Does anyone else know?" he finally asked.

"So far, just Hank and Bernie," Charlie said, motioning to the waitress and cook/owner.

"Well, I'll be damned. Congratulations. I couldn't be happier for both of you."

"Thanks, Joe," they said in unison.

"Now, eat before everything gets cold," Helen said.

Joe took another mouthful, but kept looking at the couple and shaking his head. When his plate was almost empty, he said, "I guess this qualifies as eloping."

"I guess it does," Charlie said. "Since both our parents have a problem with us getting married, we decided to just go ahead and do it. Not bother to wait and try to convince them that this is what we want and don't give a damn what they think about it. This way, they'll either accept it or not, but there won't be any arguing about it because it'll be over and done."

"There's likely to be repercussions," Joe said, wiping his mouth with his napkin. "What if they try to get it annulled?"

"There won't be any grounds for that," Charlie said. "We'll make sure of that before we ever tell them we're married. In fact, we plan on going right to our apartment after the ceremony."

Joe sighed and stared at his empty plate.

Finally, he looked at Charlie. "I don't know if this is the smartest move you've ever made in your life. I know it's not the most diplomatic one, but I know how much

354

you guys love each other and want to get married, so I'd be honored to be your witness."

"Thanks, Joe," Charlie said, shaking his hand.

Helen slid out of the booth to give Joe a kiss on the cheek, while Bernie and Hank applauded from the counter.

"Sorry," Hank said, "couldn't help overhearing your conversation."

"Eavesdropping is more like it," Bernie said.

They all laughed and Joe asked Bernie for a refill and the check.

"I just want to freshen up a bit," Helen said.

"It's in the back on your left," Bernie said, refilling all their coffee cups.

"Listen, Joe," Charlie said, "while Helen's gone, there's something I need you to do."

He outlined their plan to get married at the city clerk's office, then go down to Elizabeth Seton Chapel to get married by a priest. He gave Joe fifty dollars to "donate" to the priest.

"And just in case that doesn't do the trick, tell him Helen's pregnant."

Joe's eyes opened wide. "Is she?"

"No, of course not. But he doesn't have to know that. And it will probably assure that he agrees to marry us. It means a lot to Helen to get married in the church."

"Okay. I've got no problem with telling a little white lie. She'll probably be pregnant by next week anyway. Leave it to me."

"Thanks, Joe."

Helen returned to the table just as Bernie handed Joe his check. "Yours is on the house," she said to Charlie. "Congratulations and good luck to both of you."

"Thanks, Bernie," Helen said, "and thank Hank for us." She looked around, but he was back in the kitchen

355

filling orders for the early birds who had come into the store.

Charlie grabbed the check from Joe. "It's on me."

Both men left a generous tip on the table and the three of them left for the city clerk's office.

First in line, they became husband and wife before nine o'clock. Then they walked downtown to the chapel and after Joe's brief conversation with the priest there, they were married again in the church.

Walking down the steps from the chapel, they looked across the water to the Statue of Liberty.

"She's beautiful, isn't she?" Helen asked.

"Yep, but not as beautiful as you," Charlie said.

"Okay, you two lovebirds," Joe said, "I'm not going to be a third wheel any longer. I just want to know when I can tell Peggy. She'll have my hide if she finds out before I tell her."

"When will you see her?" Helen asked.

"After her shift today."

"You can tell her then. That will give us plenty of time to do what we have to do, and tell our parents."

Joe turned as red as the stripes on the flag blowing in the breeze.

"Right. Okay then. I'll see you soon. And congratulations. All the best." He shook Charlie's hand, gave Helen a kiss on the cheek, and walked away.

"Want to go home, Helen Sanders?" Charlie asked.

"More than anything."

The couple spent the rest of the morning and early afternoon exploring each other's bodies, napping, and munching on Hank's muffins. Late in the afternoon, they showered and dressed.

"Ready to confront your parents?" Charlie asked.

"I am," Helen said. "Don't forget to bring your suitcase so I can pack all my clothes."

"Got it right here."

They left their apartment and walked up 8th Avenue to Helen's parents' home. They timed it to get there after her father came home from work, but before Peggy arrived.

"Mom? Dad?" Helen called, opening the front door.

"There you are," Aggie said. "Just where did you go off to so early this morning you didn't even have time for breakfast? And where did you get that suit? Oh... hello Charlie."

Aggie said all this in one breath. Paddy set his newspaper aside and looked at the couple standing in the doorway. He spotted Charlie's suitcase and frowned.

"Charlie. I'm afraid you're not welcome in my home anymore. So, I'll be asking you to leave."

"That's too bad, Mr. Campbell. But I want you to know, you and Mrs. Campbell will always be welcome in our home."

Ignoring Charlie's answer, Paddy looked at Aggie. "What did I say about him taking to the road again and leaving our Helen all alone? There he stands, brazen as can be, with his suitcase. Ready to take off for who knows how long. I told you he'd leave her. It's glad I am I didn't give my blessing to their marriage."

"That suitcase is for my clothes, Dad," Helen said. "Charlie and I got married this morning."

Aggie squealed like a stuck pig and put her hand to her mouth.

"YOU WHAT?" Paddy bellowed and jerked out of his chair, glaring at both of them.

"We got married," Helen said again, her chin held high. "And now, I'm going to pack my clothes and we'll get out of here and you won't ever have to see us again if that's what you want."

Aggie cried quietly and never moved from the sofa.

"I'll wait in the hall for you," Charlie said. "Come get me when you're packed and I'll carry the bag. I'm sure it'll be too heavy for you."

"All right."

Paddy stood in the center of the room, sputtering, at a loss for words. Charlie closed the door behind him as he left the apartment. Aggie ran to the girls' bedroom.

"Whatever were you thinking, love?" she asked Helen.

"I was thinking that Dad's too stubborn to change his mind and that I didn't plan on spending days, weeks, or maybe months trying to convince him otherwise. I love Charlie and he loves me. That should have been good enough for both of you. It certainly was for me."

While she spoke, Helen continued to empty her clothes from the closet and neatly pack them.

"But to go off and get married? Just like that? No priest? No family?"

"I'm sorry you couldn't be there, Mom. I really am. But you obviously agreed with Dad, or you would have said something before now. And we did get married by a priest right after the civil ceremony."

"Without the banns being announced?"

"Yes, Mom. Seems you can buy anything you want if you have enough money."

"Oh Helen." Aggie sighed and plopped down on the bed next to the open suitcase. She pulled a hanky out from her sleeve and wiped away the tears rolling down her cheeks.

"I think that's everything. I know there are still some things I'm missing, but maybe Peggy can bring them to the apartment as she finds them." She closed the lid and snapped the locks shut. "I'll get Charlie."

"Paddy," Aggie called, "come carry Helen's bag to the door."

Paddy stood in the doorway and shook his head. "I wouldn't have thought this of you, love. You've always been the sensible one. The one who obeys all the rules without questions. But to run off and do this against my will. I don't know what to think."

"You don't have to think anything, Dad. It's over and done and you can't do a thing to change it. I'm sorry you feel the way you do. Like you said, I've spent my life obeying all your rules. But it's time I stood up for what I want and what I believe is best for me. I hope someday, you'll rethink how you feel about Charlie, but until then, I won't be coming where he's not welcome. Bye, Mom."

She leaned over, kissed her mother on the cheek, grabbed her purse, and walked out of the room. Paddy followed with her bag.

At the door, he grabbed her arm. "I'll look into getting this marriage annulled."

"I wouldn't do that, Dad. There's no grounds for an annulment. I entered into it with my own free will. And we've consummated our commitment to each other. I made sure of that before we came here just in case you thought you could pull a stunt like what you just proposed. We're married, Dad. Accept it or not, but I plan on staying married to Charlie for the rest of my life."

Helen grabbed the handle of the bag, threw open the door, and stepped out of the apartment for the last time.

Paddy trudged over to his chair and fell into it, his hands covering his face.

A while later, Aggie came out of the bedroom still wiping away her tears.

"I hope you're happy with what you've done, Patrick Campbell. I don't know how you're going to live with it, but don't come looking to me for comfort. And to think, all this because you can't forget something that happened decades ago and an ocean away. And something that lad had no part of. Or his parents either. But because of your pig-headedness, we've lost another of our girls."

Aggie stood in front of Paddy stiff as a pillar.

"I'll not have it. I'll not lose our Helen to your pride. You may not be able to admit you're wrong and apologize for being a fool, but I'll have no part of it anymore. I'm going to go to their apartment tomorrow and beg her forgiveness, and by all the saints in heaven, I can only hope she'll give it. That's what *I'm* going to do, Paddy, whether you like it or not."

She plodded down the hall to their bedroom, leaving Paddy sitting in the ever-darkening living room.

Standing on the sidewalk, Helen looked up at the apartment windows one last time.

"Now we just have your parents to talk to," she said, taking Charlie's arm and walking down the street.

"Don't worry about them. I'll go see them tomorrow morning."

"Shouldn't I come with you?"

"Not necessary. I know them well enough. They'll accept the fact that we're married and before you know it, they'll be knocking on our door with a wedding present. You can take that to the bank."

"Okay. If you say so."

"I do. Now let's get a cab. This suitcase is heavy."

About an hour later, Paddy knocked on the closed door of their bedroom.

"Aggie, love, can I come in?"

"Aye, Paddy. It's your room as much as it is mine. I've no right to keep you out."

Paddy opened the door and saw Aggie sitting slumped on the bed.

"Oh, love, it breaks my heart to see you like this in such pain."

"Aye, it's pain, it is. For it feels like I've been stabbed right through my heart. She was our first-born and I can only hope she'll see it in her heart to forgive me for not standing up to your sooner and showing you your own foolishness."

"You're right, Aggie." Paddy sat next to her and pulled her close. "For I have been foolish, taking my past grievances out on the lad. Do you think it would be too much to ask for them to forgive me too?"

Aggie looked at Paddy for the first time since he had knocked on the door. "I think it would be a grand thing if you were to do that."

Paddy nodded. "Then after supper, let's take a walk, stop in at the church, and light a candle. Maybe a prayer for their happiness would help ease the way to their forgiveness."

Aggie gave him a kiss on the cheek and patted his knee. "Aye, love, maybe it will."

CHAPTER TWENTY-NINE

"You know, Joe," Peggy said, "now that we're engaged, you can wait for me in the lobby without creating a scandal. You don't have to hide out on the sidewalk, but wherever you wait, I'm always glad to see you."

"I enjoy getting some fresh air. I'm cooped up all day in gyms and saloons, and believe me, the air there is less than fragrant. Not that the city streets are much better, but at least there's a breeze. Now, why are you glad to see me today? Aside from the fact that I'm the handsomest man in this city, and the one who adores you?"

"I don't know about the *handsomest* . . ."

"I'm deeply offended."

Peggy laughed and said, "All right, you are. Are you happy now? Can I finish what I started to say?"

"I'll be quiet as a mouse."

Peggy shook her head and went up on tiptoes to kiss his cheek. "Let's walk to the playground where we can sit for a minute. I've been on my feet all day."

They headed downtown to a nearby playground. At this hour it was almost empty and quiet. On the way,

Peggy told Joe about her day and asked about his. But once seated, she became deadly serious.

"Joe, I keep thinking about Gino, Carolyn's... boyfriend? Isn't there anything we can do? Anyone we can talk to about him?"

Joe sat still as a stone except for the frown on his forehead that deepened as Peggy waited. He shook his head and kissed her forehead, "No. There isn't. I know you want to help her, but I'm afraid she doesn't want anyone's help. She knows how to reach you, or Helen, if she needs to, but for now, it's best to let sleeping dogs lie."

Peggy snuggled in closer to Joe's side, and they sat for a few minutes absorbed in their own thoughts.

"Now, how about something pleasant?"

"That *would* be nice."

"Come on then. I have a surprise for you." Joe pulled her up from the bench and led her out of the playground.

"Where are we going?"

"It's a surprise," he said, whistling for a cab.

"Tell me. Please? Please?"

"Nope. You'll just have to wait."

They got into the cab and Joe gave the driver an address.

I don't remember ever hearing that address before. Where are we going? He can be so infuriating at times. But I do adore him.

She looked over at Joe who sat there, a self-satisfied smile on his face, humming a jaunty tune.

"Are you kidnapping me?"

"Be patient, my love."

Peggy wore the face of an angry five-year-old who's been told she can't have any more cookies. Joe looked at her, saw that face, and let out a hearty laugh.

"You don't seem to like surprises."

"I only like them when I know what they are."

364

"We're here," the driver said.

Joe took Peggy's arm and led her into the building.

"Where are we?"

"Patience, my love, patience."

"If you say that to me one more time, Joe Hayes, I'll scream. Then you'll have to deal with all the people who come to rescue me."

"I'll take my chances," he said, opening the elevator door and ushering her inside.

The car lurched and wobbled and after what seemed like an eternity to her, it jerked to a stop.

"Are you sure that elevator's safe? Aren't there stairs here?" she asked.

"Of course, there are. But this is faster and easier on my old legs."

He led her down a door-filled corridor and stopped in front of the one marked 5A. "Here we are," he said, unlocking the door.

"Where, exactly?"

"Your future home."

Peggy stared at him slack-jawed.

"Go ahead, go look around," Joe said, beaming. "Of course, if you don't like it, we can find another place."

Peggy walked down a long hallway to a large living room that looked out onto a grassy courtyard situated between the two wings of the building. Sunlight poured through the open windows and made the lace curtains glisten and dance in the breeze. A velvet upholstered sofa and easy chair faced the marble fireplace as well as mahogany end tables and a coffee table. Peggy turned and looked at Joe, amazement and love in her eyes.

"Keep going. There's lots to see. The kitchen's to your left."

The spacious kitchen had a range, refrigerator, sink, and large work counter. A wooden table and four chairs sat in the center of the room.

"This way, my love." Joe led her back down the hall past the bathroom to the first bedroom. "This will be our room," he said a blush coloring his cheeks.

A large bed covered with a floral chintz counterpane dominated the room, which was also filled with sunlight. A wardrobe and chest of drawers took up the rest of the space, while the lace curtains fluttered at the edges of the open window.

"One more room." Joe led her further down the hall. "This will be your study. At least, for as long as you need it. Then maybe it can be a nursery." His face had now bloomed full crimson.

Peggy looked at a sturdy desk, and the wall of bookshelves already partially filled with books. She wandered over to inspect them. Medical textbooks filled one shelf. Some that were so expensive she could only access them at the hospital's library. She fingered the spines carefully; afraid they might turn to dust if she allowed herself to believe they were real.

"Well?" Joe asked.

She turned and ran into his arms, her face wet with tears. "This is the most wonderful surprise I've ever had. You thought of everything. Even my books. But how did you know which ones to buy?"

"I asked around. You're not the only doctor in the city, you know. And I thought you'd appreciate these more than an engagement ring."

"Oh Joe, I do and I love you so much, and I promise I will make this the happiest home in all of New York."

Joe fought to hold back the tears that her joy brought on.

"When did you ever... I mean how could you have done... I'm so astounded."

"Do you think I spend all my time standing outside the hospital waiting for you?"

"But you only asked me to marry you a couple of days ago."

"The night I met you, I knew I would ask you to marry me. The next day, I went to the building manager and asked if I could swap my one-bedroom apartment for a two-bedroom so you could have a study. He agreed and I've spent the last few weeks picking up bits of furniture and getting the place ready for today."

"You are a marvel, Joe, and I must say very self-confidant that I would say yes."

"I guess you could call me the ultimate optimist." He smiled at her, a twinkle in his eye. "If there's anything you don't like, or want to change, that's fine. You can buy whatever you want."

"It's perfect. I wouldn't change a thing."

"I left plenty of room for more books. I'm sure there are some others you'll need or would like to have."

"I can't believe you bought all these books," she said, wandering back to the shelves. "They must have cost you a fortune."

"Consider them your engagement and wedding present."

She pulled one of them off the shelf and placed it on her desk. "*Gray's Anatomy*," she said in a reverential tone. "I'm glad I still have my gloves on. I wouldn't want to get even the tiniest smudge on these pages." She opened the cover and ran a finger down the title page.

"It's yours now, Peggy. You can do whatever you want with it. Mark it up. Spill coffee on it."

"Bite your tongue. This is like a Bible to me. Maybe even more important than that." She looked at him over her shoulder. "Joe, you've made me so happy."

"That's all I ever want to do, Peggy." He walked over to her, pulled her into his arms, and kissed her with a longing he had kept at bay since the night they met.

"And as soon as I catch my breath, I have another surprise for you."

"Another? You're going to spoil me."

"Well... this one isn't really *for* you. It's just about something that happened today."

Peggy tilted her head to the side and opened her eyes wide. "I'm all ears."

"Helen and Charlie got married this morning."

"What! They got married? Are you sure?"

"I was their witness. So, yes, I'm pretty sure."

"You were their witness? Why didn't you tell me this was going to happen? Oh . . ." She smacked his chest. "I could've been there. I could've been her maid of honor. How could you keep this from me?"

"Slow down before you blow a gasket. I didn't know myself until this morning. Last night, Charlie asked me to meet him at some coffee shop downtown at seven this morning. He didn't say why and I didn't ask. When I got there, they laid this bombshell on me. Of course, I agreed to be their witness. It was all over before I had even processed what was happening."

"But where? How? In a church? Tell me everything."

So, Joe pulled her into the living room and they sat on the sofa while he told her all about the morning's events.

"Well, I'll be damned," Peggy said.

"That's exactly what I said."

"Wonder how Mom and Dad are going to feel about this."

"That, my love, will be interesting."

Peggy stood and pulled Joe to his feet. "C'mon. Let's go."

"Where?"

"To see Helen and Charlie. We have to congratulate them."

"Hold on. Don't you think we should leave them alone and let them enjoy their wedding night privately?"

"Oh... I guess I wasn't thinking. You're right, of course." Peggy sat down again, twirling her fingers around one another. "Can we go there tomorrow night?"

Joe roared laughing. "You can't wait to hear all about their big day, can you? But let's give them some time to breathe. Saturday good enough?"

"Great! Now... what should we get them for a wedding gift?"

Joe sighed. "I have no idea, but I'm sure you'll tell me, then make me promise to pick it up tomorrow, which I will do. Now, can we go to dinner? I'm starved."

"Me too. What are we waiting around here for?" Peggy jumped up and headed to the door.

Joe followed, shaking his head the whole way.

CHAPTER THIRTY

On Saturday afternoon, just as Helen finished putting their lunch dishes away, the doorbell rang.

"Are you expecting anyone?" she asked Charlie.

"Not me. You?"

"No."

She shrugged her shoulders and buzzed the downstairs door open. They stood at their apartment door to see who was coming.

"Oh!" Helen's hand flew to her mouth. "It's my parents. I can hear them talking on the stairs."

Charlie stood even straighter than usual and braced himself for whatever would come next. Aggie rounded the last flight of stairs and looked up at the newlyweds. She put her head down and climbed the last few steps, Paddy right behind her.

As soon as they reached the landing, Charlie shook both their hands. "Welcome to our home. Come in."

"Mom." Helen opened her arms wide and Aggie gave her a hug. Releasing her, she turned and gave Charlie a quick hug. Helen stood on her toes to give her father a kiss on the cheek, then took his arm and led him into the apartment.

Once the four of them were inside, an awkward silence fell over the room.

"We just finished lunch, but I have plenty of cold cuts. Can I make you something?" Helen asked.

"No, love," Aggie said. "We've eaten."

"A cup of tea, then?"

"That would be nice."

"Come in here and sit at the table." Helen led the way to the kitchen and put the kettle on.

But before they sat, Paddy said, "We've come to apologize."

Aggie shot him a look that would freeze most men in their tracks.

"Well, me especially, since your mam just went along with what I said." He shuffled his feet and twisted his cap in his hands.

"Charlie," Helen said, "take Dad's cap and hang it up. Mom, give Charlie your purse. He'll put in on the hall table. You sit here, Mom. Dad, you can sit next to her."

Once everyone was settled, Paddy continued. "I was wrong to go blaming you, or your family, for things you had no part of, and maybe didn't even know much about. Aggie made me see that. We came here for a better life. A place to raise a family away from the battle going on back home. And what did I do? I brought the battle with me. And made you out to be an enemy."

"No—"

"Let me finish, lad. I'd no right to do that to you, your family, or Helen. And I'm sincerely sorry. I'd like us to start over and bring you into our family like a son, but if you can't agree to that and want to throw me out on my ear, I'll understand. I was a fool and I'll accept the fact that you won't abide fools. There. I've said my piece."

He sat with his hands on his thighs, ready to bolt upright if need be.

"Mr. Campbell, I said it on Thursday, and I meant it. You and Mrs. Campbell are always welcome here. I have to say, I didn't appreciate the way you treated my parents. Or the low opinion you seemed to have of me, thinking I'd leave Helen for a chance to box again. But that's neither here nor there. The fact of the matter is that we love each other and your blessing would mean a great deal to us. So, as far as I'm concerned, let bygones be bygones and we'll start fresh from today."

He stood, walked around the table, and shook Paddy's hand. Paddy stood, clasped Charlie's shoulder, and gave it a gentle squeeze.

"You're a good man, Charlie."

The kettle's whistle blew.

"Perfect timing," Helen said. "Charlie, would you get some cookies from the cupboard and put them on a plate while I fix the tea?"

"Sure, sweetheart."

While they went about their tasks, Aggie squeezed Paddy's hand and smiled at him.

"Mr. Campbell? Would you like a little something with your tea?" Charlie held up a bottle of Irish whiskey.

"Oh... maybe just a wee bit for a toast."

"Great idea. Maybe one for each of us," Helen said.

"And Charlie, now that you're part of the family, I think you should call us Paddy and Aggie. No need to stand on formalities."

Drinks, tea, and cookies on the table, Charlie lifted his glass. "To Aggie and Paddy."

"To Helen and Charlie," Paddy said, "all the best for a long and happy life."

They clinked glasses and took a drink.

"Helen, the apartment looks lovely," Aggie said.

"Thanks, Mom. When we finish our tea, I'll take you and Dad on a tour."

The women talked about the furnishings and how, where, and why they got them while the men listened and sipped their whiskey.

"All right. Time for the tour." Helen collected their plates and put them in the sink. Just as they walked into the living room, the doorbell rang for the second time that day.

"Who could that be now?" Helen buzzed the downstairs door open and, in a few minutes, Peggy and Joe bounded into the apartment. Peggy threw her arms around Helen.

"Congratulations! I should really be mad at you for not telling me your plans, but I can't be. I'm so happy for both of you." She grabbed Charlie, hugged him, and gave him a kiss on the cheek. "What did Mom and Dad say when you told them? You did tell them, didn't you?"

"She did." Paddy's voice boomed from the living room.

Peggy winced and made a face. "Why didn't you tell me they were here?" she whispered to Helen.

"You haven't given me a minute to get a word in edgewise."

Peggy hurried into the living room and gave each parent a kiss on the cheek.

"Hi. I didn't expect to see you here."

"Obviously," Aggie said. "When did you find out they were married?"

"Thursday night. Joe told me. He was their witness."

"And," Joe said, "I didn't know their plans until that morning. These two kept everyone in the dark."

Charlie put his arm around Helen's waist and gave her a squeeze.

"I was just going to take Mom and Dad on a tour, want to come?"

"Absolutely," Peggy said.

"You girls go ahead," Paddy said. "I'll stay here with Charlie and Joe."

"Joe," Charlie said, "we were having a toast to celebrate our marriage. Can I get you a glass?"

"It would be rude to refuse, wouldn't it?"

Charlie poured each of the men a drink and as they sipped, they listened to the women oohing and aahing over each room. When they returned to the living room, still chattering about the apartment, Charlie pulled a couple of chairs from the kitchen table so everyone could sit.

"More tea, anyone? Peggy? Joe?"

"Not for me," Peggy said, "but as long as everyone's here and celebrating, Joe and I have an announcement of our own. We're engaged." She held onto Joe's hand like it was a life preserver in the middle of the ocean.

Aggie's mouth dropped open. Paddy raised his eyebrows, then stood, and walked over to Joe. He stuck his hand out and said, "Congratulations. I hope you know what you're getting yourself in for. She's got a mind of her own, this one does, and she'll not be a meek mild wife. More like a penned-up bull always butting the gate."

"Dad! I am not."

"You certainly don't go along with the tide, girl. Look at you now. In medical school. How many other lasses do that? And do you plan on giving it up to become Joe's wife?"

"No, of course not."

"Ahh. Only proves my point."

"We've already discussed all that. Why Joe even has a whole room in his apartment for me to use as my study. He even bought some medical books for me."

375

Right after she said that, Peggy's face flushed.

"So, you've been to his apartment, have you?" Paddy asked.

"Just the other day," Joe said. "I wanted to surprise her and see if she liked it. Otherwise, I'd have to start looking for another place."

"And when do you plan on this marriage taking place?" Aggie asked.

"As soon as the banns can be announced," Peggy said. "All right, Joe?"

"Whatever you want, my love."

Peggy looked at her parents who both seemed to be amazed at her news. "Dad? No objections?"

"No. None at all. I've learned it doesn't do me any good to buck my girls. They'll do as they please, and if I object, it just gets Aggie mad at me. So, I best keep my mouth shut and keep peace in the home."

"About time you learned your lesson," Aggie said.

"Well, I for one think this calls for another drink," Charlie said.

"Tell you what," Joe said. "Before we all get a little tipsy, why don't I take us to dinner?"

"You may as well start calling us Paddy and Aggie, too," Paddy said. He shook his head and sighed.

Weeks later, while they ate dinner, Peggy brought up the subject of Carolyn and Gino. Again.

"Isn't there anything we can do?" she asked.

"I don't think so," Joe said. "Gino's not a small-time bookie working the docks, you know. He heads up an organized network of criminals. And he's got the police tucked away in his pocket. So, they're not going to be any help at all."

"But Hank, our beat cop—"

"Did you and your mom a favor going down there to look for Carolyn. But he didn't try to bring her home, did he? And he won't. Not if he knows what's good for him. I think Carolyn's all on her own now."

"This is terrible. If only we hadn't gone to the Copacabana."

"Now don't think that way. If it wasn't Gino, it'd be someone else like him. He's just her style. All flash. She'd never be happy becoming someone's wife, taking care of him and their home, and maybe children. No, she's one who's always going to want to be out on the town."

"But she seemed happy about getting an apartment uptown. She would have had to settle down then."

"I don't think that was in her plans. Settling down, that is."

"What do you mean?"

"I think she thought of it more like a hotel room, but one she could call her own."

"I don't understand."

"Peggy, mistresses or kept women or whatever you want to call them, like Carolyn has become, don't think of their apartments or houses as homes. Just a place where they can be with their lovers without sneaking past hotel desk clerks. They expect dinners out, or a cook to make them, and maids to do the housework, and their own car and driver. Plus, plenty of money to spend and nightly entertainment. No, Carolyn's idea of settling down and yours are as different as me and Gino."

Peggy didn't answer him.

He makes a lot of sense. But does she really think men will cater to her for her whole life?

"Joe, what do you think will happen to her?"

"Like I've said before, eventually Gino'll get tired of her, or she'll become too demanding of his time, or his

377

money, and he'll toss her out like a pair of old shoes. If she's lucky."

"Then what will she do?"

"I don't know, my love. Listen to me, Peggy. You've done all you can for her. You've tried to help. She doesn't want the kind of life we've planned together. She thinks you're the chump, willing to settle for a simple life with a man who loves you. She wants a life filled with excitement and danger. Gino's perfect for her. And if she's plays her cards right, and I think she's clever enough to do this, she'll stash a little bankroll for herself and have enough jewelry and furs to pawn to keep her out of the poor house for the rest of her life."

"That all sounds so dirty."

"It is. But she's walked into Gino's swamp now and she won't get any cleaner staying there, as that seems to be what she wants to do."

"If I could just see her, talk to her, tell her what you said about Gino. Maybe she doesn't realize how bad he is."

"You get that thought out of your head this very minute. Charlie and I already tried to do that, and it did no good. When we were at the Copa, she may not have known what he was like, although I doubt that with my heart and soul, but she knows now. She's met the goons who never leave his side, and she's been with him down at the docks. Believe me, he didn't go there for the sea air. She knows. And she's made her choice. If you go barging in there to rescue her, she'll turn you away and Gino won't appreciate you interfering in his business. The man has no conscience, no soul. There's nothing but a big black hole where all that should be. The man's black as pitch. Not one redeeming quality about him. Leave them be. Carolyn knows where her family is if she wants to find them."

Peggy gazed around the restaurant at the other diners.

Why couldn't Carolyn be happy with a man like Joe? Why does she always have to go towards danger? But, he's right. She's all grown up now. Her decisions are her own.

She shook her head to clear her thoughts.

Peggy's wedding day finally came to the Campbell household. All the frenetic activity to prepare for this day culminated in a gaggle of women in the living room making sure the ladies' outfits were perfectly fitted. Paddy, with the wisdom of a long-married man, stayed in the safe refuge of his bedroom. It wasn't until one of the neighborhood boys barreled into the apartment to tell them the limo was downstairs that the women began to leave and peace settled over the household.

"Thought they'd never get out of here," Paddy said, emerging from his sanctuary. "Never heard so much chatter in my life." He walked down the hall and stopped at the entrance to the living room. Tears welled in his eyes as the three most important women in his life stood waiting for him.

"I've never seen a more lovely sight. You all look grand, you do. Like three goddesses come down to bless me with a vision of what heaven will look like when my time comes."

"Would you listen to his blarney, girls? Have you been sneaking a wee nip or two back there in our room?"

"No, Aggie, love. It's just that heavenly you all are."

"Thank you, Dad," Peggy said, her cheeks a rosy pink. "I hope Joe feels the same way."

"If he doesn't, then he doesn't deserve you, and I give you my blessing to walk away from him and out of the church to find someone who appreciates you the way he should."

"Dad, I wouldn't walk away from him just because he doesn't think I look beautiful."

"Maybe you should," Paddy said, adjusting his tie.

"You look quite dapper yourself, Dad," Peggy said.

"It wouldn't do to have me walking my best girl down the aisle in my overalls, would it?" he huffed.

The three women looked at each other and laughed at the image of Paddy in his work clothes and Peggy in her wedding dress walking down the aisle in Saint Columba's.

"No, it certainly would not, Paddy love. But you look as handsome as the day you first caught my eye, you do."

"And you're as lovely as the fair lass I fell in love with," he said, walking over to them and giving each a kiss on the cheek. "Well, best get downstairs before the car leaves, thinking you changed your mind, Peggy love."

Peggy reached out and squeezed her mother's and Helen's hands. "Let's go. We don't want to keep everyone waiting."

The foursome descended the stairs and came out of the apartment house to find all the neighbor children huddled around the stoop waiting to catch a glimpse of the wedding party. A chorus of oohs and aahs accompanied them down the steps. The little girls jumped up and down with excitement. The boys gaped wide-eyed at the entourage. Some of the older ones yelled their good wishes and all waved furiously as the car pulled away from the curb.

Although only a short walk to the church, Paddy had rented a limo so the ladies could arrive with pristine shoes and dress hems, not soiled by the usual muck of the city streets. In minutes, the car stopped and Peggy looked out to see the steps of the church filled with onlookers. Some she recognized, but most she didn't.

The usual assembly of gapers here to see what the fuss is all about today. Makes me feel like a celebrity.

As the Campbells gathered at the bottom of the steps to the church, the crowd yelled out to them.

"You look beautiful, love."

"Best of luck to you."

"A regular faerie princess, she is."

"If only I were twenty years younger."

"Try forty, you old fool."

Laughter and good wishes surrounded Peggy as she walked up the steps and entered Saint Columba's vestibule.

Aggie made some last-minute adjustments to Peggy's veil, and said, "There you are, love, perfect as a picture. All set?"

"Yes, Mom."

"Well then, I'll be seeing you after the ceremony."

Aggie walked through the lobby doors and up the aisle to her spot in the first pew. The organ began to play, and as soon as she was seated, the ushers held two doors open for Helen to walk up the aisle. Joe and Charlie stood at the altar rail waiting. Helen gave Charlie a smile and he gave her a wink as she moved to the left side of the railing. Then the doors opened again, and Peggy and Paddy began their procession to the front of the church. Everyone rose, and Joe walked over to the center of the aisle so he could watch Peggy walk toward him.

He looks so handsome it takes my breath away. I do love him so much.

Joe's beaming glow radiated love that everyone in the church could feel. When they reached him, Paddy gave Peggy a kiss on her cheek, shook Joe's hand, and placed Peggy's trembling fingers into it. Then he joined Aggie in the front pew.

Father O'Leary said the Mass, making sure he gave a brief homily. Years of experience taught him that everyone wanted to get to the celebration and he had no intention of delaying them, or himself.

After Mass, he began the recitation of their vows and when it came time for their responses, Joe's voice boomed his, "I do," to the accompanying titter of some of the congregation, while Peggy's whispered response could barely be heard past the front pew. Charlie gave Father O'Leary the ring, which he blessed, then handed to Joe to slip on Peggy's finger. Final blessings brought the ceremony to a close, and the couple, glowing with happiness and love, turned and walked down the aisle to the vestibule. When they reached that sanctuary, Joe pulled Peggy into his arms and kissed her with previously withheld rapture.

"There, that's better," he said. "That little peck at the altar would never do to seal our marriage."

"How sweet," a woman said, stepping out from the shadows

"Carolyn!" Peggy said. "What are you doing here? How did you know I was getting married?"

"Rosemary told me. At least she hasn't turned her back on me like my family has."

Helen and Charlie came into the vestibule as she said this.

"Carolyn," Helen said, "we didn't desert you, you deserted us."

Two men came out of the shadows and stepped in front of the vestibule doors to prevent anyone's entrance or exit.

Ignoring her older sister, Carolyn turned back to Peggy. "So, decided to marry the old man, huh? I wanted to see this for myself. I can't believe you really went through with it. Afraid you'd wind up a spinster like

Helen? Better be careful with him tonight. You don't want to be a widow by tomorrow morning."

"You bitch," Peggy said. "You wish you could have as good a man as Joe, instead of a gangster."

"Oh, I could have had your husband if I wanted. I know he interrupted my tete-a-tete with J.P. at The Pierre that day just so he could meet me. But I prefer virile men, not ones with one foot in the grave."

"Or maybe he prefers a decent woman instead of a whore," Helen said.

Carolyn raised her hand to slap Helen's face, but Charlie grabbed her wrist. "I wouldn't do that if I were you. In fact, since you haven't succeeded in whatever you thought you'd accomplish here today, you might want to think about leaving with what shred of dignity you still have left, if any." He threw her arm away from him.

"You bastard. I hate you." Turning to Helen, she looked her up and down. "I knew you'd wind up being the spinster in the family." She flashed her left hand in Helen's face, a large diamond ring on her third finger, gold bracelets dangling from her arm. "Gino wants to marry me. I haven't said yes yet, but I took the ring. Can't turn down a present like that now, can I? But you. Always a bridesmaid, never a bride, huh? Isn't that how the saying goes?"

"No, Carolyn. Charlie and I were married a few months ago. Seems like you're the family spinster now."

Carolyn's face turned purple with rage and she stormed out the church door to the car waiting at the curb, Gino leaning against it. The two goons guarding the vestibule doors followed her.

"Peggy, love, are you all right?" Joe asked.

"Never better." She took a deep breath and smiled up at her husband.

Joe pulled her into his arms and kissed her again.

"Joe," Peggy said, her face turning scarlet, "what if people see?"

"And what are they going to say? It's only a husband kissing his wife. Isn't that right, Charlie?" he turned and asked his best man who stood next to them, Helen on his arm.

"No law against that," Charlie said.

"The two of you are incorrigible," Peggy said, fiddling with her dress.

"Congratulations, Joe." Charlie shook his hand. "May I kiss the bride?"

"A peck on the cheek, nothing more," Joe said.

Charlie roared. "Afraid she'll leave you already? All the best, Peggy." He gave her a chaste kiss on the cheek.

Helen hugged her sister and gave Joe a quick kiss before their parents and friends surrounded them. Peggy's head spun with the whirlwind of people, greetings, and overall joy that filled the small space. Meanwhile, as the well-wishers left, they gathered along the steps of the church awaiting the couple's departure.

"There's a great crowd of people outside waiting to cheer us off to the party, my love. We're about to face the world as Mr. and Mrs. Hayes, and I want everyone to envy my fortune in having the sweetest most beautiful woman in the world as my wife. Are you ready?"

"I am Mr. Hayes."

"Then let's get to the celebration, Mrs. Hayes."

Joe placed his hand on the small of her back and led her out of the church and down the steps to their new life.

Charlie and Helen, now the old married couple, held hands and watched them leave.

"I hope they'll be as happy as the three of us are," Helen said, squeezing Charlie's hand.

"The three of us?" Charlie looked at Helen, his eyes full of questions. "Wait a minute, you don't mean you're pregnant, do you?"

"That's exactly what I mean."

Charlie picked her up and spun her around. Helen threw her head back and laughed.

"No one could be as happy as we are," Charlie said, kissing her. "Now, let's get to that celebration. Theirs and ours."

About the Author

Although born in New York City, where she spent most of her life, Eileen Joyce Donovan has lived in six states and visited most of the others. She earned her MA in English at Northern Arizona University. In one way or another, she's been writing her entire life, whether it was imaginative stories for friends, or advertising copy for industrial clients.

But she never felt her stories were "good enough" to be published. At the persistent urging of her husband, she finally agreed to seriously edit and revise one of them and take the plunge. Although accepted for publication, the book never made it all the way to print. However, this gave her the courage to pursue her dream of becoming a published author.

Years later, her persistence paid off and her traditionally published debut historical fiction, *Promises*, won the 2019 Marie M Irvine Award for Literary Excellence. *A Lady Newspaperman's Dilemma,* released in 2022, won the 2021 When Words Count nationwide competition. Her short stories have appeared in various anthologies, including the 2021 *Chicken Soup for the Soul, Blessings of Christmas*.

She lives in Manhattan, New York and is a member of Authors Guild, Women's National Book Association, Women Fiction Writers Association, and The Historical Novel Society.

CPSIA information can be obtained
at www.ICGtesting.com
Printed in the USA
JSHW081959190223
37952JS00001B/5